Initiate

The Shadow Atlas Book One

Jenny Sandiford

VELIKOR
PUBLISHING

JENNY SANDIFORD

THE SHADOW ATLAS

INITIATE

Contact: jennysandiford.com

Cover design by Miblart

Developmental Edit by The Two Step Approach

Line Edit by Haley Willens

Proofread by Lucy Bowlby

ISBN (ebook): 978-0-6454449-0-2

IBSN (paperback): 978-0-6454449-1-9

First Edition: May 2022

To my Mum, who always took me to the library.
Thanks Mum!

CHAPTER 1

S HADOW MAGIC BURNED DEEP in Azalea's chest. She
doubled over, eyes forced down to the dead leaves of the
forest floor as she pressed her fist into the base of her ribs, willing
the dark magic to stay in, and for once do what she bloody
well asked. There was no time for delays. She needed to get this
cleansing ceremony over with so she could do something useful
with the full moon's power, like contact her dead father's spirit.

Taking a deep breath, Azalea straightened up and did her best
to ignore the Shadow Magic twisting inside. *Just stay down-*
. Around her, wind roared through the trees like a legion of
restless spirits, ancient branches groaning in protest. It's just
wind, she told herself as energy prickled her neck. She pulled her
yellow, plastic raincoat in tighter and squinted into the rain, her
numb fingers doing little to brush the wet tangle of hair out of
her eyes.

"Wait up, mum!" Azalea called into the wind as a fat raindrop
hit her nose. For the middle of summer, it was bloody freezing
and just her luck that they were out there in a storm at midnight.

Azalea jogged to catch up to her mum, Leda, who hadn't even
noticed that she had fallen behind.

"Get a move on. We don't want to miss the peak of the full moon. I'm doing this for you, you know," Leda shouted over her shoulder.

"I know," Azalea said with a frown, wanting this to go smoothly. If she said what she really thought—that her mum clearly had no idea how to get rid of Shadow Magic—it would not go down well.

Instead, Azalea focused on the smells of the ancient forest, breathing in the fresh rain as it mixed with the rich forest floor. This was their forest, an untraceable spot in the English countryside hidden from the modern world. A place with deep rooted connections to ancient magic.

Closer to the center of the forest the rough oak trunks grew wider and the glow of cute blue mushrooms set eerie light down the ever-narrowing path. Itching to check the time, Azalea's fingers hovered over her phone in her pocket. Must be pretty close to the full moon's peak now, though she couldn't see it through the thick weather she knew 12:44 am was the prime time. Her mum glanced back and frowned as if she knew what Azalea was thinking. "Don't you take out that phone. You'll wreck your forest sight."

"I wasn't going to." She resisted rolling her eyes, unsure why her mum insisted on speaking to her like a child rather than an eighteen-year-old. Instead of the phone, Azalea's fingers curled around the cool metal of her lucky pocket watch, tracing the silver filigree border. It was a gift from her dad and her lucky charm—well, it was in theory, it hadn't brought her much luck so far.

The unexpected chill of energy spread to her chest, and she swallowed hard. There were spirits nearby. Azalea crept closer to her mum and kept up her pace.

"This is it," Leda said as the muddy path gave way to grass.

Earthy scents filled the air and Azalea did her best not to stand on the mushrooms that grew in delicate circles around the clearing, lighting up the misting rain with their pretty blueish glow.

Linking arms with her mum, they stepped onto the spongy grass toward the center of the clearing. A stone circle marked the heart of the forest and bordering the clearing were silver birch trees, their usually bright trunks dulled like a black and white movie in the shades of night.

As they stepped between two moss covered standing stones, whispers danced on a breath of wind. *Super creepy.*

Azalea's gaze darted to the tree line.

"What was that?"

"Just forest sounds love, no need to be so jittery. This will all be over in a tick."

Azalea wasn't so sure. As they made it to the center of the clearing, her eyes focused on the trees on the other side. She did her best not to crush her mum's arm as figures stepped out from the tree line.

"I don't want to alarm you, Mum, but there's a shit load of spirits over there," Azalea said, pointing to the trees.

Leda frowned. Their usual day-to-day life involved ignoring the fact that Azalea could see spirits. It was no secret that her mum hated Shadow Magic and everything that came with it. But right now, these ones were very real to Azalea, and she very much wanted them to stay away.

"We've let this Shadow Magic persist far too long. Grab the salt there, Petal. You'll be rid of this darkness soon enough."

As much as Azalea wanted to believe that, she had zero faith that this ceremony would work. At least she knew that salt would keep the spirits out of the circle. She grabbed it from Leda's hemp backpack and didn't wait for instructions. Racing around in a wide circle within the standing stone border, she poured the stream of salt out of the box until the circle ends met.

"Done," she called out as Leda appeared next to her. Azalea always felt tall when her mum stood next to her. Leda was short and squat where Azalea was tall and lean. *Lanky as a beanpole*, her grandmother, RoRo, always said. Which was a silly thing to say, because Azalea was the spitting image of RoRo—both with their waves of brown hair and stormy gray eyes.

Leda chanted over the circle as the spirits moved closer, their gloomy silhouettes standing out against the lighter trees. Azalea held her breath as a few stepped toward the circle. *Nope, too close.* She took a step back, and her mum followed suit.

"Are they near?" Leda asked.

"Yup," Azalea squeaked. Her voice higher than she'd intended it to be. Shadow Magic curled up her spine and she pulled her shoulders back, as if she could squash it back down and contain it. Leda began digging through her bag, setting up an old chopping board next to the pile of firewood, which was now rather soggy.

More spirits stepped toward the circle. Close enough that Azalea could see their normal human faces, most were solemn and confused, some appeared afraid—but they weren't human anymore. Somehow, she just knew. A shiver prickled the hairs on her arms as unease washed over her. *Stop being a baby*, she told herself. They were only spirits, after all. They didn't even look different from living humans. They weren't gray, or see-through, or covered in blood, and their clothes were whatever outdated fashion they died in. When she saw them out in the daylight it was hard to tell that they weren't actual people, that was until they spoke. It was the macabre, repetitive questions about lost loved ones that gave them away. That and the persistent cold that hung off them like unshakable fog.

"Right-o, Love. I've got it all set up," Leda said as she stuffed newspaper and dry kindling from her bag into the base of the woodpile. On the chopping board sat a soggy white feather, a chipped earthen bowl, a plastic bottle of water, a bright white candle, and several bunches of dried herbs tied with straw. Leda lit a match, and the kindling crackled to life with pops and sparks. As the newly birthed flames licked at the damp wood, fire won over water and ribbons of steam curled into the night air.

"Lovely," she said, with hands perched on her hips.

Firelight danced in Azalea's vision as she forced a smile, staring into the flames. *Let's get this over with.*

"Hand me the sage, would you, Petal?"

The fire crackled and Azalea pulled herself from the flames trance. She bent down and passed Leda the sage and wondered how long this would take. The spot where she could contact her dad was back toward their cottage a few fields over and she hoped he would hang around past the full moon hour so she could still make it. He wasn't like the other spirits. He was in another place, a place she could only communicate with when the veil was thin. A full moon was perfect.

"No need to look so worried, Petal. Let's get on with it then." Smoke wound around Leda like vines. She might not be a mage like RoRo, but she had some sort of power that came from being the Guardian of the Forest. While Leda was set on her daughter becoming the next Forest Guardian, Azalea wanted nothing to do with it. If it weren't for this Shadow Magic problem, she would be off to uni in London already and looking forward to many nights at the pub with her best friend, Isaac. She'd be getting pissed on the weekend instead of going to freezing cold forest ceremonies.

"Come sit," Leda said as she lowered to the ground.

Azalea's raincoat crinkled around her as she sat cross legged, her knee resting against her mum's.

She jumped when Leda took her hand.

Her own hand was a frozen rock against her mother's natural warmth. They had always been that way. Azalea cold when Leda was hot. Azalea rushing when Leda was still. Azalea stubborn and unyielding while Leda moved with the tides of the earth. Azalea closed her eyes.

Leda rested their joined hands on their knees. "Now calm your mind. Connect with the forest's energy, reach out to the Earth and the Goddess. Fill your body with light. Do you feel it?"

Azalea shuffled on the gritty, saturated earth. "No," she answered truthfully. She tried—as she had tried several times before—but it never worked as much as Azalea wanted it to. Today wouldn't be any different.

Fiery magic rushed through her veins as if she'd had some sort of energy shot. She tensed and tried not to grip her mum's hand as she imagined inky tendrils reaching out from her chest and weaving through her limbs. Shadow Magic was a part of her now, not something that could be wished away. What she needed was to learn control.

Slow breaths, she told herself. *Shove it back down and ignore it*. But the more she ignored it, the more it threatened to explode from her hands and blanket the night with more darkness. Part of her wanted it to. But everything about it was unknown, dangerous. What if she lost control near her mum? What if she hurt her? She wasn't sure what the shadows were capable of.

She shoved the magic down deeper.

Her eyes shot open as desperate voices from outside the circle cried out. They weren't just calling for their loved ones anymore . . . they were calling to Azalea. A chill crawled up her back. This was getting way too weird.

As she tried to still her racing heart, the Shadow Magic pulsed inside her, threatening to burst out with each beat.

"Just focus your mind, connect with the earth," Leda said.

Easy for her to say when she couldn't hear the crazy dead people calling out for help. Though she didn't have the foggiest idea what they wanted help with. And why were they asking her?

Azalea ground her teeth and did her best to focus on the forest, on the moon, on the Goddess Ninhursag, hoping that if there was a goddess, she would do something to help.

Leda spoke in a low, hypnotic voice. "Great Goddess, we call upon you. On this night, in the glow of the full moon, we draw upon your ancient power. As protectors of this ancient forest, we ask that you bless this daughter. Aid in her battle against the shadows and withdraw this dark magic. We honor you."

Leda poured the water into the clay bowl and with floaty hand movements lit the candle and swept sage through the flame until smoke drifted out and went straight into Azalea's face. Azalea's fists pressed hard into her knees. The magical fire snaked up her spine, sending her bolt upright.

Okay, one more attempt to clear her mind. A pool of water in a silent cave, deep and endless, filled her thoughts. She coerced her mind into the cave. But whenever she tried to calm her breath or still her heart, the fire inside wrapped its tendrils around her spine and pushed. She bent over, breathing deep. Clearly this wasn't working.

"You won't channel any of the moon or forest energy slouching like that. Sit up straight. Align your chakras."

"I can't, Mum. I think I should leave." Whatever energy was out there only seemed to add to her Shadow Magic, not calm it.

"Nonsense, just try again." Leda threw some herbs into the fire.

Smoke itched the back of Azalea's throat, and the burning herbs had her head spinning. Nausea rose, and she struggled to breathe. Trying not to cough up a lung, she shuffled backward, away from the smoke. Leda wrinkled her brow. "What's wrong, dear?"

"I can't hold it in," Azalea said. She had to get out of the circle to protect her mum.

Leda sat upright as if realizing what she meant.

Azalea stood up and stumbled back. "I'm sorry Mum, but I've got to go. I'll find my own way to fix this."

"Just stay a little longer. Give it a chance." Her eyes pleaded.

"I can't. There isn't time. I know you want to help, but talking to trees and goddesses in the middle of the night isn't going to fix me. I need to learn to control it. If Dad was here, he would want me to learn. At least he would teach me." She regretted the words as soon as they left her mouth.

"Your father is dead because of Shadow Magic. He would have led you down a very dangerous path, Azalea. It is not one I want you to follow," Leda said, not in a cruel way, but as a mother desperate to help her daughter.

"I know . . . but it's too late! I know you want to protect me from it, but I need to know the truth about Shadow Magic." As she held her hands out the fire inside her spread through her limbs. She clenched her fists, but couldn't stop it. She got up and raced to the edge of the salt circle.

"Move!" she screamed at the spirits on the edge, and they scattered away like spiders. "Stay away," she warned as they stared at her. The circle would protect her mum if something went wrong. Magic sparked through her, spiraling up, fueled by her growing panic.

"What's happening Azalea?" Leda asked, clutching her sage bundle.

"Just stay in the circle, Mum!"

Azalea stepped over the salt as the magic forced through against her will. Hands spread out in front, she stumbled back. The magic rushed out. The waves of shadows turned her veins as cold as ice, but at the same time freed her. The release of all that power felt so good.

Leda flinched and shook her head from side to side. "No, no, no. It wasn't meant to be this way," she said as her face turned ashen.

She knew this wasn't what her mum wanted, but she couldn't help it.

She turned her palms upward as shadows surged from her hands and rose like a billowing cloud above her. Azalea opened her eyes to witness the power torpedo into the night sky above, darkness merging into more darkness.

A sob came from inside the circle.

Azalea gritted her teeth as the muscles in her chest and arms finally released—the magic died down and the last of the shadows trickled from her fingers. Her hands fell limp at her sides like wrung-out rags.

"Oh, Azalea." Her mum was at the edge of the salt circle as the shadows cleared.

"It's okay, mum. I'm going to fix this." At least her mum had seen the extent of her problem now. She rolled her shoulders and stood up, eyeing the spirits who had shied away. That might keep them away, for a while at least.

"Come back in the circle, dear," Leda said.

"I can't. I've got something I need to do. See you back at home."

Her mum would be fine. The spirits would ignore her, and she could get on with her other ceremonies for the full moon.

Azalea glanced back at the spirits before sprinting into the darkness of the trees. This was it. She had a good feeling about tonight; she was about to find her answers . . .

CHAPTER 2

A ZALEA HIT THE PATH and sprinted through the trees, ignoring the eyes that followed her. Branches whipped her face, not moving out of her way this time and blood pounded in her ears as she ran faster, blocking out all sounds of the forest.

The pulse of the invisible moon's energy lingered in the air. She could still make it to the meadow in time. Trying it her mum's way hadn't worked. It was up to her dad now. Hopefully he had some miracle solution, but she wasn't holding her breath.

Speeding across the dark field behind their cottage, grass whipped at her legs as the familiar smells of night air hit her face, fragrant hedgerows of honeysuckle and jasmine clashed with cowpats and rain. She arrived at the lone standing stone and leaned against it as she caught her breath.

A loud croak from above made her flinch. The obnoxious calls broke the spell of the night air. Three dark silhouettes of crows sliced through the night sky. *Super creepy.* She had seen way too many of them for her liking in the past week.

An icy chill settled in the air, and she was glad of her blood-warming dash through the forest. She pressed her back against the stone, its coolness trickling into her skin through her raincoat. Pressure weighed on her eardrums, and she froze.

A voice emerged.

"Zaely, are you there?" His voice was faint, like whispers through a wall. Her hands trembled and a lightness spread through her chest. *He was here!* She leaned into the rock as if that could help her hear. He wasn't like the other spirits. She couldn't see him, but he could project his voice through from the other side. Kind of like talking through a closed door.

"I'm here, Dad." She squeezed the pocket watch and tried to still her racing heart so she could hear. Azalea had been ten when he died. She liked to think she could recognize his voice, but the truth was that she had few memories of him. He had never lived with them. His visits had been infrequent, and he never stayed long, because apparently his work was *too important* and *too dangerous* to have a family. Azalea didn't know much more than that. She had never cared.

But this voice was his. He knew things only her father could know. She still had memories of his warm smile and kind eyes as he turned up on unexpected visits with gifts of a new book and a special pocket watch each time. The watch in her pocket was the last gift he gave her. The first time she heard his voice through the rock, she had tested him. He passed by describing the watch in great detail, even recalling their conversation about how to take it apart and fix it so it would work again.

"Good, I don't have much time. I'm glad you came," he said.

"I need your help, Dad. The spirits, surges of power, the shadows—it's getting out of hand. I'm worried I could hurt someone." She bit her lip and glanced around. No spirits yet.

"There is no need to fear your gifts. I might have a way to help you learn to control it."

Heat radiated through her chest.

His voice strained. "You must find the Shadow Atlas, my book. It will show you a path forward. Your mother had it. She knows it has power and probably hid it with your grandmother."

Okay . . . a book. Not what she was expecting, but if it helped, she was all in. "What does it look like? How do I use it once I find it?"

"You will know it instantly. It will only reveal itself to someone worthy and of our family's bloodline. Once you have it, it will show you how to bring me back."

"Wait! What do you mean, bring you back?"

"Back to the world of the living. Then I can teach you everything you need to know. It's my only hope. I'm weak, Zaely. I can't keep this up much longer. The equinox will be my only chance to come back." His voice trailed with a faint hiss as a weighted silence filled the air.

Azalea's breath hitched as she realized what he was saying. "You mean—"

"I mean you can perform necromancy. You will be a powerful Shadow Mage, Azalea. But you must master the basics alone. The Shadow Atlas will guide you." His voice turned rushed, almost harsh.

Questions stampeded across her mind. Why would he think she was capable of this? How was raising the dead even possible? Where was he now? How would she explain this to her mum? Why hadn't she seen this book before? Also, the equinox was only two and a half months away . . .

Her mouth was dry. She couldn't get any of her questions out. Suddenly, she wished someone was there beside her, Isaac, RoRo, *someone* to tell her she wasn't crazy.

Her dad spoke as if he had read her mind. "Your mum won't approve of this, I'm sure. She never wanted you to follow in my footsteps. But the book is rightfully yours. It is the key to obtaining the knowledge. You're strong enough now."

A jolt of fear shot down her spine. Was she considering this?

"But how? I don't know any magic and literally have no control." The words trembled on her lips. Seeing spirits was one thing, but raising someone from the dead seemed a little above her league. Was that even possible? The only thing she knew about Shadow Magic was from her uncle, he could control shadows and spent his time hunting some sort of dark creatures. Too bad her mum had cut off contact with him several years ago.

The logical side of her brain told her this was crazy. But isn't this what she wanted? A way to control magic. Having her dad back would be a bonus, though she didn't really know him. Leda never spoke of him, but his coat still hung at the front door. Surely, she would be happy if he came back, right? Or was this a trick?

There was a long pause. Her stomach dropped. He couldn't have run out of time already.

"You can do this." His tone deepened. "I promise I will answer all your questions in due time. We'll have all the time in the world, but do not speak to your mother of the book."

"Right. . ." Her brain switched gears, all synapses firing at once and forcing her to the only possible decision: she had to do it. Yes! She would bring her dad back from the dead. *Why not?*

The wind picked up once more. Azalea reached out as if to grab his voice somehow, but he was gone. The spark of energy from the air was gone.

"Please don't go. I can't do this alone." She choked on the last words.

There was no reply. Azalea slid down the rough stone to slump into a pile on the sodden earth. She pressed her fingers into her eyes, rubbing them until she saw stars. Was that real? Should she be trusting a mysterious voice in a rock, or should she be checking into the loony bin?

At least she had two things to go on now: a mysterious book and a deadline. It was July now, that meant around two and a half months till the autumn equinox. The night air seeped into Azalea's bones, along with the realization that she might be going crazy.

She closed her eyes and summoned a deep breath. The clouds weighed down on the field, darker than before and threatening rain again. She lost track of how long she sat there, staying until fat raindrops hit her forehead and her bum was numb from the wet ground.

Forcing herself up, she wiped off her muddy jeans. As she stood in the bleak, soggy field, she had never felt more alone. But hey, what did she have to lose? Time to hunt for a mysterious book to raise her father from the dead. No, she wasn't crazy at all . . .

CHAPTER 3

AZALEA LEANED INTO THE yellow mandala-patterned cushions in the window seat which overlooked the wild cottage garden. Her mum crouched over a newly composted garden bed, digging at it with a vengeance that didn't seem fair to the poor seedlings.

Last night's adventure clouded her mind like a dream, and with only a few hours' sleep, Azalea could barely keep her eyes focused on her laptop screen—or the thousand tabs she had open about necromancy, none of which seemed helpful. This was one thing the Internet didn't have the answers for.

She needed to find the Shadow Atlas.

Craning her neck, she checked that Leda was still busy. The first step was to see if her mum hid it in their house somewhere. Her hunt started in her mum's bedroom. She checked all the obvious hiding spots, under the bed, in the secret floorboard where Leda kept her good jewelry, in the cupboard filled with floral dresses.

Nothing.

The hallway cupboard was the next obvious place to check. Incense aromas wafted out in a cloud. It was an everything cupboard—Tibetan healing bowls and essential oils were stored with old running shoes, bags, beach towels, and linen, all with the same sandalwood smell. Azalea shuffled everything out and re-stacked it roughly. Still no book, but at least the cupboard was tidier.

Their cottage was tiny, with two bedrooms upstairs and an open living area and kitchen downstairs—there weren't many places a magical book could be hidden . . . Well, not ones Azalea wouldn't find. She'd lived here all her life and had found every nook, cranny, and hidey-hole as a nosy child, often with the help of Isaac.

Next, she searched her own room. It was the messiest place in the house, therefore the perfect hiding spot. Perhaps the book had been under her nose the whole time? But after two hours of putting away clothes, mounding up washing, and discovering old school notes she had needed months ago for her exams, she came up empty-handed.

"Zaels!" a voice called from downstairs with loud knocking.

"Coming!" she yelled to Isaac. She frowned at her room. It was now the tidiest it had been in years, which was certainly suspicious.

She trudged downstairs. The book had to be at RoRo's house.

"You're looking rough," Isaac said cheerily.

"Thanks, Mr. Obvious." She didn't need to look at him to know his hair would be perfect or that he was wearing some sort of fancy sweater and ironed trousers thanks to his butler or someone. "Want a cuppa?"

"Yes, but normal tea please. I'm not in the mood for fancy flower stuff," Isaac said.

Azalea stepped into the kitchen and reached between the mismatched jars of dried herbs and teas to flick on the bright blue kettle. Isaac made himself at home at the small dining room table that was scarred with melted candle wax and knife cuts from various craft and kitchen projects, but he was used to it and leaned back like he owned the place. Azalea liked to think of him as the brother she never had, and her mum always treated him as such. He appeared more himself in their tiny kitchen than he ever did up at his giant manor house.

"I'm guessing you were up late doing some sort of witchy-woo full moon ritual?"

"You know it. Mum dragged me out to the forest in the pouring rain. Don't ask."

Isaac was the only one of her friends who knew about magic. They'd spent too much of their lives together for him not to notice, and he was the only one she could talk to about her abnormal problems. She'd learned via multiple disasters-slash-rejections from ex-boyfriends and so-called friends, that it was better not to mention anything to do with ghosts or magic. People might say they are open-minded, but when faced with the truth, they all shut their minds like a church door on science. She was better off without their drama anyway.

Azalea brought the tea pot to the table, her mum's own blend of black tea. A side business she had on the go right now—- *Leda's Leaves.* She poured them two cups as her little cat Faraday wound around their legs. "Nearly forgot the biscuits," she said, hopping up again to grab the jar of chocolate digestives, her favorite. She poured the tea into two floral teacups and immediately dunked a digestive into her cup for just the right amount of time.

"So . . . I've ordered two motorbikes. They should be here before I leave. So how about it? Joy rides? Get you out of the house for once."

"What? You bought us *motorbikes*? You know you have too much money for your own good, right?"

"Well, technically one's Issy's. But she won't want to use it," Isaac said with a shrug as he dunked a biscuit into his own tea.

"I'm guessing your lovely sister doesn't know she owns this motorbike?"

"That's not the point. The point is you need to get out more. You can't stay cooped up all day fiddling with old watches and staring at ghosts out your window. For one, it's creepy, and two, you need to live a little—and preferably in the next few weeks before I leave."

"Hey, I like fiddling with old watches. And I happen to make money doing it. My online shop had three orders this week I'll have you know. *Some* of us need to work for money."

"So you'll come riding with me, yeah?" Isaac said.

"Course. Let me know when the bikes arrive and I'll be there in a flash. There's something I've gotta do first. I need to find a magic book . . . my dad told me to." She swallowed hard. Saying it out loud sounded ridiculous. She wasn't quite sure what to feel: frightened, scared, hopeful, excited? Right now, all she felt was more pressure weighing her down.

"Your dad told you to . . . correct me if I'm wrong, but your dad has been dead since you were ten. So, is he a ghost? Did you see him? Is he here now?" His voice dropped to a whisper and his eyes shifted around the room.

She shook her head as Isaac sat up straight as if her dad might appear any second. "Spirits can't get in here. It's warded. I explained it to you before."

"Right—" He shook out his shoulders but didn't seem to relax. Azalea told him everything about the night before. She explained about needing to find the book and bring her dad back, then filled him in on her plans to find the book at RoRo's as soon as possible.

He sat there in stunned silence for several seconds. "Well, what are we waiting for then? Let's go. I want to see this book before I leave. I can't miss all the fun."

She smiled. Everything was so easy with him; he didn't even question her craziness anymore. "Hold up, Mr. Wannabe Wizard. RoRo's away for a few days, but I plan to ask her as soon as she's back. In the meantime, I'll keep searching here. Don't worry, I'll tell you as soon as I find it."

"Good. Well, in the meantime, let's get back to your necromancy research so we have some good background foundations. You never know what story might have got it right."

))) ● (((

Azalea sat bolt upright, dripping in sweat. Shadows spiraled around her bed like a black, misty tornado. *Not again . . .* She crunched her knees up to her chest.

"Mum!" she called toward the bedroom across the hall. A black cat with a white diamond on his forehead appeared at her side and nudged her arm. Faraday always knew when she needed him. She slid her legs forward a little, and he crept into the narrow gap on her lap. Squeezing her eyes shut, she let the calming purrs rumble through her.

Just over a week had passed, and her Shadow Magic was building up worse than ever. The ritual in the woods, or the full moon, or something had put it in overdrive. Her sleep suffered the most. Nightmares about unrelenting spirits and suffocating shadows plagued her dreams. And it didn't end when she woke up. Shadow Magic pressed on her chest and burned until shadows escaped and engulfed her room.

The scent of sage smoke hit her nostrils. She stayed frozen. Waiting. Her mum rushed into her room. Despite the fact that she could see how bad Azalea's magic had gotten, she still thought she could fix it.

She needed to find that bloody book soon. The Shadow Magic made her feel less in control than ever, but losing sleep was making her miserable and made everything seem hopeless.

"Nearly clear," Leda said.

Azalea cracked an eye and let out a breath. Leda's bright floral tea towel snapped away the shadows as she muttered protective chants. Sage smoke overtook the darkness and the light from the paper lamp shade filtered the world back to reality. Azalea shook out her freezing fingers and leaned back against the bed with a long exhale.

Faraday stretched off her and circled a spot and went back to sleep. She stroked his head as Leda perched on the edge of the bed.

"My poor sweet pea, it will get better soon," Leda said.

"It's not getting better, Mum. Much worse, in fact." Denial about her experimental treatments was her mum's new way of life. This week's experiments had been infusions of ashwagandha, reishi mushrooms, holy basil, valerian, and chamomile. It was clear from her selection of adaptogen ingredients that Leda's target was her daughter's mental health, rather than a cure for Shadow Magic.

Leda put a hand to Azalea's forehead and frowned. "Hop into my bed and get some sleep. We can change the sheets tomorrow," she said.

Azalea's shirt was plastered to her back and she didn't fancy sleeping in her sweaty bed any longer.

"When will RoRo be back?"

"Tomorrow, I think." She smiled and stroked Azalea's cheek.

"I'm sorry Mum, I'm trying." Azalea wished this Shadow Atlas would just turn up and fix all her problems. She'd searched all week and was sure it wasn't here.

"I know you are, dear. Just get some sleep."

Azalea just nodded and peeled the sheets off her as she stumbled to her mum's room. Hot tears crept from the corners of her eyes as she fell into the bed and pulled the patchwork quilt over her head. Faraday circled the crook of her knee.

Shadow Magic was ruining her life.

Clenching her fists, she told herself to suck it up. Tomorrow she would go to RoRo's house, and tomorrow she would find the Shadow Atlas.

)))●(((

The next morning, Azalea dressed in comfortable black running tights, a purple razorback top, and tied her long hair into a high ponytail. She could almost dismiss the nightmares and shadows as foolishness in the light of day. But her strained neck and floppy limbs reminded her otherwise.

RoRo would finally be back today, and she could finally search her house.

Squinting, Azalea stepped out into the too-bright sunlight. She trudged down the uneven stone steps. Wisteria perfumed the air as she swept through the curtains of purple flowers that draped the cottage. The back path led through the most unnatural garden in England. She kept her hands to herself as she passed garden beds of tropical orchids, mystic alpine roses, and narrowed her eyes at the rare jellyfish palms that had stung her more than once. Pausing at the edge of the willow fence to check for spirits, she saw none were close, so she set off.

Today was the day. She had her lucky pocket watch and was feeling good about this whole thing.

RoRo's house was on the farthest side of the forest, near the village of Leighton. Before the Shadow Magic started getting out of hand, Azalea had spent every Saturday morning at the Leighton market with RoRo selling her balms and elixirs to locals who swore by her remedies. She missed that.

Marching through the clearing of bluebells, fat bumblebee-dragons buzzed around Azalea's head. They wouldn't hurt her, but she re-tied her hair into a messy bun to stop them from getting tangled. One hovered near her face, its fat bumblebee body bobbing up and down as its tiny dragon head darted in every direction. They had brains filled with fluff, but they were adorable critters.

A chill brushed her skin. A small crowd of spirits had gathered on the path behind her. She left the bumblebee dragons and darted into the trees. RoRo's wasn't too far. The walls of her place had protective magic embedded into the stonework, same as her and her mother's cottage. RoRo had always said they were reasonable enough wards to keep spirits out, and so far it had been true.

RoRo's workshop came into view as Azalea slipped out of the forest, not looking behind. With a breath of relief, Azalea leaned on the heavy door and shoved it open.

Trailing her fingers through the rows of hanging herbs, Azalea breathed in the familiar mix of melting beeswax, rosemary, and earth. Home. She'd always loved the old stone workers' cottage. It was like a Victorian pharmacy mixed with an out-of-control greenhouse.

Azalea pushed her way down the narrow aisles to the back work bench. She kept her elbows in close to avoid the important clutter on all surfaces; glass jars filled with fresh balms, bubbling liquids distilling into flasks, and a strange new copper apparatus belching steam.

"RoRo? Are you in here?"

"Down this end!" Her voice was muffled by the jungle of plants.

Another corner and another isle of plants, Azalea stopped abruptly at the brewing station where RoRo was standing over a hissing pot. Leaning over, harsh steam singed Azalea's sinuses. She gagged and jerked away.

"What is that?" Azalea said, scanning the room for a more pleasant smell.

"I'm making a sleep tonic, my dear—a strong one at that." RoRo smiled and planted a kiss on Azalea's cheek. "You're a bag of bones, and look at those rings under those lovely eyes." She shook her head and made those tut-tutting sounds. "Is your mother not feeding you well enough? Or is it all that running you're always doing?"

"I'm fine RoRo," Azalea said as she found a clump of lavender to hold to her face. "Can't you smell that?"

"I'm used to it. Now what brings you here? Have you come to help me organize my saffron threads in order of length? It's something I've been meaning to do for a while."

"Um—no," Azalea said with a small laugh. She'd made the mistake once before and regretted it. Her fingers had been stained orange for weeks. "I came to . . . fix your toaster . . ."

"Is that really why you came here?" RoRo asked with a knowing look.

"Um, no. I wanted to ask you something."

"Fire away, love. I'm all ears," RoRo said.

Azalea bit her lip. Where to start? "Right. Well, how about I make us a cuppa first?" Azalea said, side stepping to the next bench over.

"That sounds lovely. Tea's under the cat over there." RoRo pointed to the white puffball named Lizard.

Azalea busied herself making tea, not sure how to start the conversation. She set the kettle boiling and eased the box of tea from under the cat. She felt RoRo's eyes on her.

"Your magic is growing strong. It's natural, you know. Has your Echo Magic improved at all?" RoRo asked.

"I don't *have* any plant magic or any other types of Echo Magic, as far as I can tell. But the Shadow Magic is getting stronger by the day. Mum won't listen to me."

"You don't have to do everything alone, Petal. Sometimes it's best to ask for help," RoRo said, eyes back on her brew.

Azalea focused her attention on rinsing out the teapot in the giant farmhouse sink. This was her chance.

"I do need help. I know Mum's trying, but I need to figure this Shadow Magic out for myself. I heard there's something that might help me . . . a book." Azalea didn't dare look at RoRo. A weighted silence hung in the air.

"And where did you hear this?"

"My dad . . ."

RoRo straightened up. Azalea could feel her eyes searching.

"Oh. I see. How odd. I know you can see spirits, my dear, but Samael is the last person I'd thought would appear as one. Best not to question the ways of the gods. So, what did he say?"

"He said to find the Shadow Atlas, that it would help me learn to control my powers," Azalea said, choosing not to add the part about raising him from the dead. She suspected RoRo wouldn't approve of that.

"He always had that book with him. We never knew what it was. After he passed, we never did work out how to open it. Of course, your mother always assumed it was full of dark magic, said it was best to keep it locked away. I always thought it was a journal. He was always writing in it. Perhaps he wrote something in there to help you? Did he say what?"

Azalea shook her head. "I assume he wrote out instructions or something? I nearly messaged Uncle Fabian to ask about it, since you were away. But that would only make things worse with Mum. She'd be so pissed if I talked to him. I mean, she's still dark on him and he hasn't been over since last time when he told me about Shadow Magic in the first place." Azalea realized she was clutching the teapot and placed it down.

RoRo's steely gray eyes, a mirror of Azalea's, drilled into her as if searching for something more.

"Your mum wanted something different for you. She kept things from you for your own protection. She loves you. But either way you look at it, Shadow Magic is in your blood. There's no point in hiding from it or denying it any longer. I think if the book can help you, you should have it."

"You won't tell mum?" Azalea asked.

"I won't. That's up to you. But you'll have to be careful. Use what you learn to do good, not harm."

Azalea nodded as a smile broke her lips. "Thank you, RoRo!" she wrapped her arms around her grandmother in a big hug.

RoRo tensed. Azalea leaned back to study her grandmother's face. She noticed how similar their features were. The same oval face, pale enough to get sunburned even on an overcast winter's day, and the same sprinkling of freckles across their cheeks and nose. But more than that, RoRo had a constant look of weariness that she did her best to hide. Azalea recognized the exact look in herself. And those gray eyes had secrets.

"Can you tell me more about magic? What am I missing?"

RoRo turned to the tree behind her and as her hand reached out, a perfect plum grew from the branch and dropped into her hand.

"Bloody hell, that was amazing." Azalea stared at the perfect fruit.

"Your mother doesn't want you to become a mage, but there are more of us out there than you know. In London there are communities of mages, and many more around the world. I realize I've been wrong to hide it from you for so long."

"So that's why you didn't want to be the Forest Guardian. You became a mage instead?"

"I couldn't be a Forest Guardian for the same reasons as you, dear . . . the power. I felt its pull. I wanted it more than anything." RoRo stared into the pot, her eyes glassy as if she was remembering.

"I don't want power, RoRo. I just want my life back."

RoRo gave a sad smile. "That's what I thought too. Just remember the important things in life, like being kind and helping people. Like helping your old grandmother fix her toaster," she joked.

"I'd hardly call you old, you don't even have one wrinkle," Azalea said, for the first time realizing how strangely young RoRo looked. "But I will fix your toaster."

"You're a good girl Azalea. Now finish making that tea and we'll go dig up this book."

CHAPTER 4

// I'll finish my tea and you fix the toaster before I hunt down this book," RoRo said as she made herself comfortable at the long kitchen table filled with melted candles of varying heights.

"It'll be fixed before you know it," Azalea said, feeling enthusiastic for the first time in days. She glanced out the kitchen window and her heart skipped a beat as a raven swung down across the doorway. Hanging in the gutter, it glared at her with beetle black eyes. Its head tilted to the side.

"Ravens can't open windows, can they?" Azalea said as she swiped the curtain shut.

"Don't be silly, dear, not if they're locked."

Azalea checked the latch on the window and turned to the toaster. It was an easy fix. She took the toaster apart, cleaned out all the crumbs and grime, polished the electrical contacts, then put the whole thing back together. RoRo insisted on making toast with homemade strawberry jam, just to be sure it was fixed. Azalea finished her lukewarm tea.

RoRo ate slowly, and Azalea sat there tapping her foot.

"Can we please get the book now?"

"Patience is a virtue, my dear." RoRo finished her toast and finally gave a flick of her head to follow as she marched off up the hallway. Azalea jumped up. They stopped at a plain wooden door. *No way that was there before.* She'd spent her childhood sprinting up and down this hallway of familiar worn stone.

RoRo opened the door and Azalea peered over her shoulder to find an antique store's worth of crap shoved into a space the size of a broom closet. Grabbing a torch from the nearest shelf, RoRo clicked it on and stepped in. Azalea followed, and as she entered the small space, a familiar fire ignited in her chest. A glint of silver shone as her phone light scanned over a shelf piled high with mismatched goblets and tea sets.

"Watch the bell there, Petal."

Azalea turned in the narrow space and pain flared up from her toe as it crunched against something solid. She looked down and scowled at the large bell sticking out from under a shelf.

Feeling returned to her toe, as a dark flash darted into the cupboard. Faraday leaped to a shelf and trotted across a collection of porcelain animal figures. Yellow eyes drilled into her own. How he knew when and where to turn up, she'd never know.

"Hello, Mr. Faraday," RoRo greeted the tiny black cat. "I see you've found what we want."

He let out a 'brrp,' as he circled atop a box pressed against the back wall.

"Off," Azalea ordered the cat.

Stretching dainty paws, he trotted to the edge of the box in his own time and folded himself into a space between some rusty chains on a bookshelf.

Yanking off the blanket, RoRo sent a smokescreen of dust into the air which soon cleared to reveal an ornate chest carved with intricate phoenixes and dragons across the top. Azalea squeezed into the gap next to RoRo. Creaking open the chest, the smell of leather and old linen drifted up. The warmth inside Azalea grew like flames spreading across oil and into her limbs.

"Are you alright, dear?" RoRo asked.

"Yup, I'm good," Azalea lied.

"Dive in there. I'm sure it's in this one."

Frowning into the dark chest and ignoring the ache, Azalea handed her phone to RoRo to hold up for extra light. Lacy tablecloths scratched at her skin and smells of musty sheets filled the air as the tingling of magic spread to her fingers.

This was it. She was going to have all the answers soon. Just over two months till the equinox, but she still had time, and now she had hope. She threw linen over the sides and dug deeper.

Sparks of heat nipped at her fingers. This was it. Just a little more.

Soft leather kissed her fingers for a second. Balancing on the edge of the chest, she ignored the sides cutting into her guts as she reached in further. The Shadow Magic surged from her chest and rushed toward her hands. She froze and knew what was coming next. She closed her eyes.

This time, it was different. There were no shadows, no swirling darkness. The energy surged into the book as she grabbed it, and warmth engulfed her body. She was as light as a dandelion seed. Grasping the book, she rocked her way out of the chest.

Azalea rubbed her abdomen where the edge had left a hot, painful dent in her skin. She beamed at the book. Her hands trembled as RoRo passed her the phone and she ran the light across the cover.

"That's the one," RoRo said.

Azalea's fingers brushed the dark leather. At the center, an emblem of a golden snake shone up at her. She breathed in the smell of leather and something else—an unusual scent for a book—the smell of ice, and distant snow; of changing weather.

"Well, open it dear. The suspense is nearly killing me," RoRo said.

"Hold your horses, I'm getting there," Azalea said, grinning. She opened the front page to find illuminated script radiating with the very words she had been hoping to see—*The Shadow Atlas*. A thrill of adrenaline shot through her. "It's lovely, isn't it? Let's hope your father isn't leading you astray. Just remember, all magic has a price," RoRo added with uncharacteristic seriousness.

She hugged the book to her chest and kissed RoRo on the cheek. "Everything will be fine, RoRo," Azalea said, very much hoping that was true.

))) ● (((

Warm lamplight filtered across the bedroom as Azalea flipped onto her stomach on the sheepskin rug. Isaac lay next to her on his back, staring up at the beams they'd scratched their names on as kids. As promised, she had invited him over to check out the book for the first time.

Ignoring the piles of washing and uni paperwork strewn across her desk and bed—which Isaac was used to anyway—her focus was entirely on the book.

She turned the Shadow Atlas over in her hands, and Isaac rolled over to lie next to her.

"It's very small, isn't it? More of a notebook, really. I was expecting something large and bejeweled. Perhaps the media has led me astray once more," Isaac said with an over dramatic sigh.

"Stop being so judgmental. I'm glad it isn't. This can fit in my bag, much more practical. But honestly, it's quite heavy for being so small," Azalea said.

It felt almost alive, and she couldn't help but trail her fingers over the smooth creases in black leather. One finger hovered over the raised emblem of a snake, its golden body coiled in a perfect spiral with its head at the center. Eyes of tiny gemstones that she swore were a reddish-purple color when she found it, were now as green as a dewdrop sitting on moss.

"Let's open it," Isaac said, tapping a drum roll on the floorboards with his hands.

"Yes . . . we should." Apprehension crept in. What if it didn't have the answers? She stared at it for a long minute, half expecting the snake to move. When it didn't, she pressed the emblem firmly, and it gave a click as the metal clasp flipped open.

"It's gone," she said in disbelief. The front page she had opened to earlier had disappeared. The fragile mottled paper mocked her with its blankness.

"I thought you said it had writing in it?"

"It did!"

"Wait, it's doing something," Isaac said. Both of them leaned over the book. He was right. Black ink crept onto the page as if someone were writing.

The words *Feed me* appeared in flawless calligraphy, big enough to cover both pages.

"Feed it what?" Azalea sat up as she got an idea. "At RoRo's it took my magic. Maybe that powers it or something?"

"Go on then, ask it," Isaac said as he rolled up to sit cross legged next to her. "Feed you what?" Azalea asked slowly and clearly. It didn't change. The words *Feed me* darkened as the ink started running down the page.

"This is kind of creepy. Maybe try writing in it?" Isaac suggested, scooting back ever so slightly.

"Chicken," Azalea teased. But he was right—the writing was creepy.

She got out a pencil so at least then she could erase it if it didn't work.

Feed you what? she wrote, very messily compared to the elegant ghostly script.

Blood or Magic. I enjoy both.

"Disturbing much?" Isaac said, pulling his hands into his chest as if the book might bite him. "Well, just give it some magic, then."

"I can't just make magic happen, in case you forgot." She looked at her hands, for once hoping the Shadow Magic would come out. It didn't.

"Blood, then. Give the vampire book some blood. Why not?" Isaac said.

"*You* give it some blood," Azalea snapped back. If it was her dad's book . . . she should trust it, right? It's just . . . the sight of blood always made her more than a little woozy.

"Stop being a baby and do what the book says, come on." Isaac nudged her with his shoulder and hopped up and went to her desk.

"You're far too excited about this. Do you think we should trust it?"

"Yes. And you should be more excited. We have a magical book that possibly has all the answers to your life's questions. This is going to make a great story one day."

"You can't write any of this down, Isaac."

"I know, I know. I'm not. It's all up here," he said, tapping his head with the end of a craft knife he found on the desk. "Here. Just prick the end of your finger." He handed it to her.

She swallowed as nausea rose up at the thought. "You do it," she said, shoving the knife back at him and holding out her finger.

She squeezed her eyes shut as his warm fingers wrapped around her palm, and she tensed, waiting for the pain. "Get on with it!"

A prick of heat flared into her finger.

"All done." Isaac hovered her finger over the book as she opened her eyes. Droplets of ruby red fell onto the parchment.

"That's more like it," Isaac said as Azalea's eyes blurred, not wanting to see her own blood leaving her body.

"Gosh!" she exclaimed, the blood instantly forgotten. Illuminated borders of shimmering gold, vibrant deep blues, velvety reds, and verdant greens materialized on the page in elegant patterns, the *"Feed me"* slowly absorbed into the central blankness of the page.

"Bloody hell, that's brilliant," Isaac said. The awe spread across his face . . . she felt it too.

With shaking hands, Azalea flicked through the pages. Page after page now revealed intricate illustrations that embellished meticulously inked maps. She soaked in every word, every image, every map. Flicking, flicking. More pages. More maps. Maps of their forest, maps of the village, several maps of London. All up to date with modern roads and houses.

"Isaac. Why is it all maps?" she said, trying to keep calm. None of this was instructions on how to raise someone from the dead or control Shadow Magic.

"Obviously I have no idea. Maybe it needs to warm up to you? Or you need to ask something specific?"

Suddenly, the page went blank. Azalea flicked through, but it was all gone. She grabbed the pencil. *How do I control shadow magic?* she asked it.

Feed me.

A wave of anger rolled through her. She pressed her finger to the page where a little dried blood left a smudge. "That's all you're getting," she said.

"Way to tell it, Zaels," Isaac whispered sarcastically with a pat on her shoulder.

I do not serve the weak. The text faded instantly, leaving nothing but blank pages.

"Stupid bloody book!" Azalea shouted, and slammed it shut.

"Maybe it doesn't like your blood," Isaac said.

"You're welcome to give it yours," she said as Isaac scrunched up his nose. Dark thoughts crept across her mind like weeds. Was this all some sort of trick or cruel joke?

Footsteps echoed outside the door. Azalea snatched up the book and shoved it under a pile of clothes.

"Why are you two on that disgusting floor? And how in the world did it get so messy in here so fast?" Leda said, frowning at the mess.

"It's fine, Mum, I have a system."

"You could do with a better system." She shook her head, her eyes darting around the room as if she was looking for something. "I made Cornish pasties if you lot are hungry."

"I'm always up for a pastie," Isaac said as he sprung up. Azalea quickly followed Isaac out before her mum asked any more questions.

CHAPTER 5

R AIN DRIZZLED ON WITHOUT a break, same as the past few days. Everything was soggy, and Azalea didn't feel very summery as she crunched up the sloping gravel drive toward Isaac's house. Even the weeping willows seemed to drag more than usual. Weaving through the curtain of willow leaves, Azalea took the shortcut that led behind the manor house.

It had been weeks since she'd found the Shadow Atlas. She'd been squeamishly feeding it blood in the hopes that it would reveal something useful. She'd studied every map and every bit of gibberish text it chose to show her. When she flicked to one map, it often replaced it with another. Just thinking about it sent her stomach twisting with anxiety and rage. Last night, she nearly threw the book in the fire when it refused to display anything and told her, *I will not allow one so unworthy to gaze upon my pages for another minute.*

She was out of ideas and patience. What she needed was to blow off steam. Her feet sank into soggy grass as she hopped over a stile and jogged toward the barn, glancing back in case of trailing spirits. It was all clear.

She made it to the decaying wooden barn out of the rain and shook out her yellow raincoat. Though there wasn't much point in trying to get dry now, her jeans were already soaked through. Her eyes adjusted to the dim light from the cracks in the barn as Isaac's footsteps crunched up the drive and he burst in looking pleased with himself.

"Got you this. Thought you'd want to look the part." Isaac handed her a black leather jacket dotted with raindrops.

"This is amazing! Thanks, Isaac." She hugged him and hung her raincoat on a nail and slid her arms into the fleece lined sleeves.

"Well, you only brought it up every single time we ever saw someone in a leather jacket, so it was a safe bet. And now you have an excuse to wear one."

"You know me so well." She kissed him on the cheek. He was good at presents. "So, are we going to take these bikes out?"

"You know I just got them so I could pretend to be a bad boy to impress girls?" Isaac said.

"You actually have to ride them to do that. I'm here now, so let's do this." She eyed up the motorbikes.

"It's not you Zaels. It's just . . . the weatherman . . . he didn't mention it would rain today, and you know how I am with getting my hair wet." Isaac breathed out an easy laugh.

"The helmet will crush your precious hair, so no need to worry about that." She picked up a leather glove and slapped him across the shoulder. "Get on with it. I haven't got all day. I've got to get back to my research."

He threw the other glove at her face. "You've certainly got the biker chick attitude down. How's the book going? Any luck?" He threw his leg over the bike as if testing out the seat.

"I'm sure it's just fucking with me for a laugh," she said, sure that was true.

"It does have a rather dark sense of humor. Not to worry, a ride will do you wonders. Maybe it'll like the taste of adrenaline in your blood? Give it a bit of a thrill when you get home."

Azalea let out a snort. "Worth a try. I've got to get some watches done too. I need to sell about a million of them to pay for uni."

"Well, that's very boring of you, you know. It's about time you had some fun."

She rolled her eyes. "Whatever. Let's get a move on then. If this is my one shot at fun, I won't have you screwing it up. On your bike, city boy." She kicked out the stand from the blue Suzuki.

"You know we could both be city people if you actually moved away instead of studying online. You should come back to London with me. I've got lots of friends you'd like, or you could go to Edinburgh since you already got in there," Isaac said as they pushed the bikes out onto the road.

"You know why I can't. And that's the beauty of online study. I don't have to go to Edinburgh to study there. Plus, I've met some of *those* friends, Isaac." She stopped and fastened her helmet. His friends from his boarding school were all spoiled, rich wankers, and he was very much one of them when they were together. She preferred this version of Isaac.

He just shook his head and revved his bike loudly, then lurched forward with a wobbly start. They were off.

As promised, more rain came, but it didn't stop them. Village after village rushed by as they pelted along narrow country roads. Adrenaline pumped through Azalea's veins as blurs of cows flashed past. The smell of exhaust and wet road filled her senses. Miles ticked by like heartbeats. As they sped up, Isaac's whoops of laughter merged with the roar of the bikes.

Leighton loomed just over the hill. Spitting rain lashed at Azalea's helmet as she sped up. Isaac wouldn't win this. They never discussed a race, but it was always a race with Azalea, and she would reach the village first. Isaac would slow too much on the last corner for sure. That's where she'd catch him.

The corner came up fast, but Isaac wasn't slowing down. Azalea's heart dropped to her stomach. His bike slid out from under him, screeching on the wet road. Ravens shot out of nowhere, pelting him from above. Before Azalea could take a breath, he slammed into the stone wall.

A scream spilled from her lips as she revved the engine to reach him. *No. No. No!* The ravens continued to dive into his collapsed form.

Her bike slid out as she hit the brakes hard. Tumbling off, she lurched toward Isaac.

She couldn't get close to him, so she threw clumps of dirt at the ravens till they backed off, though temporarily, she suspected. *Please don't be dead,* she repeated in her head. Horrible thoughts clawed at her mind as she crawled across the ditch to his still body. Holding her breath, she reached out for his hand. He groaned and nearly gave her a heart attack.

"Ouch," he said, with his eyes squeezed shut. Thank the gods he was alive.

"Bloody hell, you scared me," Azalea said as her heart raced a mile a minute.

Isaac pulled off his helmet and began wrestling with the bike. "I can't move it." He winced.

Trying to keep an eye on the sky for more bird attacks, Azalea scrambled up the bank and took the weight of the bike so Isaac could slide out. The birds had retreated to a nearby stone wall. They just sat there, cocking their heads from side to side like robots.

"Those bloody birds attacked me. That is not normal," he said, as he ran a muddy hand over his grazed cheek and into his hair.

"I know. I saw them," she said. "Are you okay?"

He slid back in the mud, leaning on Azalea. "I'm fine." He looked at his hands as if they weren't his own. There was blood, but she couldn't tell where it was coming from. He must be in shock. His usually perfect hair was a mash of sticks and grass, and he wasn't complaining about it.

The ravens began inching themselves along the wall in a line, getting closer.

"We need to go," Azalea said, warning bells going off in her head like fireworks. These birds weren't right.

"Let's just wait for someone to drive past," Isaac said.

"No. We need to get to the forest now." And she meant right now. The birds were like tigers, ready to pounce.

Isaac got the message. "Is this a weird magic thing?" he asked with his arm curled around her shoulder, and he winced as his foot hit the ground.

"I don't know. Just get a move on," Azalea said, more to herself than Isaac.

He was the same height as Azalea, but far more solid than her slight build.

"What have you been eating?" she joked.

"Oh, you know, roast peacock, venison, porpoise, the usual Tudor delicacies worthy of my father's taste," he said through pained breaths.

She did her best to hold his weight as they staggered toward the forest while the ravens launched into the sky and circled. Lower and lower. The forest wasn't getting any closer. With a screech, the birds attacked. Feathers and claws everywhere. Steely wings slashed at Azalea's cheek as she ducked and dragged Isaac down. They only seemed to be going for her though.

More talons came at her, and she raised her arms in a pitiful shield. A scream split from her lips as ribbons of skin raked from her arm. Twisting like fighter jets, they shot back into the air.

"Move, now!" she yelled and somehow pushed Isaac over the stone wall, then vaulted herself over. Each footstep toward the forest was like wading through water.

Ravens bombarded them relentlessly, but the tree line was close. Claws tangled in her hair and dug into her scalp. She dragged Isaac as the magic flames swirled within her chest. What good would shadows do her? She pushed them down, wishing she had some useful magic.

Azalea let out a sob as they finally reached the forest. She leaned against the bark of an old ash as Isaac's eyes glazed over, then closed for a long second. She shook his shoulder and strained to hold his weight. "Stay awake, Isaac. Please."

The ravens didn't enter the forest, but their cries continued high overhead. Blood trickled down Isaac's arms and face. Azalea tried to ignore the blood. She probably didn't look any better. Isaac was swaying. Pulling him deeper into the trees, they both collapsed to the earth. Isaac winced at his swelling wrist, then looked up at Azalea, his eyes half-lidded and glassy.

"Zaels, your face. There's blood." Isaac pushed the blood-soaked mess of hair out of her forehead, plastering it to the top of her head so she could see. "Those birds were attacking us," he said in disbelief. "We ought to call animal control or something. Was it magic? Is there a magical animal control? Do ravens carry rabies?" he asked, eying up her arms.

Azalea ignored her own pain. The gouges in her arm were fizzing and burning, as if someone had poured acid on them. "I don't know, but I think they've gone now. Where else are you injured?" She pulled Isaac's boot, but he screamed as she shifted his foot. Her brain was growing fuzzy. "Sorry."

She untied the laces and shifted the shoe off as gently as she could, while Isaac mumbled under his breath. A monster of a bruise bloomed on the side of his ankle, and it was swelling. Together, they shuffled back to a tree root. Leaning his head back against the tree, he hissed under his breath as she adjusted his leg.

"We need to get ice on this and get you back." She didn't recognize this part of the forest, and now Isaac was shaking. He tried to pull his phone out of his pocket, but there was no point. The forest blocked all signals.

Something moved behind the trees, and Azalea froze. The bushes rustled as Faraday and Lizard slunk out from the undergrowth as if they were expected. They trotted over, avoiding the puddles.

"This *is* magic related, isn't it?" Isaac said, his head heavy on her shoulder.

She glanced across at him. "I think so, but I have no idea what it is." His eyelids drooped. "Keep talking. You need to stay awake. I think the ravens had something on their talons, something's poisoning me," she said.

Faraday rubbed his head on her leg, then started clawing a nearby tree root. "Faraday. Can you please go home and get my mum," she said, knowing full well he was a cat, and even if he understood, he might not be inclined to help.

Faraday wound around her legs then batted Lizard on the head and ran into the bushes. Lizard, always slow to react, lowered his ears, then dashed after Faraday.

"Were you just talking to your cat? Is he magic?" Isaac asked sleepily.

"Yes, I was talking to him . . . I don't know if he's magic though. Sometimes he seems to understand. Either him or the forest will get my mum." She watched him closely, hoping the forest alerted her mum where they were. Faraday wasn't much hope.

"Stay awake, dammit, Isaac!" Hopefully he didn't have a concussion.

She shook his shoulder, and he lazily opened his eyes. Her head became suddenly heavy, and she let it loll against Isaac's shoulder. Her eyes wanted to shut, but her skin was boiling underneath it. There were scratches on her arms; angry red lines forked out like lightning from the gouges oozing with blood. She swallowed slowly, her tongue thick and heavy.

It was her fault Isaac was here. Guilt washed over her. She should have been at home figuring out the Shadow Atlas, then none of this would have happened. She only had a month left now. Instead, she told herself she deserved a break, but in truth, she was just being selfish. She didn't deserve to have her dad back, didn't deserve to learn Shadow Magic, didn't deserve to become a mage.

Her head was pounding. She couldn't stop the tears creeping into her eyes. All she wanted was to sleep.

Something was shaking her. "Azalea, wake up!"

Hot fingers were pulling at her eyelids. Light seared her vision. Groaning, she tried to look for Isaac.

)))●(((

Azalea struggled to focus on the hazy forms looming over her.

"She's waking up, Leda," a familiar voice said.

"Azalea, Petal. Can you hear me? We need you to wake up."

Straining against a blinding light, Azalea forced her eyes to blink.

"Drink this." Someone shoved a cup to her lips, and she drank. She'd never been so thirsty in her life. Sharp bitterness hit the back of her throat, and she spluttered half of it back up. The mint did little to mask the horrid taste.

Slowly, she came around. RoRo was next to her on a kitchen chair, holding the drink. Leda perched at the foot of the couch, her face red and eyes blotchy. The yellow flowery curtains, low beams, and bookshelves came into focus. She was on the sofa in the living room.

"What the—" Azalea started.

"You were poisoned, dear," RoRo said before she could ask.

Oh, that's right. Killer birds. Azalea raised a bandage-covered arm that reeked of strong and unfamiliar herbs.

"Where's Isaac?"

"He's fine. We took him to the hospital, and he's all patched up and at home sleeping. He's got a sprained ankle and a few bumps and bruises, but no poison like you. He'll be fine.

"Poison . . . wait, what?"

"The ravens. They had poison on their talons. You'll be happy to know you weren't paranoid this whole time. They were targeting you," RoRo said, smoothing out her long floral skirt with a pained look in her eye. "But enough of that. Drink another cup and get to sleep. You need rest to heal. Let us worry about the ravens," RoRo said.

Azalea noted the false reassurance. They were keeping something from her.

She forced down another cup of the disgusting concoction. "They came out of nowhere. Why did they attack Isaac like that?"

"They were testing you. Seeing if you would retaliate with Shadow Magic," RoRo said.

"I didn't. I don't know any useful Shadow Magic," Azalea said.

"They should leave you alone now. You've failed their test, though someone will come to check up on you, no doubt. To make sure you really did fail."

"Who? Why would they do that?" Azalea asked, but her brain was clouding over.

RoRo stroked her cheek and stood up. "Later dear."

A tide of drowsiness washed over her.

Her eyelids drooped. RoRo and her mum moved to the kitchen around the corner, and Azalea strained her ears. She could just make out their voices.

"How do you think they found her?" RoRo said.

"I don't know, but she should be safe here if they come. The house is well warded."

"You're in denial if you think that's true. They'll try to recruit her if they find out she lived through this, and once they find out who she really is, she'll be in much deeper water. She isn't safe anymore."

"I can protect her."

"You aren't a mage, Leda. Don't be foolish. She needs real protection."

"Don't do it Mum. Don't let me lose her as well."

"I'm calling Fabian," RoRo said. "He can keep her safe."

Her mother's sobs drifted into the living room as Azalea fought to stay awake.

CHAPTER 6

FEED ME.

Azalea dabbed a cotton bud into the cut on her arm and smeared the blood onto the page.

How to I bring back my dad? She wrote in the book for the ten thousandth time.

It replied with blood red ink:

A veil, a girl, a spirit lost.
From blood they once were tied.
Blood for blood is the cost.
Let shadows be your guide.

No shit. She needed Shadow Magic, that much was clear, and it had told her that before. She felt like it was just mocking her now. Nothing useful, just random maps and stupid riddles.

She flicked to the next page on the off chance it would be helpful. At least the poison from the day before was well out of her system now. She'd been hungry all day and was more awake than ever due to an overdose of sleep. But she was still under strict orders to stay in bed.

She found yet another map of London and rolled her eyes. Exhaling through her nostrils, she shut the book. What reason did it have to hide things from her, anyway?

She leaned over to check her phone. She had been messaging Isaac all day, and he kept claiming he was fine. If anything, he was thrilled by their adventure and glad to have the story. But still, she hated to have put him in danger.

A knock sounded at the door downstairs. Azalea strained her ears. Who the hell would be here after dark? Pushing back the blankets, she pulled on a zip up-gray hoodie and black jeans from the mountain of clothes on her chair. The material tugged against the bandages as she eased the sleeve over her arm. She tiptoed across the room and dodged the squeakiest floorboards.

A familiar voice echoed up the stairs and through the old cottage walls. *Uncle Fabian.* This guy had a death wish if he was showing up unannounced. Surely, he learned from the last time.

Within seconds, her mother was yelling.

This was worth hearing. Slipping through the door, Azalea inched to the top of the stairs and peered through the gap in the banister like she used to do as a kid.

Fabian didn't look at all himself; he looked rough. A dark trench coat trailed around him, and tangles of dark hair hung loose around his shoulders, not the slick, tamed back look Azalea was used to. His eyes locked on her mother's with an intensity she had never seen. Her mum was gripping a tea towel covered in daffodil patterns, she was still dressed in her dirt-flecked gardening overalls.

"The sentinels have found her, Leda. What don't you understand about that? They're looking for anyone with even a hint of Shadow Magic, testing them. The House of Ravens *will* come for her and recruit her, and when they find out who her father was—I don't want to know what they'll do," Fabian said bluntly. "She has a chance to get away now. We can make them think the poison killed her. Make them think she was too weak."

"I won't let them take her! She's better off without any Shadow Magic. We can suppress it. I've read all about it and have all the right herbs and rituals. We just need more time," Leda said.

"Herbs and incense aren't the answer here, Leda. She needs to learn proper control." Fabian's usually smooth, suave voice was desperate. Rooted to her spot, Azalea clutched the banister for support.

"No. I've protected her all these years and I won't give up now. She's better off without all that. I can train her to use ambient Echo Magic like me. As hard as it might be for you to believe, not everyone wants to become a mage. As much fulfillment can be found in serving the forest and the goddess."

Azalea swallowed. *Um, no. Had her mum been listening at all?*

Fabian scoffed. "For you, maybe. But she isn't like you, Leda. Can you not see what is happening? She's pulling ambient Shadow Magic from miles around and with it comes all kinds of trouble. She's drawing in spirits, and she drew in the ravens. She has to learn to control it. You should have called me sooner."

"I didn't want to call you at all. You know nothing about her, Fabian." Azalea caught the hint of a waver in her mum's voice.

"That's because you told me I wasn't welcome here." His hands curled into fists that he pressed hard into his sides.

Azalea jumped as something touched her leg. She gripped the rail just in time to catch herself. But it was just Faraday. Fabian was about to get himself kicked out, but she needed him to help her first.

She straightened up and stepped into the light. "Do I get a say in all this?" Her breath caught as her uncle glanced towards the stairs. His eyes were jet-black, no whites, just solid black.

"You might as well come down," he said.

She swallowed. Her mouth was dry as she walked down the stairs. This wasn't the uncle she knew, this was the side they all kept hidden from her. It felt like vines were wrapping around her guts and pulling. Her mum's usual rosy cheeks were drained of color.

"Hi, you're looking a little rough," Azalea said as her uncle pulled her into a firm hug.

"Good to see you, little Azalea, though you're not so little now and not looking so good yourself either." He released her and looked her up and down.

She smiled and folded her arms. "Actually, this is the best I've felt in weeks," she said. She didn't have to look at her mum to know what she was feeling and how much she didn't want Azalea to leave.

"Your mum and I were just discussing some options for your future," he said.

"I heard." Azalea glanced at her mum who was nibbling her lip like she did when she was worried.

"Good, you're up to speed, then. I have two options for you. You can either come with me to my house and I can try train you when I'm around. Or you can go to the Tower and join their Initiates program for Echo Magic."

Azalea twisted her mouth at the words *Echo Magic*. That was the opposite of Shadow Magic, wasn't it?

"Or you can stay here where I can protect you. RoRo can improve all the wards on the house. I promise you it will be safe," Leda said, her eyes pleading.

"You can't make promises like that, Leda," Fabian said.

Azalea bit her lip and turned back to her uncle. "How would learning Echo magic help me? I thought the whole point was that I don't have plant magic like Mum? Can I even use it?"

"Yes," Fabian replied quickly. "You should have abilities for both types of magic. The problem you have now is the ambient magic in the surrounding air isn't enough for you. Some people reach a point where they require raw magic. Many who don't seek to use the power, like your mother, can resist the pull and be content with using the little magic in the air around and never need anything more. You'll have Echo Magic abilities in there somewhere," Fabian said.

"And this would fix me?" she asked, letting hope flutter in her belly.

"You don't need *fixing*, Azalea. But it would be too much risk leaving you without training. The sentinels—the Ravens—have already found you, so either way, you need to get somewhere safe and learn some control."

"And you can teach me?"

His lips drew to a thin line. "I'm not around much, Azalea. I'm away for months at a time. I can guide you, but you would be alone a lot. It wouldn't be ideal."

The fluttering died down. There was always a catch. Plus, Fabian's house—her father's ancestral home, Blackbourne Manor—was in the middle-of-nowhere countryside. There were no towns, no Universities, no people, and no pubs.

"And what about this program at this tower? Isn't there somewhere else that teaches Shadow Magic?"

"There may be a chance you can learn *some* Shadow Magic there, but no promises. The only other place to learn is with the House of Ravens, and they just tried to kill you, so it's obviously not the best option."

"So how will learning Echo Magic help?" Azalea asked. None of these options sounded great. But if she could learn control, it would be worth it.

"By learning Echo Magic techniques, your body will build up resistance for Shadow Magic as well. Make it easier to use either type." He shrugged. "It's better than nothing. And at the Tower you would be in training with others your age. Most go to uni during the day and train in magic at night," he said.

Azalea rubbed her forehead. If she went with Fabian, she would be alone all the time in his big house—not so different from her current life. Even so, she would be learning magic. The Tower intrigued her, though she knew nothing about it. Staying at home was not an option. She didn't want to live like this anymore. Her concentration flicked back to Leda and the growing panic in her voice.

"I will not have her turning into another narcissistic mage. You're all the same. She needs to get her education and have a normal life." Leda rung her hands around the tea towel.

Azalea's chest tightened.

Fabian looked at Leda with pity. "Her life won't be normal if she has to hide here. You would condemn your own daughter to a life of mediocrity just because of your own selfish fears?"

Leda's sniffed. "If it keeps her alive, then yes. I will not be *that* mother standing over her only daughter's grave, wishing I had done more to protect her."

"Becoming a mage isn't a death sentence but staying here might be if the House of Ravens finds out she's alive after their little test," Fabian said as he shook his head in frustration.

The whites of his eyes were returning to a smoky gray as he stormed past Leda into the kitchen. He opened cupboards until he found the good whiskey. Azalea was surprised her mum didn't stop him as he poured a generous amount into the nearest teacup. "She would be better off as a mage, and you know it."

"Like Samael was?" Tears silently ran down Leda's cheeks, but she still managed to glower at Fabian drinking her whiskey.

Tension hummed in the air, and Fabian's eye twitched at the mention of his brother's name, Azalea's father. She wondered why her father hadn't reached out to Fabian. Surely he could bring her dad back to life easily? He rolled his neck slowly and poured another drink.

"I don't want to stay here if it will put you in danger, Mum. And I need to learn magic," Azalea said. "But I also need to think things over first."

"I'd be worried if you didn't," Fabian said. "You're not asking nearly as many questions as you should."

A zillion questions bombarded her brain, but she couldn't pin them down. It was a lot to take in and fear was doing its best to stop her.

"Where exactly is this tower?" she asked, ignoring her mum's disapproving looks.

"It's in London." He stared at her as if she were an idiot. "The Tower of London, actually. I'm sure you've heard of it," he said a little too sarcastically.

"You mean the *actual* Tower of London?"

"Obviously."

She clenched her jaw. What the hell about that was obvious?

"People live there?"

"Yes. And have done for centuries now. It's a community of mages from various backgrounds. It's also the biggest magical hospital in England, an archive for historical documents, a research center for magical artifacts, a base for the Initiates' training program, and a seriously well defended fortress. They've got some secret shit going on in there too, but I'm out of that loop now."

"Okay . . . this is sounding crazy." Living at the Tower of London sounded like a fantasy story. A much better experience than rattling round in an old house by herself or staying here and going mad. London would also have several sites she could use on the Equinox, a better chance of helping her dad. But it would also be one of the most haunted places with its dark past of executions and mass graves.

"What about the ghosts?" she whispered, knowing it sounded silly.

"Most buildings are warded against spirits. You should be fine," he said, not seeming to care. Maybe she should be worried . . .

"Can I bring my cat?"

"Sure," he said with a shrug.

Azalea's heart hammered against her ribcage like a piston. She had to take this chance. She wasn't learning any magic at home. The Atlas was no help. At least if she went to the Tower, she would have a better chance of finding what she needed and learning something to help bring her dad back.

"I'm going upstairs to wash my face and think about this. I'll let you know what I want to do when I come back down." Without looking at either of them, she darted up the stairs and into the bathroom. Cold water focused her mind as she splashed her face. She sat on the bathroom floor for ten minutes knowing she had to make a choice. Slowly, she got back up. There was only one thing to do . . .

CHAPTER 7

// I WANT TO GO to the Tower to learn Echo Magic," Azalea announced from the stairs.

Leda drew her hand in as if she'd been punched in the gut at Azalea's decision to leave. She made no attempt to hide the misery that spread across her face.

Fabian slammed down his drink in triumph, and Leda shot him a withering stare. "That settles it. Let's go." He pulled a knife from his belt.

"What? Right now?" Her stomach dropped. This was happening and happening fast.

"Of course. This place doesn't have nearly enough wards." He eyed the small living room suspiciously. "Go on then, pack your stuff."

Leda's arms fell to her sides. Azalea knew she felt betrayed.

"Just promise me you won't end up like your father," Leda said as she pulled Azalea into a hug.

"I'll be careful, Mum," Azalea said, her voice steady, but her hands were shaking. She didn't even know what happened to her father, and now didn't seem like the right time to get answers.

"I better go pack," she said as she peeled herself off her mum.

As she turned away, hot tears crept out, and she wiped them with her sleeve. She didn't want her mum to hate her, but she knew she had to leave. After running up the stairs, she pushed the door to her room harder than necessary. Faraday flattened himself and blinked at her.

The Shadow Atlas peeked out from under her pillow. She wrapped it in a purple sweater and stuffed it into the bottom of her largest sports bag. What did people usually pack when they only had minutes to leave their life behind?

She needed all her watches. The cash would be crucial if she was heading for London. She'd probably need to find herself a job of some sort too. Her savings account wasn't too healthy. She carefully placed loose dials, watch hands, lugs, springs, and tiny rubies from her desk into their designated homes in her purple tackle box and arranged her tools in their rollable leather case, then set the box by the door.

She threw open her wardrobe and stared blankly at her clothes. Apparently, (according to the many life-hack articles the Internet had sucked her into) in an emergency, it was best to just grab the laundry basket if you needed to leave in a hurry. Her washing basket was empty, but the clothes covering her floor were perfect. She stuffed as much as she could into the bottom of the bag knowing she would have enough t-shirts, underwear, socks, and workout clothes to last awhile, and they would be things she actually liked—not back of the closet crap. She added a few more sweaters from the washing pile, then some clean clothes on top to last a couple of days.

Her eyes glanced over her room. Faraday sat up to lick his paws, pretending not to care, but he watched closely. Her head was fizzing inside and the cuts on her scalp and arms were prickling. What else to bring? She grabbed some jeans, tights, a coat, her favorite pillow, and toiletries. She packed up calculus, physics, and mechanical engineering textbooks, plus stationary and her sticker covered laptop. She grabbed all her chargers and stuffed them in her backpack along with Faraday's favorite mouse toy and his purple cat bed. Was that it? Her whole life was in two bags?

She scanned the room. All she really needed was Faraday and the Shadow Atlas. Preparing to leave, she looked at the items on her bedside table. There was Gerald, his giant round eyes staring up like a lost puppy, though he was actually a brontosaurus. Isaac had won the toy dinosaur for her at a fair when they were six. That silly dinosaur had to come with. Priorities. She squished him in the top of her big bag and zipped it up. Done. She wouldn't get to say goodbye to Isaac. He would be at uni next week anyway, which was just down the road, at least he'd be pleased at that.

Staring at the mirror with false confidence, she tied her hair up and told herself she was doing the right thing. Heaving her tackle-box and bags down the stairs, she half expected her mum to yank them off her and drag her back to her room. Her uncle stood in the middle of the room, pacing. She dumped her big bag next to him while she slipped on her yellow canvas shoes and grabbed her leather jacket.

Fabian nodded at her. Azalea looked for her mum to say goodbye. But she wasn't there. Azalea bit the inside of her cheek to stop herself from bursting into tears. Was she doing the right thing? Leda stepped out of the pantry with a flax shopping bag.

"I packed some tea, biscuits, bread, honey, cheese, ham, some nectarines, apples, and a few jars of homemade piccalilli and chutney to get you through." Leda clutched the bag to her chest before handing it to Fabian.

"Thanks, Mum." Azalea kissed her cheek and pulled her into a final hug.

Leda wiped a tear from Azalea's face. "Stay safe, love."

She turned and went outside, back to her garden. Before Azalea could rethink, Fabian pulled her to the center of the room and raised his knife. Azalea froze in shock.

The rippling metallic blue blade drew her like a moth to a flame, so did the glowing gemstones in the handle. Unable to look away, she watched as Fabian carefully drew the knife through the air in one practiced sweep. This graceful motion cut a perfect arc. In what, she couldn't say.

The air rippled, revealing a darkness from somewhere else. The cut in the air was a doorway, its curtain of shadows moved like silk but dissipated like coils of smoke at frayed ends. A breath of icy air came from the darkness. It had the familiar smell of distant snow and frozen rivers that called to her.

Fabian, unfazed by this doorway to nowhere, acted as if he were holding a door to a lift. One hand resting on the edge of the silky shadow, the other reached out to her bag. "The wards here are shit. I shouldn't be able to open this here. Hurry up now, pass me that bag." He nodded to the big one on the ground, his eyes once again all black.

Speechless, Azalea did as she was told. Freezing air filled the room. She could see her breath and when she stretched her fingers, they went numb, but that was nothing new. Shadow Magic seemed to have that effect on her. In a daze, she stood for a moment, then panic shot through her.

"Faraday!" she yelled up the stairs. Her uncle looked at her impatiently as she ran to the kitchen, her hands shaking as she stuffed a few packets of cat food in her bulging backpack. She'd probably need a litter box. Digging around in the back of the cupboard she found a spare disposable one from the time Faraday had to stay inside after a cat fight left him banged up. They were both in for some changes it seemed.

"Come on, get a move on." Fabian nodded toward the darkness. She kneeled down as Faraday trotted down the stairs. In much the same way as Fabian, he seemed unfazed by the large, shadowy void open in the living room.

The black cat jumped onto her shoulder, and she used one hand to stabilize him. Azalea swallowed her nerves as she watched the shadow ripple. Faraday's purrs rumbled against her ear, allowing her to relax, but only a little.

Fabian took her free hand, guiding her toward the darkness. Her heart hammered away, and she gripped his hand, feeling like a kid on their first day of school. He smiled. "It's called a Hollow."

He gave her hand a quick squeeze and, side by side, they stepped into the black void.

Azalea felt a shiver glide down her body as the darkness sealed behind them. She gasped a breath of chilling air and her eyes adjusted to the sudden darkness. A glimmer of blue light lit her uncle's face. The ground was spongy like moss and glowing ever so slightly. He released her hand, but she wasn't scared anymore.

She watched him make another cut with his glowing knife and a wave of damp musty air rushed toward her from the new doorway. She took a breath, ready to step out into her new life.

CHAPTER 8

A ZALEA STEPPED OUT OF the Hollow into air thick with the smell of stagnant water. Somber light painted shadows across the rough tunnel wall and only the drip, drip of water cut through the silence. Fabian was still at her side, thankfully, and the shadow door sealed behind them.

Faraday leaped from her shoulder, and they followed Fabian around dirty puddles that looked more like bottomless sinkholes scattered across the uneven, cobbled floor.

"Come on, I can't stay here long."

"What? You're not even staying the night?"

"Sorry. Got places to be, love."

Great. He was abandoning her already. "Where are we then?" she asked, not about to let him know how much that bothered her.

"One of the tunnels under the Tower. This one leads to the Hospital."

The smell alone told her it was old. She hoped the whole place wasn't like this dank tunnel.

"This doesn't look like we're meant to be here. Is this part even open to tourists?"

Fabian ran a hand through his hair and shook it as if he were trying to get sand out. It looked like he might have more than sand in there. It was a bloody mess. "No, this is a great little secret, a loophole in security one might say. It's the only place you can make a Hollow on the Tower grounds. The whole tourist attraction thing is just a cover, anyway. The House of Owls runs this place, but there's a lot more to it and you'll be wanting to stay on the right side of them. They're a very powerful magical House and they've made this into one of the biggest communities of mages in London. They've rounded up talent from all over the place and from different Houses too. Though none from our House, elitist bastards." He glanced around.

"I'm finding this a little hard to take in," Azalea said. "What are these Houses? I'm guessing they aren't physical houses, right? How many communities like this are there?"

He stopped and raised his eyebrows like he didn't want to waste his breath explaining. "They aren't *actual* houses. Houses are made up of people— families—all with the same lineage of magic. There are eight Houses, four are Shadow Magic Houses and the other four, Echo Magic Houses. Each has unique skills in magic. The House of Owls are experts in knowledge and mind magic, hence all the research and training here." He checked his watch and then his phone, frowning at it as he stopped.

"As for communities, there are various ones around the world. Magic doesn't come from any one ethnic group or area. London has more mages than anywhere else though, it's a bit of a magical hub here. Lots of history, lots of places to blend in, lots of ways to make money. A few thousand people I'd guess, maybe ten thousand? Not sure, I don't go to any of the networking things. Too many arrogant pricks for my liking."

"Am I supposed to know all this already? What House am I in?"

"Calm down, you'll catch up. But we shouldn't stand around here gas-bagging. Come on."

"No!" She grabbed his arm. "You need to explain this to me now. I need to know what's going on. How many people live here? Where do they live? How will I fit in?" Faraday wound around her, frankly too calm for this new situation.

Fabian took in a controlled breath. "Fine. Around 300 or so live at the Tower. Mostly in the outer fortress wall along Mint Street, in the inner fortress wall houses, and in several of the towers. They're modern enough flats, so don't get your knickers in a twist. You won't be living in a prison cell. There's also an underground complex down here with a lovely cafeteria that also serves as a pub. There are offices, a library, archive vaults, meeting rooms, a gym, and training rooms.

"The old hospital above ground is now flats, and the real hospital goes deep underground below. It's huge. What else?" He tapped his foot and checked his phone again. "Our family's magic is the House of Snakes, but I need to get you tested to confirm it—" He froze.

Voices echoed from up ahead. Footsteps heading their way. Fabian swore under his breath, clearly annoyed. "Yeoman Warders coming—I can't be seen, but you'll be alright. If they ask, say you're here to see Danni." He vanished, like he became part of the shadows. Azalea was left blinking in disbelief, trying not to panic. She raised her hand and waved it through where he'd been standing.

Faraday chirped reassuringly. Azalea stood tall, trying not to freak out and gripped the straps of her backpack to hide her shaking hands. Bright red, formal uniforms rounded the corner. There were two men, one tall and bored looking, the other short and frowning, as if he didn't want to be there. Sweat pooled under her arms, but she walked toward them.

"Where'd you come from?" the taller guard asked. They stopped in front of her, eying Faraday.

"Back there." Azalea pointed to the end of the tunnel. "I'm here to see Danni—" She froze. *Was Danni male or female?* "I'm expected . . ." she answered, before they could ask anything else, hoping that much was true.

The guard raised an eyebrow at his partner. "She's always bloody late. And she didn't register your arrival, we'll 'ave to take you to the office." He checked his watched and sighed. "What's your business here, anyway?"

Azalea swallowed. *Nope.* She had nothing.

The click of heels on stone charged toward them. A woman with fiery red hair, pale skin, a pink dress, and a clashing yellow beret stopped in front of them and doubled over to catch her breath. She looked up with a glowing smile, but more noticeably, she had a blazing fireball cupped in her hand.

"There you are, love!" She ran up and gave Azalea one-armed hug, transferring the fire to the other hand. "Sorry I'm late, you know me," she laughed. "Hiya boys, thanks for finding her for me. Running a bit late—you know how it is."

"You didn't register her. Thought you agents were meant to be organized," the smaller guard said, stone faced.

"I know! I'm *so* sorry. Got my days mixed up. Do you mind if I do it tomorrow? She's just staying with me tonight. I promise I won't let her go anywhere else."

"Fine, be sure you do," the tall guard said, probably more interested in going to have a cup of tea than sorting out paperwork. The other bloke scowled.

"Have a good one," he said, as he flicked his head to his co-worker that they were leaving. The short man narrowed his eyes at Azalea. She held his stare until he turned and walked off. He was probably jealous that she was taller than him.

As the guards left, Azalea let out a breath and looked around for her uncle. The woman busied herself patting Faraday as he wound around her legs. "You're a strange pussycat, aren't you?" she said, bopping a finger on the white diamond on Faraday's head.

Azalea cleared her throat, about to speak, when her uncle appeared at her side. "Alright?" he said.

"Where the hell did you go?" Azalea hit him in the arm as she tried to squash the panic from her voice.

Fabian rubbed his arm. *What a baby.* She hadn't hit him hard.

"Fabian, you old dog!" The woman stood up as her fireball disappeared with a wave of her hand. She threw herself on Fabian, then stepped back from the hug and punched him on the same arm. "What are you doing, leaving this poor girl to face the guards alone?"

"I wouldn't've had to, if you turned up on time like I told you to," he growled.

This woman had balls. Fabian was an intimidating bloke, someone you wanted to stay on the right side of. They clearly knew each other well.

"Well, you didn't exactly give me much notice." She looked Fabian up and down and narrowed her eyes. "Besides, I clearly recall you saying you would never set foot in this cesspit again." She paused, raising her eyebrows.

Fabian's lips pressed into a thin line, his solid black eyes glaring at her. "Something like that."

"That's right! You said the Tower was no more than a bunch of brain-washing Owls that had me under their thumb. And here you are crawling back." She tut-tutted and flashed a wicked grin. "And who's this lovely lady? I see you've lost your manners since you left our unit, Fabian."

He blinked, then regained composure. Azalea suppressed a smile.

"I believe I said they were a bunch of brain-washing wankers, which, as far as I know, is still true." He nodded toward Azalea. "This is my niece, Azalea Sharp."

"Zaels, this is Danni Fletcher, a friend of mine who lives here. She works for the government. She's an agent for the Paranormal Justice Unit," he said like he had an unpleasant taste in his mouth.

Danni smiled sarcastically at Fabian. "He's just jealous. Used to be one of us until he got kicked off the force. But here I am, still selflessly protecting the unwitting public from dangerous magic."

"And I'm off doing the dirty work and protecting everyone from being overrun by far more dangerous creatures—gallu." Fabian turned to Azalea. "They're a type of spirit wraith."

Azalea had no idea what that meant. But she added it to her list of things to find out about.

"Yes. Well, let's not turn this into a pissing contest, for Azalea's sake." She turned away from Fabian. "It's lovely to meet you Azalea. Now let's get out of this horrid tunnel. We wouldn't want the guards to find your uncle. He's rather unpopular around here, you see. He's the reason why they stopped letting people from the House of Snakes in." She winked at Azalea, and Azalea instantly liked the woman. Bonus points for anyone who could make her uncle pout like a schoolboy.

"Those arseholes shouldn't have stolen priceless artifacts from my family," he mumbled under his breath.

Azalea knew this wasn't the right time to ask. Danni ignored his comment and Azalea followed them up the tunnel and through an unassuming wooden door. A stone staircase spiraled its way into the wall at the end, but they turned toward the brightly lit lift. The world moved from the ancient to modern in an instant.

Up on the third floor, the bright white bricks of the hallway had no leaking walls and no moss. They entered the flat and Azalea's eyes adjusted to the modern, white design that shone at her from walls, ceilings, and sleek handle-less kitchen cabinets. Perhaps what was once a minimalist, orderly flat was overrun with vibrant family life; scattered kid's books, hot wheels cars, and soft toys infiltrated every surface making it warm and welcoming. There was even a faint scent of cinnamon and cookies in the air. Faraday walked in as if he owned the place and curled up by the fire.

"Welcome to our flat. My wife, Maiken, did the decorating, in case you were wondering. If it was me, it would be all Ikea." She laughed. "The twins are in bed, so don't be too loud or we'll never get rid of them. They love visitors and especially love our Fabian."

Azalea couldn't imagine him around kids and smiled at the thought.

Danni pointed them toward the white kitchen island while she made tea. "So, what's the story here? You're not looking your normal self, Fabes. You've got dirt on you and your hair's all ratty."

"I haven't exactly had time to get home, I had to go off and rescue this one," he said, raising an eyebrow as if displeased. Azalea knew better and gave a hint of a smile.

"Well, it's nice to have you here, Azalea. I assume Fabian's brought you to join the Initiates Program? He mentioned some time ago that you might turn up sooner or later," Danni said.

"That's why we're here. I've got a rather large favor to ask you, Danni," Fabian said.

Fabian updated her on the situation as Danni poured tea into Tower of London teacups. Fabian's explanation didn't clarify the situation any more for Azalea, but it must have meant something to Danni. As he told her about the raven attack, the color drained from Danni's face, and she placed her cup down with shaking hands.

"I heard the House of Ravens was on a big recruitment push. I'm guessing she takes after your side of the family?" Danni glanced at Fabian.

"Yes, it seems that way, but I'm also hoping she has Echo Magic abilities from her mother's side," Fabian said. "Her grandmother explained to me on the phone how Azalea's Shadow Magic has been manifesting, and it seems her mother has been trying to cure her of it. I'm hoping learning Echo Magic here will help her balance it out."

"I'm still not clear on all this. What is this House of Ravens and why would they try to recruit me? And for what?" Azalea asked.

"They're a Shadow Magic House . . . more of a cult, really. But they don't take kindly to anyone from the House of Snakes, which is our family's House. Our magic isn't so different from theirs, but there's a feud they won't drop. Right now, they are looking for kids to recruit for training as spies and assassins," Fabian said, and surprisingly he was being dead serious. He sipped his tea as if that were a perfectly normal statement.

Danni nodded and Fabian continued, "We can't risk them finding you. They wouldn't accept you once they found out who your father was." Fabian shuffled uncomfortably. "Your dad clashed with Korbyn Dumont, the head of the House of Ravens. He blamed your father for the death of his wife, which wasn't true. But it started this feud and Dumont's still at it."

"I thought these House wars were in the past. It's all so . . . archaic," Danni said.

Fabian nodded. "Most families are mixes of several Houses now anyway. It's just the Ravens keeping up these barriers and we are being forced to do the same to survive. Our House isn't doing anything to provoke them. Many House of Snakes families are going into hiding to avoid them. It's absurd."

"My dad didn't have anything to do with her death, then?"

"No, he didn't," Fabian said with a look that told her to drop it.

Azalea wanted to know more, but she changed the subject. "What magic does the House of Snakes have, exactly?"

He put his cup down. "We can manipulate shadows in a few ways. Like this." A wall of darkness appeared between her and Fabian and she flinched. "Shadows can have substance if you get good enough at it."

She poked her finger into the veil of dark air. It was thick and resisted her touch, but she couldn't feel anything. It was nothingness.

"So it's like a forcefield then?" Her finger tingled and the fire in her chest sprang to life. She stiffened and fought it back down. No way she wanted to lose control in front of her uncle.

"If that analogy works for you, then yes, but it's so much more." The wall of shadows disappeared, and Fabian was standing right in front of her once more. "I can use it as a shield or to cloak myself to remain unseen—as I did in the tunnel. We can also create portals to the Hollow, communicate with spirits—and back in the day, also necromancy. That's illegal now, though. But don't worry about that. I can teach you Shadow Magic later. Just focus on Echo Magic while you're here."

An icy chill shot through Azalea's veins. *Necromancy was illegal.* Shouldn't her dad have told her that? She panicked and changed the subject again.

"So . . . these Ravens won't be able to get me here? What about my mum?" Azalea asked. It seemed five new questions arose for every one he answered.

Danni gave a reassuring smile. "This is the safest place in London. They won't be able to find you here, and the wards are top notch."

"She's right and I'll make sure your mum is safe, too. They should think you're dead from that poison and they don't know your name. The Ravens will be watching the house, waiting to see if you survived the attack. They'll report back if you aren't there, hopefully assuming you're dead."

Azalea's hands were clammy. She had a horrible feeling about this whole thing. She took a breath. "Okay." She nodded. "So why am I here if you said House of Snakes weren't allowed here? How am I supposed to learn Echo Magic?"

"I'm banking on my theory that your bloodline isn't just one House. Yes, I'm sure you are part of the House of Snakes, same as me and your father. But your mother's side of the family descends from the House of Bees—which focuses on plant magic. Your grandmother is a powerful plant mage, so I'm betting you've got some of that blood in there too."

Azalea's head was starting to throb, but she sipped her tea like a person who was not about to have a mental breakdown. She needed to know more, needed to know if there was hope for getting her dad back. "So, this necromancy? You said it was illegal?"

"It was made illegal hundreds of years ago, but some people still practice. It's what makes our house rather unpopular, especially with the House of Owls. They like to think themselves superior to the other Houses," Fabian said.

Danni coughed and raised her eyebrows at Fabian.

"Also, I may have got us all banned from here for a recent disagreement about the artifact they stole from us." He clenched his fists on the table. "I know those bastards have it."

Danni patted his hands and did her best to hide a smirk. "You blasted down several walls and threatened to hold the Crown Jewels hostage. You're lucky they didn't have me arrest you."

"You what?" Azalea said.

"I don't want to talk about it. Besides, you have House of Bees blood, they will let you in." Fabian pivoted around and headed for the kitchen. "You got any liquor in here?"

"Nope," Danni called back and winked at Azalea. "So anywho, what do you think about all this? I can find you a flat here. Are you studying right now, or working? It'll be safer for you to stick around here. And not go out unless one of us is with you. You know, kind of like prison," she said apologetically.

"That's fine. I'm starting uni online soon and I can look after myself," she said, half lying. She had no idea how to cook or pay rent. "I want to learn magic and I won't cause trouble."

Danni smiled, her eyes speckled with fire. "Okay, then it's all settled." She stood up and started clearing teacups. "You can stay with us till I find you a flat in the Tower somewhere." She gave a sharp nod.

"She needs her bloodline confirmations done too," Fabian added. "Her mum never wanted it done, but she needs it so she can join the program."

"Oh. Okay, that shouldn't be a problem. You'll want to leave some bribe money if you want to keep her House of Snakes records off the book. It'll be safest if the Ravens can't track her," Danni said.

"Fine, a little extra cash won't hurt the process. But I expect you to pay me back," Fabian glanced at Azalea as he took out a wad of cash from inside his coat.

Butterflies stormed around in her stomach. Was he serious about paying him back? It was hard to tell with him. Either way, she didn't want to be in debt to him. She would pay her own way. Screwing this up and being a burden wasn't part of her plan.

She nibbled on the shortbread that Danni offered. Her questions could wait for later.

The hard drive in her brain was full for the day.

"It's getting late. I'm going to have to make a run for it soon," Fabian said. "Here, this is for you."

He slid an ornate box across the bench. Azalea opened it and pulled out a knife like her uncle's. The short dagger's blade rippled blue and gray, its bone handle was inset with black, purple, and blue gemstones, and the other end had a huge antique key sticking out of it. She clicked a black gemstone and the key shot back into the handle, and the knife clattered out of her hand onto the bench.

"Careful with that. It's your father's dagger-key, and it's called an elemer. You use it to cut into a Dimension to draw magic out, and this one used to belong to your great grandfather," Fabian said, smiling strangely to himself. "Don't even try to use it till you've had real training and passed your tests for class. Keep it in the box. I'll get you a training elemer to start with next week," he said.

"Can I do what you did opening the shadow door? And what do you mean, cut into a dimension?"

"No, you can *not* open a Hollow. *No Shadow Magic.* Raw Magic comes from other dimensions, Shadow Magic from the Shadow Dimension, Echo Magic from the Echo Dimension. It's simple. Someone will teach you about it in time," he said, as if it wasn't important. It sounded extremely important to her, but judging from his impatient pacing, he wasn't going to hang around to explain anything else.

"Are there spirits in the Hollow? You know . . . ones that aren't here like the ghosts," she asked, hoping for a hint of where her dad was and how she could pull him through.

"No. Some are in the Shadow Dimension. The Hollow is like a sub-dimension in between, not much in there. Sometimes wraiths and spirits find their way in there via various loopholes, but it's not common. It's my job to hunt the gallu that get through."

That must be how her dad contacted her. *So, it was possible.* "Okay, thanks."

Fabian tapped his knuckles on the bench. "I'm heading off. Be good, Zaels." He kissed the top of her head. "And thanks, Danni. Say hi to Maiken and the girls for me." He kissed her cheek. "I owe you big time. Also, I'll pay for your rent and fees for this month, Zaels, but after that you're on your own."

"All good. I've saved up a little for uni, I'll be fine." A little as in a few months' rent . . . she'd need to up her watch restoration game if she was going to stay. She squeezed her dad's watch in her pocket, for luck.

Fabian smiled and looked as if he wanted to say something else. Instead, he kissed her on the head, then turned and left without another word.

Nerves took over again. Alone and with a new level of financial and magical problems on her hands, Azalea suddenly wished she was back in her bedroom ignoring it all. It was hard to believe her mum was over two hours away now and probably hating her. Forcing a smile, she turned to Danni.

"No worries, love. We'll get you sorted."

Azalea nodded and forced back tears. She was stronger than this and she was going to master Shadow Magic and look after herself from now on . . . somehow.

CHAPTER 9

F ABIAN WAS USED TO carrying dead bodies, it was a necessary skill in his line of work. This particular body wasn't too heavy and hadn't developed a smell yet, which was always a bonus. Slicing out of the Hollow, he tossed the corpse ahead of him. He stepped out as the tear of darkness sealed behind him.

He breathed in the cool night air. It was fresh with the recent rain that had rolled through and there was also a pleasant cemetery aroma to it. *Shit, better get moving*, he realized as he checked his watch. He had to attract a gallu tonight. He needed to be catching one or two a month and he was already behind. Losing his contract and the cash that came with it was not an option right now. Not when he'd promised to pay Azalea's rent for the month and gave her the money he'd allocated to his House of Snakes emergency fund. He was sure he'd done the right thing with her. Leaving her at the Tower was her best bet. Secretly he was glad she chose to go there. If she'd decided to stay with him, she'd end up just as screwed up as he was. He was no teacher, and certainly not a role model.

He shook away those thoughts; he needed to concentrate. As far as spirit wraiths went, the gallu were the nastiest, but the

House of Eagle paid top dollar for them and this one would be worth it.

He glanced down at the body bag. A shame. This one was young. Freshly dead that day from a car crash. His spirit would be like a roast dinner to a gallu.

Fabian heaved the corpse across the well-kept Edinburgh cemetery. The gallu had been spotted in the area the last few days by some local mages and he was more than ready for it. It was an active enough cemetery, with quite a few fresh spirits wandering around. That would help. Of course, it wasn't as good as hospice or a hospital, but it was far less public, and less messy.

Time to set his trap. He unzipped the body and placed it in an open patch on top of a fresh grave. Next, he pulled out a small leather bag of black diamonds, not to use as protective wards like usual, but in reverse as a cage.

He padded across the damp grass, placing the diamonds in strategic locations. He'd just have to seal the ward with one more diamond to trap the gallu.

For good measure, he placed eight sapphires on top of the grave—he couldn't afford to lose them. But spirits loved blue sapphires.

Gripping the cold stone, he hauled himself on top of a nearby mausoleum to wait. His hipflask weighed heavy in his jacket pocket. A sip wouldn't hurt. He leaned against the angled roof and took a long swig of whiskey. Then just one more. He wouldn't need much magic to get the gallu. It was a weak one after all.

He checked his phone to see there were no messages. He hadn't expected any anyways. Azalea would be safe with Danni and Maiken. She didn't need him.

A dart of movement caught his eye. Warmth spread through his right hand as his spinel ring warmed and pulsed between gray and blue like a tiny, faceted moon. One more sip of whiskey and he crouched, ready to spring.

A black shape lurched out from behind a tree, its oily body trailing across the grass. Its thick head tilted from side to side as if listening, though it had no visible ears.

Shit. The creature was far more solid than he'd predicted. It had been a wisp of a wraith last time. He ground his teeth, pissed off that he'd let it get away for so long. A few more feedings and it would be fully corporeal. He could not let that happen.

Fabian's heart slowed as the gallu shuffled across the lawn toward the dead man, its head tilted with the usual jerky movements.

A chill in the air settled as spirits started converging on the sapphires. The young lad's spirit was sitting calmly on top of his body, lounging there with his legs spread out as if he was on the couch watching television. Stupid boy didn't know he was dead. Fabian had no time for spirits. They should have left when they had the chance.

The gallu sped up. It flicked its head around, frenzied by the gathering spirit buffet. Fabian's muscles were set like springs. Just a few more meters. The gallu paused. They weren't stupid creatures by any means, but their hunger always won out over sense. It made a straight line for the boy.

It slid into his trap. Fabian jumped into the diamond barrier and sealed it with the final stone. The gallu glanced up, but its meal was too enticing.

It shot toward the boy, much faster than Fabian expected. Oily tentacles stretched from its globular body, and it began tearing off chunks of the boy's spirit. It slurped and sucked them through its protruding tubes. Each mouthful adding more mass to its bulging form. Each morsel making it more and more solid.

Fabian had to act. He pricked his thumb with his elemer and cut to the Shadow Dimension. He switched the blade to face the gallu and pulled magic into him from the key. Raw power surged through him and into the night air with a roar of purple light. He pulled through waves of magic as it left a pleasant sear across his veins.

The gallu continued to tear the boy apart. His screams shattered the night calm, though only Fabian could hear them. Hands shaking with the pressure of the spell, he drew through more power and forced his will onto the gallu. *Break, you bastard. Break!*

Vibrations of magic hummed through his body, right to his ear drums and heart. He held back the wave of nausea that came with it. He was going to rip this mongrel apart.

A crack, and something gave. The fracture crept across the gallu's oily hide and grew, splitting like a lobster shell. Fissures opened up, revealing its true form, a pathetic wisp of a shadow. Fabian stormed toward the creature and pulled a bottle out of his pocket. The inky black liquid sloshed inside. He thrust the bottle toward the creature, as close as he could get without getting its toxic ooze on him. It screamed as the bottle connected. It writhed and hissed as it forcibly coiled into the glass vessel then dissolved into a harmless stream of smoke. The hollow shell of a body melted onto the ground in a pile of black tar.

Placing the bottle in a different pocket from his flask, he patted it proudly and rolled his neck. That was a close one . . . too close.

"Do you know what time it is? I think I'm late for a buck's party," the spirit boy said. A jagged hole gaped where his arm had been and he was half propped against the headstone, his torso ripped to shreds.

"You're dead, you pillock. Get it into your thick head. You were nearly absorbed into a fucking gallu. Getting to a bucks party is the least of your problems, mate," he said.

"Are you having a laugh?"

"Your fucking arm was torn off, you dimwit!"

"Alright mate, calm it down."

Fabian clenched his teeth. He didn't need to talk to the spirits. Fresh ones were the worst. They had no idea they were dead. Some retained a hint of humanity, though most sunk into a dark place, roaming around searching for answers, no longer remembering key places and details from their lives, all the while getting more and more unsettling.

He collected the sapphires off the body and gave the finger to the ungrateful, dead boy.

"You're a wanker, you know that? You could at least tell me what I'm doing in a graveyard," the boy called after him.

He stormed off to collect the diamonds. At least gallu had no interest in gems. Spirits however, were the opposite and were drawn to blue sapphires. A gemstone unique in aiding communication with the dead. Fortunately, the spirits couldn't pick them up.

Once they were safely in the bag, all he had to do was take the body back and drop the gallu bottle at the House of Eagle's lab. He had no idea what they did with them, and frankly, he didn't care. As long as they kept them in the bottles, it wasn't his problem.

As he tried to stuff the body back into the bag, he heard a soft thud on the grass behind a grave. He crouched behind the marble stone, elemer out. He wrapped a shadow cloak around himself and the boy. A woman in a masquerade mask of woven shadows was leaning on a gravestone.

"I know it's you there, Fabian. You might as well come out."

He recognized that voice. *Kat.* She was one of Korbyn Dumont's minions and a bloody good assassin. In the past they had put their house differences aside and had become almost-friends. Well almost-friends with benefits. Until Samael was killed. They hadn't spoken since. Like hell he'd listen to her now, and he sure as hell wouldn't let her trick him again. She'd used him for information and now his brother was dead. His eyes adjusted further to the night. No waiting around this time. He sprang from behind the marble stone with full force. She ducked and rolled out of reach.

He had no training in real fighting— but was seriously starting to wish he did. Rudimentary skills from pub fights and unfortunate mix-ups with disgruntled husbands were all he had to go off. At least it was better than nothing.

This woman was half his size, but she knew what she was doing. If she wanted to kill him, he wouldn't have a chance. Usually, he could pull up some passable defensive fire magic, but not after having whiskey. He could barely use Echo Magic at the best of times. There was zero chance if he'd had a drink.

She was yelling something at him as he ducked behind a gravestone, and she did the same. He stumbled over some bricks and hit his shoulder. Wincing, he tried to remain quiet. She cast a net of shadows around herself as she sneaked behind him.

He lunged where he guessed she would appear. He caught her arm with the blade of his knife. Twisting around, she kicked his feet out from under him and the ground came up to hit him hard. Swearing loudly, he flipped over and kicked out to stand up.

Hot pain shot through his side and soon after sticky blood coated his hand. The bitch had sliced him. Rage tore through him as her eyes trailed him like a stalking cat, no doubt hoping he would collapse so she could drag him through a Hollow. Not a chance. He stumbled toward her, clutching his side and blindly slashing his elemer in front of him. She stepped out of his way.

He stumbled forward, getting a mouthful of fresh grave dirt. This was not going as planned.

She crouched next to him.

"Fabian, listen to me."

"Not bloody likely. You just stabbed me." He reached inside his coat, but he was too slow. She kicked him over and stood with a boot pressed into his chest.

He grabbed her foot and somehow twisted it and rolled away. His side was on fire and he was losing too much blood.

He'd have to leave the body. He cut into the Hollow as the woman rushed toward him.

"He's going after the relics, Fabian. You need to be prepared," her voice echoed behind him.

"Nice try, you crazy bitch." He wouldn't fall for that again. His leg popped through, and the Hollow closed. Whatever she said was a lie, or some sort of plan she concocted to distract him. He checked to ensure the bottle of gallu was still in his pocket and in one piece. To his relief it was. Too bad he had to leave the body behind. He got out his phone. Perhaps he'd lost more blood or was drunker than he thought—phones didn't work in the Hollow.

He gripped his side and cut a rough tear out near the gates of Blackbourne Manor and rolled out. He checked the wound and was surprised to see it would only need stitches. Tomorrow he'd call Maiken. For now, he called Colin, his groundskeeper/handy man, to come fetch him as he started the long walk up the drive.

CHAPTER 10

AZALEA SLID ASIDE THE thick curtains and squinted into the crisp morning light. *It wasn't a dream.* She was at the Tower of London, and all the BBC documentaries she binged since childhood couldn't prepare her for the real thing. The White Tower was right there in the center. Sharp lines of sunlight outlined the light stone walls, turrets, and jagged ramparts that rose into the clear sky.

A shiver trickled down her back as two black dots—ravens—hopped across the manicured lawns. She shook off the unease. Those weren't the same birds; she was safe here.

She tried not to scratch the itchy claw marks on her arm.

Her head snapped toward the door as it clicked open. Two little girls with brown, frizzy hair peeked through the crack. Both girls had bright silver eyes. Must be another magic thing. Azalea smiled at them and gave a small wave.

"Can we feed your kitty?" the one on the left asked shyly.

"I'm sure he would love that," Azalea said as she grabbed a pouch of chicken flavored wet food from her bag. Good to see Faraday was already settling in.

"Thanks!" The girls exploded into giggles, then sprinted off, thundering downstairs.

Figuring she should head downstairs if everyone was up, Azalea dug into her disorganized bag, hoping she'd packed enough clothes. She pulled out clean dark jeans and a maroon t-shirt with buttons at the top, and quickly got changed. She sent a quick text to Isaac after she'd finished getting dressed: *Got loads to tell you! Main thing is I moved to London. Fill u in later.*

And one to her mum: *Hey Mum. Just wanted to let you know I got here safe. Please dont be too mad at me. I'll be fine. Luv u xoxo.*

Her mum messaged back instantly: *I'm glad to hear it. Please stay safe. And don't trust anyone. You can always come home remember. Love you.*

Nice try, Mum. Azalea thought as a message came through from Isaac: *WTF! How did that happen? Tell me everything.*

She didn't even know where to start. She'd call him later. Swiping the messages away, she shoved the phone in one pocket and her pocket watch in the other. She took a deep breath before heading downstairs.

The twins were sitting at the table eating breakfast, and their eyes, which had changed to deep brown, lit up when they spotted her.

"Good morning," she said. The girls waved enthusiastically, their mouths too full to answer. Danni leaned against the bench next to another woman who was cooking eggs.

"You're up!" Danni said. *She must be one of those mythical morning people from books.* Azalea smiled to herself. Danni wore dark skinny jeans, and a tailored pink tweed blazer. "Azalea, this is Maiken." Danni put her arms around the other woman, trapping her in a hug as Maiken tried to pile scrambled eggs onto plates.

"Lovely to meet you Azalea. Here, have some eggs. How did you sleep?" the woman asked, as she escaped Danni's grasp and handed Azalea a plate. Azalea couldn't help but stare. Maiken was beautiful, even dressed in plain scrubs. She was probably in her mid-thirties, like Danni. Her face was composed and serene, with the same hair and deep bronze skin as the twins. Breezing around the kitchen, she radiated an air of control and power.

"Thanks." Azalea retrieved the plate with twice as much food as she usually ate. "I slept very well, thank you. I think I needed it after the past few days. It's all been a bit of a shock."

"I'm sure it is," said Maiken. "Just let us know if you need help with anything. We have a soft spot for Fabian. Any family of his is family of ours."

"Thank you, that's kind of you to say," Azalea said, surprised at how welcoming these strangers were and how she felt quite at home already.

"Azalea, this is Ava and Zoe. They're going to a fun activities group today, aren't you girls?" Danni said. They nodded without the enthusiasm of their mum. Azalea and the two women joined the girls.

"But Mummy has to go to work," Zoe said, wrinkling her nose.

"Maiken is a doctor here. The hospital is right under us," Danni said, beaming with pride. "And lucky for you, I've got the day off work so we can get your tests all done."

Azalea froze at the mention of tests. It must have shown on her face, because Maiken patted her hand. "It's nothing to worry about. You'll be fine. They just take a little of your blood and add it to a solution. The color it turns indicates what Houses you have magic for."

Azalea nodded. It wasn't the blood test she was worried about. It was learning if she had Echo Magic or not.

They finished breakfast, and Danni ran off to find her keys. If Maiken was calmness and order, Danni was the exact opposite. She radiated chaos. Maiken dressed the girls while Azalea went to get her things together and put on her leather jacket (which was by far the newest thing she owned) and her yellow canvas shoes. Everyone headed for the door while Danni hunted for her keys, until Azalea spotted them in a plant.

Maiken and the kids left for work and their summer activities group, while Azalea and Danni headed outside. The smells of the city washed over Azalea—coffee aromas mixed with exhaust fumes and freshly cut grass.

"Ready for a quick tour?" Danni said.

Azalea nodded with a wide smile but held in the squeal of excitement bubbling below. Isaac would tease her for being a nerd, but it was hard to believe she was *actually* inside the Tower of London before it opened to tourists. This place was riddled with ancient scandals, dead kings and queens, and countless enemies and traitors that had never made it out. Death soaked into the very walls and earth. She could feel it. Which also meant there were spirits lingering around, her uncle mentioned some of the buildings were warded, but that wouldn't stop them wandering around everywhere else.

Looming over them, the White Tower swayed against the sky. Danni's knee-length boots clicked along on the stone as they followed the edge of the grass. A raven croaked from above. Azalea twitched as it flapped down to a nearby bench and stood unmoving, its dark eyes set on her.

"Don't worry about the ravens. These ones live at the Tower, they won't hurt you."

Azalea wasn't so sure about that. She kept an eye on the enormous bird.

"It's said that if the last raven were to leave, the Tower would crumble to dust and great harm would befall the kingdom," Danni said cheerily.

Shivers sent Azalea's spine ramrod straight as they crossed the grounds. There were spirits here, for sure. Azalea did her best to listen as Danni pointed out the buildings, but the bitter coldness clawed its way under her skin, growing with every step as she sensed them getting closer to the spirits.

"So that was the hospital we just left. It goes a lot further underground than you would believe. The part above ground is all flats. This is the Waterloo Barracks on the right. Part of it is open to the public so they can see the Crown Jewels. The other parts are all House of Owls offices and archives." They walked past another impressive building with turrets that matched the White Tower.

Azalea's skull prickled. Yup, spirits were nearby, and lots of them.

They neared an old chapel, the *St. Peter ad Vincula Royal Chapel*, according to Danni. She couldn't see any spirits, but she was sure they were there somewhere—as sure as the ice crystallizing in her bones. She wanted to walk faster.

Would it make Danni uncomfortable if she mentioned spirits? If necromancy was illegal, surely seeing spirits wasn't a good thing, either. She didn't want to give people reasons to ask more questions. Tucking her head, she kept walking.

Azalea tried to take in the names and details of every building they passed. Houses butted up against each other, making the inner walls of the fortress all centered around the White Tower. Some were stone, some black and white Tudor style, others were made up of dark brick—a mismatched castle courtyard. She forced herself to note details to distract herself from the spirits: rosemary in a big pot, an alley leading behind the chapel, a glass pillow on a circle monument . . .

A woman watching her.

Fierce eyes locked on Azalea. She swiveled around, but too slowly. The woman knew Azalea saw her, and the image of her elaborate Tudor-style dress was instantly stamped into Azalea's mind. Yup, definitely a spirit, and a creepy one at that.

Fortunately, they were moving away from the chapel and Azalea tried to distract herself by asking Danni questions, hoping the strange woman wouldn't follow. She didn't dare look back. Danni was more than happy to spout random knowledge about the Tower. Three-hundred and eighty-four people lived in the Tower of London. Most were mages and their families. They worked as Yeoman Warders, House of Phoenix Guards, historians, researchers, doctors and healers, apprentices, metal workers, and a few were students studying magic. Much to Azalea's disappointment, they didn't wear robes or wizard hats, but dressed like normal people.

As they passed the Bloody Tower, Azalea was feeling herself again. She made a note to steer clear of the chapel in the future. She'd only seen the one spirit, but she was sure there were more around. They avoided the front gate, instead wandering the opposite way through a side door and popped out next to the Thames on a busy walkway.

Danni charged through the crowds, apparently not noticing the sheer number of people. "We aren't walking far. The blood-line test can only be done at one place: Eagle Tower. They have a specialty lab."

Azalea took in a breath. Everyone knew Eagle Tower. It dominated the London Skyline, towering over all with its impressive black and gold, Gothic facade. It screamed of hidden mysteries lurking inside.

Danni chattered about life at the Tower as they wove through the crowds. Azalea tried to focus on her words, but rushing people and distractions caught her eye in every direction. She focused on stepping one foot in front of the other.

They arrived at the foot of a massive staircase. Formidable eagle statues glared down at them as if they might attack any second. Glass doors led to a lobby like any fancy office building from TV. Danni hurried them to the lifts at the back. She pulled out a dagger like Fabian's—an elemer—and tapped the blade to the glowing panel and selected the 20th floor.

"All the bottom floors are normal offices. Twenty and up are restricted to magic. The lab we're going to is the top science lab for magic research and that sort of carry on."

They stepped off the lift and Azalea froze. Her first reaction was to take a photo to show Isaac or her mum, but she knew she couldn't. Isaac wasn't supposed to know about any of this, and she wasn't sure if her mum wanted to know what she was up to.

It was a lobby from another world. A fully grown forest climbed into an endless expanse of darkness and stars. It was higher than Azalea could see, but the forest below remained light, all enclosed by never ending walls of glass. Thousands of colorful lanterns drifted up on invisible columns of air between the trees.

On the edge of the forest, reception desks grew out of the ground as giant slabs of stone with waterfalls running down the sides. Nestled in the trees was a coffee shop surrounded by long wooden tables filled with people on laptops and phones going about their business like this was totally normal.

"I thought you'd like it," Danni said, smiling. "Come on. There's a mall above these levels. The shops there sell anything relating to magic—anything that's hard to sell outside of here. We can go there later. The other floors are offices and apartments. Most people living here are the House of Eagles—that's sky, water, and air magic. They hang out here 'cause there's good coffee and an amazing bakery."

Azalea blinked in disbelief. They came here for *pastries*?

They crossed two moon bridges as silvery fish darted in the clear water beneath. They reached the center of the forest where four glass lifts grew out of the floor in the shape of a four-leafed clover. Danni touched her elemer to the panel and selected the 60th floor.

Azalea's ears popped as the lift rose into the starry ceiling. They stepped out into a white reception area where a receptionist who didn't seem at all magical greeted them and sent them down the corridor with directions to Dr. Lamb's office.

Danni's boots echoed up the long hallway, but she didn't seem to notice. Azalea wiped her sweating hands on her jeans. This was the part in the movie where she got captured by scientists and became infected with a horrible zombie plague.

The doctor's office seemed normal-ish, and Dr. Lamb seemed like a normal guy. She wasn't exactly sure what she was expecting. Hopefully, he was a real doctor. A periodic table was taped to the wall, catching Azalea's attention. It wasn't like the ones she had learned about in science class—it had an extra row of elements.

The doctor gave a passive-aggressive cough, matched with a frown. He indicated they should sit down and slid a pamphlet and a form across the table. Azalea skimmed over the form and signed it.

Dr. Lamb began explaining the pamphlet in a slow drone. Azalea half-listened but mostly studied the pictures. She flicked to a page of animal icons, the symbols of the eight Houses of Magic. House of Snakes, an elegant purple snake with a black background. There were three other Shadow Magic Houses surrounded by black: a white Deer (healing magic), a raven (sleep & dream magic), and a winged Bull (divination).

The other four Houses had white backgrounds for Echo Magic. Azalea ran her fingers over the pictures one by one. An owl (mind magic), an eagle (air & weather magic), a phoenix (fire magic), and a bee (plant magic). She needed that little bee.

She focused her attention back on the doctor. "From our research here, we know the magic in our blood is the result of a genetic mutation. The mutation activates a gene that allows us to channel and manipulate power in certain ways as it passes through the body," he said, glaring down his sharp nose.

Danni was not looking impressed with the doctor, so Azalea slid her the pamphlet to distract her. Azalea wanted more information, but listening to this guy and the way he was looking down at them made her want to punch him in the face.

"Now, these 'gifts' the 'gods' bestowed on us are unique to each blood line—" he said with air quotes.

"Yes." Danni cut in and the doctor pursed his thin lips. "I'll add something in here. Azalea's new to all this, you see." She smiled at the doctor, and Azalea had to stop herself from laughing. Dr. Lamb glanced at the clock and continued to frown.

"When the gods left our world, they each chose a family to bestow their powers on. This meant their legacy would live on in mortals left in this dimension. Each of our eight Houses represents the magical lineage of one ancient god and each House has an affinity for particular types of magic. Although many of the skills cross over between the Houses, you always have an advantage in your own House's magic type."

"What's your House's specialty?" Azalea glanced at the picture to check.

"I'm from the House of the Phoenix. I'm best at fire magic, but if I try hard enough, I can do other forms of magic. It just doesn't come naturally." Danni shrugged. "Maiken is from the House of the White Deer. She is amazing at healing magic, but struggles to catch a fireball when I throw one at her."

Azalea stared at her. *They could throw fireballs? So many questions.*

The doctor scowled. "Yes, yes." He adjusted his cuff-links and turned to Azalea. "If you believe that sort of thing about 'gods'."

Danni pressed clenched fists into her legs at his air quotes. "I think you'll find most of us do."

"Yes—well, in *reality* your blood has genetic markers to tell us what House your ancestral bloodline is. Usually, the same as one of your parents, sometimes a mix of both, and rarely, a mutation from further back in your ancestry may pop up."

Danni sat stiffly with her arms crossed. "Can you just tell us how the test works?"

"Very well." He sighed. "I'll take a drop of blood to add to this solution. The color and reaction—according to that chart you have there—will confirm your ancestral lineage. Questions?"

"How does it work if you have two Houses? How will it know what color to turn?" Azalea asked, her legs bouncing against her chair.

He looked at her as if it were the stupidest question ever asked. She scowled again, wanting to punch him in the face. She secretly hoped Danni might do it.

"The solution will determine the weakest magic first as there will be less resistance. Your dominant magic will show last. The color and strength of the reaction will show how strong your magical affinity is. Let's get started."

He placed a rounded flask of shimmering blue liquid on the desk between them. He removed the crescent moon crystal stopper with a pop.

Azalea's heart rate kicked up a notch. She had to be in the House of Bees. She had to be able to stay at the Tower.

The doctor took her hand. He held a pen with a needle on her thumb and punched it quickly. A tiny ruby bead appeared. He held her finger over the flask and let two drops fall into the blue. He swirled the flask around unceremoniously and put a plaster on Azalea's finger.

She held her breath and leaned in to stare at the swirling liquid.

House of Bees, House of Bees, House of Bees. She glanced at the pamphlet. *Please change to green!*

The doctor went back to typing on his computer. Azalea jumped at a small *pop* and smoke puffed from the flask. The liquid turned sludge green, and Azalea let out a shaky laugh and briefly closed her eyes. She might have plant magic after all. Her mum and RoRo would be proud.

Danni clapped and hugged Azalea from the side.

"Well done, well done," the doctor said. "The House of Bees. I haven't seen one of them in a while. A most noble and productive form of magic, plant magic. A very respectable House, young lady."

Azalea forced a smile as relief settled over her. The doctor obviously wasn't expecting a second house as he turned to his computer and started typing once more. Azalea stared at the flask, waiting for a second pop.

The seconds dragged on, and the magic burned in her chest as if wanting to burst out and reveal itself. For the first time she felt a desire to harness the magic instead of fear it and she knew right then that she didn't want to hide from her Shadow Magic, she *wanted* it. She *wanted* to embrace it, to bring her dad back and prove herself. Prove she was worth sticking around for this time.

She stared at the vial as Danni chatted away to the doctor. He printed off a letter and handed it to Azalea with a nod. As she read it, she chewed on her lip. It said she had passed the test for magic and officially possessed Echo Magic from the House of Bees bloodline. A good thing, but still . . . unreasonable thoughts flitted into her mind. Perhaps her Shadow Magic wasn't strong enough or something was wrong with it? That would explain why the Shadow Atlas wouldn't show her anything useful.

Out the corner of her eye she could see the horrible green swirling around. She jerked back as a deafening explosion rattled the air. Heat swept over her as she shielded her face with her arm. The flask wobbled on the table and deep purple smoke erupted and billowed across the room. The liquid inside was a seething purple mass. If the color and strength of reaction showed how strong her magic was, like the doctor said, then there was no doubt she had strong Shadow Magic. Hopefully, that was a good thing.

She covered her mouth to hide her smile as her eyes watered. It had been an impressive explosion. Coughing and spluttering, the doctor flashed his elemer, and the smoke was sucked into a vortex from nowhere.

Flustered and sniveling, the doctor backed against the wall, wringing his hands and muttering.

"I think we should go," Danni whispered as she got up off the floor.

They moved toward the door, but the doctor rushed to block the way.

"I can't let you leave. I'm obligated to report anyone who tests for Shadow Magic, *especially* if they come from the House of Snakes. I'll have to hand you over to the House of Eagle's High Council. That was one of the most powerful reactions I've ever seen." He looked appalled.

"Sorry, mate, but we have somewhere to be. How about we don't include that little detail from the record and there's a grand in it for you? That would be nice, wouldn't it?" Danni didn't skip a beat.

"You can't bribe me. I'm a scientist."

Wasn't he a doctor? Azalea watched his brain ticking over the options.

"Well, *Mr. Scientist*, I'm sure they don't pay you very well, so I'll make it two grand and we'll be out of your hair. You can buy a new science machine and this young lady doesn't get her life ruined by telling the world about her Snake Magic. Everyone wins."

His eyes narrowed as he lunged for the emergency button near the door. But Danni was faster. She blocked his path. A fireball flared to life in her hand, and the doctor crashed into the corner of the steel bench in panic. His hands scrambled at his jacket, presumably for his elemer, but it was on his desk next to the computer. Realizing his mistake, he struggled to regain his footing.

It all happened so fast. Azalea stood there frozen as Danni extinguished her flames and had the doctor in hand cuffs and on the ground in seconds.

"You'll never get out of here," he spat.

"I think you'll find we will." Danni poured something in his mouth. His eyes closed, and his head lolled to the side.

"What the hell was that? He's not dead, is he?" Azalea asked. Hopefully she hadn't put her trust in a serial killer.

"He'll be fine. It's a new memory potion I got from work. The lab guys said it was safe to try." She shrugged and started pulling the doctor along the floor. "Give me a hand, would you?"

"Um. Sure." After all, it was perfectly normal to help a woman you met yesterday who could shoot flames from her hands move a magically drugged doctor onto his computer chair.

Danni positioned him so he looked like he was napping on the job and took off the handcuffs.

"At least we still have the bribe money," Danni said cheerfully as she checked whatever he had written on the computer, then started rummaging through the cabinets of vials and bottles. Was she going to rob the guy now?

"What are you looking for?" Azalea asked, not sure if she wanted to know the answer.

"Got it!" Danni said.

"Do I even want to know what that is? And will he really be okay?"

"Course he will. It should only wipe an hour or so from his mind and the lads at the lab have never steered me wrong. Rinse out those flasks in the sink and then we can go. This little potion is for you. It's kind of an initiation to your House . . . well, *Houses* in this case."

Azalea moved the glassware to the sink and poured out the now sludgy liquid, careful not to let any touch her skin. Danni set the room right as if they'd never been there—like a pro.

"What exactly is your job?" Azalea asked.

"Mostly desk work these days. I haven't been in the field as much since we had the twins, but I do join in on the occasional investigation. Right, let's get going. We can chat on the way home."

The elevator ride down was painfully slow. Each ding had Azalea holding her breath, imagining guards storming in.

"Just stay calm," Danni said as they walked through the forest lobby that now felt like a minefield.

"Why are we even doing this? What would happen if he recorded that I was House of Snakes?" Azalea whispered.

Danni kept a light smile on her lips as she walked with a spring in her step. "From what Fabian told me in the past, your father kept your existence a secret for your own protection, of course. There's no record of you in the archives so best you stick with your mum's last name so no one will make that connection while you're at the Tower."

Azalea's heart stopped a beat. Her father kept her existence a secret? Was he ashamed of her?

"Why would he hide me?"

"So Korbyn Dumont wouldn't find you. If you were added to the records now connecting you to your dad, Korbyn would know your dad had a kid and would likely come after you to finish his whole revenge thing."

"But he didn't get revenge. My dad wasn't murdered."

Danni gave her a sad smile. "Of course he wasn't, love."

Was everything she had been told a lie? She was eighteen-bloody-years-old and felt more like a kid than ever. She wasn't even sure she wanted to know more. Numbness shrouded her as they entered the next lift. She didn't even realize they were outside until the noise of trucks squeaking breaks shocked her back to reality.

"Let's get you back. That's enough excitement for one day," Danni said.

Azalea just nodded and trailed after Danni like a ghost.

CHAPTER 11

THEY MADE IT BACK to the Tower. Azalea wandered through the sea of tourists in a daze, struggling to keep up with Danni. Relief washed over her as they made it back to the quiet living room where Faraday was happily napping on a very white chair he was bound to leave fur on.

A second after they sat down, Danni was up again. "Maiken just messaged. She said to bring you down to the hospital right now to see something."

"What is it?" Azalea's mouth went dry.

"I'll explain when we get there, but I suggest you come."

Rushing out of the apartment, they took the stairs rather than wait for the lift. The smell of antiseptic and herbs hit Azalea as Danni pushed open the doors. Azalea kept close as people in white coats with colored cuffs rushed around the sterile hallway. There were no windows; only closed doors. Azalea followed Danni into a hospital room.

People clustered around a bed. Most were in doctors' coats, but one man stood out. He was young, and eye-catching in a charcoal-gray designer coat with the collar turned up. Azalea couldn't help but stare at his eyes. They were black as obsidian, right to the edges.

Danni nodded toward him. "That's Torin, he sometimes helps Maiken in extreme cases like this. He's a Shadow Mage from the House of Ravens."

Azalea instantly tensed up.

"Don't worry. He's the only one here, and he's a defector. He's been exiled from the House."

Azalea stared at him. Maybe a little too much. He was gorgeous, no doubt about that, despite his demonic eyes. He had golden brown skin and closely shaved hair. He also had a nicely shaped head, which made a difference when someone had hair that short. But his severe expression drew away from his charm. Everyone stood back from him, darting looks between each other and shuffling nervously. He ignored them all, his focus entirely on whoever was in the bed.

"I need everyone back at their stations!" Maiken shouted. Two of the white coats raced off, their cuffs both amber-colored. Maiken was the only one with blue cuffs. She appeared to be in charge.

Danni pulled Azalea against the wall, and Maiken glanced in their direction. "Keep her here. I want her to see what burnout looks like," she said to Danni. This was a different woman to the calm Maiken she had met in the kitchen that morning. This was a no-nonsense doctor you wouldn't want to argue with.

Danni whispered, "Burnout is when you overdo it with magic, or try magic with no experience. It's an amateur mistake, but a deadly one."

Azalea made herself small. Animal-like moans escaped the patient's lips as he writhed across blood-stained sheets. Swallowing back a scream, Azalea couldn't look away, but nearly threw up at the sight of that much blood. It streamed from his eyes, staining his cheeks dark, dirty red. His skin crackled and blistered with burns, and the coppery smell of blood and singed flesh hit the back of Azalea's throat. She took in sharp gasps of air.

A whimper came from the corner. Azalea nudged Danni. "There's a girl over there. Should I see if she's okay?"

"Stay here. I know her. The boy on the bed is her brother, Erik," Danni said. The girl had flattened herself into the corner, shrinking away. Danni picked her up, and the girl clung to her, sobbing. She carried her across the room and past Azalea. "I'm going to find her dad. Are you okay here?"

"Why do I need to see this?" Azalea asked, wanting to leave with Danni and the girl.

"Because this is something you won't forget. You'll have a vivid image of the consequences if you push your magic too far."

Nodding, Azalea bit down on her lip. Danni left, and the door swung shut behind her. Alone and way out of her comfort zone, Azalea tried to blend in with the wall once more. She stared at the Shadow Mage, Torin, forcing her mind away from the horrible scene. He was much nicer to stare at than his unfortunate patient.

A small scar split his eyebrow in two in a piratey kind of way, like a miniature sickle. It was difficult to guess his age. Maybe early twenties? His nicely trimmed beard made him look a little older. Still, too young to be a doctor. He was so still, if beads of sweat weren't pin-pricking his forehead, he could be a robot. His eyes were locked on the patient, his hand hovering over the boy's chest.

Maiken watched from the other side of the bed. Azalea jumped when Torin moved and an elemer appeared in his hand.

Dark tendrils began flowing from his blade. His magic looked just like hers, though he was controlling his. Her mouth fell open as ropes of shadows wrapped around Erik's arms, legs, and chest, pinning him to the bed.

Wiping her forehead, Maiken rolled her neck and nodded toward Torin. The other two doctors moved back as the patient arched his back and his screams ripped through Azalea. The shadow ropes held him effortlessly.

Torin held both his hands above the boy's chest, one wrapped around his elemer. He closed his eyes, and the screams died down. In that moment, Erik went limp.

Maiken, gripping her own silver and white elemer, placed her hands on either side of Torin's, just above Erik's heart, and the shadows mixed with the light like a braid growing out from the two blades. Maiken's eyes glazed over, all black. Then light flooded into Erik's skin.

A pulse of energy moved through the air, thumping like a heartbeat. The other doctors stood by Maiken, watching calmly. Bloody hell, this was intense. How were they all so calm? If anything, this was a good lesson not to study medicine. At least engineering didn't come with this level of stress, she hoped.

Maiken fell backward. A doctor caught her, and the others moved her to the next bed over. Her eyes squeezed as she crunched into a ball, and Azalea glanced back at Torin. His hand was on the boy's forehead, but he pulled it away quickly. Torin turned, and Azalea froze as his pupilless eyes locked with hers.

He turned away and said something to Maiken. She squeezed his hand, and he left the room without so much as a nod to anyone else.

A woman wearing a white coat with amber cuffs wiped blood from Erik's face as he groaned.

Azalea did a double take. No way . . . he was healing right before her eyes. His raw skin turned bright pink and the bubble of burns smoothed out, and before she knew it, he had healthy tanned skin.

Azalea glanced at Maiken, who caught her eye. A spiderweb of glowing, red veins branched out from her eyes across her dark skin. Azalea froze, but Maiken smiled reassuringly as a doctor handed her some water and a pile of pills.

The boy sat up. He had a crooked nose and dried blood caked through a matted nest of brown hair. He had big shoulders, built like a rugby player, and seemed to be around eighteen as well. But how in the world was he still alive?

His gaze caught Azalea's. *Eeek! Where to look?* He sat rigid with his jaw locked as his eyes burned into her. Did he not know he nearly died? She held his gaze, not wanting to show she was scared. He turned away when the doctor spoke.

Azalea exhaled as Danni came back in with the girl and an older man. Erik's face softened as the little girl scrambled onto his bed, into his arms. Stroking her hair, she clung to his chest. It's lucky they hadn't walked in a minute ago.

"Come on. I'll check Maiken, then we can get out of here," Danni said.

"Yes please," Azalea squeaked. "I hope Maiken's okay. What did she do?"

"She'll be fine. She knows what she's doing," Danni said, though Azalea got the impression she didn't approve. "She puts so much into healing; it takes its toll on her. All magic has a price."

Azalea inched closer to the door and waited as Danni talked softly to Maiken. She gave Maiken a kiss, then nodded her head toward the door. Azalea followed her into the hallway.

"You okay?" Danni asked as they made their way back.

"I'm not exactly sure. What just happened?" Azalea said.

"Maiken wanted you to see what burnout looks like—when you overdo magic."

"So, he did that to himself?"

"Yes. A little too cocky for his own good, and showing off, no doubt. He's not cleared to practice unsupervised, and he'll be lucky if they let him in the program now."

"My program?" Azalea asked as they stepped into the lift.

Danni dug around for her keys. "Yes. He should be in your class. He lives here too. He's from the House of Phoenix, like me. His dad's the best metal smith in England. He makes elemers." She held the keys up triumphantly, then shook her head. "Erik should have known better."

"So, what happens to him now? Will there be side effects?" Azalea asked, glad to be away from the antiseptic smell.

"If you overtax your magic like that, you usually die. The magic that Maiken poured into him has its own consequences. The price for life is always life." Danni said bluntly. "Magic has a way of balancing things."

"So he was that close to dying? How does it balance?"

"He will be drawn to seek out blood. A sick joke of the gods, if you ask me. He's lucky Maiken was there. She's one of the few healers strong enough to restore a body from burnout. She also pays the price for healing him. But it's a temporary side effect for both until their magic balances."

"So, are they like vampires or something?" Azalea asked as sweat beaded into her palms.

"In the olden days, that's what they would be, but without the fangs. Today we have medicines that keep them in balance, so they don't hurt people or drink blood," Danni explained. Her hands were shaking. Clearly, she was more rattled than she let on.

"Wow. My mum kept a lot from me, but I'm starting to see why." She wished her mum was here to help her understand. They stepped out of the lift, and Danni let them into the flat. "How does magic even work? Is it safe?"

"It's safe if you do it right," Danni said as she flopped onto the sofa. Azalea sat in a stiff armchair, waiting for an elaboration of some sort as Danni continued. "Magic is like electricity. We siphon it through our bodies and it comes out as something else. Our intention and spells turn it into focused magic. The key is building up resistance so you can channel more . . . without dying."

"And how am I supposed to do that?"

"A shit load of hard work," Danni said. "You have to be at peak physical and mental condition before they'll even let you touch magic. So be prepared for some extreme training."

"But once I pass the training, I can do magic?"

Danni rubbed her chin. "There's a lot more to it. Lots of theory and you have to keep training up your whole life. You'll be fine, don't worry. There's a few other things you should know before you decide. Maiken was going to explain the details later, but I can give it a go since she'll be sleeping for a while. But first we should have a rest, I'm knackered." She rolled her neck against the back cushion.

"I think I need a nap," Azalea said, her head pounding against her skull.

"Good call. Here, take this up. I'll probably lose it." She tossed Azalea the small potion bottle they got from the doctor. "You'll need to take this potion once you decide if you're in."

"What is it? Like, what does it do?" Azalea studied the small vial. The green glass stopper was in the shape of a tiny dragon, and the liquid inside moved in opalescent spirals.

"It's kind of like a protection thing. It confirms your Houses officially and signs you up. Sorry, I suck at explaining. Don't decide now. We can talk about it more when you've had time to think and had some rest."

Azalea tucked the vial into her pocket, thanked Danni, and made her way upstairs. She already knew what she wanted, and she wasn't going to chicken out of it now. Being in this place full of mages and people who knew how to use magic had her nerves on edge. What if she lost control of her Shadow Magic now? Would they all hate her? The sooner she had this under control, the better. Plus, discovering there was a Shadow Mage at the Tower was a bonus. Maybe he could teach her? One thing was for sure, she was drinking that potion now.

CHAPTER 12

A FTERNOON SUNLIGHT SPILLED THROUGH the small windowpane as Azalea perched on the edge of the bed and rolled the tiny vial across her palm. Faraday wound around her back and let out a chirp, glancing between her face and the vial.

She rubbed her pounding temples as she pulled out her phone and sent a quick message to her mum: *All is going good here. Don't need to worry about me. Love you.*

Mum: *That's nice dear. Love you too. RoRo says hi.*

Azalea laughed to herself, typical Mum response when she didn't want to know what Azalea was really up to.

Shit, she'd forgotten to message Isaac back from earlier. Oh well, he could wait for now.

"Right. I'm going to take it. It's the only way I'll learn Shadow Magic, so there's no point in putting it off," she said, wondering if she should ease up on talking to the cat. Faraday growled and dug his needle-like claws into her leg. Shoving him off, he tumbled across the bed. "What the hell!" she yelled. "You never growled at me before, you little shit."

She narrowed her eyes at him. "Sod off. I'm doing it." She pulled the dragon stopper off and downed the glowing liquid in one quick shot. Faraday hissed at her and bolted out the door.

The air grew heavy. Her throat tightened, and she struggled to pull in a breath. Blood pulsed through her ears. Clawing at her throat, she fell back on the bed, and scrambled for something, anything. Black spots morphed across her vision as a crushing weight squeezed her lungs.

She fought the darkness until struggling was too hard. She let herself sink away.

)))●(((

Azalea stood in front of a pyramid. Giant steps rose high out of an endless desert of golden sand. Walking toward it, a pathway of stone blocks rose out of the earth. Two figures stood on the steps of the temple, and she walked toward them.

The sun dipped into the rolling sea of sand and Azalea's bare arms soaked in the warmth radiating around her. She frowned at her arm. The scratches she'd had that morning were gone.

Around her, a strange silk gown flowed like water. Not something she would have chosen, but it was pleasantly cool against her skin. Her footsteps were silent, and as she walked, enormous stone pools rose out of the ground, filling with water that reflected the orange and pink sky.

Azalea reached the base of the pyramid, where the women on the stairs stood like statues. She floated toward them as if she were in a dream. The woman on the left stood tall with her shoulders back and her chin high like a queen. Her skin shimmered silvery-gray, and her sleek metallic-black hair trickled over sharp collar bones like water over a ledge. Her hand looked like it had been dipped in mercury. This woman placed a clay bowl on the step and rose.

The other woman's lithe frame moved with equal elegance as she placed a second bowl on the step. Her skin was the color of golden wheat and her hair was as green as a meadow, rippling like wind through long grass. They wore similar dresses to Azalea's—the silk moved with light and colors that seemed alive.

They gestured for her to come forward.

Azalea somehow knew what to do as she reached the steps. She kneeled at the bottom and bowed her head down until it touched the step above. She waited as silence rested on the hot desert air. The metal-handed woman spoke, and Azalea looked up.

"We welcome you, daughter of mortals. You consumed the elixir of the gods and summoned us to bear witness as protectors."

They bowed their heads, and Azalea dipped her head in response.

"I am the Ereshkigal, Goddess of Death and The Dead. I greet you as a daughter of the Great House of Snakes."

Azalea bowed again.

The other woman nodded to the Goddess Ereshkigal. "I am the Mother Goddess, Ninhursag. I bestowed the gifts of plants and herbal wisdom upon your ancestors. I welcome you as a daughter of nature to the Honorable House of Bees."

Azalea wasn't afraid but felt like maybe she should be. Her mind was dulled like it was filled with sand.

"Thank you for this honor. Is this a dream?" she asked.

"Yes," Ninhursag answered with a smile. "We are in the Great Desert of Dreams, ruled by the God Zakar."

Ereshkigal glared down at her. Her gaze was venomous but restrained, as if a demon might rip free from her at any second.

"I'm in a different world in a dream?" Azalea said.

"It is something mortals often find hard to perceive. This is a land where only one's subconscious may travel, but that makes it no less real," Ninhursag said.

Thank god, or gods, that the Goddess Ninhursag seemed friendly. Azalea didn't want to have to explain running out on her mother's equinox ceremony. Ereshkigal was the opposite. She oozed darkness and terror.

This was not a person—er, goddess—to mess with.

"You have been summoned to accept the Mark of the Gods," Ereshkigal said. "Upon taking the Mark, you will abide by the laws of magic and use this gift with only the intentions of goodness and kindness."

Azalea stared up at her and nodded. The goddess didn't look like she followed those rules.

"Before we ask you to accept the Mark of the Gods, we have one warning. If you accept the Seal, your path will lead to an inevitable fork in your life's journey." Ninhursag held out one hand. "One direction will lead you to the destruction of many." She held out the other hand. "The other to the destruction of one. This will not happen for at least one cycle of the sun. Choose wisely."

Azalea didn't know how to react. Either way she would be the direct cause of destruction . . . *great*. But if she backed out now, she would never get her dad back. She would miss her chance at controlling magic and would probably end up a crazy cat lady at twenty years old talking to ghosts and cats. RoRo always told her to forge her own life path . . . but was this a trick?

"Who is the *one*? And is there another path?"

"The *one* is important to you and there are many paths, but if you accept the Mark, your journey can only lead to these two places."

Was this even real? Either way, she knew what to choose. Whatever the future held, she could deal with it. Plus, this was just a dream, a place where risks lead to rewards without consequences, so why not?

"I choose to accept the Mark of the Gods," she said.

Ereshkigal's mouth twitched into a serpentine smile. "Daughter of the House of Snakes, drink from the bowl of the Gods and accept the Mark of Ereshkigal as bestowed upon your ancestors."

Azalea reached up and accepted the bowl. She brought the warm clay to her lips and drank the liquid, surprised to find it was water.

Ninhursag spoke. "Daughter of the House of Bees, drink from the bowl of the Gods and accept the Mark of Ninhursag as your ancestors did."

She drank the cold liquid from the cup.

"Turn and reenter the world as a new light between the Shadow Dimension and Echo Dimension. Daughter of two Houses."

Azalea stood and walked out toward the desert. She sensed the two goddesses close behind. She stopped beside the first pool of water and looked down into its midnight blue depths. The women stood on either side of her. She flinched as each caught hold of an arm.

They crushed her flesh until she was sure her bones would crack. Pain shot through to her spine and light seared her eyes, but she couldn't cry out. Palms burned through her skin like hot, glowing metal. Suddenly, she was falling. She hit the water. It wrapped around her like a cocoon and dragged her down, cold and unrelenting. But she couldn't fight it and the dark liquid spilled into her lungs, forcing her to continue. There was no more air.

CHAPTER 13

P AIN FLASHED ACROSS AZALEA'S vision as she struggled
to free her arms and legs. Twisting, she rolled to the side,
her arm brushing her chest, sending flares across her skin. She
kicked to free her legs but shifted too far to the side. Her
stomach dropped as she slammed into the hard floor. Footsteps
pounded closer and closer. A door opened, flooding the room
with harsh light.

"You silly goose," a kind voice said.

Azalea's head was hammering even harder than before, and
her mouth tasted of acrid vomit. She cracked her eyes to see
Danni leaning over her.

"Ow." Azalea tried to sit up, but her arm protested. Danni hoisted her from under her armpits and hauled her to the
bed. She was in her room at Danni's place. A shard of light
slipped through the curtains, stabbing into her eyes like daggers.
Her legs were unsteady, and she squinted at the bright lamp
that Danni had apparently turned on. She found her head was
cloudy, and she badly needed to pee. When she attempted to
string together the words to get Danni to help her, her voice felt
scratchy and unused.

After an awkward visit to the bathroom and back, the small amount of energy Azalea had before was now well and truly drained. She sunk into the soft pillows, barely able to move her limbs. Faraday appeared next to her, giving a firm head-butt before circling into a ball on her lap.

"What happened?" she asked.

Danni handed her a glass of water. Azalea's arm strained, and she winced in pain. Uneasiness crept over her as she studied her bandage wrapped arms. It had been a dream . . . hadn't it?

"What happened is your uncle would've had my guts for garters if you didn't wake up." Azalea didn't miss the shakiness in her voice or the dark rings under Danni's eyes.

"What happened?" she repeated.

"You took the bloody potion, and you had no idea what it was—not very clever of you." Danni pulled out her phone and started texting.

Azalea leaned back against the pillows and sipped the water, washing the foul taste out of her mouth. She must have slept all afternoon.

"I'm sorry," Azalea said, her brain started to wake up. She nodded to her arms. "What's all this?"

"You were marked. It's the Mark of the Gods."

"But it was a dream."

"Yes, and it was also real. If you had waited for us to explain it, you would know that," Danni said.

The door opened and Maiken rushed in. Her eyes softened when she saw Azalea sitting up, but the stress behind them was unmistakable. "Thank the gods you're awake."

Danni moved and let Maiken take her place on the edge of the bed next to Azalea. Maiken looked much better than in the hospital. Danni hopped on the end of the bed to sit cross-legged.

"You should have waited for us. Taking the potion is dangerous and not a choice to be taken lightly." She lifted Azalea's right arm and began unwinding the bandage. "But it's too late now. Let's see what the damage is," Maiken said.

Azalea tensed, unsure if she wanted to know what was under there. "Why are you taking them off?"

"Because they should look much better now."

"Didn't you just put them on?"

"You've been asleep since yesterday afternoon," Danni said. "It's Sunday night."

Azalea grew lightheaded. No wonder she'd needed to pee so badly. She had never slept so long in her life. Azalea focused on Maiken's graceful hands unwinding the bandages. How much of the dream had been real? She tried to backtrack through the events with the two goddesses. Both had given her the Mark of the Gods, so she assumed she passed whatever dream test it was.

But what lay beneath the bandages? Horrible burns for sure, or perhaps a brand. The memory of her burning flesh flashed across her mind.

"Will it heal?" Azalea asked, looking up at Maiken, trying to keep her eyes off her arm.

"It nearly has," Maiken said, peeling away the last strand of bandage. The smell of chrysanthemums and cabbage wafted up. Maiken gave it a wipe with something cold.

Azalea's breath caught, and she blinked at her arm as if it wasn't her own. There was no burn. Instead, a tattoo. A delicate watercolor tattoo of two pink flowers, azaleas, sat perfectly positioned on her forearm. A fat bumblebee hovered above them, and behind the flowers were the thin-lined geometric designs and tiny moons. So . . . this was weird. Brushing her finger against it, it hummed with warmth. A faint pulse of light ran through the lines as she lifted her fingers.

She looked at Maiken, whose smile had returned. Maiken gave Azalea's hand a squeeze. "I'm sure your mother would love it."

Azalea forced a smile. She wasn't so sure about that. RoRo might. It was like RoRo's flower tattoos, but RoRo's were all different types: belladonna, foxgloves, freesias, jasmine, and so many more.

"Do the other arm!" Danni shuffled her way up the bed to sit right in front of Azalea, eagerly awaiting the next reveal.

The bandage on the left arm wasn't white like the other. A tinge of yellow and red seeped through the layers to the surface. Azalea didn't miss the split-second frown that crossed Maiken's brow.

"Let's have a look." Maiken started to unwind the bandage.

The dream was coming back with surprising clarity. "What do the tattoos mean? What did the goddesses do to me?"

Danni shot her another 'you would know this if you waited for us' look. "It shows your House affiliation and what strain of magic you are competent at. The tattoos can't lie. They show the strength of your power and over time, they tell the story of your magic. It can be both good and bad. Not everyone wants to share that much information up front with strangers. Most mages keep their arms covered, either for modesty, or secrecy," Danni explained.

"Whereas others are just showoffs and love displaying their talents for all the world to see," Maiken teased, nodding to Danni's thin-strapped summer dress. Danni chuckled and held her arms in the air, showing off her tattoos. Lifelike dragons and phoenixes, with flames of crimson and gold covered her arms. The tiny geometric lines running behind the tattoo looked like molten-red steel pulsing through their own secret network under her skin.

"What can I say? I don't have a poker face. I like people knowing how great I am upfront." Danni shrugged. "I've found it's the best way to avoid conflict because no one wants to fight me. They know they'll lose."

Maiken shook her head in fake disapproval. "She has a point. But is also a brazen showoff."

Danni batted her eyelashes and smiled. Azalea remembered how quickly she had taken down the doctor, and the fact that she could make fireballs and throw them, apparently.

"You can do magic without a tattoo, but the Mark of the Gods strengthens your ties to your family magic. Think of it as the starting point on building your resistance," Danni said. She twisted her face in thought, as if trying to find the right words. "It's kind of like a boost of protection from the gods."

Maiken continued from where Danni had left off. "Scientists still haven't worked out exactly what it is, but it adds some sort of protection at a cellular level, meaning you can handle more magic running through you. That's why it's considered the first step to becoming a mage. You can't handle much power without this basic shielding of your cells."

"Old legends say that every time your tattoo grows, it's the gods honoring you with their blessings and praise," Danni said.

"The tattoos expand as you channel more magic. Your body grows the tattoos to reflect your experiences and level of power you can handle," Maiken said.

"But it also depends on what the gods think of you," Danni said.

Maiken arched an eyebrow but said nothing, she was entirely fixated on Azalea's arm.

"That's why we wanted to talk to you first. Sometimes the body reacts badly to the potion or to the Mark once it's performed. On rare occasions, people die during the process, or get trapped in the Great Desert of Dreams. It's a serious decision to make."

Azalea felt the blush creeping up her neck. She was an idiot. She thought the decision was if she wanted to stay at the Tower and learn magic or not. Maybe it was better not knowing she could have been trapped in a weird dream world. Acting without thinking was one of her not-so-lovable traits. Leda's voice always rang in her head after making some stupid spur-of-the-moment decision, but it never helped at the time. She promised herself to try to listen better in the future, to stop making rash decisions.

"I'm sorry. I should have waited for you. I just knew how sick you looked after you saved that boy. I didn't want you to have to worry about me, too." She chewed on her lip. "I guess I made things much worse."

"Remember that magic is not something to be taken lightly. You need to think things through," Maiken said.

Azalea nodded. The bandage became dark with dried blood as Maiken unwound another strip, pulling to get it unstuck. It felt hot and sticky as Maiken peeled the last strip away. The smell was the same chrysanthemums and cabbage that made Azalea gag when it mixed with the smell of blood. She squinted through one eye as Maiken carefully wiped her arm. Azalea rested her head back against the pillows, trying not to wince as Maiken's cleaning made her arm burn with every wipe.

"You can look now," Maiken said.

Azalea forced her head back up. She looked down at her arm and took in a sharp breath. It was nothing like the other tattoo, but she loved it instantly.

A snake painted her entire forearm. The snake's body was a mixture of deep azure blue and galaxy purple dotted with tiny, illuminated stars. The contrast against her pale skin was striking. Its underbelly had lines of shimmering black and silver, and its body was loosely knotted with pleasant symmetry. She touched the pulse point on her wrist where a luminescent crescent moon shone back. The serpent's head reached out to it with its forked tongue. It was different from the flower tattoo. It was bold and vibrant, but still had a delicate feeling in its thin and precise lines.

"Gosh," Danni said. "That's rather impressive."

"It's lovely. Though not as easy to hide as we hoped," Maiken said.

"What does it mean?" Azalea ran her fingers along the outline of the snake. The geometric lines behind the tattoo buzzed with silver energy streams. Her fingers tingled. The skin around the tattoo was red and hot.

"You'll have to keep it well covered. Best not to let others see. Not until your place here is secure and you've got your magic under control," Maiken said.

"It means you have strong Shadow Magic. You'll have to be very careful here," Danni said.

"Is it normal?"

"It's fine love," Danni said. But Azalea didn't miss the small glance between the two women.

"Any who, I've got good news. While you were asleep for the last *twenty hours,* I managed to find you a flat. Once you're feeling up to it, I'll take you over there. You'll like your flatmate, Evangeline. She's a lovely girl—one of Maiken's apprentices at the Hospital. She's in her second year here, so she's around nineteen," Danni said.

"But first, get some more rest." Maiken added.

"I'm fine—" Azalea started but stopped with one look from Maiken. "I'll have a bit more sleep and I'm sure I'll be much better. Thank you for looking after me."

Maiken nodded and gave a kind smile. Danni gave a quick wave goodbye, and the two women left the room. Azalea couldn't keep her eyes open. She rested her hand on the snake tattoo. The energy buzzed through her fingertips in a pleasant way. She would have another nap, then get on with meeting her flatmate and starting her search for Shadow Magic info. Just a few hours' sleep . . .

CHAPTER 14

Azalea hurried after Danni, and Faraday trailed close behind as Azalea's sports bag thudded against her thigh. Chatter droned around her as she narrowly avoided photo bombing tourist groups.

Rounding the corner of a cobbled lane called Mint Street, they passed a sign that read RESIDENTS ONLY PAST THIS POINT. Azalea relaxed as Danni led the way to a bright red door in a row of brown brick flats that were part of the fortress wall.

"I'm going to live here?" Azalea said, her eyes wide.

"You sure are. There's nowhere safer. Now . . . what number was it?" Danni said to herself as she flicked through her phone.

Azalea admired the rows of vibrant flowers in colorful mismatched pot plants that lined the pavement outside the flats, alongside a few clotheshorses and small garden tables.

"Got it! This is definitely the right one," Danni said as she pushed open the red door to a short hallway.

Azalea followed her in.

"You're the red one on the right," she said as she rapped on the door.

Azalea bit her lip. The door creaked open.

"Welcome, welcome! Hi, I'm Evangeline. But please, call me Van. I'm so, so glad you're here!" The girl, who looked around nineteen, clapped her hands and ushered Azalea and Danni in before they could get a word in. The things Azalea noticed, other than her loud voice, was Van's warm smile and big eyes with long lashes. She was very tanned—most certainly fake—and had a bright purple and yellow headband that held back waves and waves of brown hair. She was dressed in purple leggings and a tie-died sports bra.

"Um thanks. I'm Azalea Sharp," Azalea said, unsure how to deal with the burst of energy as she was hustled in.

"Come in, come in." Van shuffled them further into a compact living area that was both kitchen and dining space.

Azalea dropped her bags in the hall and shook out her shoulders. Faraday followed her, cautiously sniffing everything as he went.

"I'm so glad you're coming to live here Azalea; you have no idea. My flatmate moved out two weeks ago after dropping out of the Apprentice program. I guess it was too much work for her with all the shifts and study on top. I had no idea how I was going to keep up with rent. Then Mage Hawthorn mentioned she might know someone, and I harassed her all afternoon yesterday to get you to come over! I'm so glad you're here. Please, help yourself to some biscuits," she said without a break. They sat down. She had about ten types of biscuits and fruitcake spread across the table and was pouring them tea.

Danni dug into the biscuits, selecting a hobnob to dunk in her tea. "Like I said, Zalea. Evangeline was in desperate need of a flatmate, so it's your lucky day if you're keen," Danni said.

Azalea smiled as she picked out a chocolate digestive and nodded.

"Is this all right for you? I know it's rather small and pokey, but I'm sure we'll get on just fine. I have to warn you that I work nights. But I'm out dead during the day, so you don't have to worry about being quiet," Van said.

"It's perfect," Azalea replied. "Thank you for letting me stay. I've had a lot to get my head around and this is a life saver." A life saver, but also terrifying. She was now under pressure to come up with rent money, learn to cook food somehow, and do her own washing. Her savings from selling watches over the past years would be gone within a month of paying bills. She needed a job, and fast.

"Lovely jubbly!" Van said with a happy squeal. She danced to the kitchen and flitted back with more tea.

Jeez. Azalea wasn't used to living with strangers, especially one so excitable. Hopefully, this was just a first meeting thing. Van topped up the tea and Azalea opted for sugar to boost her energy and then snuggled into the corner of the sofa.

Van and Danni caught up on Tower gossip, but Azalea was too tired to try to keep up with names or what was going on. Faraday disappeared off somewhere and Azalea sent a message to Isaac, promising to call him soon.

"Oh, how rude of me!" Van said in a tone loud enough to shock Azalea awake. "You'll be wanting to see your room. Come on then." She jumped up and spun around with the grace of a dancer. She darted off. "Oh look! Your kitty has already found his spot."

Azalea followed the cooing sounds and found Van fawning over Faraday, who was lapping up the attention. He had indeed found his spot, right in the center of the double bed.

"Wow, I was half expecting this to be a dungeon since its inside the castle wall," Azalea said with a laugh.

"It was. Trust me," Van said. "It was in desperate need of brightening up. No way I was sticking with the hideous red wallpaper and disgusting seventies carpet." She shuddered. "This is brand new carpet, and you can see the east moat out there if you look through the not-window." Van nodded to the small cross shaped slit where a splinter of light sneaked through. The room had a cozy cave-like feel to it, it was small and simple, but it had a desk, a lamp, a cupboard, and a bed. It was perfect.

Evangeline showed Azalea the rest of the flat, which consisted of a bathroom, complete with a bath, and Van's own room right next door.

"I best be off now," Danni said as the girls re-entered the living room. She'd polished off a good pile of the biscuits.

"Thank you for all your help," Azalea said as Danni jumped up.

"No worries, love," Danni said. "Just be careful," she nodded toward Azalea's left arm. "And pop over for tea anytime and for Sunday roast." She hugged Azalea, and Evangeline sent her out the door with some fruitcake.

Azalea tossed her bags in her room and found Van in the kitchen. She handed Azalea a map. "It's a tourist map, so you can learn your way around. You'll need to know your way around the Complex; the cafeteria—known as the caf—the training rooms, and I guess the library."

"Thanks, I haven't had a chance to look around much yet. I'd like to see the library," Azalea said, hoping it might hold answers about Shadow Magic, so she wouldn't have to ask people, or the Shadow Atlas.

"I've got to run and pick up my supplements. Trust me, you don't want to see me when I don't have them. You know, healer's curse and all." Van let out a nervous giggle.

Azalea froze up. "You mean like the whole vampire side effect thing from healing? You've got that too?"

"Only if I do a lot of healing at once. I don't get to practice very often, I'm only in my second year after all. But don't worry. I won't try and drink your blood or anything! Gosh no. That's vile—no one does that these days. That's why it's best to have the supplements on hand." Van gave a nervous laugh. "Sorry, didn't mean to scare you."

"Don't worry, I won't be scared off that easily. I really needed a flat," Azalea said with a smile. To tell the truth, she was a little nervous, but Van was reassuring, and Azalea could always lock her door at night.

"I'm glad! Not glad you need a flat . . . I mean . . . I'm so glad you are here!" She flapped her hands frantically, then cracked up laughing. "Sorry, don't worry about me. I'm not crazy, but haven't had much sleep in some time now. Moving on . . . I can let you into the Complex if you don't have an elemer yet."

"That would be great," Azalea said, having no idea what the relevance of the elemer was.

Van spent ten minutes applying makeup while Azalea quickly unpacked by dumping her clothes across her bed. Van popped her head in the door wearing an over-sized, floppy sun hat.

Perhaps it served as another one of her vampire-ish precautions. "Lovely. Let's go," she announced.

Azalea told Faraday to stay, and she trailed after Van. They walked a few meters down the road and then crossed the cobbled street, heading straight for the stone wall of the inner fortress. Azalea was grateful for that extra wall blocking her from the chapel. It was a large enough barrier to keep spirits on their side and hopefully well away from her.

Just when Azalea was about to question why they were facing a giant wall, Van tapped her elemer to a stone and it lit up. The stones cascaded inward to reveal a staircase.

"Holy shit, that was amazing," Azalea said, blinking into a dry, well-lit tunnel, which was much nicer than the last one.

Van beamed. "So, this is an entrance to the Complex. It's all underground. Just follow the hallway and you'll be in the caf, they have great coffee and sandwiches. All the doors off the far hallway are training rooms, the gym, and meditation rooms. Go to the end and you'll find the library. It's got enormous doors and looming silence . . . you can't miss it."

Azalea blinked at the stairs. "Thanks," she said, not quite believing it was real.

"Oh, silly me! Here's your key." Van handed her a key with a pink puffball keyring. "See you tonight," she said as she skipped off, leaving Azalea staring into the tunnel.

She tiptoed down the stairs and flinched when the staircase groaned and retracted as she stepped off. She followed the bright light and emerged into an expansive room. She was expecting some sort of military style mess hall, instead she found an enchanting underground courtyard.

Skylights filled the space with bright natural light, though that was impossible as the White Tower must be directly above her. At the center of the courtyard, a circular waterfall cascaded from the false sky ceiling and collected in a natural pool, complete with reeds, water lilies, and frogs.

The room smelled of fresh bread and earthy forest floor. Her feet sank into a spongy carpet of grass.

"Don't get too comfortable," a voice sneered behind her. "People like you don't last here long."

Azalea spun around to find herself face to face with the patient from the hospital. He wasn't covered in blood this time, but she recognized that stare and his cold blue eyes.

"People like me?"

"Yes. People who know nothing about magic."

"You're hardly one to talk. And too bad," she scoffed. "I'm not going anywhere." She looked him up and down, taking note of his overly styled, ash-brown hair and arrogant posture. He was clearly well aware of just how attractive he was. Just as Azalea was aware of how much of a wanker he was. She knew his type instantly. He was just like Isaac's snobby friends from school, and she would not be bullied by some rich-kid arsehole. This wasn't high school anymore.

"We'll see about that." He took a step closer and brushed past her. "This is going to be fun," he said, as he strutted away.

Azalea shook her head. *What a dick.* He was probably scared she would tell people about his little mishap. She didn't have time for drama. What she needed was to keep to herself and find some useful information on Shadow Magic.

Walking through the huge cafeteria, Azalea spotted families spread out on picnic blankets as kids raced around the pond and parents chattered away. She wondered if her dad had ever been to places like this. Would he have taken her and her mum on a picnic? Sat around like a normal family? She doubted it. He had been the one to leave them. She headed for the hallway on the other side of the courtyard.

She found all the rooms Van had mentioned but went straight for the vault-like doors at the end.

The doors creaked open by themselves, revealing a long, low-ceilinged room with a central isle and rows and rows of books. She breathed in the thick smell of old books and let herself relax a little. With slow footsteps, Azalea peered down the little side streets of books, curved archways of stone made for cozy reading or study nooks. Some had desks with green library lamps, others had one or two puffy armchairs.

This was where she needed to be. In twenty-eight days, her dad would be there waiting. This was his one shot. He had said he'd be too weak for another chance at this so she couldn't screw it up. She would prove to him she wasn't a useless little girl. If the Shadow Atlas wasn't going to cooperate, she had to take matters into her own hands. She'd make good use of these few weeks before uni started and sit there reading until her eyes bled.

Searching with no particular method, she came across a section of books on Echo Magic and flicked through a few about plants and basic elemental magic. She wandered for another half hour, but found nothing on Shadow Magic, and nothing on necromancy or how to communicate with ancient books that didn't want to cooperate. The filing system was not at all clear. Tomorrow she'd have to work out how to get a library card.

She left the library and found her way back to the flat. Flopping down onto her new bed next to Faraday, she called Isaac to fill him in.

"You'll never guess where I am," she squealed into the phone.

"Somewhere in London I'm hoping?" Isaac replied.

"Yes. The Tower of London, to be exact!"

"Great. Love that place. Did you see the Crown Jewels yet?"

"I'm not visiting. I'm living here!"

"Unless you suddenly got twenty-two years in the armed services and have been hired as a Yeoman Warder, I'm calling your bluff."

"Trust you to know more about the traditions than me. No, it's actually a secret community of mages. But you can't tell anyone. Non-magic people aren't meant to know about this stuff."

"Wait . . . you're serious?"

"Dead serious."

"Bloody hell. Not a conspiracy I would have picked to be real."

She told him everything about Fabian whisking her away and getting her magic tests done until he was up to date enough to help. "So, what do I do about the Shadow Atlas? It still won't work."

"Can't you ask someone there?"

"There is one guy I saw that's a Shadow Mage, but he didn't look very friendly."

"I dunno, Zaels. Don't get yourself into trouble. Maybe try feeding it more blood? Or take it to the library to see if it gets on with the other books? I'm probably not the right person to be asking, you know."

"Thanks anyway. I'll just keep trying."

"So, when can I come visit?" Isaac asked.

An unexpected chill raced down Azalea's spine. Something told her it wasn't safe for him, and she listened to her gut. "I dunno Isaac. I need to get settled and scope this place out first. I don't want to put you in danger if I can help it."

"That's no fun. Well don't keep me out of the loop too long or I'll be knocking down your door and making a scene."

"It's scary that I can actually see that happening and you getting dragged off by guards." She laughed. "It won't be too long. Just get settled at your new place and we'll sort something out later."

They said goodbye and Azalea stared up at her new, unfamiliar bedroom ceiling. She unwrapped the Shadow Atlas from her hoodie, but couldn't face any more blood and decided to try it tomorrow when she'd had a decent sleep. She tucked it under her pillow with her dad's pocket watch and set about unpacking.

CHAPTER 15

AZALEA GROANED AS VAN dragged her into the grassy moat at 6am the next day. It was only Tuesday morning for heaven's sake, and it was way too early to be awake, and not to mention waaay too early to be training. Waking up to a room full of shadows hadn't been the greatest start. Van hadn't seemed to notice though.

Danni hadn't been lying when she said you needed to be in top physical shape to do magic. These people took it too far. Azalea tried not to stare at their Instagram-worthy bodies of lean muscles and zero fat.

Van tugged on her hand and steered her through the crowd toward the back. She shivered as the morning breeze skimmed across the back of her neck. The city smells were unfamiliar; noxious car fumes and wafting coffee aromas made her feel both sick and wish for coffee.

"How are you this awake?" Azalea asked as Van bounced around and stretched.

"I'm a night owl." Van giggled. "I was working all night at the hospital and just finished up my clinical research assignment before you woke up. I nailed it, by the way. This is my wind down."

Azalea glanced around. Most people were older than her, but she spotted Erik and a group of people around eighteen- or nineteen-years-old near the front. She was too slow to move as he turned and spotted her. He nudged a red-headed guy next to him and pointed right at her. The other guy narrowed his eyes and glared at her. *Great, another arsehole to stay away from.* She thought she'd escaped the witch hunt when she finished high school. Her so-called friends had ditched her when she first started talking back to spirits. She didn't need any of them then, and this was no different.

She ducked behind the group and was grateful when the whistle blew, and everyone spread out. Within three minutes Azalea wanted to die. She was dripping with sweat just from the warmup, and it only got worse. There were sprints, push-ups, crazy ab straining moves, things that hurt her legs, wobbled her arms, and used muscles she didn't even know she had.

As the rest of the group did their millionth burpee in a row, Azalea lay face down in the grass, not caring that it was wet with dew, or that a bug was crawling toward her mouth.

"Come on, Zalea," Evangeline yelled. "Just the stretching now." She pulled Azalea off the grass.

They finished stretching, and Van dragged her up as her muscles protested. "Come on, better keep moving. You have a quick shower and I'll drop you at the meditation room."

"The what now?"

"Initiates have to attend every day, so you might as well start now. It'll help in your first week. It's fun!"

Azalea groaned as the wet grass beckoned her into its chilling fingers.

She made it to the shower and Van dropped her at meditation. She survived by not talking to anyone and dozing for the thirty-minute allocated time. Not a good start, but the best she could do with her past-exhausted body.

Back at the flat, Azalea made a bacon sandwich from what she found in the fridge and a strong cup of coffee to bring herself back to life. Van's snores echoed through the door as Azalea sat at the tiny dining table when a letter on the bench caught her eye. An envelope with her name on it. She slipped it open to find a timetable of classes starting the following Monday. *This was getting real!*

Timetable- Y1 Initiate- Azalea Sharp

Practical and Theoretical Magic Training- Training Room C

7:30 pm – 9 pm—*Monday – Friday*

Theory—10 am – 12 pm—*Saturday*

Practical—1 pm – 3 pm—*Saturday*

- Initiates are required to attend one physical training session per day and one meditation period.
- You will not conduct any unsupervised practical magic until you pass the physical fitness test.

Wishing you the best in your studies.

Archmage Norwich, Grand Master of the House of Owls and Tower of London

Holy crap, that was a lot of lessons on top of starting her degree in electrical and mechanical engineering, *and* needing a job on the side. She tucked the letter away. *Take it as it comes* would be her new mantra.

She spent the rest of the day tracking down how to get an ID in the Barracks office. Danni had said all people working there were mages, but they seemed like normal boring office people.

No capes, magical amulets, or glowing staffs. Disappointing. If she became a mage, perhaps she could start up a more wizardly fashion trend.

In the meantime, she returned to the library to hunt down some books. She managed to track down the books she found the other day, plus a few on Shadow Magic and returned home with them.

Her time had not been well spent. Two hours later and it was clear the Shadow Magic books were bullshit, all written by people who clearly didn't have Shadow Magic and didn't like anything to do with it. Slamming the book down, she winced, remembering Van was still sleeping. "Sorry," she whispered into the air, hoping she hadn't woken her. She'd have to go back and dig deeper. There couldn't be an ancient magical library without a section of dark magic.

Pulling the Shadow Atlas from under her pillow, something felt different. She put aside the pocket watch and flicked open a page to find new golden borders and glowing scripty writing.

A snake, a bee, you found the key.
But time is running out.
A church in which the trees are free.
Is where you'll face your doubt.

Woah! It was saying stuff! Gripping the book, she blinked a few times to make sure it was real. The ink stayed there, and she quickly grabbed her phone to snap a photo. She got one as the letters faded away and was surprised the picture worked.

"What key?" She shook the book, but it remained blank. *The pocket watch.* It had been with the book all night. She snatched it off the bedside table and placed it on the blank page and got her pencil. She guessed facing her doubt meant bringing back

her dad, so she had to find a church with free trees? She'd deal
with that later.

"How do I bring back my dad?" she whispered as she wrote
out the question.

A new golden script appeared.

When dark and light align as one.
The Hollow nears this plane.
The land, a breath, a tiny sun.
A drop, ignore the pain.

She had no idea what that meant, she snapped a photo. It
didn't say anything more after that, but at least it was talking to
her now and the pocket watch had some luck after all. Finally,
she had something to work with.

)))●(((

Bright shards of morning light splashed across the kitchen table.
Azalea grumbled and flicked the curtain to block it out. Two
days in and she was trapped in a mouse's wheel. Two days of
torturous training had her muscles turning on her. Two days of
being tormented by nightmares and shadows, and the Shadow
Atlas hadn't talked again since. All of this had her ready to snap
at someone. She slumped into the kitchen chair when a rap on
the door had her sit bolt upright.

She opened the door, revealing nothing but a small package
on the doorstep. Frowning, she went inside and stripped back
layers of butcher's paper to find a smooth wooden chest. Lifting
the silver latch, the shine of a new elemer caught her eye—the
training elemer her uncle had promised to get her. She ran her

fingers over the sleek black handle and the bumps of inset jewels. Bright sapphires and amethysts with clean cuts sat next to black cabochons that shone like insect eyes. She clicked one black stone and a key shot out the other end, fast as a piston. She bounced the handle in her palm, the dagger blade at one end and the key at the other balanced perfectly. But how did the mechanism work? Her uncle would probably be pissed if she took it apart.

Azalea,

I'm sorry I couldn't stay. My work will have me away for the coming month. You've got my number—message if you get into any real trouble. Please listen to Danni and Maiken and go to them if you need help. Do not leave the Tower. It isn't safe.

Do your best to master the basics and your magic will start to balance. We will deal with everything else later. Don't tell anyone about your Shadow Magic. It'll be easier for you. Trust me.

Please be good.

Fabian.

Rude. Sending a half-arsed letter was hardly protection. She scrunched up the paper and tossed it into the bin. If he couldn't be bothered coming to check up on her, then he could hardly expect her to follow his rules. She'd promised herself she would stay at the Tower. She didn't need him treating her like a child. The magic surged in her chest and caught her off-guard. Shadows streamed from her hands and slunk around the dirty dishes, engulfing the kitchen, and pinching out every inch of light in the room.

She didn't move. Fists closed at her sides. The darkness was everywhere. *Please stay asleep, Van!* Azalea thought as she tip-toed through the shadows, feeling her way to her bedroom.

Now was *not* the time to panic. The shadows coursed ahead of her and filled her bedroom. She smashed her toe on the corner of her dresser and hobbled to her bed, then scrambled across until leather met her fingers.

Come on, come on, do something useful for once! She shook the book like a crazy person. Faraday head-butted her arm, and she pulled him to her chest and squished her face into his fur. She wished her mum was there with her sage smoke and tea towel.

The stream of darkness meandered its way toward her, and shadows formed currents like the slow pull of the tide. The Shadow Atlas suddenly grew warm in her hands. She stood there, stunned, as the book began soaking up the shadows. She held it out in front as she moved back to the living room, collecting shadows on the way.

Eventually, the room cleared. She kissed the book. "Thank you, you might earn your keep yet," she told it. Perhaps it was warming up to her, that, or it just wanted to eat Shadow Magic.

CHAPTER 16

AZALEA GRIPPED HER PHONE as she swung open the door to Training Room C. It was hard to believe she was in one of the many rooms crammed beneath the Tower of London, but here she was, at her first Theory of Magic lesson with no idea what to expect.

The door crashed behind her. The echo bounced around stone walls and heads snapped in her direction. A group of over-dressed students gathered around a table that looked made for ancient Viking feasts. The guys were wearing sports coats and the girls wore tight dresses that were presumably from designers Azalea wouldn't recognize anyway. What she did know, though, was that it made her feel well underdressed in her usual dark skinny jeans and leather jacket.

She didn't breathe as each of her footsteps echoed across the flagstone floor of the long room. No one moved or said anything as she approached. She kept her eyes up but ignored them, instead taking in the massive room with a small classroom plonked down at the end. A teacher's desk and a digital white-board stood at the back wall. There were no desks, just the enormous table sitting on a rug worthy of Buckingham Palace that covered half the room.

Azalea reached the table and sat herself down at the far end of the long bench.

"Who are you?" said a blond girl with noticeably large boobs. Azalea tried to look at the girl's face, but she couldn't help thinking about how the dress was not appropriate to wear around other humans in the light of day.

"I'm Azalea Sharp. I'm in this class." She held eye contact with the girl and hoped she was in the right place.

"Oh, we didn't know anyone else was coming. How lovely," she said, not at all sounding like she thought it was lovely. She flashed a look back at the others, then turned to Azalea once more. "I'm Livia Frost, House of Owls."

Azalea shook her hand. "Nice to meet you," she said, not sure what to make of the fake niceness. The others stared at her expectantly. "Oh, um. I'm in the House of Bees," she added, hoping that was what they were waiting for.

They turned away in a hushed whisper before Livia turned back. "Lovely, we don't know any Bees. We were worried you might be an airy fairy Winged Bull, or something worse." She gave a dramatic shudder. Azalea glanced at Erik, who was perched on the far end of the table, his eyes fixed on her.

Azalea just smiled and took out her notebook and a pen and placed them by her phone. Livia sat beside her, and two other students moved across the table opposite her. Sitting up straight, she forced a smile.

"Let me introduce everyone," Livia said. She leaned back to reveal a lad with blond curly hair who was reading a book next to her. "This is my younger brother, Elam. He's some sort of genius apparently. That's why he's in this class a year earlier than he should be." Elam didn't even look up when Azalea said hi.

"Don't mind him, he fancies himself a philosopher. We don't even start uni for another three weeks," Livia rolled her eyes. "This is our cousin Millie Norwich." She nodded toward the mean-looking girl with eyebrows that were way too drawn on.

"Hey," Millie said, narrowing her eyes.

"And this is Ambrose Miller." Livia gestured toward the tall boy with red hair she'd seen with Erik in the mornings. He leaned back and crossed his arms.

"You shouldn't be here," Ambrose said with a frown. His eyes drilled into her and she could feel something pushing on her mind.

She pushed back. *Was he trying to read her mind? Was that even a thing?* She did her best to blank her thoughts, just in case, and pulled her eyes away, but it left her with a cold chill trickling down her neck.

"I don't think that's up to you," Azalea said.

"We'll see," Ambrose said. He was one to stay away from.

"Play nice," Livia said, hiding a smirk, but continued on.

"And of course, we can't forget Erik Faber, brooding so handsomely down the end there. He's a Phoenix," Livia said. The same house as Danni. Hopefully he couldn't shoot fire from his eyes because he sure as hell looked like he wanted to.

"Hi," Azalea said. Cursing how high her voice went.

Millie changed her stance and flicked her brown hair back as Erik looked their way.

"Hi," he said back with a sneer. He jumped off the table to sit at the far end of the bench. Millie straightened herself up and didn't take her eyes off Erik. But Ambrose moved faster and took the seat she clearly wanted. Millie pouted as she took the middle seat between Ambrose and Elam. Azalea was glad she was separated from Ambrose and Erik. Whatever the issue those guys had with her was, she didn't want to know about it.

"So, how did your magic manifest?" Livia asked, as if it were a normal question. The whispers from the others died down to listen. "You wouldn't believe what happened to me!" she said before Azalea could answer. Azalea swore she could feel the eye rolls cascade up the table.

"See, me and Elam were walking through Hyde Park and this man walked right past me and made a comment right to my face about my tits! Can you believe it?"

Azalea could believe it. Livia's cleavage was extremely visible to anyone who had eyes. "So, what did you do?" she asked politely.

"I called him a bloody pervert, of course! He was right shocked, though. You should have seen him. Right, Elam?"

Elam let out a sigh next to her.

"I wanted to give him a good slap, but Elam looked at me like I was mental. He *apologized* to the man, who *apparently* hadn't said anything at all! Elam dragged me off and told me I was nuts. But it turned out it was my magic manifesting. I could read minds! And it just happened to start out by reading that dirty bastard's thoughts. Turns out I should've given him that slap after all." She laughed and looked to Azalea for a reaction.

Azalea did her best impression of shocked, though it probably wasn't convincing. "So, can you all read minds?" Azalea asked, shifting uncomfortably.

"Yes, all of us from the House of Owls can. But don't worry, we won't read yours. It's very rude—we only do it to non-magic people."

Elitist much? Were magic snobs a thing? Azalea forced herself to stop thinking. Now was not a good time for them to start reading her mind.

"So, what about you? Any good stories? The others are all pretty boring, and Erik refused to tell us about his." Livia waved her hand at the others. Azalea could feel Erik's death stare from the end of the table. Swallowing hard, she pushed her brain into gear. She couldn't tell them about the spirits or shadows.

"Um, well, I woke up to the vines from a plant in my bedroom trying to strangle me," she said with a shy smile, hoping this was a legit story.

"That's brilliant!" Livia said. Millie made a scoffing sound.

The door creaked open, and Azalea was let off the hook. Dainty footsteps clacked across the stone. A woman with mousey brown hair tottered over. Azalea's eyes followed her as she reached the desk, but the others didn't look up or stop talking, and Azalea couldn't help but listen in.

"Have you seen how hot Mage Dumont is? Do you think he's single?" Millie said.

"You know he murdered a bunch of people, right?" Erik replied.

"He's too old for you either way, Mills," Livia added.

The woman cleared her throat with a weak cough. "Eh hem. Quiet please."

"He's only like 22, isn't he? Why does that matter? Elam, *Elam*," Millie whispered loudly. "You've seen him, yeah? He's fit, right?"

Elam ignored her and continued reading.

"I heard he's an Azurite Mage, so he must be older than 22. He's dangerous. You best keep away from him," Livia said in a serious tone.

"Grandmother is only keeping him around in case he becomes useful one day. Liv's right, you should all stay away from him," Elam said, looking up from his book for only a moment.

Erik leaned in from the other end of the table. "I heard she got him out of prison early and he signed some sort of life debt to the House of Owls."

"Well, I heard he's working on a secret mission. He only works alone and never talks to anyone," Livia said.

"That's not true. I've seen him talking to Mage Fletcher before," Erik said.

"Anyway, my point was," Millie began loudly, "I wonder if he's single?"

Livia laughed. Erik made a gagging sound.

"Didn't you find enough lads out clubbing last week? Mage Dumont wouldn't even look at you," Erik said. Millie picked up Azalea's book and hurled it at Erik's head. He ducked just in time.

"Why do you have to be such a wanker all the time?!" Millie said.

"Just trying to keep your expectations real, love," he said.

Azalea sighed and stepped over the bench to retrieve her book. How was she involved in this boring nonsense already?

"So, do you have a boyfriend, Azalea?" Millie asked, leaning in to block Erik from view.

Azalea shook her head and pursed her lips, then turned toward the bewildered teacher. If she even was a teacher, she wouldn't get anyone to listen the way she was going.

This fragile bird of a woman didn't look like she could lift a feather, let alone levitate one. *Was that a thing they would learn?*

"Please class, if you would listen, we can begin."

Azalea tapped Livia on the arm. She turned and blinked at Azalea, who nodded toward the front.

Livia turned and sat with her hands neatly folded on the table and stared down the teacher. The whispers died down, and the teacher cleared her throat once more.

"I am Mage Abigail Shepard. I'll be your tutor for Theory of Magic and Practical Magic for this year. I am from the House of Owls, as are most of you. We also have two students from other houses, but not to worry you two. This year we will all be learning the same things—the basics of Echo Magic. We'll be starting with elemental magic." Her voice was soft and calm.

Azalea's hopes for learning real magic felt like they were slipping away. Mage Shepard droned on about being safe with magic and how to stay fit and live healthy. And the rules: no drugs, no alcohol, no sex—it all unbalances magic somehow. All Azalea heard was, *this will be a slow and boring year, and there's no way you'll learn enough to resurrect your dead father in less than a month.*

Her grip on her pen tightened so much as the lesson went on, it was nearing snapping point. They spent most of the time writing out notes on all the stuff Maiken and Danni had already drilled into her. She rubbed her thumb over the concealed snake on her left arm. A dull pulse of energy answered back. She snapped her hand away and focused back on the board.

After the notes, they moved onto the red rug and spread out in a circle. Mage Shepard led them in a brain-numbing meditation with the instructions of deep breathing and focusing their House symbol in their minds and holding it.

Azalea had no idea how to do that. Plus, she was trying to block out Millie and Livia's embarrassing attempts to flirt with Erik and Ambrose and was busy making sure no one was reading her mind.

Every time she tried to clear her mind thoughts piled up like a poorly stacked woodpile. How was her mum doing without her? What was RoRo up to? That she should message Isaac. Did the medicine that healers take really stop them wanting to drink blood? What would she have for dinner? Her phone buzzed in her pocket, finally breaking her from her spiraling.

Azalea pressed her fists into her knees and tried to shuffle, to get feeling back in her bum from the hard ground. Her eyes peeked open. Their teacher had her eyes closed. She looked over at Millie, who was on her phone.

Screw it. Azalea slid the phone out from her pocket. She saw a message from Isaac and smiled.

Hey Zaels. Any progress on the you-know-what book? You know I'm in London now, right? You too busy for me? Me and the lads found a new local already. We're there after Sat cricket if you want to pop down for a pint.

She bit her lip. A pint with Isaac was exactly what she'd need at the end of this week. But she couldn't leave the Tower. That would be irresponsible, and she was being an adult now. Plus, she was so short on time for her dad. The pub and Isaac could always wait. She glanced around. Erik had his eyes shut, but she was sure he had been watching her.

Sorry, Isaac. Rain check on the pint for now. I need to sort out this stuff with my dad first you know . . .

A heavy weight settled in her gut. As much as she wanted to see Isaac, she also didn't want to drag him into her crazy new world and get him or herself in trouble. Avoiding him was the best strategy for now.

She slid her phone back into her pocket and glanced at Erik. He was looking at her and shaking his head slowly. What was with this guy? Surely, she'd proven she wouldn't say anything about his stupid near-death experience. Her phone buzzed again.

Isaac: *No worries. Let me know if you need help or a useless sidekick or whatever. Miss you.*

She messaged him back with the riddles from the Shadow Atlas. He was studying literature, so maybe he could work them out. Smiling at her excellent delegation skills, she closed her eyes.

She tried to block out Erik and focused her mind, imagining a bee floating in the vacuum of space. Time dragged by. Instead of the bee, a glowing silvery serpent appeared. She willed it to change to a bee, but it didn't want to. It felt right. Its body sparkled with luminescent stars and purple light as it slithered in the fluid pattern of an infinity sign.

Her arm grew prickly and warm, her hand shot to cover it and her eyes flashed open. She didn't dare roll up the sleeve on her shirt, but she felt the magic in the tattoo moving. Was it meant to do that? She closed her eyes again, trying to force a bee image into her mind. But every time she tried, it changed to the snake.

Time to stop trying. Now was not the moment for shadows to pop out and wreck her first class. She kept opening her eyes to check her hands. So far, so good. Around her, the others shuffled, and she heard the faint beep of messages coming through.

Livia was whispering to Elam, who was ignoring her. He seemed to be an expert at that.

"Well done, everyone," Mage Shepard said, as if she believed it.

"I hope you all imagined your House symbol and successfully held onto it. This is the first step in forming a spell cloud."

Azalea fixed her full attention to Mage Shepard. The others shut up as well.

"Does anyone know what a spell cloud is and how it works?"

Elam's hand shot up and he spoke before he was prompted to. "It's an image you form in your mind to bring together magic. Your think up the spell and then add in power symbols that represent your intentions and then send it out."

Mage Shepard opened her mouth, but Elam kept going.

"You use an elemer to cut into the Echo dimension, then pull through the power to fuel the spell and then just do it. Easy."

"Yes. Very good Elam. Thank you. But it isn't *easy*," Mage Shepard said, looking a little flustered. "A spell cloud is the basis of performing spells. At the heart of the cloud, you will always have your House symbol. This is the root of the spell and is the point you build from. You must keep this strong in your mind and draw power into it. Think about the spell you want to perform with crystal clear intention. Can anyone tell me what power symbols are?"

Elam didn't even bother to put his hand up. "Power symbols are parts added in to make up the spell. Things like water, fire, movement, light, growth, strength—anything you want to add into a spell. You just need to learn the symbol for it and visualize it."

Livia rolled her eyes, but Azalea was hanging onto his every word.

"Thank you, Elam," Mage Shepard said, not adding anything further as she pulled a bag from behind her. "Now, how about I show you some examples?"

Mage Shepard pulled out a fluffy toy owl and a bag of what looked like mahjong tiles. She reached her white elemer in the air and clicked out the key from the other end. With a snap of her wrist, her elemer cut into the air, exposing a tiny flicker of light. The toy owl was suddenly floating in the middle of the circle.

"Let's pretend this toy owl is the center of the spell cloud in your mind."

Azalea's breath hitched. She was seeing real magic!

"Each of these tiles has a different symbol of power on it. But let's start with the basics." She added two tiles to orbit around the owl like an atom. Bubbles appeared from nowhere.

"The symbols of power are ancient. Each has a name and a meaning, but few know them all and they can be interpreted in many ways."

The bubbles began rising and spinning above their heads, gaining speed. Mage Shepard's face was confident and determined, nothing like the woman who first walked in.

"The two symbols I've added to my spell cloud are air and water. As you can see, I've chosen to make bubbles. But I could just as easily make a spell to help me breathe underwater, or to dry my hair. I could have made a rain cloud."

The bubbles zoomed upward and smashed together overhead to form a mini rain cloud.

"What makes a spell work is your intention. You form the spell cloud in your mind and add power symbols to give yourself a basic set of instructions. You then make a cut into the Echo Dimension."

She held her elemer to the air once more and cut it to make a tiny light glow at the end of her knife blade. She turned the blade, and the key connected with the cut in the air.

"You draw the power from the Echo Dimension with the key end like so."

A new level of energy filled the air with an underlying hum that vibrated through Azalea's bones. A pulse of energy shot from Mage Shepard's elemer, straight into the mini cloud.

A rush of air blasted across the room. The cloud shattered, and droplets hung like tiny lanterns above them. They danced across the high ceiling, moving faster and faster until they were hurtling around before being sucked into the tight funnel of a tornado in the center of the room.

Azalea held her breath. She felt a push on her mind and straightened. She forced up mental shields like RoRo had taught her when she was a child. She'd always thought it was a game, but she knew better now. The vortex of water rushed in front of her as someone tried to force their way into her mind. She pushed back and hid all her thoughts behind a solid vault. She didn't dare look around, but she was sure it was Ambrose.

The tornado lowered into the circle as the students inched back. Azalea's head was pulsing with tension. The tornado exploded and rainbow light shot in every direction as if they were inside a colorful lamp. The force pulled away, and Azalea held out a hand to catch the rainbow mist as it descended around them. *So pretty!*

There was a sudden flash of heat, and the air was thick with steam. The cloud, tornado, and rainbow light had vanished. Millie let out a squeak and Azalea jumped.

Mage Shepard sat calmly with her hands and elemer in her lap.

"The possibilities with magic are endless," she spoke softly, and this time everyone listened. "We are only limited by the amount of magic we can channel and the strength of our minds."

"When can we do proper magic?" Millie asked, breaking the silent wonder of the room.

"Soon enough. To start, we will practice basic elemental magic without cutting into the Echo Dimension. We will just use low level ambient magic that is always present."

Millie groaned. Azalea would have groaned too if she were Millie. She didn't exactly look like she was keen to do magic or could pass a fitness test. A tug pulled at her mind again. What did this prick want?

"If you make a large cut with the elemer into a dimension, can you go through, like a Hollow?" Azalea asked, her vault holding strong.

Ambrose scoffed, and Millie giggled. Azalea didn't care. She wanted to know.

"No, it isn't possible as it is with a Hollow. Only a tiny cut can be made from this dimension to the Shadow or Echo Dimensions, just enough to draw magic through. Anything larger will close instantly. It's the same as if someone tried to open a Hollow on Tower grounds with the wards. It just isn't possible, and only someone with Shadow Magic can access the Hollow," Mage Shepard explained with a smile.

"Thank you," Azalea said, ignoring her classmates' stares. Her head was pounding.

"We won't be starting anything until Friday. I expect you to all begin memorizing the symbols of power. Start with the first twenty elemental symbols—we'll need the basic ones this Friday—and practice your meditation as well. Off with you all now," she said, shooing them off.

Azalea was glad to get out of there.

CHAPTER 17

S EVERAL DAYS WHIZZED BY. Azalea woke sweating and surrounded by shadows every morning. But each day, she was more determined to find answers to help bring her dad back. The Shadow Atlas cooperated occasionally, but only when it felt like it, and only when she fed it well. It was in a particularly good mood one morning after clearing her room of shadows that she got a new bit of riddle:

Summon from the shadow lands.

A power strong and true.

Call to one who once knew love.

And he will follow through.

It wasn't exactly revolutionary, but she added it to her list of clues.

It was Saturday, and instead of the preparation reading for uni she had planned on doing, Azalea sat in an alcove in the library in a green armchair with a book titled *The Power of Power Symbols.* She was well hidden from Millie and Livia who were on the other side of the room, whispering away.

Using the little side table, she practiced drawing out all twenty basic elemental symbols and their unfamiliar shapes onto flashcards she'd ordered online that week for her uni work, but this seemed a more pressing need.

The basic symbols, plus the thousands of others in the book, seemed to be a mash-up of everyone's favorite symbols across the world. There were hundreds for fire alone. Some looked like Norse runes, some were Celtic knots and spirals, others were Sumerian cuneiforms, and others were ancient Greek and Chinese symbols. It would take a lifetime to learn them all, but at least if she learned the basics, and some extras that looked like they worked with Shadow Magic, she'd have a better shot at helping her dad. Her thoughts flicked to Isaac as she continued drawing onto her cards. Hopefully he was having a bit of luck with the riddles she'd sent him.

In the afternoon, Azalea winced as the aftereffects of past days' training protested in every muscle. But she would pass that fitness test if it killed her. Today she added a run and a round on the obstacle course to her training. Her hands were blistered from the monkey bars, but she needed her upper body strength to improve. More pushups was the answer. She could add them in between job hunting online and putting together watches for a new order tonight. At least being busy stopped her thinking about things and the countdown to the equinox. Just seventeen days to go. *Dammit*, now she was thinking about it again.

))))●(((

Azalea darted through the rain to the tunnel and was ten minutes early to class Tuesday evening. Her training elemer sat ready in front of her. Elam was already there, and they aimlessly chatted about the power symbols they had learned that week. Mr. Braniac was a few hundred ahead of her.

The others filtered in, and Mage Shepard wasted no time getting started.

"We will train in pairs today for safety reasons. Take turns and watch your partner."

She placed Ambrose with Elam, and Livia with Millie. It was just Azalea's luck to be placed with Erik—but at least it wasn't Ambrose.

They moved to the red patterned carpet and sat opposite each other and focused on the water bowl between them.

"Now the task is simple. You have a bowl with one water droplet between you. Form a spell cloud in your mind and pull in whatever power symbols you feel you need," Mage Shepard explained.

Azalea shuffled in her seat and wished she had brought a cushion like Livia.

"Now use the key end of your elemer to draw on the low-level magic around you. You summon it into yourself and send the power out of the elemer to the water droplet."

She could feel Erik's eyes on her. Judging, or cursing, or whatever evil thing he was doing. He was from the House of Phoenix, so at least *he* couldn't be reading her mind. Well, she hoped he couldn't.

"You will pass the water drop to your partner and place it gently on the palm of their hand. Then practice guiding it between you using your elemer."

It was way harder than it looked! Nervousness and excitement fizzed up her brain, making it much harder to quieten things down and keep her mental shields up. Beating Erik was the goal here. Ignoring him for the time being though, she focused on the bee in her mind. The power symbols she wanted were clear. She'd spent the last two days doodling them in every white space in her notebooks.

Erik leaned in toward the water. It vibrated in the bowl, but didn't budge. *Not such a hot shot now.* She closed her eyes and had the image of the bee clear when her thoughts shattered.

"You don't belong here, you know," Erik said under his breath.

Her eyes shot open. "I don't see you moving the water any more than I am."

"That's because I've got fire magic. It doesn't go well with water. If you were from the House of Bees, you'd do that in a second. You're a fraud."

"I am not. I'm just brand new at this and practicing responsibly. Unlike some people." She bit back her anger. She would remain civilized and not stoop to his level.

"You have no idea what you're talking about," he said.

"You're lucky Maiken saved you. You'd be dead if it wasn't for her," she whispered. "I'd be a bit more grateful if I were you."

"I'd be a bit more careful if I were you. Ambrose has something on you, and someone wants you out of here."

"Who?" Azalea asked. She was sure it was all talk, trying to throw her off her game . . .

He just shrugged and went silent, and Azalea tried not to let his comment rattle her. She didn't want to get wound up by him. Next time Ambrose tried something, she would tell Mage Shepard.

The water droplet started moving, but it wasn't her doing. *Oh hell no.* There was no way he would win this. She forced everything into one intention; move that bloody water drop.

The snake appeared in her mind before she could tell it to leave. She knew what she wanted. Dark symbols appeared around her spell cloud. Their meanings were clear, though they weren't the ones she'd drawn.

Without hesitation, she pointed her elemer at the water drop and it rose in the air. Just a little push with her mind and it shot straight toward Erik, laced with her pent-up rage. He let out a screech and doubled over as if he'd been shot.

Growling, he sat up with a hand over one eye. "What the hell was that?" he yelled.

Mage Shepard was next to him.

"She did that on purpose," Erik said.

"Let me look," Mage Shepard said in a soothing voice.

Azalea cocked her head and studied his face. He wasn't faking it.

Wincing, he took his hand away. His eye was streaming and the white part was all bloodshot.

"I didn't mean to," Azalea said, shocked at her own power, but also a little thrilled by it.

"It's nothing to worry about, dear. A little too much enthusiasm, perhaps? I'll get Erik checked out with a healer. That's enough for tonight. Off with you all, we can practice again next week."

Everyone left and Azalea walked back through the caf. Controlling that water was amazing! It was so easy, so right. Yet it hadn't come from the bee. The shadows stirred beneath her palms. She clenched a fist. She'd have to be careful in the future.

Though the reality was, the Shadow Magic was what she needed to help her dad. If she had to break a few rules to do that then so be it.

)))●(((

By Friday night Azalea's head was hazy from Echo Magic drills and she wasn't any better at it, even after two weeks of classes. The pressure was building. Too many new things; pressures of needing money for rent and food and watch parts. Plus, her judgey classmates, Van's over-enthusiasm about everything. She was a gasket waiting to burst.

There was no time for crying in the corner now, though. She had a quick ham sandwich for dinner and flicked through a book she'd found hidden in a back section of the library: *A Concise Guide to the Hollow*. She hoped it would have insight on how spirits traveled between worlds. She slammed it shut on the first page. Apparently, elemers were frequently made with the bones of one's dead relatives. What-the-fuck.

She remembered Fabian's strange smile when he said the first one he gave her had belonged to her granddad. Discomfort crawled up the back of her spine. *Disgusting*. She read yesterday that blood could strengthen magic. She already knew that from her book and its vampire tendencies, but using body parts was taking it too far.

The box with her father's elemer sat on her bedside table. *Yuck*. But she'd need that power to bring back her dad. She'd take every bit of help she could get. She glanced at her pocket watch on the desk, a reminder of time running out. Just two more weeks. Or . . . two more weeks till she saw her dad if she chose to be optimistic. Unfortunately, she wasn't one of those glass half full people, and now she was late for class.

Azalea was the last to arrive. Shuffling onto the hard bench, she avoided making eye contact with Erik across the table. Mage Shepard explained they were making nice, safe bubbles tonight.

All Azalea's focus was on forming a nice green spell cloud with a bee in the center. It took most of the class just to get a vague form. It was fuzzy, but there. She pulled forward power symbols relating to water, movement, and air, then added them to the hazy bee and held her breath.

Holding the spell firmly, she pushed a perfect bubble through the air and floated it across to Erik. She was doing it!

Erik was supposed to be ready to catch it on his hand. Instead, he shuffled back. Her lips pursed together. Just a little further. She strained her mind to its limits. Erik moved his chair back again and smirked.

Dick move. Rage blistered under Azalea's skin. *Enough.* She pushed forward one more time. But instead of catching the bubble, Erik popped it with his pen.

She slammed her fist into the table.

"Why are you such a twat all the time!" she exploded.

"Because you don't belong here," he said without missing a beat. He leaned back in his chair and glanced at Ambrose, who nodded.

"Screw this." She knew she was overreacting about a bubble, but she was well past caring. These past two weeks had been too much. She grabbed her stuff and stormed out of the room.

Tears blurred her vision as she ran through the tunnel toward her flat. What the hell was she doing here? She had managed to make a bubble, her first time using Echo Magic, which was a small victory, but her heart sank, knowing it wasn't enough. Her Echo Magic was weak, and she had zero control over Shadow Magic when she wanted it. It just rolled in like a storm whenever it wanted.

She had just two weeks left to raise someone from the dead! What the fuck?! Why the hell did she agree to this and think she could do it? She stopped and leaned against the tunnel wall and rubbed her temples.

No, she told herself. *You're better than this. Quit this whinging and get on with it.*

Two minutes of calming breaths and staring at the blank wall later, she found herself at a mental crossroads. Either go home and eat a shit load of chocolate digestives while watching Studio Ghibli movies, or get her arse to the library and scavenge up some bloody answers.

She spun around on her heel. Answers it was. It was only 9pm, and the library was open till midnight.

CHAPTER 18

A ZALEA WALKED BACK THROUGH the caf. The only people in there were three Yeoman warders getting on the piss at the bar, and Millie and Livia who had only just entered and sat down at a picnic table—eyes glued to their phones. They ignored Azalea as she walked past and she ignored them right back, thankful they didn't call her out on her outburst.

The smell of books welcomed Azalea into the library. She could see that Elam was arranging himself in her usual alcove. Great, now she needed a new spot. He gave a small wave with a twitchy smile as she hurried past.

She headed for the section right at the back in the corner, the place where the dark magic books were tucked away on shelves as if someone wanted them out of sight.

She rounded the corner, not expecting anyone to be there. "Yeep!" Heat filled her face. Yes, she had just made that embarrassing sound out loud. "Sorry, I didn't expect anyone to be in here," she said.

"Obviously," the man said, raising an eyebrow.

Wait, she recognized that eyebrow with the tiny sickle scar. *Torin. The Shadow Mage.*

He looked back down at his book as Azalea's heart raced and her mind blanked. He knew Shadow Magic. She didn't need a book if he could help her.

Play it cool Azalea, she told herself. "So . . . Maiken told me you're a Shadow Mage. That's um . . . interesting." She tried to lean casually on the shelf, but a book caught on her sleeve and hurtled toward the floor. Trying to catch it like a ninja, she lurched forward but hit her elbow on the end table, toppling it sideways. She let out a squeak. Before she knew it, she was being hauled out of the way by Torin's firm grip. A whiff of star jasmine drifted over her, sweet and strong, the smell of home in summer after dark. She blinked, looked up, and he was standing there holding a lamp.

"Whoopsie daisy," she said. Good one Azalea. Way to act normal. No way he was going to help you now.

"No harm done," he said, setting the table and lamp right again. He had a long gray coat on, same as the first time she saw him, very fancy. It looked good on him. "And yes, I'm a Shadow Mage. Most people around here do not find that interesting. Quite the opposite."

"Well, I'm new here. I'm trying to catch up on the whole history of magic thing." She picked up the book from the ground and placed it back in its shelf. *Now stay,* she told it—in her head of course.

"You'd be wise to stay away from this section and from Shadow Magic. It won't make you any friends."

"Are you just trying to get me to leave this section because you were here first?"

"No, I mean it. Stay away from Shadow Magic."

Okay, so it was clear he meant it. "I'll keep that in mind, but just out of interest, for academic purposes, of course. Do you know where I can find any decent books on practical Shadow Magic?"

He paused for a second and frowned.

Yes, it was the opposite of what you just said, Mister.

"No. You won't find anything like that here, it's all rubbish," he said, picking another book off the shelf.

"Oh, okay, well, what are you looking for?"

He let out an audible breath and started skimming through the pages. "If you must know, I'm looking for folklore. Part of my research. Now, if you don't mind leaving me alone. Please mind the lamps on your way out."

"Well, actually, I have my own research to do. I have a project to do about the House of Snakes and on necromancy in particular. So, I'll be browsing here until I find something useful." She was banking on the fact that he didn't know the Initiates' study curriculum. His expression changed when she mentioned necromancy, just for a microsecond, but it was enough to know he knew something.

"Necromancy is illegal. I suggest another research topic if you want to pass your class."

"Do you know much about it? Anything that I might be able to use in my project?"

"Yes. That it's dangerous and more people died attempting it than were ever brought back. Not a very practical form of magic if you ask me. High risk, low rewards." He slammed his book shut. "Now if you'll excuse me, I've rather lost my appetite for researching tonight. Goodnight." He gave a gentlemanly bob of his head.

"Wait," Azalea said as he brushed past her, "Just one more thing."

He stopped and half turned around.

"Do you need special tools for a necromancy spell? Hypothetically, of course."

"Hypothetically, no. Just the usual elements in a salt circle." He paused for a second and gave her a suspicious look but continued. "An elemer, of course, and blood. It has to be done with blood magic. And usually, some sort of binder to the earth—a gemstone of some sort. But strong Shadow Magic is the key. Also, the right time and place. A good celestial alignment, a thin veil, and a full moon always helps." He stopped as if he caught himself. "Of course, it's difficult to line all these things up and get the spell right as well. Hence all the failures. I suggest you stick to the theory side."

"Thank you so much," Azalea said, practically leaping with joy inside. So worth bumping into him and looking like an idiot.

"Maybe don't tell anyone I told you this," he said and just as quickly twisted around, stopped to readjust the lamp, and marched off.

He was a strange fellow. Nice to look at though, and perhaps useful again in the future. She raced to the nearest desk and wrote down everything he said. With a list of things to look up, she wasn't going to take his word for it on all the books being rubbish. She was bound to find something. Though his comments on mortality statistics from necromancy seemed rather concerning. Still, she wouldn't be deterred that easily. The risk of bringing her dad back would be well worth it.

CHAPTER 19

AZALEA GRIPPED THE TRAINING elemer tightly as she watched Mage Shepard pour a salt ring around the training area. Silence fell across the group. The two House of Phoenix guards stationed outside didn't ease her nerves. Everyone in the class had passed their fitness tests, Millie only just. Two weeks of hard training had been worth it for this moment. Finally, to feel that raw power. Her fingers tingled with excitement, but she was also terrified.

Colorful cushions dotted their way around the large red rug, each with a pure white candle in front of them.

"Now, you all have your training elemers?" Mage Shepard scanned the group as they positioned themselves. "These differ from a mage's elemer, as they have dampening properties of quartz sand filling. This restricts the amount of magic that can be pulled in and let out. But don't be tricked into feeling safe. It's still enough to do damage to yourself and others, so always keep your intentions clear at the front of your mind and don't lose focus."

Azalea nibbled her lip. Mage Shepard cleared her throat, looking reluctant to continue.

"Now the process is simple. The elemer has two ends: a blade and a key. You can click them inside the handle with the push of a button. Please practice this now."

Not-so-subtle groans echoed around the group. They had all done this a thousand times already. They clicked away impatiently until Mage Shepard was satisfied. Something started chipping away at Azalea's mind, then a voice sounded in her head: *The House of Ravens knows what you are. A Snake amongst the Owls.*

Cold fear washed over her. *Ambrose.* She tried to put up her mental shields and pretend she hadn't heard anything. But her mind felt like it was crumbling. How did he know that?

I may be an Owl, but Ravens pay well for loyalty. No need to worry your pretty head, though. A nobody snake girl is hardly a matter for them to waste time on. But I'm watching you. Remember that.

Her eyes met his. A sneer spread across his face and Azalea's heart plummeted to her feet. Pushing her mental barriers up like a castle fortress, she forced him out of her mind in panic, trying not to get up and run screaming from the room as she did so.

Her eyes blurred as she stared into the red carpet. A fight-or-flight debate raged in her head. The Ravens knew she was here. *Bad.* But they weren't doing anything—maybe just watching her or waiting for the right time to act. So maybe they didn't know who her father was? *Maybe good?* Perhaps she was just a lowly Snake who slipped through the cracks . . . hopefully that was the case. Either way, Ambrose was dangerous, and it was time to tell Mage Shepard. But after class, and very carefully.

Azalea straightened her shoulders and smiled toward Mage Shepard as if she hadn't a care in the world. She wouldn't let Ambrose know he got to her.

"Now I will demonstrate how to cut into the Echo Dimension." The room grew silent as the clicking of elemers stilled. Mage Shepard held the dagger blade out at eye level. Tension rippled in the air as the knife made a hazy slice—like a wavy mirage, with a line of light at the center.

"Now you see, I've made a small cut here," she said as if it were a cooking show. "It uses a great deal of energy to cut into a dimension so it's only possible to make tiny cuts. Just enough to draw out a touch of magic. You make the cut, then flip the blade around so the key end connects with the opening. You then draw the energy through the key and convert it into a spell using the spell cloud you already have formed in your mind. Is that clear?"

Azalea's eyes fixed on the tiny cut in the air held in place by the knife. She could feel the energy charging out from it. It was nothing like the weak magical energy that was all around them. It felt like the force of lightning compared to a static shock.

Everyone nodded enthusiastically.

"I will make the cut for you, and you can pull the magic through yourselves."

Azalea sat up straighter.

Mage Shepard went around the group one at a time so they could try to siphon magic under her close supervision. Everyone else was told to practice lighting candles in the meantime so they could compare the difference between the weak background magic and the direct Echo Magic.

She studied her classmates' faces as each person felt the power. Her heart sped up as their eyes grew wide and hungry as Echo Magic surged through them when it was their turn. Their candle flames roared into life, blasting toward the ceiling.

Azalea swallowed. It was her turn. She focused on the candle.

Mage Shepard made a tiny cut in the air and Azalea raised her hand and carefully aligned the key of her elemer with the cut and aimed the blade at the candle.

She focused on a simple spell cloud to light the candle. The key pulled the magic into her hand and as it touched her, it awoke every cell in her body with fireworks. It sang through her blood and lit up light like a power grid through her muscles, seeping into every inch of her skin.

Her eyes closed as the trickle of power gave her new life.

Azalea's future was set in stone that second. She would be a mage and nothing else mattered. As the power of life and death flowed through her, she felt the great oceans currents from afar and the churning earth deep beneath their feet. She felt the very ripples of air as if it were alive around her, and the singing of trees and plants outside. It was intoxicating.

Then it was gone.

She blinked back to the room. Holy shit. Had the others felt that when they did it?

They looked at each other, breathless, speechless, with the same giddy, power-drunk looks on their faces.

She could tell who had followed the rules—if this was truly their first time feeling raw magic. Erik and Ambrose both sat there smugly. It was obvious they had both drawn magic from the Echo Dimension before today, and they weren't doing anything to hide the fact.

Azalea shot Erik a look that wiped the smugness right off his face. He had no right to sit there looking like that when his premature attempt at magic had screwed up so spectacularly. The image of his damaged body in the hospital was still sharply burned into her mind and he would certainly still be feeling the vampire-ish after-effects.

"That was a taste of true Magic," Mage Shepard said. "A gift that must be respected."

"From this point on, if I find *anyone* abusing Magic, there will be consequences. I have been lenient up until now, but there is real danger from here. You will act as adults and in return, you will be treated as adults. Clear?" she said sharply, a very different side of the easy-going teacher they'd seen so far. They all nodded. Mage Shepard's eyes lingered a little longer on Erik and Ambrose.

Everyone got up to leave, but Azalea lingered behind, slowly collecting her things.

"Mage Shepard?" Azalea asked as the others left the room.

"Yes, Azalea? How are you fitting in here? All right, I hope?"

"Yes. It's fine. Well, no. I have a problem with Ambrose." She paused. "I think he was trying to read my mind. He's been doing it since I got here. I don't think he likes me much," she said with a weak smile, feeling silly for tattling to the teacher. But he'd given her a real reason to be scared now.

"That's quite an accusation, Azalea."

"I know. But I'm sure of it." Though she couldn't exactly explain what he had said.

"You're new to all this. I'm sure you just need a good sleep. Magic can be draining, but can also make one paranoid," she said as if she were speaking to a child. "Especially surrounded by all this new information. You're down the rabbit hole and don't know quite what's possible anymore," she said sweetly.

Azalea wrung her hands around her bag's strap. Was this woman for real? Was she actually saying this bullshit and believing it? Azalea might be new, but she wasn't imagining anything.

"If he was reading my mind, what would happen to him?" Azalea said through gritted teeth.

"Well, I'm sure he wouldn't be. He grew up here. He knows the etiquette as well as any mage would. It is forbidden to read minds without express permission from the person, he would be expelled from the program if he did so."

Just lovely. Now she needed proof. No way Mage Oblivious over there would listen to her when she'd known Azalea's classmates since they were young. She probably couldn't stand up to them, anyway. Worth a try, but Mage Shepard was clearly not the solution.

"Well, I'm sure I was wrong then," Azalea said with a plastered on fake smile.

"Not to worry. You'll catch up to the others soon. Go get some sleep."

Azalea spun around on her heels and marched out of the room with hands clasped in front of her so she didn't throw any candelabras back at her teacher.

))).(((

Both the practical and theory lessons were more interesting after that, though Azalea's respect for Mage Shepard had dropped and her paranoia had skyrocketed. She hadn't been able to get hold of her uncle on the matter of mind reading and threats. She didn't want to tell her mum about it. She'd just worry and ask her to come home. RoRo had practical advice and gave her some good tips on meditation techniques to block mind reading. For now, that would have to do.

The Theory lesson the next day was on everything that could go wrong with magic. A plan to scare them, Azalea suspected. But Elam was the only one who seemed concerned, though it could be that he wanted to explain things to the class and show off his genius brain. In the next practical lesson, they made their own cuts into the Echo Dimension. A lot easier said than done.

Every time Azalea tried, she ended up cutting into a Hollow or the Shadow Dimension. She worked this out quickly. They each had a distinctive smell and feel about them. She couldn't even find the Echo Dimension to cut into. It wasn't exactly a problem she could bring up in class, but least Ambrose wasn't there today.

Sweat prickled Azalea's forehead as she focused intently on her elemer blade. Not just from the effort of finding the right place to cut, but the fear of slipping up and ripping into the Shadow Dimension in front of everyone. Her snake tattoo warmed, and she pulled at her sleeve and sat up straight to focus. Last time she looked at it in the shower she swore it had grown, its tail now rested in the crook of her elbow. Her leather jacket was now a constant companion to hide her arm.

Her blade snagged once more on the Hollow. It was easy to recognize, and felt like cutting something right next to her, like fine silk. She pulled away the blade but got a whiff of snow and deep winter she knew from her trip with Fabian.

Azalea tried once more. She focused her elemer in front of her and made the tiniest prick into the air. It was the Shadow Dimension this time. It felt more distant than the Hollow, almost like cutting into a mushroom, and rather satisfying. A sliver of faint purplish-blue light radiated from the tiny cut, and she breathed in the smell of storms and electrical energy that called to her.

Azalea quickly let go. It sealed itself instantly, thank the gods. She glanced around, heart pounding, her chest brimming with pent up fire, wanting a way out. She squeezed her hands into fists and calmed her breath.

No one seemed to have noticed. *Close one.* At least she knew what not to cut into now. But she had to find the bloody Echo Dimension.

She poked around in the air, trying to feel for something different. She blocked out the sounds of success from her classmates around her.

It was like stabbing around in a dark room, trying to pin down a flapping flag. She whittled the blade into the air in front of her, feeling silly. It kept catching on the other dimensions, wanting to cut through. But she didn't let it. Instead, she searched further into the space for a distinct feeling.

Her arm was heavy. Elam and Livia were making tiny cuts of thin green and yellow light, barely noticeable unless you were looking. But they were doing it.

Finally, her blade snagged on something. She froze and held the elemer in place. It was like thick leather that didn't want to budge. She forced the knife in further and pushed her shoulder into it. A thin prick of green light appeared. But then it was gone.

She had done it!

For the next half hour, she focused on finding the leathery Echo Dimension. She discovered the best way to make a cut was to do one hard push and imagine pinning it, then work on the cutting part. She got a slice of green light a few times, but it didn't want to yield to her.

One thing was evident: she would need a heck of a lot of practice. At least she had a starting point now, but the days were ticking down. She needed to be able to do Echo and Shadow Dimension cuts without thinking. Then all she had to do was master Shadow Magic in a matter of weeks and get the Shadow Atlas to tell her what to do. What could go wrong?

She got back to the flat after class and joined Van for a strange red smoothie that turned out to be beetroot, not blood. Van flitted off to work and Azalea slumped into the cushion mountain on the sofa. She checked her phone to find a train of enthusiastic messages from Isaac. Still hungry after the smoothie, she threw a frozen dinner in the microwave, then called Isaac.

"I worked it out!" Isaac yelled.

"Wonderful! What is it?"

"The riddle. Well, an idea. Didn't you read my messages?"

"No. I just got in. That's why I called you."

"So, the second riddle, *'A snake, a bee, you found the key. But time is running out. A church in which the trees are free. Is where you'll face your doubt.'* I have some ideas about where it could be. You said it had to be somewhere with energy, so a church does seem right. Temples and churches are powerful sites in most religions, so could work with your equinox power theory. I looked for churches with tree affiliations: giving away trees, donating trees, or supporting tree planting, etcetera."

"Okay . . ."

"Right, but I didn't find anything too convincing. Then I started looking up abandoned churches where nature was taking over. Where trees are free. I found one right near you, Zaels. It can't be a coincidence! Nature and a church would have great energy, I'd imagine."

Forgetting all about her food, she darted into her bedroom and grabbed the Shadow Atlas and flipped it open. "You're brilliant Isaac! Where is it? Let's see if the book will help now."

"It's St. Dunstan in the East. Just up the road from you."

Azalea flicked to speaker phone. He could be onto something this time. She pricked her finger with the needle she'd started keeping by her bed and bit her lip as a drop of blood splashed onto the page. She put the pocket watch on the book—still with no idea how it helped—and wrote *St. Dunstan in the East autumn equinox.*

"What's it doing?" Isaac said impatiently.

"Shut it, it's doing something, hang on a tic. It's a map of London. It's coming clear now," Azalea said, but as soon as she did, it started fading. "No, no, no!" she yelled at it.

"What?"

"It disappeared."

"Did you give it some blood and put the watch there?"

"Yes. Now it's saying *feed me.*" She let out a disgruntled sigh.

"Give it some magic. You said you'd been practicing, right? Just make some shadows pop up or something."

The snake on her arm grew warm at the thought. She wasn't meant to make cuts into dimensions unsupervised, but she also wasn't meant to attempt necromancy. She shut her bedroom door and got out her elemer.

"Are you still there, Zaels?" Isaac asked.

"Yup. Just getting in the zone," she said, sitting cross-legged on the bed as she raised the dagger blade.

She cut into the Shadow Dimension and twisted the elemer to the key.

Shadow Magic flowed into her, along with the smell of storms before the rain, thick with humidity and electrical energy. She pulled the tiniest amount of Shadow Magic to her and closed her eyes.

Every cell lit up with glorious darkness, laced with purple fire. It felt like coming home. She pulled a little more. The flames of purple fire wrapped around her limbs, her heart, and her mind. It wasn't scary anymore, as long as she embraced the shadows.

Pain shot through her leg like tiny stabbing needles. She drew a sharp breath, opened her eyes, and released the magic. Her room had become a vortex of black, swirling shadows. They swallowed every inch of light, but somehow Azalea could still see. She sucked in a breath. This was so much more than the usual wisps.

She looked down at Faraday and frowned at him.

"Zaels! Azalea, are you there?" Isaac's panicked voice screamed from the phone.

"I'm still here," she said calmly, though her heart was racing.

"Jesus, don't do that to me! I thought a Shadow Demon killed you or something. I was about to come over there."

"Faraday scratched me . . . also, I don't think Shadow Demons are a thing," she said. Perhaps he had been doing a little too much esoteric research. She glanced at the pocket watch on the book. Several minutes had passed without her knowing. Deep gouges in her leg seeped with blood. She winced, but . . . *waste not, want not.* She scooped some of the blood off her leg with the side of the elemer blade and wiped it onto the book. Yuck! Blood was still disgusting, no matter how useful it was.

"You sure you're okay?" Isaac said.

"Yup, quite alright," she said, perhaps a little too enthusiastically. She felt anything but alright. Her hands were shaking, and there was a real risk she might vomit all over her bed. She let out a breath and focused back on the book. The moment she touched it, the book began soaking in the surrounding shadows.

"Oooo, it's eating the shadows!" Azalea exclaimed.

"Yes!" Isaac said. She imagined him punching the air dramatically as he often did in triumphant moments.

Her room was cozy, filled with shadows. She could see everything in a comforting black and white, like an old movie. But the book needed them more than she needed room ambiance. Taking off her leather jacket, Azalea jumped up and started wafting the shadows toward the book as if it would help. It didn't but jumping around made her feel more useful.

Faraday gave her a judgmental look, curled up on the bed and went back to sleep. Azalea's arm tingled. The stars on the tattoo snake's belly sparkled. It looked happy, well, as happy as you can imagine a snake looking.

"What's it doing now?" Isaac asked.

Azalea tumbled onto the bed to the book.

"The map is changing. It's got extra grids on it . . . now some weird symbols on the side. Power symbols, I think! Parts of it are pulsing with light now. I think I know what it means. It's like it's on the tip of my brain!"

"Look for St Dunstan in the East. Is there anything around it?"

Studying the map, the shadows in the room seemed to pour into it, powering its new colors and symbols. "There're power symbols and runes, now there's dates appearing on the sides. I think it's working! Yes, there's something at St. Dunstans. It's all blue! Do you think that's the energy there?"

"Maybe. Take some photos and send them to me."

Azalea scrambled for her phone with excited fingers and managed to get the camera up and get a few snaps as the book faded back to blank. "No! It's going already. And I fed you so much, you ungrateful door stop." She glared at the book.

"This is good. We're getting somewhere now," Isaac said. "I've got to go, but let's talk tomorrow after we've had a think about it. You've still got eight days. We can work this out." He would never back down from a puzzle or a mystery. She knew if anyone would help her figure this out, it was him.

They said goodnight, and Azalea lay across the foot of her bed, knowing she should put a plaster on her leg and go eat her frozen dinner. She couldn't get the shadows out of her mind. It was the first time she felt real control. Well, not *control*. But for the first time, she wanted to keep going. But she had broken Mage Shepard's first rule—always have an intention. She'd just called through shadows at random with no spell cloud and no real intention. It was probably a good thing Faraday snapped her out of it. She couldn't wait to try it again.

CHAPTER 20

A ZALEA STRAINED HER SENSES as she poked around in the air. She wanted to find the Echo Dimension on the first go for once. She needed to have that control in six days if she had any chance. Just six days left until the equinox.

It was Wednesday night, and the third night in a row she had spent sitting up till 1 am practicing dimensional cuts. A hot chocolate sat next to her bed, and her room was in shambles. Her dirty laundry had maxed out her chairs and it now cascaded into pools on the floor.

She blacked it all out and focused on finding the Echo Dimension. Why did it always fight her? She had to pin it down and hold it just to make a tiny cut. Then the tricky part was spinning around the elemer in time to catch the green prick of light with the key. She had only managed it a few times, but she recognized it now—Echo Magic smelled of sunlight on a meadow and baking summer earth.

It was the opposite with the Shadow Dimension. It called to her, *screamed* to her. All she had to do was hold her elemer out, and it was there. It *wanted* her to cut into it. Wanted to give her the rush of liquid power. Her elemer often found it subconsciously when she wasn't even trying—just holding it and day dreaming was enough. It was addictive, intoxicating. But also, dangerous. Every time, she felt like she was just on the edge of control.

Azalea took a sip of her hot chocolate but spat it back into the cup. *Yuck.* It was cold. Faraday moved onto her knee, always watching. She needed a break.

Van wasn't home, so it was unlikely she would be disturbed. A good time to try again with the Shadow Atlas. Reaching under her pillow, she pulled up the book and propped up the pillows on the bed. Then she tugged a fluffy blanket over her knees and set the book in front of her.

She performed her new ritual of cutting into the Shadow Dimension and purposefully calling through shadows (*with* intention and a spell cloud). She pricked a finger to draw blood and wrote *Good evening*, hoping it wouldn't be in a mood to insult her or reject her.

Her words dissolved into the pages and were replaced with what she took as a friendly greeting, *Good evening, unworthy Initiate.*

It seemed to be growing on her, at least. Grinning, and ever hopeful, she wrote out her request.

Please all powerful book, show me how to bring my dad back. She'd noticed in the past that it responded well to compliments. This time, she was in luck.

Slowly, a map of the Tower of London general area appeared. Faraday forced himself onto her knee once more. The purring of the cat helped keep her focused and calm. Familiar grids, patterns, and symbols showed up. Sections of London were pulsing, and the brightest was St. Dunstan in the East.

She held her breath as more writing appeared. Then something new. Down the side, a list of moon cycles and celestial events materialized and . . . a new riddle! The full riddle, it seemed.

"You marvelous creature! I knew you liked me," she said as she kissed the book, and took a photo in case it disappeared, then read through the lot.

A snake, a bee, you found the key.

But time is running out.

A church in which the trees are free.

Is where you'll face your doubt.

Yes, she had the key—the watch—and the location.

A veil, a girl, a spirit lost.

From blood they once were tied.

Blood for blood is the cost.

Let shadows be your guide.

Straight forward, that one.

When dark and light align as one.

The Hollow nears both planes.

The land, a breath, a tiny sun.

A drop to break his chains.

After discussions with Isaac and from all her time spent obsessing over Torin's tips, she assumed this referred to the four elements, or the drop could be blood. She'd read up on the practices of blood magic and knew she'd need to tie it into the spells by adding it to the circle, her instruments, and her own energy points, just to be safe. Torin also said she needed a binder—a gemstone. One thing she still had to find.

Summon from the shadow lands.

A power strong and true.

Call to one who once knew love.

Alone, one passes through.

She'd figured that meant a summoning spell, one she didn't have yet. And presumably, only her dad could come through, no one else. Which sounded good.

Speak the words for those long gone.

Speak them loud and clear.

But beware of shadows lost.

For darkness brings more fear.

This one was new, and a little ominous. She had no idea what that meant.

More words soaked into the page.

Now my Mageling, the words you shall speak, "With my voice I call thee, with my blood I bind thee, with my power I draw you forth. Cross the Hollow barrier."

She snapped a photo as the words dissolved once more.

So, she had the spell. A pleasant shiver ran through her and tingled right through to her snake tattoo. This was starting to feel real, and a bit scary. Also, the book was calling her *Mageling* now? It must have appreciated her kiss. Better than *unworthy Initiate*, she supposed. It was still hard to tell if it liked her or was trying to sabotage her.

Why are you helping me? she wrote, thinking it was safer to ask now she had more info.

I do not help. I serve the shadows.

Okay, so not so helpful. She'd had enough riddles for the night. *Well, thank you anyway.*

Carefully shutting the book, she placed it under her pillow, not wanting to get on its bad side again. She glanced at the time. It was nearly 3am. Where the hell had the night gone?

The last of the shadowy mist swirled around her. A faint smile crept to her lips as she lay back on her pillows and imagined the moment her dad would step through. She was ready now, and she would make him proud.

CHAPTER 21

T HE DAY HAD FINALLY come. Jitters buzzed through every cell in Azalea's body. This was it—the Autumn equinox—the day she brought her dad back. The week had rushed past in a daze of Shadow Magic, late night phone calls with Isaac, and a serious overdose of tea and coffee.

They had gone over the riddles again and again and come up with a plan for a ceremony at St. Dunstan in the East to take place right on the equinox hour. She was sure it would work, and for once she wouldn't have to hold back on the Shadow Magic; she could use it. Of course, Isaac had wanted to come, but she made him promise he wouldn't. If things went wrong she couldn't risk hurting him, or getting him mixed up with all this.

She called her mum for a quick chat. She wanted to hear her voice; you know . . . in case something went wrong with the whole necromancy thing. Her mum insisted on telling her all about the equinox ritual she had planned for that morning. Azalea listened patiently, eager to get on with her own ceremony. Once she hung up the phone, she felt oddly alone.

She slipped on her purple hoodie with a zip down the front. Hopefully, it would prove lucky. Pulling her hood over her ponytail, she left out the main tower gates, straight up the center of a tourist group. The Tower had just opened, and no one would notice her slipping out. She suspected the House of Ravens had better things to do than watch out for her day and night. Once outside, she called Isaac.

"I'm out now. I'll call you when I'm done," she said as she passed the tour groups and crossed the road.

"That's all you have to say! What if it all goes pear-shaped? I don't know why I listened to you. I should be there."

"Because you're a good friend who respects my wishes and knows I'll kill him if he comes anywhere near here while this is going on. It'll be fine. We have it all planned. Bye Isaac," she said, desperately hoping that much was true. She felt guilty for leaving him out, but it was better than him getting hurt if things did go wrong.

Trying to keep a normal pace, Azalea crossed the road, crunching through autumn leaves gathering in the gutter. Only half an hour till the exact equinox. Half an hour till she'd have her dad back and everything would be different. Everything would be better.

She went over the ritual in her mind as she kept close to the brick buildings. Salt circle first, then set out her four elements, then blood for binding along her energy points, then all she had to do was summon a spell cloud and say the words from the book. She could do this.

Swallowing back the sick feeling rising in her throat, Azalea marched up Great Tower Street as the eyes of strangers pierced into her like thorns. They didn't know what she was about to do; but it felt like somehow, they knew, or that someone was following her. Panicked questions and cold sweat crawled across her. What would she say to her dad? Would he be normal after being dead so long? Would he look like he did when he died?

A shiver shook her back to reality, and despite her fast walking, she was freezing. It was far colder than normal for September, it almost felt like it could snow.

She took a stabilizing breath and turned down St. Dunstan's Hill, a small street with red brick buildings and barred windows. The black iron gates didn't look friendly. She wondered if it was a sign to turn back. Her mum always taught her to look for signs. She ignored it though and forced her feet up the old steps of St. Dunstan in The East church, or what was left of a church.

Woody vines wound themselves over the entrance and archways, taking back the church for their own. Green and brown leaves crept through empty windows and over crumbling walls with no roof. It was how she imagined a church should be, open to nature.

Golden leaves littered the floor, and the sound of traffic was replaced with birdsong and the wind rustling the treetops. A small park grew inside the church walls. There were no pews or organs, but there was a circle of cobblestones surrounded by park benches that made a nice gathering area. Stone walls penned in the trees that reached toward the sky.

People sat drinking their morning coffees, all fixated on their phones. But she had planned for this. Taking a seat on the edge of the cold stone wall, she plucked out a bottle from her backpack. No one was watching. She stilled her rapid heartbeat and focused on forming a spell cloud to make bubbles.

Azalea forced a cut into the Echo Dimension and directed her blade toward the bottle. She drew the liquid into her army of bubbles and sent them out across the courtyard.

0

88JENNY SANDIFORD

One by one, people grasped their noses and shot sideways glances to their neighbors, each too polite to blame their fellow coffee drinkers for the smell. Their faces turned red, and they left abruptly. Azalea stifled a giggle, at least that eased the tension a little. Sulfur and garlic bubbles were a good trick—and—an idea of Isaac's.

Accepting that she was doing this, she tried not to freak out. Her hands shook and her palms were slick with sweat already. Testing the air with her elemer, she found the mushroom-y Shadow Dimension and, without hesitation, made a sharp cut and summoned a mist of solid shadows before she could chicken out. It was easy. They wanted to be let out. But keeping control was *not* easy. Her elemer hand strained until a shroud of eerie darkness covered the courtyard, a wall of semi-solid shadows. Hopefully enough to keep people out.

The grassy patch next to the paved circle was a good spot. She cleared the area of leaves with her foot and placed her backpack down. Not long now. Extracting Van's largest mixing bowl, Azalea poured an entire bag of salt in.

She checked the time. Just a few more minutes.

With a hint of hesitation, she removed a Tower of London tea-towel and unrolled her dad's elemer. Her fingers hovered above the bone handle, but a training elemer couldn't pull through the power she needed for this spell.

She forced herself to pick up the elemer and rested her familiar training one at her side. A faint buzz ran through her fingers. Crossing her legs, she faced the bowl and held her dad's elemer over it. It was like trying to psych herself up to jump into cold water. She took five fast breaths and quickly counted down.

Four, three, two, one—she went to slide the blade across her palm but paused. *Why did people do it that way in movies?* Instead, she pricked her thumb with the tip of the knife—much more civilized. She let out a squeak. *Still bloody painful.*

Her fingers were so cold she had to squeeze to get the blood out, but once it started, it was fast. Her hand hovered over the bowl. Unsure how much to put in, she let the blood fall in droplets as the salt greedily ate it up. Van wouldn't be wanting this bowl back.

She stirred the blood in with the blade of the elemer. Hopefully, it was enough. Putting her thumb to her lips, the metallic, salty taste awakened her to the reality of the situation. Was she doing the right thing? Panic set in for a second. What if she died doing this? Would she come back as a weird ghost? She rubbed her temples. No. She could do this. She had to.

Snapping out of her momentary rush of self-doubt, she stood up and sprinkled the salt in a wide circle around her, big enough to open a Hollow inside. Next, she placed a plastic water bottle, a yellow beeswax candle, a bright dandelion in a pot, and a white feather next to each other on the grass. Pouring the water into a wooden bowl, it didn't escape her notice as to how similar this was to her mother's ceremonies. She lit the candle and sat back.

Swallowing, she took in a nervous breath. It was now or never. Her thumb throbbed, and the cold was seeping in deep. Next, she unzipped the front of her hoodie, exposing her chest to the icy wind. It was necessary, but she was overly conscious of the fact that she was only wearing a bra underneath.

She checked the pocket watch. It was time. She tucked the watch into the top of her bra, then tried to squeeze out more blood from her thumb. It hurt, but nothing came out. *Shit. Shit. Shit.* She needed to do this now.

Tightening her grip on the bone handle of the elemer, she took a deep breath and sliced across her palm, just like in the movies. But it was nothing like the movies. Gasping from the sudden pain, she dropped the knife and clenched her hand, pressing it into her chest. It hurt like a bitch, throbbing and pulsing, and there was a lot of blood. Hot and sticky, it dripped out the creases of her hand and trickled down her arm. She had nothing to stop it, so she pulled down the sleeve of her hoodie and scrunched it in a fist.

Her brain wasn't keeping up. She remembered she needed the blood and held her hand over the elements. The dark stream trickled across the items, much more than she intended, and the bowl of water turned deep red. Trying not to throw up, Azalea opened her palm and gathered the gruesome paint on her index finger to dab messy patches onto each of her seven energy points, starting at her forehead.

She was feeling a little woozy.

Copying the motion she had seen her uncle do, Azalea drew a full circle in the air with the bone elemer. It cut through to the silky Hollow with ease. The rush of icy wind told her it had worked.

How far away would her dad be? She had no idea how big the subspace of the Hollow was. Sitting by the shadowy doorway, Azalea closed her eyes and cleared her mind. A snake hovered in a purple nebula of magic and grew as she focused on the spell. With great concentration, she visualized symbols from her book for resurrection—blood, life, spirits, binding, and all the elements. With this, she mixed her memories and feelings of her father and the sound of his voice. It all wove together in a tapestry in her mind.

A soft rush of the wind from the Hollow swept over her.

She made her cut into the Shadow Dimension and twirled the blade in her fingers, aiming the dagger straight into the Hollow.

The magic hit her with crushing force. Lightning and ice pulsed into her violently, as if every muscle and cell in her body was being seared with liquid fire. This was nothing like the training elemer. Fear squeezed at her chest as the Shadow Magic bored its way through her and into the Hollow. She couldn't breathe, nor could she stop the raw power. But she didn't want to. She had to do this. Pushing back the pain, she focused on nothing but the spell cloud. It held strong in her mind, pushing the magic into the dark void, and she screamed for her father to come to her, yelling the words into the darkness. "With my voice I call thee, with my blood I bind thee, with my power I draw you forth. Cross the Hollow barrier!"

She screamed it louder and louder.

Her vision blurred. A figure moved inside the Hollow. She called again. It was him. It had to be.

Just hold on a little longer, she told herself. He was coming. The flow of energy was consuming her, tearing at her cells as she squeezed her eyes shut tighter. She forced the spell cloud to hold in her mind, but it was cracking up. She was cracking up. Her arm didn't have any strength left, and each breath was harder than the last.

The figure was moving toward her. The blue haze of light from the Hollow faded away as he loomed over her.

"Hi dad." She let her body relax, and the spell in her mind dissolved into nothing. She had done it. Her eyes wouldn't open, but she knew he was there.

"Azalea," he said. She felt herself slipping away. But she had done it . . .

CHAPTER 22

T ORIN FLICKED HIS COLLAR up against the icy breeze. This weather did little to improve his mood. He nodded to the Yeoman Warder at the main gate and attempted a smile, but it was met with narrowed eyes and a grimace.

He started along the Thames, reliving the meeting he had just had with Brandon, his supervisor. It was clear the Archmage would never be satisfied with his progress. She wanted the task completed yesterday. *Unreasonable bitch.* Too bad it would take at least a year. Ancient relics didn't just grow on trees, especially the ones she was after.

Ridiculous people with unreasonable expectations is what it was.

Torin hadn't been fond of taking up the task, especially when it involved living at the Tower of London amongst a community of people who hated him. But like Danni pointed out, no one else would hire him, not with his history. But he'd been given a second chance and avoided life in prison thanks to Danni and the House of Owls. He wasn't exactly in the position to turn this down.

Urgent footsteps sounded behind him. He braced for an attack, his hand already at the knife on his belt. He spun around. Not an attacker, a student.

"Sir, Mage Dumont." The lad was as tall as him, and by the looks of him, a rugby player. He realized he knew him. It was the idiot from the hospital with burnout. He stood there, out of breath, his eyes wide. "You have to come with me! It's Azalea. I think something's happened to her." He motioned for Torin to follow as he turned to take off.

Torin looked him up and down. "Calm down. What's happened?"

People were staring. *Great, just what he needed.*

"It's Azalea. There were shadows all around her. I went in, but it was hard to see and then I heard her scream."

A chill shot through Torin. He shouldn't get involved. It would only lead to more trouble for him. The lad turned away and started running, obviously expecting Torin to follow.

Torin searched the crowd for someone more qualified, but all he saw were staring idiots. He had no choice but to go.

Blood pounded through his ears as he thought of everything that could go wrong. If something was wrong, he'd certainly make it worse. He took off after the boy.

They reached the ruins of a nearby church; the courtyard was filled with shadows and the thick, prickling energy of Shadow Magic hung about. The cold air almost masked the smell of a recently opened Hollow, though most people wouldn't recognize it for what it was.

Torin called in the shadows with a flick of his wrist and sent them to form a more solid barrier around the courtyard. He then cleared the central area of shadows. That's when he saw her. A body splayed out across the grass, surrounded by a wispy shadow mist.

The girl lay inside a crude salt circle. Her open jacket revealed intentional marks of dark blood against her ghostly skin, and a black cat was nibbling at her fingers. Torin glanced around to see that the circle remained unbroken. Either the person who did this escaped through a Hollow or she had done it herself. He couldn't imagine why.

Torin grabbed the boy's arm and yanked him back before he stepped in the circle.

"Look where you step, you idiot," he hissed.

The boy's face drained of color.

"What's your name?" Torin tried to get him to focus.

"It's Erik."

"Erik. Run back to the Tower, go to the Hospital, and find Mage Hawthorn. Tell her it's an emergency and to meet me in the Hospital tunnel. Go now."

Erik nodded, took one glance back and sprinted through the gap in the shadow barrier Torin opened.

Torin re-checked the barrier. It was strong. The glow of morning light settled at the tops of the stone walls. What in the gods' names was this girl up to, and why was he the one here to clean it up?

Torin held his elemer over the circle and made a neat cut across his thumb. He let one drop of blood fall into the salt.

He hoped the girl's circle was weak, and that she hadn't known what she was doing. Torin took a deep breath and kicked the salt with the point of his shoe. A whoosh of freezing air shot past him as the circle opened, nearly bowling him over. He shut his eyes to the piercing wind, hopefully that was the only defense she had up.

Dropping to his knees at the girl's side he lifted her slender wrist. It was light as a bird's wing, the skin almost blue and tissue paper thin. Dark blood stained her fingers and there was no pulse. He knew it was too late. She was already gone.

His stomach sunk. *This was bad*. He could not be found with this girl if she was dead. They would blame him, and it would all be over. His throat grew thick—she reminded him of Kira. Kira with the same long dark hair, that image of her lying there on the forest floor with her blank eyes staring past him. It was stamped into his brain, making it impossible to forget or to forgive himself. He pushed those thoughts away. He hadn't been able to bring Kira back, but maybe this time it could be different.

Her face was so devoid of emotion and pain that she looked peaceful, and for a moment he envied her. Suddenly he realized he knew her—*the girl from the library*.

He also knew exactly what she had been attempting. *Necromancy*. He glanced around the circle. It looked like necromancy or at least spirit summoning because he couldn't see a body.

His heartbeat increased, pounding in his ears. *He was so stupid! Why couldn't he keep his mouth shut?* She hadn't been just a cute girl hitting on him; she had wanted to know about Shadow Magic.

He pulled up her right sleeve where people usually had their House tattoo. *House of Bees*. Foolish girl. No wonder she screwed this up. Even the best Shadow Mages in history had struggled with necromancy. She didn't have a chance. How did she even have Shadow Magic abilities?

A sharp pain shot across Torin's hand. He instinctively lashed out and met the soft body of the cat. He looked down at it and it yowled.

"You little bastard!" Torin looked down at the blood streaking across the top of his hand.

The blood sparked his memory again. This wouldn't be a repeat of Kira. He slammed the memories back to the deepest part of his mind. The guilt never left him, and he couldn't handle adding to it. This time *would* be different. This time he could bring her back. She wasn't Kira, but she sure as hell didn't deserve to die for following his stupid advice.

His elemer rippled blue as he felt for the previous Hollow and sliced straight into it. There was no time to waste. The breath of the Hollow kissed his skin. *Home*. This was his domain. The freezing temperature and faint blue light inside usually brought calm. But not this time. His heartbeat thrashed against his ears so loudly it blocked out all sound.

Torin scooped up the girl. She was light as bird bones and cold as death. Her long brown hair twisted around her neck as if it was trying to strangle her, but he felt faint magic bleeding out of her. He could sense it as he stepped into the Hollow, so there was still hope. If she was trying to summon a spirit from the Hollow, then that's probably where hers would have gone. The cat trailed along next to him.

Torin placed her on the soft ground inside the Hollow. The cat watched him examine her. She had blood on her energy points, explaining why her jacket was open in the freezing cold.

He eased her sleeve from her fist. Her hand was sticky with blood as he peeled her fingers back revealing a wide gash across her palm. Whoever she was trying to summon, she was obviously serious about it.

Squeezing blood from the cat scratch on his hand, he added streaks of his own blood to the energy points on her body: one on the top of her head, another at her throat, over her heart, solar plexus, lower abdomen, and turned her over to place the last drop at the base of her spine. He stripped off his coat and shirt and did the same to himself, hoping it would be enough to bind the spell and have a point to call her back to.

Taking the leather pouch from his coat on the ground, he selected a natural brown zircon. He placed it on her stomach and took a deep breath, clearing his mind, despite the growing panic. The spell cloud he summoned was a deep blue. A focused raven stood at the center.

He summoned a complex combination of symbols. It was ill-advised to use magic from multiple Houses on any sort of spell, but it wasn't the first time he'd done it. He would rather risk it all than get blamed for another death.

He pulled resurrection and necromancy symbols towards him—*Snake magic.* From his own House, he summoned symbols of darkness, night, and dreams to give him power. From the House of Bees, he used earth symbols for binding and from the House of the White Deer—healing magic to restart her heart.

The spell circled in his mind, arranging itself into a new, powerful form.

The symbols balanced, and he was ready. *Please don't let her spirit be too far away,* he prayed to any gods listening, then cut into the Shadow Dimension, a tricky thing to do from a Hollow and a dangerous way to fuel a spell that shouldn't even be possible. He forced all his will into it. *By my will, it will be. By my will, it will be.*

The surge of energy flowed through him, activating the spell, and poured out into the girl.

She was out there somewhere. He could feel her.

"Azalea!" he bellowed into the Hollow. That's what Erik had said her name was. He screamed her name into the darkness. The magic wasn't just flowing through him, he was pushing it along, willing more and more power to go into the girl, and it was working, pulling her back. It had to work . . .

CHAPTER 23

"**Y**OU ARE HERE WELL before your time, child."

A strange voice. Azalea's head was fuzzy, but the pain had gone. In fact, she couldn't feel anything. Her eyes shot open to see someone, or *something*, standing over her.

A man? He was tall and spindly, much taller than anyone she'd ever met. His skin was gray, almost blue with a metallic tinge, and his face was stretched a little too long, but his sharp features fit it well.

"Where am I?" Her voice felt wrong, distant. She tried to move her arm, but found it strapped down. She was on a hospital bed. The strap didn't even budge as she struggled against it, and the man lightly pressed her chest to keep her down. It didn't take much pressure.

"Your spirit has separated. Your body remains in the land of mortals, but you are with us, here in the City of Stars. I am Damu." His voice was serene, and he spoke with an accent she couldn't place. There was a lot of strangeness about him. He reminded her of the Goddess Ereshkigal, from her dream. She relaxed a little—that's what this was. A dream.

"The being you called has taken your place in the mortal world. The balance is reset." He bowed to her and took a step back as if that explained everything.

"Can I go back?" she asked weakly.

He didn't answer. She glanced around, trying to work out where she was. It could be a hospital or lab. *Just a dream*, she reminded herself as panic shot through her. The room had shimmery black walls, but one was all glass, and through it, she could see a group of strange people staring at her. They certainly weren't human, and she glared right back at them.

Some had horns, one had glowing golden eyes, many had long hair that was the color of moonlight, it even seemed to glow. Their skin ranged from scaly to metallic to one that looked like it was made of water. She narrowed her eyes at them, but they continued to stare. She didn't care for being treated like a zoo exhibit.

Damu stood at a bench of instruments in front of a wall covered in test tubes and beakers filled with colorful liquids. He turned to her with a look of fascination in his eye.

"I want to go back. Please send me back now." She tried to move her arms again, but they were as useful as dandelion stalks.

"We can't always get what we want, little one. You have been sent here to help us. A most fortuitous day."

A lump caught in her throat. She didn't care what kind of day it was. She wanted out, and this Damu guy needed to start talking some sense. Was this some weird House of Ravens prison? Had they captured her while she was freeing her dad and injected her with something? She hoped her dad got away at least.

"Please let me go back. I'm not part of any House wars. I'm still new to all this and I just want to learn magic and see my dad. Please let me go. Please . . ." Her voice cracked. She sounded pathetic, but she was out of energy and out of options. "If this is a dream, I want to wake up now!" she yelled at the people in the window.

A jolt of energy surged into the room. The air crackled and fizzed, and Damu's face lit with surprise.

"It seems it was not your time after all, little one," Damu said. "If you agree to help us, I will assist in your return." He looked over his shoulder. A smiling woman nodded at him with a slow, unnerving blink—almost like a cat.

"Just send me back," Azalea said, her mouth slow to form the words. Had they drugged her? She felt herself slipping away.

A too wide grin crossed the man's face. Smiling didn't suit him. "Do you want to know the price?"

"I don't care, let me go." Something wasn't right. She was being pulled against the straps on the bed.

"Very well." He bowed. "You will know the price soon enough. A fair price for balance and a great service to the City. Yes, a great honor."

This guy was a crack pot, and this was a fucked up dream. Her desire to get home was growing stronger, a deep ache in her heart turning into a painful pull.

Her mind was blurring. Whatever drugs they had given her must be kicking in. She tried to sit up. "Okay, please let me go," she pleaded, feeling like she was being torn apart.

The man bowed and nodded to an old woman who entered the room. She looked like him—long, thin, and pointy, but with hair that rippled midnight blue with tints of galaxies and stars.

The woman stepped forward. Her hands were coppery and metallic, different from the soft skin of her arm that was dark as deep space and speckled with spiral galaxies and bursts of colorful nebula. She placed the metal hand on Azalea's heart. She couldn't feel the woman's hands. It was as if they were made of air.

A low harmonic chant echoed across the room, coming from the woman.

Azalea's insides grew warm, then flared with a white hot, stabbing heat. She heard herself screaming, but as an echo from far away.

A powerful pull yanked in her chest, as if an electromagnet was switched on and she couldn't fight it. The air crackled louder, and a dark shape formed in the middle of the static. She wasn't sure what was real.

Everything suddenly muted to dulled silence.

The woman released her hands. A violent jolt rattled through Azalea's body, and she was jerked away as if she were being hurtled through a tornado.

CHAPTER 24

T ORIN FELT SOMETHING GIVE. Something had answered his spell. Hopefully it was the girl, not a wraith or demon. He held on but was unsure how long he could sustain this level of power. A force was being drawn to him. Suddenly, a jolt hit his chest, and he was thrown back as the air crackled around him. It then turned still, leaving behind a strong electrical smell.

He scrambled over to the girl and found the cat was licking her cheek, but she wasn't moving. Time to go. This sort of power could draw unwanted attention in the Hollow.

The girl sucked in a loud breath. Torin sank to his knees beside her. She was alive. A weak pulse fluttered where his fingers rested on her neck. Definitely alive.

Her eyes opened wide as if she suddenly remembered something, and they were jet black, the same as his own would be. Torin held her down as she tried to sit up.

"You're safe," he said, trying to sound reassuring. "I'm going to take you to the hospital once I'm sure I can move you."

A sharp pain shot through his chest as her hand latched onto his. He didn't have time to pull away and he doubled over at the squeezing sensation in his chest. No doubt a side effect of the magic. It was a miracle they were both alive.

He sat up.

"Are you alright?" she asked.

"I should be the one asking you that," he said. "You know you were dead, right? What the hell were you doing?"

She just looked at him in confusion, then spotted the cat and relaxed a little. Her dark eyes turned to a steely gray as the magic slipped away. Then they closed, and she fell back.

He had no time to waste. Torin cut back through to St. Dunstan in the East and pulled her through. The cat stuck close to her. He placed the girl on the ground before pouring the bottle of water over the salt circle and rubbed it into the grass with his foot. He put on his shirt and gathered up her bag, shoving the scattered items inside. Then cut another Hollow, picked up the girl, and stepped through the darkness. The pain in his chest grew stronger. He held her tightly, then focused on the hospital tunnel and cut through.

Maiken was waiting, calm as ever, with a stretcher bed. He stepped out to see Erik was there as well.

"She's alive—just," Torin said, seeing the desperation on Erik's face.

Erik stared down at her. "I was sure she was dead."

"She was very close." Torin dumped her onto the bed, surprised he hadn't dropped her earlier.

Maiken gave Torin a sideways glance. "Let's get her upstairs. Erik, back to your house for now. Come back tomorrow."

Erik shuffled from one foot to the other. Torin could tell he wanted to say something, to accuse him of something. He stared down the boy with his darkest look. A spark of fear rose in Erik's face. *Good*, the boy wouldn't push him.

"You've seen she's alive, off with you now and not a word about this to anyone until we can ask her what happened," Torin said.

Maiken got them to a room with two beds. Torin trailed along, quite sure he was about to collapse. He hadn't been this close to burnout in years.

"Lie down, Torin," Maiken said. Her voice was stern kindness. He did not want to cause her more problems by collapsing on the ground. She didn't ask him what happened, and he didn't tell her. He wanted to make sure the girl would be okay. Would she have brain damage? Did he even call the right spirit back to her? He had no idea.

He fought the sleep tugging at him, his eyes locked on the bed next to his. It rapidly blurred and darkened.

CHAPTER 25

"**B**LOODY HELL," AZALEA GROANED as she rolled over, glad to be free of nightmares that had plagued her sleep. Her eyes shot open, suddenly remembering her dad. She had to find him. Battling the sheets, she struggled to sit up, realizing how sore every inch of her body was and how dry her mouth was. Instead of finding water, her eyes landed on a man. She froze seeing it was Torin, the Shadow Mage. What was he doing here?

He shuffled in his chair as if unsure where to look, then got up to leave. But before he could, the curtain flicked back, and Maiken appeared.

"Good morning," she said without any warmth, but went straight to Azalea and started checking her over.

Azalea tried to greet Maiken, but her mouth and brain were barely cooperating with one another. She mumbled something along the lines of *good morning*. This must be how it felt for an astronaut returning from the ISS. Whatever had happened to her, gravity was now hitting her hard. Tunneling blackness threatened as she tried to focus her eyes.

"What happened?" Azalea said. She moved her mouth around, trying to find some saliva.

"It's good to see you awake," Maiken said, then turned to the man. "Alright, Torin?"

Torin did not look alright at all. He had a sour look on his face, and he didn't look at all like a model in his fancy coat this time. His dark eyes were sunken, his previously well-trimmed beard had stubble around the edges, and he was wearing a rough woolen sweater, the sort a fisherman might wear.

He nodded to Maiken but said nothing. It was clear he didn't want to be there.

Maiken handed her a cup of water. "You have Torin here to thank for being alive."

Azalea glanced at him. She remembered the salt circle, her dad's elemer, the blood on her hands, and most importantly her father's voice. She was sure she had heard him. But reality and dreams were grafting together unreliably. She remembered a tall man and a woman with copper hands. That last part was definitely a dream. In either reality, she didn't recall Torin being there.

"What happened?" she repeated.

Torin cleared his throat. "You died is what happened," he growled.

Maiken peered out the curtain and shot a look at Torin. "Careful what you say." She picked up a tablet at the end of the bed and began writing on it.

She *nearly* died, must have been what he meant. But none of that mattered right now. "My dad? He came back? Is he here?"

A look of disgust twisted Torin's face. Maiken almost dropped the tablet. She spun around and rested her hand on Torin's shoulder, keeping him in his chair. Azalea's stomach dropped.

"You stupid girl!" Torin hissed. "Do you have any idea what you were doing? How dangerous necromancy is? Not to mention illegal." He shook his head. "Calling a bloody spirit. I should have trusted my gut when you were asking all those ridiculous questions. Assignment, my arse."

He clenched his free hand as though he wanted to strangle her. She was glad Maiken was there, though her expression wasn't far off Torin's.

If it had worked, none of this mattered. Her dad would be out there waiting for her. Azalea swallowed down a lump. Her eyes pleaded with Maiken silently. She didn't dare look at Torin. "Please, just tell me. Is he alive? Is he here?"

Torin slammed his fist into the chair arm. "No, of course he isn't! It's not possible. You can't just call back a spirit without a body, it's hard enough to just call a spirit. Do you have any idea what I had to do to bring you back?" His nostrils flared; his jaw locked in rage.

This wasn't adding up. Hadn't Damu sent her back from her dream? She was just asleep, not dead. "But the man in my dream, he said I'd released a being to our world and . . ." She stumbled about the words. "I agreed to something." It sounded ridiculous out loud. But the memories were becoming clearer. She knew her father was out there somewhere, whatever this guy believed.

Torin glared at her. "I'm telling you, he didn't come back. Your friend came and got me, and you were dead when I found you. I opened your circle first and no one else was there. No one left and if they had, I would have seen them."

She shook her head in disbelief. "You're wrong." Tears welled in her eyes. "My dad came through. He said my name. Maybe he is just a spirit. But I know he's out there," she said.

So, she'd failed at bringing him back to a body, something the Shadow Atlas hadn't thought to mention. But she could still find his spirit and help him.

Azalea let out a shaky breath. Maiken moved to perch on the bed and wiped Azalea's face with a wet cloth.

Torin folded and unfolded his legs, then stood up and paced the room. After a minute, he suddenly stopped and leaned on the rail and spoke in a low whisper. "Azalea, it's important you don't tell anyone what happened. You'll be expelled from your program and forced to move out of the Tower, not to mention locked up for necromancy." It wasn't just anger, there was real fear in his eyes. "As would I, for bringing you back."

So that's what it was. He was worried about getting himself fired or locked up alongside her.

"You should be grateful for Torin. He's put everything on the line to do what he did," Maiken said harshly. "What Torin did for you is more than anyone could ever ask. You should be dead, Azalea. Don't you understand? The burnout you suffered would have killed an experienced mage. I can't even explain it. It's a miracle he brought you back and a miracle I was able to reverse the damage. You were worse than Erik, though it didn't show on the outside." Maiken was flustered and near tears.

Guilt stabbed at Azalea's chest. "I—I'm sorry," she choked out. "Thank you, both of you," she said weakly.

Torin stood to his full height and threw the curtain back to leave. Maiken raced after him, catching him near the door. Azalea couldn't see but heard them whispering.

"That girl is going to get me kicked out of here," he said.

"No, she won't. You're a good person Torin—you deserve to be here, and so does she. Don't listen to everyone. I know you won't tell me what you did, but I'm warning you to be careful around her. Only we know what happened and we can tell the Archmage it was burnout after attempting to wield too much Echo Magic."

"It's hard to believe an Initiate got that far attempting Shadow Magic and necromancy, of all things. She must be nuts. Her father can't be out there. You need to get her to understand that, and the sooner the better."

He might be some infamous Shadow Mage, but she knew what she heard.

"She has no background in magic. She's new to all this. Cut her some slack and be thankful you're both alive. If she truly thought she could bring her father back, she just lost him all over again."

Azalea's stomach dropped. He couldn't be gone; she was sure of it.

"I'm not getting any more involved in this. Keep an eye on her."

The door shut and Maiken came back through the curtain.

"Don't use Shadow Magic again. Focus on the Echo Magic and your studies. I thought showing you Erik's burnout would be enough to scare you but no, now you've experienced it firsthand. I hope you understand the danger and the consequences."

"Consequences?"

"What you didn't see was Erik's recovery. You'll be weak for some time, magically and physically. Plus, you'll have to take blood supplements to subdue the cravings and be careful around others to make sure you don't hurt anyone."

"You mean like vampire cravings?" Azalea said. She didn't want to be a vampire.

"If that's what you want to call it. It's the magic trying to balance inside you, and it may make you more irrational. Something I suspect you don't need. But do your best and do not attempt any Shadow Magic." Maiken gave her a look of pity.

"I'm sorry Maiken. I was so sure it would work. I thought I knew what I was doing."

"Well, if anyone knows Shadow Magic, it's Torin. I trust his word. He's an Azurite Shadow Mage, the youngest in decades. You shouldn't question him, and you shouldn't say a word of this to anyone. This is serious, Azalea."

True—Torin was a Shadow Mage. So maybe he did know what he was talking about. But maybe there were other explanations, too. Ones he didn't know about.

))) ● (((

Azalea awoke to Van standing at the end of the bed, frowning at her chart. She must have been off duty, as she was wearing a thin strapped bohemian dress in all shades of pink and purple.

"Hey Van," Azalea said as she sat up and tried to ignore the violent hunger pains burning through her. Van put the chart back and Azalea noticed the network of veins in Van's left arm, pulsing and rushing with blood. Her eyes fixed on it and her hunger only increased. She wanted to bite Van. Her skin crawled at the thought.

"Eyes off the goods. Here, take this." Van reached out for the two blue pills and a glass of water. "No biting."

So, these were the side effects in action. She eyed Van's soft looking skin, her arm with a tattoo of a white deer and red roses came closer. Azalea was ready to lunge. Perhaps a tiny bite?

No! What the hell was she thinking? Instead, she took the pills and downed them faster than anything she'd ever eaten.

"Shit. I nearly bit you," Azalea said as she slammed the glass back down.

"You wouldn't have gotten me. I'm faster than you think. A bit rough, isn't it? Anyway, I came to see you to say your friend Isaac dropped in. Or more accurately, he stormed around the Tower, asking every Yeoman Warder in sight if they knew where you were and demanded to see you."

"Shit. Isaac!" Azalea threw her legs over the side of the bed. "Where is he?"

"Not to worry, Love. Lucky for you, I came across him and took him to our flat for a spot of tea and a calm down. I sent him on his way with the promise you were alive and well."

Poor Isaac. He would have been frantic. "Thanks Van. I owe you one."

"Oh, not at all. He was sweet and obviously cares for you a lot. Invite him over any time." She winked and picked up her bag.

"Don't go, Van. I need to get out of here. Can you put in a word for me with Maiken please?" Her dad could be miles away before she got out of here. Who knows how far he might get?

"You're on your own there, Love. No way I'm going against Maiken's orders, and you'd be wise to follow them. Bye bye!" She waved in farewell without a hint of sympathy and skipped off.

Before Azalea had a chance to sink back into her pillow or plan her hospital escape strategy, Danni charged into the room.

"I am so mad at you," Danni said with her arms across her chest, but it lasted about a second before she was on Azalea in a lung crushing hug. Azalea swore she could smell the blood pumping through Danni's neck as she draped over her. She held her breath until Danni got up and perched on the edge of the bed.

"I'm so sorry, Danni. I know I screwed up big time. I didn't want to get Maiken in trouble. I hope she's okay."

"She's fine and her job is safe for now. You gave us a real scare." Danni sat down and proceeded to give Azalea all the same telling offs and warnings as Maiken had, making Azalea's guilt twist her stomach into tighter knots.

Azalea bit her lip, hard enough to draw blood. She savored the salty metallic taste. *Eughh, sick*. All she could say was, "I'm sorry." It sounded pathetic and meaningless.

"Just be aware that the Archmage can have you expelled at any time if she finds out the truth."

"But Erik wasn't."

"Erik has connections you don't have."

Azalea swallowed. She couldn't get expelled. She needed to stay in London to find her dad. "I won't do Shadow Magic anymore," Azalea said, believing that was what Danni wanted to hear.

"Well actually, I had another idea. Though you may not like it." Danni glanced around and lowered her voice. "Instead of ignoring your Shadow Magic, I think you should learn some basic control. That way, you'll know what is and isn't dangerous. It was wrong for Fabian to just dismiss your abilities all together."

"But he said he couldn't teach me. Is he coming back?" Azalea asked, suddenly full of hope. He was the next best thing to her dad teaching her.

"No. He's away for a while," Danni said as her shoulders slumped for a second, then straightened up again with a bright smile. "Even better. I was thinking that Torin could teach you!" She clapped her hands as if it were a brilliant idea.

Azalea's heart sank. "Um . . . It's a lovely idea, Danni. But I'm *certain* he hates me. Why would he want to teach me?"

"Because he's my friend, and it's in all of our best interests if you don't do anything else dangerous due to lack of proper knowledge and control."

"And he agreed to this?"

"Well, no, not yet. But I'm sure he will."

"If he agrees, then I'm in," Azalea said, meaning it wholeheartedly. If she could get even a little more control over her Shadow Magic, she wouldn't have to fear it, even if it involved being around Torin. She could use it to find a way to help her dad.

"Lovely!" Danni exclaimed. "Gods know you need to learn some control, girl. Shadow Magic requires a great deal of focus. You're not demonstrating that so far. We'll all be dead from heart attacks by the end of the year."

CHAPTER 26

TORIN SLIPPED BACK IN the main gates right before the key ceremony began. The bellows of the Yeoman Warder rang out behind him as he passed Beauchamp Tower. The Tower certainly had a lot of ceremonies and rituals he was yet to get used to.

Wood smoke lingered in the air as he passed the chapel leading to the courtyard below his tower. He took two steps at a time up the east wall, to his sanctuary. Jingling the old key in the lock, he twisted it and kicked the door in just the right way to open it.

Stepping in, he was met with the autumn chill that had seeped into his office. The smell of books told him he was home, and he let his shoulders relax as he placed his coat on the stand and his bag on the large antique table that he used as a desk. He took the steep spiral of stairs to his living room, put on the kettle, and filed through his stack of ready-made Tesco's meals in the fridge.

A loud knocking sounded downstairs. It had to be Danni. He started the microwave and went down to let her in.

"Alright, Torin?" Danni said in a cheery voice.

"Maiken sent you, didn't she?"

"What, no?" she said.

"Come in. I'm just having dinner, but I'll make you a cuppa if you've already eaten."

"Let me guess?" she said excitedly. "Curry?"

Was he that predictable? He just shook his head, and Danni followed him upstairs and into the fragrant smell of chicken tikka masala that drifted over from the microwave. Danni darted around his kitchen, grabbing mugs, and ducking into cupboards.

"Biscuits are above the fridge," he said, knowing that's what she was looking for.

She pulled down the Hobnobs. Plain, not chocolate. Why people had to cover perfectly good biscuits in chocolate, he had no idea.

"Sooo," she said, with a look that said he was in for trouble.

Torin frowned at his curry as Danni set down a pot of tea. This was about the girl.

"What you did for Azalea was amazing. You, of all people, must understand what she's going through," Danni said.

"I was never stupid enough to try and bring someone back from the dead without a body," Torin replied, poking his fork tensely into an unidentifiable vegetable.

"No. But you did stupid things when you were younger. Very similar things I might add . . ."

"Because I thought I was doing the right thing."

"And so did she," Danni said as she poured them both tea from the waiting teapot. There was always an answer with her. "I was just hoping you could teach her some Shadow Magic basics. You know, just enough to learn some control and keep her out of trouble?" she leaned in and gave a cheesy smile. "Pretty please?"

"No," he said without even thinking. "Bad idea. That girl should be nowhere near Shadow Magic."

She steepled her fingers and tapped them against her lip. "I see your point. But we tried that and look what happened. She just needs a little guidance, just the basics. Or maybe scare her off it?"

He glared at Danni, but knew it had no effect on her. Scaring the girl could work.

"Come on, Tor. She needs help and you're the best there is."

"I'm the *only* Shadow Mage at the Tower."

"Exactly. Perfect for the job!"

"I'll think about it."

"Right-o. Well, I shall leave you to it. Thanks for the cuppa. Let me know when you decide you want to teach her, and I'll let her know." Danni hopped up.

Torin shook his head. The truth was, the girl was a danger to herself and to Danni and Maiken. He didn't have a choice, and Danni knew it. He had to be sure she wouldn't tell anyone what happened and to find that out he needed to be close to her.

He showed Danni out, then went back upstairs and jumped in the shower, hoping the steam would clear his head. The past day had been a nightmare. Constantly looking over his shoulder, half expecting the Archmage to walk up and tell him to get packing. Or worse, have Danni arrest him for participating in necromancy.

His muscles ached. His whole body was drained of magic. Stepping out of the shower, his eyes fell on his reflection in the mirror. His left pec of previously unmarked skin was now deep blue with a bright ivory moon set on top. A strange place for a new tattoo to appear. Even stranger was the fine pattern of intricate knots within the moon, all glowing like silvery moonlight.

At this point, he was too tired to care. What he needed to worry about was getting ahead on his relic hunt so the Archmage wouldn't fire his arse. He didn't have time for this Azalea or her juvenile magic. He would agree to teach her, but after he was done with her, she'd either be bored to death or scared to death. Then she'd have to give up on Shadow Magic.

CHAPTER 27

F INALLY, AFTER A WEEK cooped up in a hospital bed trying
not to bite people and wanting to go find her dad, Azalea was about to be free. She stuffed Gerald the dinosaur, her
main companion for the week, into Van's floral duffel bag and
downed her last hourly supplement.

The whole week she'd been expecting the Archmage to walk
through those doors and tell her she was expelled from the Initiates' Program. But she never came, leaving Azalea in a constant
state of anxiety. The cover story was a mental breakdown, and
one she was happy to go with as it was verging on true.

She'd made sure to text her mum, Isaac, and Fabian multiple
times throughout the week, so no one would come to check on
her or would worry about her. They all thought she was fine.
In reality, she was crumbling inside, but despite her weakened
body and newfound lust for blood, she hadn't given up on her
dad. This was her shot to go find him. She just needed to get to
the Shadow Atlas.

Turning to leave, she nearly crashed into Erik.

"I thought you were dead." He looked at his hands, then
glanced up at her. "I'm glad you're not." His usual confidence

wasn't there, and to her further surprise, he handed her a box of chocolates.

She tilted her head, wondering if she'd heard right. "Me too. Um, thanks for the chocolates, and for getting help that day. I *would* be dead if it wasn't for you." It felt weird to be thanking Erik. She tucked the chocolates into her bag and hoisted herself onto the edge of the bed, still feeling a little unsteady. Erik did the same and sat down right next to her as if they were friends.

"No worries. And I didn't tell anyone, if that's what you're worried about."

"Thanks. I won't be doing anything like that again." She *had* been worried and sure as hell didn't trust him. "Why were you following me?"

"I saw you leave the Tower. I dunno what it was. Just a bad feeling, I guess. It was something Ambrose said before. It made me worry and he seems to think you're a spy. But I see now your secret is your Shadow Magic, right? You're not trying to hurt anyone?"

Azalea shook her head. "No, of course not, and I'm not a spy." Why would Ambrose say that?

"Well, it seems he's way off. Just watch out for him, all right? I don't know who's feeding this load of bollocks to him, but you don't want to be on his bad side."

"Thanks," Azalea said, wary of anything coming out of Erik's mouth.

He nodded at the supplement bottle on the bench. "It's a bitch, isn't it?"

Who was this new friendly Erik? "Are you being nice to me because you know what it's like to want to bite people?"

He shrugged. "Maybe. I know what that feels like. It's only just wearing off now. It really made me more of an arsehole, so good luck with that. I nearly bit the whole lot of you the first day of class. Annoying bunch of twats."

Unsure how to respond, she stayed silent, and Erik was quick to fill the gap. "So, if you need anyone to talk to just let me know."

Surprised at his sudden niceness, she turned and met his gaze. His blue eyes locked with hers and she found that the usual coldness was gone. Instead, she found warmth and a relaxed smile. An unwelcome blush bit into her cheeks. She must be losing it if one cute smile had her forgetting what a dick he had been.

"Thanks," she said.

"No worries. I'll save you a seat in class when you're ready to come back. And don't worry—you can trust me." He hopped up.

"Oh, okay. See you then," she said, feeling like she'd forgotten how to speak full sentences.

With a small wave, he walked out the door as Maiken marched in.

"One last checkup before I release you," Maiken said, pointing to the bed.

Azalea didn't complain. The faster this was over the better.

Maiken went about her exam, checking every inch of Azalea's body to make sure all signs of burnout were gone. The cold stethoscope met Azalea's skin and Maiken stood back and tilted her head. Azalea raised up on her elbows to see what was wrong.

"Did you have this tattoo before?" Maiken asked. She ran a finger over a tiny moon that had appeared above the small mound of Azalea's left breast.

A cold sweat formed across her body. "That definitely wasn't there before," Azalea said. It was right where the dream woman had placed her hand.

The moon had a weak silvery metallic glow, and she could see intricate knots at the right angle. A night sky washed out in watercolors behind it.

Maiken dismissed it. "Must be the first extension of your tattoo," she said, nodding to the flower tattoo on her arm. "It's pretty. Though odd that it isn't on your arm. Tattoos usually grow close to each other."

Azalea knew it wasn't part of either House tattoo—it was something else entirely. Another weird magic thing to worry about later.

))) ● (((

Azalea spent the next few days sleeping and trying to get the Shadow Atlas to talk to her. She needed its help if she had any chance of finding her dad. But, of course, it was ghosting her. The book remained totally blank, not even asking to be fed. She suspected she had been so drained of magic it couldn't sense her, and she didn't want to risk drawing blood and triggering her weird blood craving. Her new thing of wanting to eat raw meat was bad enough.

Not being able to do magic, or use the Shadow Atlas, was frustrating, but also a chance to start sorting out her life so when her magic came back, she could find her dad. She started with calling her mum. It was a relief to hear her voice, but the guilt rose in her chest as she thought about how close she had come to death and her mum had no idea. She was careful to avoid all topics relating to magic. They chatted about Leda's garden, RoRo, and how Azalea was fairing at uni (she lied a little about that—the truth was she was way behind in her studies). At least things felt back to normal between them.

After getting out of hospital, out of desperation to pay rent, Azalea reluctantly started a data entry job online.

Another week of boring recuperation passed, and Azalea got the shock of her life one morning. Isaac turned up on her doorstep. Of course, he ignored all her messages to stay away, but she had never been so glad to see anyone in her life. He stood there on the front steps with a dopey grin on his face.

"You freaked me out, Azalea," he said as he crashed into her in a hug that showed just how worried he had been.

"I'm sorry Isaac, I'm so glad you're here." She squeezed him back. "I don't think the book gave us the whole truth."

"You think?" he said sarcastically. She dragged him inside and filled him in on everything that had happened. Exhausted and drained from reliving the ordeal, she was glad when Van bounced into the room.

"Hey guys," Van said with a smile directed at Isaac and poured herself a sludgy green juice. They had met while she was in hospital.

"Zaels filled me in on her near-death experience," Isaac said.

Azalea facepalmed. "Isaac, I told you, you weren't meant to know about any of this."

"Yes, but Van already knows."

"But no one is meant to know that you know."

Azalea held her breath, worried she would get in trouble for telling someone about magic. But Van just giggled.

"Don't worry. Your secrets are safe with me." She winked at Isaac. "It's nice you have someone to talk to about all this, Azalea. But how about we give you a rest now. I can take Isaac on an exclusive tour of the Tower, well, all the non-magic parts."

"Sounds great!" Isaac said, not even trying to hide his extreme enthusiasm. He jumped up and gave Azalea a kiss on the cheek. "Get some rest."

"Oh, and take these vitamins." Van placed a large bottle of multivitamins on the coffee table. Azalea thanked her and waved them goodbye.

Once they left, Azalea was glad to shut her eyes and sink into the sofa. She didn't tell Isaac or Van she was going to find her dad once her magic returned. This she would keep to herself for now.

))) ● (((

It wasn't until two weeks after she left the hospital that she was cleared to join her evening magic classes again, but she was under strict instructions from Maiken not to do any magic, only theory. She wasn't sure she was ready anyways but was scared she would never find her dad again and needed to get back into it.

Her first Theory of Magic class was exhausting. Trying to stay awake was hard enough, let alone focusing on Mage Shepard talking on and on about the rules of dueling tournaments. It was nice just being there though, even if her classmates were darting strange looks all around her. She ignored them and offered no explanations.

Millie and Livia both shot her death glares when Erik sat down next to her and said hi. At least he wasn't being a total wanker now, but his change of heart was weird. Her near-death experience seemed to have more impact on him than his own. Ambrose ignored her as if she wasn't there, and Elam was too engrossed in his study to talk to anyone. As they packed up to leave class, Azalea was ready to fall asleep on her feet. All she had to do was make it past the caf and through the tunnel, but as soon as she stepped out, she saw Danni by the pond, waving.

Trudging across the caf, the smelled of earthy ground and water reminded her of her forest and her mum. A pang of loneliness grazed over her. A frog jumped off the pond's edge as she reached Danni.

"Okay, here's the thing," Danni said. "I talked to Torin again. He's not exactly happy about it, but he agreed to teach you."

Nervousness crashed over Azalea. "When?"

"So, you need to go right now. I said I'd get you after class and if you don't turn up, I'm pretty sure he'll change his mind."

Azalea's brain whirled a million miles a minute. "What do I do?"

"Don't panic. I can walk you over there, and I'm sure it will be fine. You don't need anything. Just listen to him and follow instructions. You can do that, right?"

Azalea nodded. Of course she could, there was no doubt about it. She would be the perfect student —if she could only stay awake.

Instead of going through the tunnel home, Danni led her upstairs through the Barracks and out into the chilly night toward the chapel. Azalea froze up as they got closer to the old church. Eyes of spirits followed them as they passed. Azalea had a feeling they knew she could see them. She tried to avoid eye contact but couldn't help but look.

What if her dad was one of them? He might not remember her. She had to look. Scanning through them, none of them looked like the photos of her dad. Her eyes locked with a young woman's. A sense of recognition flashed across the woman's face. "Ho there, you girl. Have you seen George?"

Azalea's eyes darted to the pavement. Thankfully, they turned the corner down an alley right next to the chapel, and Danni led her up the steps of the wall to the corner tower.

He lived in a tower. *Yup, jealous.*

Torin answered the door, and he did not look pleased.

"Delivered as promised," Danni said.

"Please come in," he said to both of them.

"I must be off. I'll leave you two to it. Ta ra!" Danni nudged Azalea in the doorway and was off down the stairs before either of them could protest.

Torin gestured for her to enter his office. She hesitated, then followed him in.

"Please take a seat at the desk there. I'll be back in a minute. Please excuse me." There was ice behind his overly polite words. It was clear he didn't want her there.

He went upstairs and Azalea let out a breath. The room held an uneasy silence, but the office was very comfortable, with a faint smell of wood smoke that hung in the air. There was a big table with a laptop perfectly centered from either end. Next to it was a neat pile of notes and a line of pens arranged by length and color. Even the phone charger cable was wound in a neat spiral. He was one of *those* people.

The circular floor was old flagstones, covered with colorful Turkish rugs, and bookshelves covered every spare bit of wall. She didn't dare touch the books. Judging by his obsessive organizing, he would know if she touched anything, especially any of the interesting looking artifacts on the shelves. The stairs spiraled up to her left, and next to them was a fireplace with a comfy looking chair she wanted to curl up in and go to sleep.

Seating herself in the very straight-backed chair at the desk, she shuffled uncomfortably as footsteps sounded down the stairs. Torin placed a cup of tea next to Azalea and heaved a gigantic pile of books off a shelf and plonked them down next to her.

"You can start by reading these," he said.

"Okay, thanks," she said, unsure how else to respond. Torin went back to work on his computer opposite her. The silence in the room was deafening. It was too quiet to drink her tea for fear she would disturb Torin. She wanted to thank him for saving her and for agreeing to give her lessons, but she didn't know how to start.

After an hour of reading, her eyes felt like rocks. Her first night back at class had been exhausting enough. Now this. She just wanted to go to bed. But Torin hadn't said one word, and she wasn't going to break the silence. Shuffling in the hard wooden chair, she thought about how old it must be—some fancy antique that was not at all practical for sitting for long periods of time, *but perhaps he knew that.*

Another half hour passed. He was testing her. He had to be. The next book she picked from the pile sat open, still on the first chapter: *The Physiological Effects of Rapid Magic Inundation*.

She'd flicked through the first pages but read nothing. He'd obviously chosen it to prove a point. Diagrams of bursting cells, overloaded synapses, pictures of damaged human organs, and corpses of people who had suffered burnout were plastered across every page. She got the point: she was an idiot and should be dead. Irritation bubbled under her skin and hunger burned in her chest. The veins in Torin's hands were lovely. His long, slender fingers danced over a book at his side. She wondered what they would taste like. What his blood would taste like.

Whoa! She caught herself. Super inappropriate thoughts.

She couldn't face any more reading but refused to show weakness. So, she pretended, studying Torin out the corner of her eye—not thinking about biting him (much)—just noticing him. He was so still. So focused. So fit. She shook her head and told herself to wake up. But her eyes were drawn back to him. He looked too young to be a mage and too serious to be that young. She wondered what he was working on. *What did he even do?* Something to do with artifacts or history, she suspected—judging by the history books and artifacts everywhere. *Duh.*

He pushed his chair back and Azalea jumped.

"That's enough for tonight. Come back after class tomorrow and you can continue."

Pushing back her own chair, she stood up and shook out her hands as blood trickled back to her sleepy limbs. She slung her bag over her shoulder and turned toward the door, which Torin had already opened for her. Azalea stopped next to him in the doorway.

"Thank you for saving me. I know this isn't what you wanted, but I am grateful. So, um, thanks . . ." she said.

"You're very welcome," he replied, as if she had thanked him for opening the door.

She gave a weak smile and stepped through the door.

"Azalea," he said.

She turned back and held her breath, sure he was going to tell her he didn't want to teach her.

"Take care," he said, as if he actually cared.

She felt a smile tug at the corner of her lips. "I will. Bye, Torin." She waved and trudged down the stairs. Perhaps he didn't hate her. She swore she would make this up to him somehow.

In her short-term daze, she'd forgotten all about the chapel. There were more spirits than before. She glanced at them and felt the icy cold sweep over her. Her legs reacted before her head. She was done with tiptoeing around them. She sprinted past, not bothering to look at any of them, and ran all the way home and slammed the door behind her. Her heart battered against her ribcage.

If the spirits were catching onto her, that would make life hard. She could worry about that tomorrow. Right now, she needed sleep.

CHAPTER 28

A ZALEA WAS BEGINNING TO resent Practical Magic classes. She sat there spinning her training elemer on the desk and sulking as they waited for Mage Shepard, Erik, and Ambrose to arrive. Another Practical Magic class with no practical magic. But her mental shields were stronger than ever with all her free time to practice. Ambrose couldn't get through at all and sat there looking pissed off most of the time.

She half listened as her classmates chatted around her. It was hard not to. Millie's voice was so high and piercing. Azalea worked extra hard to keep her temper in check.

"I hear a new gallu has been hunting in London. The hunter hasn't been able to catch it so far," Millie said.

Azalea felt a chill run through her and turned to Millie, her annoyance replaced with curiosity. "I've heard my uncle mention those. What is it?" Azalea asked.

The girls exchanged a look before answering. "You don't know much, do you Zalea? A gallu is a spirit wraith, a dark creature from the Shadow Dimension that feeds on human spirits," she said in an overly exaggerated voice. "They wait for the freshly dead and eat up the spirits, growing more and more real every day, until one day they reach their corporeal form and can start killing people to create more dead souls to feed on!" Her voice grew more and more dramatic. "Then when they're strong enough, they call their brothers from the Hollows and flood the earth with gallu until the whole world is taken over and everyone is dead!" She stopped abruptly, slamming her hands on the table.

Livia rolled her eyes. "That's why there are gallu hunters. They don't let them get to the corporeal stage and catch them one at a time. It's not possible for them to grow in numbers."

"I read that they can retain the memories of the spirits they eat. They get smarter as they consume more spirits. They can even use the memories of the spirits' loved ones and go after them," Elam added in.

Millie dismissed him with a wave of her hand. "But seriously, it *is* weird that one's in London and hasn't been caught yet. They usually get the ones in populated areas straight away."

Livia nodded. "Oh well, hope they get this one. What an exciting job! I wish I knew more about them."

"I could ask Torin. I'm sure he knows all about them," Azalea said, also wanting to know more.

"What? Do you mean Mage Torin Dumont? You know him?"

Azalea froze. *Torin Dumont.* A moment of realization washed over her. She was an idiot and had never asked Torin's last name. She'd completely forgotten the conversation the girls had on the first day of class. All she could remember them saying was how hot he was . . . and that he was a murderer?

She needed to know more. These two as a source weren't exactly credible. "Sort of, I guess. I've bumped into him a few times with Danni." She felt her face go red. She shouldn't be talking about him.

"Is it true what they say? Did he murder a bunch of people and go to prison? Does he really know the Hand of Death?" Millie asked.

"I don't know him too well. I have no idea."

"You're blushing! Do you have a thing with him? I mean, we've all thought about it, so I can't blame you." She looked impressed.

"We don't have a thing." Azalea tried not to blush again, but knew she failed. Torin had a rough past with the House of Ravens. But a murderer? That was hard to believe.

"You so do! Come on, tell us. What's he like? You like bad boys, Zalea?"

"You talking about me?" Erik appeared at the table.

Azalea suppressed a groan. She hadn't even heard him cross the room.

"You wish," Livia said. "Zalea here has a thing with Mage Dumont."

She locked eyes with Erik, silently willing him not to say anything.

"Doubt it. Have you ever seen him with any birds? She's just covering for me. Right, love? Doesn't want to tell you about our secret affair." He winked and sat down at the table.

Azalea rolled her eyes. "How do you lot talk so much rubbish? I don't have a thing with Torin or Erik. And I don't know about him being a murderer or whatever. He's actually quite nice."

"Sounds like you like him. But say what you like. You can't keep secrets here. This place is just a village of gossips and busy bodies—we always find out in the end."

"I think there's far more interesting gossip out there than about me," Azalea said.

"I don't know about that." Erik caught her eye, and she promptly looked down at her book. She wanted this conversation to end.

Torin would know about the gallu. She'd ask him. They weren't exactly on casual conversation terms, let alone asking about his potentially-murderous-past terms, but she needed to know.

)))●(((

Azalea made it through a few more days of classes before Maiken finally cleared her to start training again, allowing her to start out with some exercise and very light magic. She was back at the start with everything, especially with building up her magic resistance.

As soon as she got back into training, life got better. She spent more time trying to get her fitness back than she did on uni work. Her meditation became more focused, and she could summon spell clouds to her mind in an instant and change between the bee and the snake more easily than before, but it was a strain.

She was more determined to learn magic, but also more wary. And with Torin's stash of Shadow Magic books, she was bound to find something that would help her find her dad.

Evangeline and her classmates were equally happy to have her back to full health. Van had been too nice to complain, but

Azalea knew full well she had been a nightmare to live with the past few weeks.

Lessons with Torin were not going well. One thing was clear: he was punishing her instead of teaching her.

It was Friday night after Practical Magic class, and Azalea sat in Torin's office, the hard antique chair digging into her back and the chair by the fire taunting her with its apparent softness. *Where was he?* It was already 9:30pm. Fortunately, he'd given her a key so she could access the books when he wasn't there, but she hadn't used it until this point.

This was a waste of time. She was sure Torin had no intention of teaching her anything real. Right now, she certainly didn't want to open the latest book: *Theories of Subspace Travel with Hollows.* The subject sounded interesting, but the way it was written was not, and there were no pictures.

Thoughts whirled around in her mind about everything her classmates said about Torin. The side effects of the healing still had her thinking irrationally at times, but she was sure it was wearing off. Still, she couldn't help but think these 'lessons' might have been better spent trying to commune with the Shadow Atlas again. She still didn't know anything about Torin.

Standing up, she stretched and casually leaned over his desk. She dared herself to go around the other side—a peek wouldn't hurt.

A photo in a black frame sat by his computer, one of only two in his office. A cute little boy, about four years old, sat there beaming, perched on a smiling woman's lap. They had the same wide smiles, golden brown skin, and bright eyes. It had to be his mother.

The other photo was of Torin graduating from university. His arm was casually wrapped around Danni's shoulder. He was smiling—something Azalea had yet to see in real life. It suited him. She giggled at the thought of trying to make him smile somehow. She wouldn't even know where to start.

It wasn't like Torin to be this late. She wished Faraday was there to talk to. He'd love Torin's office, lounging across the red rug by the fire. Perhaps she'd bring him along next time. Tapping Torin's pen on the desk, she decided to take a quick peek at what he was working on. Couldn't hurt.

She darted to check the window. No sign of Torin in the courtyard or on the wall.

Just a quick peek, she told herself as jitters flitted through her. The top page of his notes was boring, serial numbers for artifacts or something. Just a few more papers . . . all boring. Onto the desk drawer it was. She found it locked, but easy to open. Grabbing a paperclip off the desk, she unwound it and jiggled it in the lock, practice from years of her and Isaac sneaking into his dad's liquor cabinets.

An important-looking folder sat open to a page with a sticky note on top. It was a list of artifacts, a few with ticks by them. She didn't have time to read more. The unmistakable sound of the lock rattling got her moving. Slamming the drawer shut, she scrambled back to her chair to sit innocently.

"Good evening Torin," she said as he stepped inside.

He looked at her sideways. "Azalea." He nodded in greeting, offering no explanation for his lateness.

As usual, he set his computer up and started working. She couldn't help but wonder what he was hiding from her and what the artifacts were on the list he kept locked away. She also wanted to ask him about the rumors but was terrified of his response.

He looked up at her. "Why are you staring at me?"

His voice startled her, and she realized she had been staring.

"I wasn't, sorry, just thinking, I'll go back to my work now." She felt her face go red, and she stared down at her work. *No.* She told herself. *This is the time to ask him. Just do it.* "Actually, I heard people talking around the Tower and wanted to ask you something." She tried to keep her voice steady.

"They said you did some horrible things." She swallowed. "Is it true?" She held her breath, waiting for him to deny it, or to yell at her, offended.

Instead, his eyes dropped down. Much worse than being yelled at.

"Yes. I did a lot of things I'm not proud of, but I'm trying to make it right. Don't ask me any more about this, Azalea. You won't like what you hear."

She didn't know what to say. Her hands were sweating as she looked down at her book, not reading it, but trying to tame the thousands of questions parading through her mind.

Torin was a good person and there had to be more to it— a reasonable explanation. She peeked over her book at him. His own eyes were glazed over, staring at his computer screen without really looking at it. He looked so sad, and now she felt horrible for asking.

She went back to her book. The silence in the room was more oppressive than ever and she was no closer to any answers.

CHAPTER 29

"COME ON! IT'S FRIDAY. What's got you all mopey?" Van said as she flitted around the kitchen. She was on her third batch of muffins for the afternoon, not that Azalea was complaining. She was more than happy to be a taste tester, even if one flavor was beetroot and raisins.

"I'm fine. Just need to get some magic practice in before class, but I'm putting it off," Azalea said, not wanting to get into the details of why she wasn't fine. She'd been putting off trying Shadow Magic again, but the longer she waited, the more scared of it she got. She needed it to track her dad, then maybe once she found him, if his spirit was coherent enough, he could tell her what to do.

"Well, staring out the window into the rain like you're looking for Mr. Darcy isn't going to help," Van said. "How about you revive those drooping tomato plants? That'll be good practice and not too straining."

"Okay," Azalea said as she watched Van tip a large chopping board of chilies into her mixing bowl, followed by raspberries. She wondered if she should say something but decided to let the experiment continue. Reviving the tomatoes would be good practice.

Rain tapped rhythmically against the windows and the sound of Van watching *Pride and Prejudice* on her laptop faded into the distance as Azalea settled into her meditation. After a while, she opened her eyes, feeling more in the zone.

Placing the four drooping tomato plants on the coffee table in front of her, she set about using different power symbols with Echo Magic to alter the amounts of water and nutrients, and tried to speed up the growth with a few random symbols to see what would happen.

The Echo Magic drifted through her, slow and familiar. By plant three, vines of juicy tomatoes weighed down the tiny plants. She was sweating and slightly drained, but yay! Tomatoes were a win. Small successes were what she needed for the next stage.

Shadow Magic.

Van had wandered off to her room without Azalea noticing she was gone. Azalea went to the kitchen and downed some supplements and several glasses of water. She wasn't ready, but it was now or never. She hadn't used Shadow Magic since that night. But she couldn't keep living in fear.

Her hands were slippery against her training elemer. She'd just do a small trial to start. Holding out the elemer, she made a clean slice to the Shadow Dimension. Her hand shook as she flipped the blade around. Her breath caught the moment the magic touched the key. A rush of memories and power flooded her. Dizziness threatened as black pushed at the edges of her vision, but it was amazing. Intoxicating, but also terrifying.

She cut the link. It was just a taste, but she was shaking all over. She wasn't giving up that easily. She had to be ready to use it.

Taking a deep breath, she made another cut. Using the same spell cloud with the same power symbols as before, she decided to try it with Shadow Magic this time. The magic flowed through her. It was so right, so perfect—so powerful. Aiming the elemer at the last tomato plant, she drove the spell forward.

But it was different this time. It was all wrong. There was too much power.

It crashed into the plant and the leaves turned black and curled at the edges. The stem bent and sagged until the plant collapsed. Tears crept to the corners of her eyes. One by one, the other plants fell, all blackened against the soil. Instead of bringing life and vibrancy to the plant, she had brought death.

"No!" she cried as she tried to grab it, as if it could somehow come back to life. She touched a leaf, and it turned to ash.

A sob escaped her lips, and she clutched a cushion to her chest.

The poor plants couldn't come back. They shouldn't. If they did, they would never be the same.

She collapsed onto the sofa and burst into tears. What had she done? She knew nothing about real magic, but she tried something so wrong, so unnatural. It wasn't just the plants. Why did her dad tell her she could do it? Why did he say he could come back, when it was clear all along he never could?

She couldn't undo any of it. She couldn't bring back the plants, just as she couldn't bring back her dad. It suddenly felt so real, so raw. Her dad wasn't there to teach her, neither was her uncle, and Torin didn't want to. She was alone. And she was the only one who could find her dad, the only one who believed or cared that he was out there. It was all on her.

She had to get Torin to teach her something useful, and she had to get the Shadow Atlas to talk to her again. Showing the book to Torin was an idea that popped into her mind a few times but was always overruled by a strong gut feeling that told her not to.

Azalea wiped her cheeks and gathered her plant remains to take out to the compost bin. Once outside, she froze as her eyes fell on a spirit woman. She stood in the middle of the lane dressed in what was probably the height of fashion in Tudor times, a necklace with a large B hanging from her neck. Her relentless stare drilled straight through Azalea's soul. Two priests stood on either side of her. Their eyes filled with expectation—hope.

Azalea dumped the plants and raced inside. She spread salt across the doorways and windowsills and did her best to ignore the spirits on the street. She needed to stop being afraid. It was time to convince Torin to teach her real Shadow Magic.

))) ● (((

Monday evening, Azalea left class dreading having to face Torin.

Without saying goodbye to anyone, she strolled out and raced up the stairs in the Barracks, went out the main door, and appeared behind the White Tower in the dark. Rain was pelting down in buckets as Azalea dashed towards the chapel, boots flicking up water from the slick stones.

"That's most unladylike, running about in that manner," a spirit woman called as she passed close by.

"Oh, piss off!" she yelled. The spirit stepped back with her mouth agape and a hand on her heart. *Worth it.* Azalea grinned. She wouldn't remember her the next day, anyway. Azalea nearly slipped as she approached the steps to Devereux Tower.

She knocked twice before yanking the doorknob and kicked the door till it opened, stumbling into Torin's office soaking wet, leaving a nice puddle in the doorway. Dropping her bag, she shook off her saturated coat to hang next to Torin's nice, dry one.

"You know it's been raining for days. You'd think you would remember a brolly by now," he said.

"If you must know, I left it in the library two days ago," she replied.

Taking a breath, she focused on details around the familiar room so she could get her thoughts together before she blurted everything out like an idiot. Torin's office always smelled nice: pine sap, wood smoke, jasmine, books. She looked toward the comfy chair she'd recently claimed as her own. She'd given up on the table a week ago and did most of her reading by the fire. But this time, Faraday was in it.

"How did he get here?" Azalea asked, momentarily forgetting her plan of confrontation.

"He's been here all afternoon, clawed at the door after lunch and made himself at home."

"I didn't know he knew you," Azalea said.

"Actually, we met a while ago. He came with me to the Hollow when you died. He seemed rather concerned." He said it as if it were a casual topic, rather than the thing they always avoided mentioning. Azalea didn't recall Faraday being there that day.

"I found him trying to eat your fingers, then he followed me into the Hollow and wouldn't leave your side, even when we got to the hospital. Strange cat." Torin was in an unusually talkative mood. She could use that.

"Yes, he pops up in unusual places. He must like you." She cleared her throat. "Speaking of that night, I've been meaning to ask..." she paused, ready to lose her nerve and go stand out in the rain. "Why aren't you teaching me real Shadow Magic?" she straightened her shoulders, appearing confident, but terrified of his response.

He walked around his desk and sat on the edge. She felt silly standing on the doorstep, dripping wet. She couldn't really go anywhere.

"You don't want to use Shadow Magic, Azalea. Trust me."

A chill ran through her. He hardly ever used her name. It felt strange.

"I do want to. That's why you're teaching me. I clearly need to learn control." *And I want to find out where my father is*, she thought to herself, but suspected that wouldn't help with her plight. "You're the only one who can teach me."

He looked at her with pity. Anger shot through her. She didn't need this; she needed a proper teacher.

"You're not ready."

"But I am!"

"You're not," he said. "I know you were searching my desk the other day. How can I teach you powerful magic if I can't even trust you?" He took a step toward her. Wow, he was tall.

She looked at the ground. How did he even know that? "It's not my fault. You won't tell me anything! You're the one keeping secrets. I hear all these horrible rumors about you, and you expect me to trust *you*!"

Rage flashed across his eyes, and Azalea gulped down a breath to stay quiet.

"You want to know the truth?" He stepped closer to her, his voice almost a whisper. "You know I'm from the House of Ravens. You have no idea what I went through to get my powers. I wouldn't wish it on anyone who had a choice. Our training is more horrible than anything you can possibly imagine."

A heavy silence hung over the room. Azalea heard the drops from her wet hair hit the stone floor. She backed toward the door.

"Do you truly want me to teach you Shadow Magic, Azalea?" He took a step closer. "Do you even know what that means?"

She swallowed but refused to be intimidated by him.

"I can teach you magic from the House of Ravens. But I promise you won't like it."

She didn't turn or look down like she wanted to. He was trying to scare her. He wanted to get rid of her, but she wouldn't let him. She tilted her head up and took a step toward him, close enough to see tiny flecks of gold in his deep brown eyes. "I want to learn."

He rubbed his forehead, letting out a low laugh.

"I give up. I tried—and don't you dare tell Danni anything different. She doesn't want you to end up dead."

"So, you will teach me?" Azalea's chest tightened.

"If you want to learn, I can teach you. Only because I know you'll go off and try to learn it yourself and get killed again. But don't say I didn't warn you. It won't be easy, like your training is here."

Easy? Her training was the hardest thing she had ever done in her life. She nodded furiously, worried he would change his mind. "Yes. I swear I'm ready. I want to do it and I won't let you down."

"But if I ever catch you going through my things or give me any reason to distrust you, this is over. I can't work with you if we don't have trust."

"I could say the same to you," she said.

"One day," he turned back to his desk, "—one day I'll tell you. I'm not ready for you to hate me just yet."

His face was expressionless, but she recognized the deep sadness. Whatever it was, she was sure she wouldn't hate him. In fact, she was starting to like him.

"Maybe it's best if Danni and Maiken don't know about this, though," Azalea said, biting her lip, not sure if he'd go for that. "I don't want them to tell my uncle."

He nodded. "I'm sure most families from the House of Bees would not be pleased to know their daughter was studying Shadow Magic. I don't want them lecturing me, either. But I don't like secrets and if they ask, I'll tell them."

"Thank you. I know none of this is what you wanted, but thanks," she said.

"Despite what you might think, I *do* want to help. I want you to be safe." He sighed. "Unfortunately, this is looking like the best option. At least if I'm supervising you, you shouldn't kill yourself again."

"I promise I'll make it up to you one day." She meant it.

Torin patted Faraday and noticed the large puddle inching closer to the rug.

"I'll get you a towel. You're soaking," he said as if angry at himself for leaving a wet guest in the doorway. She didn't blame him in the slightest. In fact, she was surprised he hadn't said no and kicked her out.

Azalea waited in the doorway as involuntary shivers coursed through her. She was drained from all the candle lighting she'd just done in class, and her feet were frozen in her boots. Her normal state seemed to be disheveled and exhausted these days. Torin came back with a towel and went off again. She took the towel gladly and dried her hair while standing next to the fire. Torin returned with tea and fruitcake.

Azalea accepted the tea and sat by the fire on the rug. Faraday curled up on her lap as Torin poured himself a whiskey, already looking like he regretted agreeing to teach her.

Azalea hadn't realized she had been watching him.

"You don't think this is an acceptable reason to drink? You've caused me more stress in the last month than anyone else in the past two years, and that's saying something."

"Can I have one?" she asked.

"No. You will be content with tea."

She picked up a bit of fruitcake and nibbled it. They were finally getting somewhere.

CHAPTER 30

The next night after class, Azalea sprinted up the steps to Torin's office as Faraday leaped behind her over puddles. *Shit, she was two minutes late.* That was about as bad as being an hour late with Torin, and it was the first day of her real training.

Azalea knocked and slunk into his office, once more dripping onto his doorstep. She still hadn't found her lost umbrella.

"I'm so sorry I'm late!" she yelled up at him.

He appeared on the stairs, pressing his index finger into the palm of his other hand, something she noticed he did when he was anxious. "It's fine. Have you eaten?"

She shook her head, hoping he had some food.

"Good, you'll probably throw up anyway. Did you bring the elemer?"

Was that a Torin joke? Or was she going to throw up from this? "Yup, got it here." She patted the side of her backpack and set it on the chair. Her nerves were rising. She hadn't used that elemer since *that* night. She'd only been using her training elemer, but Torin had insisted they start with the real deal today, and she wasn't about to argue.

"Now, you're sure about this?" Torin asked as he came down the stairs. "I'm not going to go easy on you."

She swallowed. "I'm sure." *Or maybe not*, her brain answered back.

"Very well. In Echo Magic training, you're learning gradual resistance by slowly adding to the amount of magic you can handle. Shadow Magic is the opposite. Training works by shocks to the body. You channel powerful streams of magic right to the edge of burnout, forcing your body to take large jumps in both recovery and resistance. You understand this?"

All or nothing—it was more her style. Her fingers and toes buzzed with anticipation. She remembered how horrible she felt after her last burnout. She certainly didn't want a repeat of that. She had died. It couldn't get worse than that, right?

"I understand. Let's get on with it."

"I'm here to supervise. But you need to recognize your own burnout. You need to pay attention to the magic and your body's response to it. You have to know when the magic is about to take over. It feels like you're at a point where every cell in your body is vibrating and about to break apart. At that point, cut your connection with the Shadow Dimension," he said.

Bloody hell, she was going to do this, willingly go so close to burnout. She remembered that feeling way too clearly, like the magic was about to erupt in her body. She'd gone well beyond that point when she brought her father back. No way she'd do that again.

"I saw you produced a cloak of shadows that morning at St. Dunstan in The East. Since you already know it, we'll use that. Follow me."

He went up the stairs, and she hesitated at the bottom, as-suming they would stay in the office as usual. She'd never been upstairs before, and it seemed overly personal to be going up there . . . Torin was such a private person.

But hey, when in Rome. She followed Torin up to a large, circular room that she was instantly jealous of. Bright antique carpets spread across the floor, mostly in shades of red touched with blues and gold. Tapestries from all over the world draped the stone walls, giving the stone room a cozy, inviting feel. Rain trickled down the pane glass windows as she glanced at the sitting area. It felt like seeing a secret part of Torin's soul. She'd imagined he would be more into minimalistic furniture and was surprised at the old deep-red couch and two mismatched red and green gingham armchairs by the fire.

She followed him to the kitchen. She suspected he may have redecorated in here since moving in, it was much nicer than her flat—regardless of the adjustments that Van had made. Black stone benches followed the arc of the wall in a pleasant half-moon curve and on them sat a line of shiny and perfectly matched appliances.

Torin pushed two dining chairs and a square wooden table to the side, leaving a large open space. *What would they be doing that needed this much space?* He rolled another rug off to the side.

Torin said nothing as he poured out a large salt circle and Azalea's palms began to sweat. Messing up his nice floor like that . . . this had to be serious. He was a clean freak, usually. Though she had seen his office in shambles twice now. He seemed to survive in two states: either extreme organization or complete and utter chaos.

"Get in the circle," he ordered as he set two chairs inside it, facing each other. Faraday followed her in and tucked himself under Torin's chair. Azalea did as she was told, and he held out a small box. Inside it a single red stone sat on a black velvet base. Its facets caught her eye with a flash of light and dragged her into its deep red heart.

"This is a five-carat, pigeon blood, Mogok ruby," he said, clearly not as dazzled by it as she was.

"It's so perfect," Azalea breathed.

"No, not quite perfect. And that is *precisely* why we need it. Gemstones have power, but the inclusions within a gemstone can alter the effect of a stone. I've borrowed it for our lesson."

"Is this from the Crown Jewels?" Azalea asked with a grin. She had seen Mage Frost, Livia and Elam's mum, who was in charge of the Crown Jewels, and didn't take her as the sort of person who would help Torin borrow one or two priceless gemstones for a student.

"That's not important." A flash of guilt crossed his face, and her respect for him instantly went up.

"As I was saying, inclusions are the secrets within a stone. If you know them, you have their power. Rubies can enhance strength and stamina, but this ruby contains negative crystal inclusions. Negative crystals give the user of the stone the power to store their own magic within and draw on it."

"Like I can save magic for later?"

"Yes. But in this case, it's more to drain it out to make room to channel more."

"Oh, okay." She bit her lip. So, draining her magic sounded fun . . .

"All you have to do is summon a cloak of shadows that will be contained in this circle. But I want you to direct all the power into the stone. Got it?" He looked calm, but he was pressing his finger into his palm again. He stopped as he realized she was watching him.

"Okay, I can do this." And she would do just that, bloody well do it or die trying. Though she trusted Torin not to let her die. *Don't make a dick of yourself Azalea,* she told herself.

She took extra time meditating.

Once her breathing slowed to a steady rate, she formed the familiar snake spell cloud in her mind. This was the one spell she was confident in doing, and she was lucky Torin had picked it. She pulled in the power symbols, then opened her eyes.

Gripping the elemer, she cut into the Shadow Dimension and inhaled as the key drew the power through her. She faced the dagger blade to the ruby, and she felt it coming as a thrill rushed through her. Magic poured out of her and into the stone, filling the circle with misty shadows. Azalea let out an involuntary shudder as the magic coursed through her. The flow became stronger, like a valve that could only let so much through before it would give.

The rush of magic began to feel uncomfortable. Okay, it was getting a little freaky. *How much time had even passed?* It felt like elephants were sitting on her shoulders, weighing her down and pushing her into the chair. Her veins shook like they might burst, and she imagined the purple magic rushing through them, pushing on every cell wall in her body, testing her.

The salt circle filled with a swirling vortex of shadows, growing denser and spinning round and round with nowhere else to go.

She had to keep going. It had been much easier when she tried to bring her dad back. There was no way she would have stopped. This was hard. She could just make out Torin's form through the shadows. She kept her eyes focused on the elemer, and the ruby, and the spell cloud in her mind. She didn't dare look around.

"Don't stop, Azalea," Torin's voice echoed around her.

Gasps of breath kept Azalea going. Bloody hell, this was hard. Minutes felt like hours. Okay, it had to be time to end this soon. Torin wouldn't let her go too far, would he? Or was that his plan? Black dots crept to the edge of her vision.

Blinking, she tried to focus on the ruby. Then she felt it. Her body humming from within. Her cells shaking apart with fiery purple magic, waiting to explode. She took it right to the edge, then cut the connection.

The shadows disappeared, and she slid off the chair but didn't hit the ground. Instead, she felt herself being lowered onto it. The room was spinning. *Thank you, floor, for being so nice and solid.* She heard Torin chuckle, realizing she had said it out loud.

He helped her sit up and stabilized her with scratchy cushions. A bucket appeared next to her as the room lurched. She grabbed the bucket and vomited up her stomach. Torin handed her a cool, wet flannel, and she pressed it into her face in relief.

"You did well for a first go. Much longer than I pegged you for. In the House of Ravens, everyone takes bets on the newbies. You would've lost a few people some money."

"I hurt," was all she managed to say.

"Can't say I feel sorry for you, or that I didn't warn you. And hey, you didn't die, so that's better than your first go."

Haha. How could he joke when everything inside her hurt? Giving him the finger would be an appropriate gesture, but she preferred to stay on his good side. At least someone was enjoying this.

"It seems you have a bit more Shadow Magic in your family than I thought. I'm surprised it didn't show up in your bloodline test."

Maiken must have left out the part about her being House of Snakes. No doubt he'd work it out soon enough. At least for now, the fewer people who knew, the better. She shuffled on her cushion and pulled down her sleeve. Even if Torin was estranged from the House of Ravens, she didn't know him that well.

He helped her up to the sofa once she could stand. "You can have a whiskey this time. It'll help," Torin said, pushing a drink into her hand.

Yes! Alcohol sounded like a great idea. Hopefully it would numb the memory of this experience. She moved the glass to her lips and let the burning liquid slide down her throat. Oh, that was nice. Not the nasty taste of whiskey, but the fizzing in her cells subsiding, like they were silenced by the alcohol.

"Now *that* is real magic," she said.

Torin shook his head. "Alcohol dulls magic. Usually, it's not a good thing."

Duh, she'd learned that the first day. She held her tongue and congratulated herself for it as she sank into the sofa. The cozy fire and soft cushions could have her out in an instant, but Torin probably didn't want her staying overnight, plus Evangeline would notice her missing in the morning—they had training at

6am. The thought of walking past all the spirits made her stomach turn all over again, but she had to get over it, to toughen the fuck up if she was going to be a mage. She bet her dad and Fabian weren't as scared of them as she was.

The whiskey warmed new life into her limbs, and she shook them out before attempting to stand up. She stumbled toward the fire, but Torin grabbed her in time.

"Whoopsie daisy," she said to herself, channeling her mum's voice. "I'm fine. Faraday will watch me." She made her way downstairs.

"You did well, Azalea," Torin said as she was about to leave. "But this is just the beginning. Tomorrow night after class, I'll need you be to be back here again." He handed her an umbrella.

Wait, what? Surely, he didn't mean to do this every night. The door closed behind her. It was only drizzling. Whoops, she'd forgotten to thank him for the umbrella, just realizing she was holding it. She kneeled, and Faraday jumped on her shoulder. Of course, she couldn't let his precious feet get wet.

The clock bells chimed midnight as she dashed past the chapel. Ghostly voices echoed around. Then they started yelling. Without looking around she kept her head down as she continued running.

A woman stepped into her path, and Azalea couldn't dodge her. Skidding on the slippery stone, Azalea landed hard on her hip, and Faraday bailed out.

The ghost woman leaned over Azalea, voluminous dress swishing around her. The top was elaborately decorated and cut to fit her perfectly. The letter 'B' dangled from her neck close to Azalea's face. Her eyes drilled straight into Azalea's soul. "You see us, don't you, girl?"

She couldn't pretend not to see her. The woman was terrifying and right in her face. Refusing to answer, Azalea slid back across the stones and jumped up. Running away was sometimes the best—and only—option. Faraday was in front of her like a guard dog and Azalea took off. This time, the spirit followed. *What the hell, lady!* Her heart thumped against her ribcage as she ran. The woman was slow in her bulky gown but called out as Azalea made it to the front door.

"On the morrow, we shall speak! Seek me out, girl. I must have words." The voice followed her into the night.

Relief washed over her as she slammed the door shut behind her. Adding extra salt to the door and windows seemed like a good idea. After that, she went straight to her bedroom, turned on every light, and jumped into bed fully clothed. *Just wonderful.* She was being stalked by a crazy ghost lady. She lay in bed, staring at the ceiling, unable to get the woman's determined face out of her mind.

CHAPTER 31

FIVE DAYS INTO TRAINING with Torin, and Azalea slumped onto the floor in his living room. *No*, she would not cry this time. After the same exercise every day, she was ready for a meltdown. She should be better at this by now, surely.

Sleep was eluding her, and the training was pushing her to breaking point. Her arms and legs were made of lead, her head was pounding, even her skin hurt. She draped herself across the bucket, not caring what was in it. She clung to it as if it were the only thing she could rely on in the world.

"Are you alright?" Torin asked.

Why was he being nice now, after an entire week of being an arsehole who apparently liked to see her in pain? It was too much to deal with. She collapsed into a sorry heap on the floor and let out a sob that broke the flood banks.

Hot tears streaked down her face, and she couldn't hold them back. *So embarrassing*. But everything since the Autumn equinox had crushed down on her with the weight of the universe. She'd never find her dad. She sucked at Shadow Magic. She hated waking up early, spirits were stalking her, and it was raining again. She was so pathetic, and she couldn't stop herself from crying.

Torin did nothing to comfort her. She didn't expect he would. He simply waited for her to stop, and she cried until there was nothing left. Now all she wanted was to sink into a pit of quicksand and disappear.

Torin pulled her bucket away. *No!* It was pathetic that her comfort was a bucket of puke. He hoisted her up, and she stood there, feeling utterly foolish. Unsure where to put her hands, she rubbed her face and refused to look at him.

Torin guided her to the chair by the fire—his chair—and sat her down. He placed a cup of tea in front of her and said, "Drink, it will help."

She sipped the tea through trembling lips. It was chamomile with passionflower and valerian root. She recognized the ingredients from a similar tea her mum made. Faraday jumped on her lap, and she began to feel silly about the whole thing.

"I'm sorry," she said. "It's all a bit much." She looked down at her hands and the plain white teacup.

"I'm surprised you've lasted this long," he said. "Most people have their melt down on day three or four. Five is pretty good. One boy in my training died on day six, so don't feel too bad."

Was he serious about the dying part? She didn't want to know. "How long did you last?"

"Day eight was it for me. Worst day of my life—well, no, that's not true. But it was pretty horrible. I cried in front of the girl I had a crush on. I couldn't look her in the eye after that."

Azalea smiled, appreciative of his attempts to cheer her up. *He shared something personal.*

"What was your training like?" she asked. She must have looked terrible, or he was feeling sorry for her, because he answered.

He poured a bit of whiskey in a glass and leaned back in the chair. "The House of Ravens start their training at age ten. The idea is to build up resistance rapidly before the magic comes through fully. It either works incredibly well, or you die," he said bluntly.

That explained why he was an advanced mage for being so young. He must have taken the mage tests at her age. "Sounds like they're training child soldiers."

"Oh, they are," he said with bitterness.

It was clear he didn't want to talk about it, but a sharing mood for him was rare. She might as well use his temporary pity for her. "So, what's your job for the House of Owls then? You might as well tell me, because I'm always here while you're working, so I'll find out eventually. Maybe I can help you?" she asked. She owed him big time now. Despite the torturous training, he was taking a lot of his own time to do it and if she could find a way to help him, she would.

He rubbed his temples. "I'm here to curate a collection, that's all."

"Come on." He was way too secretive for it to be a boring collection. "I know you're doing something related to collecting artifacts. How interesting could that possibly be?"

"They aren't just any artifacts. They're important." He eyed her suspiciously. "And it's classified. You shouldn't know about it."

Classified, aye? That was more like it. "So, these artifacts are magic?"

"Why are you so nosy?"

She shrugged. "I like knowing things. And I mean it, I want to help." She did mean it, and in her mind she was picturing a magical treasure hunt, which was something she certainly wanted to be part of.

"I'm collecting artifacts for the House of Owls. It's no more exciting than that. No more questions."

"Okay. I'm going to help you get them. I need to pay you back for teaching me. So just tell me how I can help."

"You don't give up, do you? I don't need help, but I shall tell you if I ever do."

"Nope, I don't, and that's all I ask." She smiled and sipped her tea. Things were already looking up. That was some excellent tea. She pushed her luck one step further. "Can I sleep here, please? On the sofa obviously. I don't have training or classes tomorrow, so no one will notice." She didn't want to leave the fire, but more importantly, she didn't want to walk past the chapel. She hated that Torin lived behind it and that spirit lady was always there now.

"You live two minutes' walk away. Why are you always so reluctant to leave? I'm sure it's not my charming company."

She hesitated. In fact, she did enjoy his company, well, some of the time anyway, but she wasn't about to tell him that. Telling him the truth was embarrassing. She didn't want to sound like a child, but she said it anyway. "It's the spirits . . . The chapel creeps me out and I'm scared of the dark and hate walking past it at night," she said all at once, half expecting Torin to laugh in her face.

"More than 1,700 bodies were buried around this area. There is a mass grave under the chapel," he stated factually. "But the dark is nothing to fear Azalea. Spirits won't hurt you."

That was not the best way to reassure her fears. Sometimes being lied to was a nicer option. "I know, but there are too many of them. They keep harassing me, trying to talk to me. Sometimes they follow me, and I'm scared they'll get into my flat one day."

Torin's jaw slackened. He pushed his finger into his palm. "What? You can see the spirits. They talk to you?"

"Yes, and they're bloody annoying and super creepy. One woman in particular—"

His look shifted, as if studying her or reading her mind. She hoped he couldn't do that. "Not many people can see spirits, Azalea."

Her blood chilled. Should she not have told him? She cursed her lack of judgment. Oh well, she couldn't take it back now. "I know, but I've always been able to. Sometimes in the day I think they're real people. It makes me look like a nutcase."

"Learning Shadow Magic will increase your affinity for spirits. I never thought to mention it. If you want, I can teach you how to block them. But you're too weak for that now. How about I walk you back?" He stood up.

There was a way to block them? Hallelujah! Maybe that could help with controlling her dad's spirit when she found him. She didn't have the energy to find out what it involved now, but it was a relief just knowing. In the meantime, him walking her home felt silly, but was a good solution. When she was with other people, the spirits often stayed back.

They went downstairs and stepped into the night. Having Torin next to her was oddly comforting, she couldn't face them alone this time.

It was drizzling outside. Even the weather was against her. Torin held his enormous umbrella high above their heads. The man seemed to be made of umbrellas. She must remember to give his other ones back. Holding her breath, they passed the chapel. The familiar chill caught her as she tried to make out the shapes in the shadows. She couldn't help but search for her dad's face every time.

They must have spotted her, clearly they remembered her now because they started pouring out of the church. "My child, have you seen the Bishop? He's late again," an elderly priest called to her. They continued walking. More and more moved in, lining the pathway. *Shit*. There were *way* more than yesterday.

The woman, who she now referred to as "B", appeared at her side. "Ho there! You girl, come hither. Hast thou seen George? Pray fetch him for me at once."

What made them think she could be ordered around like this? They were the dead ones. Shouldn't they be doing her bidding or something?

Azalea turned her head and had a moment of bravery with Torin at her side. "I'm sorry, I don't know George. I told you that yesterday and the day before." She realized she probably sounded like a nutcase.

B put a hand to her heart and stepped back, offended. "Thou art so bold of speech for one so young and ill dressed." She looked Azalea up and down, as she had done several times in past meetings. "Stop dallying. My brother George is known by all."

"He isn't known by all. I don't know him." This spirit was nuts. It was clear she one hundred percent expected Azalea to find George for her. Best not to engage further. Azalea tried to walk faster as Torin slowed.

"They're here? How many are there?"

"I'm not talking to myself, I swear. I dunno, maybe thirty?" She stiffened. "Why can't you see them?"

"It's not a natural gift for me. I can feel their presence, but I'd have to work quite hard to see them," he said, squinting his eyes as if it would help. He was far too excited about this.

"Can we please go? More are coming." She nodded toward the chapel. "I get sick when too many come at once and I've had quite enough of that for one night."

"Sorry. Let's get a move on then." He was smart enough to note the urgency.

He walked her all the way to her front door, asking the entire time if they were being followed. B had followed them right up Mint Street yelling, "Fie on thee!"

At least Torin was taking her seriously. She hadn't expected him to. She was used to being ignored or scoffed at when she mentioned spirits. Especially from her mum, who had banned her from talking to spirits when she was five and brought her 'friends', Alice and Belle home to play. She hadn't known they were ghosts at the time, and they had been harmless when she was a child. Growing up had changed something.

Unlocking the door, she stepped into the entrance. Torin hovered in the doorway. "You sure you're alright?" he asked.

"Yeah, thanks. Sleep will do me good. Thanks for protecting me from the ghosts," she said jokingly, but meant it.

"You should have told me sooner. We can fix it, you know. But that's for another day. Have a good sleep."

Once he left, Azalea stumbled into the living room and flopped onto the couch. A door slammed, making her jump. Evangeline appeared in the kitchen.

"Bloody hell, you scared me," Azalea said. "I thought you were working at the hospital tonight."

"Sorry, hun, didn't mean to scare you. I swapped a shift," Van said as she made a pot of tea. "So, who was that at the door? Hot date tonight huh? He could have stayed, you know, I don't mind."

Azalea scrunched up her nose. "No! God no. That was just Torin. He's been tutoring me after classes."

"You mean Mage Torin Dumont?" Evangeline twisted around to stare at Azalea. "A bit late to be studying, isn't it, and you do realize it's Saturday night?" she said suggestively.

Azalea groaned. "I honestly have no idea what day it is." Her brain had gone to mush. The last thing she could think about was doing fun stuff on a Saturday night.

"I've never seen Mage Dumont talk to another human, let alone spend time with anyone, Azalea." she raised her eyebrows. "What's he like?"

"He's fine, not like all the rumors. He's just a normal person. But not really a people person, he's barely tolerating me," Azalea said with a smile. Though tonight he had certainly shown a kinder side.

"And you're studying with him?"

Azalea nodded. "He knows a lot about history, and artifacts and stuff."

Evangeline brought over the pot of tea and a plate of chocolate digestives and mystery muffins and sat across from Azalea. "Hmm, studying artifacts on a Saturday night sounds . . . fun?"

Azalea selected a digestive. "You're as bad as Millie and Livia," Azalea said, forcing herself not to blush. "He knows all about magic and history, he's been helping me a lot." Dating anyone right now was the last thing on her mind. She hadn't gone out with anyone, let alone slept with anyone, since before her magic went out of control. That was well over a year ago.

"Interesting. Well, I'm glad for you," Evangeline said. "Drink the tea. It'll help you sleep. I've been watching you all week. I know something isn't right."

"I'm fine, just tired," Azalea said, trying to sound as normal as possible. Van was so nice. She didn't want to lie to her. She considered telling her about the Shadow Magic and everything, but it was too much for now. Perhaps another day. She suspected she knew anyway but was too polite to ask.

They drank the tea, and Van hustled her off to bed, not letting her sleep on the couch like she so desperately wanted to. She planned to sleep in the next day. A luxury after a week of sleep deprivation and torture. Her bed felt like heaven.

CHAPTER 32

T ORIN STEPPED OUT OF the gym to find his path blocked by a petite woman with a bob of snow-white hair.

Archmage Norwich. Just what he needed.

"Mage Dumont," she nodded to him. "How is your search coming along?"

She knew very well how it was coming along. He had submitted a detailed report the previous day.

"I have good intel on the Crane Relic. I plan to target it next."

"I thought you would be further along by now." Her eyes drilled into him. Searching. He strengthened his mental shields and brought select images to the forefront of his thoughts, the three jade relics he already had: the Fox, the Phoenix, and the Owl. He imagined the Crane in the private collection he tracked it to. Hopefully, enough to satisfy her questions of his dedication and make her think he was easy to read. She didn't know he took a memory blocking potion every morning.

A hint of a smile twitched at the corner of her thin line of a mouth. "Very well. I expect it before the year is through."

"Yes, of course, Archmage." He bobbed his head, and she left without another word.

Though she carried a cane, she walked with a perfectly straight back. He suspected it was for hitting people with, rather than for any assistance in walking. She was a bitch of a woman, and one he would rather not cross.

Walking back to his tower, he mulled over his plans. He couldn't go any faster. There was too much research to do. He opened the door and set his bag down, then glanced at his desk as he took off his jacket. It was a right mess. Scattered scrolls covered numerous surfaces and stacks of books grew out of the table, all courtesy of the British Museum, though of course they didn't know it.

The astrolabe alarm started spinning on his shelf. *The artifacts gallery.* No one else would know something had triggered it. He considered telling the Phoenix guards, but it would be best to check it out himself before causing a fuss.

Throwing on his jacket, he sped to the Fusilier Museum next to the hospital. He walked through the main museum without a glance from anyone, then swiped his elemer to go underground.

There was nothing overly valuable down there, not like the Crown Jewels collection. These were important archaeological finds that might not appear impressive, but their history was.

He tested the door. *Still locked.* Unlocking it, he flicked on the lights and went straight to the end of the cellar-like room.

The wooden case nestled in the stone archway was the same as every other in the room. Through the spelled glass, he counted three jade relics right where he left them. He tested the security wards on the case. They were still intact, and so they should be. There were about ten layers of protection on this exhibit.

He turned to leave, relieved he wouldn't have to explain anything to the Archmage.

"Thought you might show us the way," a woman said. A mask of lacy shadows in the shape of a skull hid her face. The shadow mask was a trademark of the House of Ravens, though he didn't recognize her. She was younger than him, a recruit after his time. The intricate black lines moved with her. Another woman, her mask a cat's face, stepped out from behind her and blocked Torin's exit.

The woman with the skull mask lunged at him. He missed the tip of her blade as his reflexes kicked in. Not an elemer, a distinctive bronze dagger, one that was known for being laced with poison.

She pounced again, driving him back and away from the cabinet. He held his ground as he dodged the knife. All it would take was a scratch. He sidestepped her and ducked.

Her fighting style was unmistakable, calculated tactics with deadly speed. So very Raven, the same as his training. He kept an eye on Cat Mask as the blood pounded in his ears. She would get a nasty surprise if she tried to get into the case.

"You won't get the relics. Do you even know what they are?" he yelled. They needed to stay here, they needed to stay safe. If anyone, especially the House of Ravens, got their hands on them it would be a worldwide disaster.

"Course we know. They'll be much safer with us," she hissed.

Torin laughed. "You're brain washed fools. My father is the last person who should have them." He fell back to the stone wall. If his father got hold of the relics, no one would be safe. At least if the Owls had them, they would protect them because it would only hurt them to open the Gateway to the Echo Dimension. Cat Mask filled the room with shadows in an instant. Torin's eyes adjusted, but not enough to account for the thick shadow mist. He lost sight of her and threw a shadow net toward Skull Mask, hoping to restrain her while he got back to the cabinet.

She burst from the darkness, her blade slicing toward him. Dodging it by a hair's breadth, he caught her and flipped her with her own weight. Her hip smashed on a bench's corner, and she hissed in pain, a lucky shot from him. But she was on her feet in seconds.

Twisting away, he sprinted toward the cabinet then swept Cat Mask's legs out from under her. She crashed to the floor, gasping for breath.

"You're on the wrong side, Dumont. The Owls are no better than anyone else," Skull Mask said as she prowled behind him.

"That's absurd." He tracked the direction of her voice. If the Owls opened the Gateway, all the Echo Magic would flood the world. It would be so strong that anyone who tried to use it would find burnout very rapidly. He maneuvered behind a row of cases. Destroying the room was the last thing he wanted.

"The Gate to the Echo Dimension will open no matter what. But whoever opens it has the control and I plan on being on the winning side," Skull mask yelled.

"Nice try." He twisted to block her attack as she came from the opposite direction of her voice. She darted away quicker than he expected. Cat Mask was up and blasting spells at the case. Each threw her back violently and built force each time. She'd be sorry if she kept doing that.

"What's taking so long?" Skull Mask yelled at her.

"Too many wards," Cat Mask yelled back.

Smoke from the explosions clouded the room. Torin's lungs screamed for air as he crouched low, trying to breathe and keep an eye on both women.

He let Skull Mask lead him to the other side of the room, as a sharp pain spread through his arm. Blood trickled down his hand. Shit. Somehow, she had nicked him. He had to get out of here. An explosion catapulted Cat Mask hard into the ceiling, cabinets shattered in all directions. It smashed Torin into solid stone and a sickening crack sounded in his leg.

Pain shot through him, but he didn't quite register it.

That explosion was loud enough for the whole Tower to hear. Backup would be there soon. Skull Mask grabbed her partner and darted out the door. *They must be working with someone on the inside.*

Torin pulled himself up, only to feel a horrible pain shoot up his leg as it collapsed underneath him. He dragged himself across the floor to the cabinet and pulled himself up. Brushing off plaster dust from his hair, he let out a breath. All three relics were still there. *They'd taken the decoys.* He slumped onto the floor and rolled up his sleeve. It was just a scratch, but a deadly one.

Phoenix guards and Yeoman Warders ran towards him. He hadn't failed. The relics were safe . . . though the room was a mess.

"They ran out that way," Torin yelled to the nearest Phoenix guard.

The poison was seeping into his blood. Fortunately for him the Hospital was nearby. Though experiences with poisoned blades reminded him that he was in for a world of pain and

weakened magic—not to mention his leg was probably broken.
Just his luck.

CHAPTER 33

AZALEA DODGED TOURISTS AS she left the Hospital building and fast walked toward the Barracks to go down to the Complex. People always looked funny at her if she ran in the Tower grounds. Perhaps it wasn't good tourist etiquette.

She had visited Torin in the Hospital. According to him, he broke his leg valiantly defending a Tower of London exhibit, but he failed to mention what it was or who was trying to steal it. Azalea had no luck digging information from him, and the more he didn't tell her, the more she wanted to find out. At least she had a temporary reprieve from Shadow Magic death training. Unfortunately, he hadn't taught her any spirit warding yet. She dodged a man in a bowler cap, unsure if he was a ghost or just a weird tourist. Her paranoia about spirits had her dodging people left and right these days, it was best to avoid them all.

For several weeks she'd been back in her old routine and was feeling better than ever. She didn't mind that it had been raining consistently and she had managed to catch up on most of her lectures and assignments for uni, plus put in a few extra hours of data entry to cover the bills.

She made her way down the stairs of the Barracks. The dueling tournament today wasn't even near the top of the list in her mind. Nerves tightened her chest at the thought of starting training with Torin again. He'd been in hospital three weeks. It seemed the poisoning he'd somehow received, in addition to his broken leg, was worse than he had initially let on. She wasn't stupid. She just hoped he would be okay.

She'd taken to visiting him after class to see how he was doing. One thing that was for sure was he did not like being in hospital. Before all that, his training had been working, but she'd lose all that conditioning if she waited too much longer to get back to it. It would be like starting all over again, and she shuddered at the thought. Even her Echo Magic had improved.

She hurried down the corridor and crashed through the doorway to find herself the last to arrive in class.

"Are we all ready?" Mage Shepard asked.

Azalea glanced at the rolled-up rugs and salt circle that took up the width of their spacious classroom. She'd been looking forward to the lesson on dueling, but now found herself preoccupied.

She watched as her classmates battled each other using basic elements from the buckets of water, sand, earth, and a brazier of fire that sat within the circle. The air was soon thick with the smell of singed clothes and wet earth.

When it was Azalea's turn, she beat Livia within minutes by forming two spell clouds at once, one with Echo Magic, one with Shadow Magic. She pelted Livia with balls of water laced with icy Shadow Magic. It was enough to drive her from the circle. Livia just stood there, eyes wide with shock, and her clothes saturated through. Azalea felt a tiny bit guilty for cheating using Shadow Magic, but it was worth it to win. Showing up Livia might be the highlight of her day.

She held out a hand, but Livia slapped it away. "You didn't have to make me look like such a fool," Livia hissed.

Bitch. Last time she tried to be a good sportsman. "You did that yourself." Azalea said, retracting her apologetic thoughts.

"Now, now girls, this is a place for learning. Shake hands." Azalea held out a hand stiffly and shook.

Erik beat Elam with a spectacular firestorm that had Elam out of the ring in seconds. Ambrose beat both Millie and Livia (who had requested a second chance match). Livia sat next to Azalea, fuming, even more pissed off now than she'd been after her match with Azalea. "The tosser used an illegal memory diversion," Livia whispered.

Azalea gritted her teeth. She had to win against Erik so she could go against Ambrose in the final match. It was about time he was put in his place.

Her match with Erik was close. She doused herself in water right from the start and extinguished the brazier before he had a chance to draw from it. But he was quick and soon had clumps of flaming dirt whizzing around Azalea, pelting her from every angle so she couldn't see. The air became unbearably hot. She squeezed her eyes to avoid the racing fireballs.

Pulling as much water as she could from the buckets, she pushed it high above their heads, panting from the weight of the water. She imagined a rain cloud, and it formed above them silently. A second later, she released it in a violent burst across the circle, dousing them and the fire. Erik just stood there, dumbfounded. She was winning! Azalea summoned balls of sand and started pelting Erik. Sand in the eyes was no joke. He crouched down and rolled out of the circle without even knowing it.

A cheer rang out from her classmate as Erik continued rolling around.

Azalea crouched down next to him. Had she gone too far? She'd thought the irrational behavior from her healing was gone, or perhaps this was her being overzealous. "Are you okay?" she asked cautiously. Just because they were outside the circle didn't guarantee he wouldn't set fire to her.

Mage Shepard was ready with a bottle of eye rinse solution. Through red teary eyes, he looked up and smiled, then reached out his hand.

Azalea let out a deliberately quiet exhale. That was unexpected. She accepted his handshake. "Good match," she said.

"It was . . . other than the near blinding, I mean, but you seem to have a thing for my eyes."

"You wish." She laughed.

He shrugged and rinsed his eyes once more. He leaned in close. "Be careful of Ambrose. Something isn't right with him," he whispered, meeting her eye with his watery red gaze. He was dead serious.

"After Azalea and Ambrose have a quick rest, we will have the last match of the day." Their teacher looked between both opponents. "No funny business." Her gaze carried a strong warning.

Azalea was wary of Ambrose. She hoped her mental shields would be strong enough against whatever mind magic he would throw at her. Ambrose could do any number of things to confuse her; plant false images, read her thoughts, increase her fear for no reason.

She sat alone and downed a few blood supplement pills with her water—it couldn't hurt. She was already feeling the draining effects of the day. The others looked far worse. They hadn't been forced to exert their power like she had with Torin. It was proof that his training was working.

It was time. She stepped into the salt circle and shook Ambrose's hand. His grip crushed her fragile bones together. *Totally unnecessary.*

"You're going down, bitch. The House of Ravens have let you live this long, but it all ends here," he hissed under his breath, too quiet for anyone else to hear.

She held his stare as cold fear washed over her. If he was serious, then she was in real danger. But Mage Shepard was there. She wouldn't allow anything bad to happen, right?

"No need for such language," Azalea said, feigning confidence, knowing it would rile him up more than an insult, hopefully start him out off-kilter. The whistle blew and Azalea sliced with her elemer, flicked it 180, and pulled the water to her as Ambrose did the same with the fire. She kept pulling the magic, keeping the Echo Dimension cut open to a steady stream.

She pointed her elemer at the stone pavers under his feet. Calling the water from the damp swampy ground that lay beneath, she formed a spell cloud, telling it to sink. Ambrose lurched forward, then dropped half a meter. Ground water and earthy sludge flowed into the temporary pool. His feet suctioned into the anoxic stench of mud.

"Sneaky bitch!" he yelled as his fire went out. But he was already scrambling up the sides.

Azalea didn't have a plan past this point. *Oh shit.* Her mind was blank. Ambrose's nostrils flared and blind rage twisted his features into something monstrous. He wanted to kill her for real. If she left the circle, chances are Mage Shepard wouldn't believe her. Her only option was to fight.

She threw wet sand balls at him, but they never made contact. He thrust every one straight back like his elemer was a tennis racket. Azalea spun around as they smashed onto the back of her head and shoulders. Arm shielding her head, she glanced to the side. Erik watched intently.

Ambrose clambered out of the pit and lunged. Catching her footing just in time, she remained in the circle. She spun around, but realized, too late, that Ambrose was on the wrong side of her.

He knocked her to the ground and straddled her waist. Was this how she was going to die? Before she even found her dad? She didn't want to be a spirit.

The crushing pressure had her drawing sharp breaths and her shoulder drove hard into the stone. She nearly stabbed him with her elemer blade in reaction. Instead, at the last second, she flicked the knife blade in and shoved the blunt end into his stomach with every ounce of force she had. He doubled over. Kicking him hard in the guts, she rolled to the side.

She clicked out the elemer blade and called up all the sand and mud to surround her in a thick tornado while she caught her breath. What the hell was he playing at? This wasn't training. It was very real. Why hadn't Mage Shepard stepped in? The outside of the circle was hazy, like he was blocking them out somehow.

Through shaky breaths, she tried to think what to do next. She could feel him probing at her mind like a battering ram. She struggled to hold him off.

She couldn't keep hiding. Taking a deep breath, she braced and pushed the sand tornado out until it blasted over Ambrose and spread to the edges of the salt circle, encapsulating them, and blocking everything on the outside. Much worse, welts began to bloom across Ambrose's face from being sand blasted. It had stopped his assault on her mind, but no one outside could see them, and her tornado was out of her control.

Ambrose appeared right in front of her, a ball of fire in his hand and a malicious look in his eye. He wasn't playing around.

Cold sweat washed over her. The House of Ravens must be paying him bloody well to do all this. His hand cranked back and thrust the fire towards her. Without even thinking about Shadow Magic, a shadow appeared in front of her. It must have thrown Ambrose off because he growled and cursed from the other side. She had made a shadow wall—*nice*. She slid around the side of the shadow and attacked Ambrose from behind.

He spun around and lunged with his elemer directed at Azalea's chest. She knew it was over. She was too slow, and he was already on her. The wind knocked out of her as her head hit the floor.

It was hard to breathe. She squeezed her eyes shut as the roar of the tornado dissipated and gritty sand and clumps of mud rained down. Her chest struggled to rise. Something heavy was on her. She was going to wake up to see Damu again. She knew it.

She cracked open an eye. It wasn't the strange dream man, but Erik with a genuine look of relief on his face. Erik groaned and collapsed onto her. She tried to wriggle out. "Erik. Erik, are you okay?" she yelled.

Erik wasn't moving. She eased him onto her lap. Someone was asking if she was okay, but her head was fuzzy. Her fingers came away sticky when she touched the tender spot on the back of her head. Livia caught her hand and held it.

"It's okay Zalea, help is coming." Something wasn't right; Livia was being far too nice.

Azalea looked at her blood covered palm. She must have hit her head pretty hard.

"Erik? Are you okay?" she repeated.

"Mmm I'm great, thanks."

Her hand rested in his hair. It was as soft as it looked. She glanced down, and a scream sliced through the fog in her head. Ambrose's elemer was sticking out of Erik's back.

"Help!" she tried to cry out. People around her were yelling.

Suddenly Maiken was there with a bunch of other fast-moving people. They whisked Erik away and hauled her onto another stretcher.

Mage Shepard was sitting on Ambrose, holding his hands behind his back, his face pressed into the stones. At least she had to believe Azalea now.

CHAPTER 34

"**I**S IT JUST ME, or do we keep meeting here?" Torin said as he caught sight of her, and an unexpected flush crept to his cheeks. *Must be from the poison.* Dismissing it, he eased onto the end of Azalea's hospital bed and set his crutches to the side. His heart raced from the short walk from his room down the hall, the effects of poison still slowing his movements. They didn't waste healing magic on non-threatening broken bones.

"Torin?" Azalea said. Her eyes shot open, and she sat upright. He moved to sit next to her, preempting her toppling over.

"Hey, Torin," she said softer, looking around. Her eyes anchored on him, and a small smile stole across her pale lips.

"Hey." He smiled back, a smile so rare he hardly remembered what it felt like. There was something about Azalea, something that made him feel light inside. It must be the relief from her waking up. Perhaps an aftereffect of the first time he sat next to her bedside, thinking she would die. He couldn't quite shake the sensation of needing to know she was okay. He should never have taken on a student. It didn't pay to get attached.

She looked around and groaned. "I thought you were in the hospital, not me. I was coming back to visit you after class." Her eyes suddenly changed from calm rainy-day gray to the deep gray of storm clouds. "Erik! Is he okay? He got stabbed!" She pushed back the blankets, scrambling to get out.

Torin moved as quickly as his poison dulled limbs would allow and guided her back into bed. She was dizzy and weak, so he needed little force. "Maiken fixed him up. He's fine, so you don't need to move."

"Why would that idiot do that?" she asked

"Why, indeed," he said sarcastically. He tucked the blanket around her and, as her long pajama top sleeve bunched up, his eyes fell on her arm. A wash of anger rushed through him. He gripped her wrist and thrust the sleeve up to her elbow. He froze as blood pounded in his ears.

She had a snake tattoo. A beautiful and treacherous snake tattoo coiled around her pale arm. A spark of rage pulsed through his hand. She tried to pull away, but he tightened his grip.

"I should have known," he forced the words out through gritted teeth. So, she'd been lying to him this whole time.

"I couldn't tell you. I promised I wouldn't tell anyone," she said, her eyes full of fear and apology.

He released her arm and took a step back. Of course she was a bloody Snake. He was a fool for thinking she was just from the House of Bees. All the signs were there: spirits, necromancy, strong Shadow Magic. Deep down, he hadn't wanted it to be true. He told himself she was like him. An outcast from the Shadow Magic Houses, someone he didn't have to worry about hating him or turning on him. He had been lying to himself. Of course, she was one of them.

"I'm sorry, Torin." A tear slid from the corner of her eye. He could almost feel the remorse and guilt radiating from her.

"My uncle said I couldn't tell. I was in danger. Our family is in danger."

He knew all this, but it didn't stop it hurting. The truth was she was hiding it from him because of his history, his family. He didn't blame her. Snakes were being hunted by Ravens mercilessly now. His father's revenge for his mother's death would never be satiated. Killing the head of the House of Snakes and their council wasn't enough. He wouldn't stop till he ended their families as well. Of course Azalea would want to keep it quiet. She was just trying to keep herself and her family safe. But it also proved she didn't trust him.

"You could have told me," he said as his voice broke, trying to quash the anger he usually did so well to contain.

"I'm sorry. I *do* trust you, Torin."

Yeah right. Another lie. Though for some unexplained reason, he felt it was true. He studied her for a second.

"Can we still do lessons together?" she asked as he realized he had been silent too long.

"We shall see. I think I'll need some time to think things over," he said. Knowing what his House was doing to hers would make it much harder to get past this. She nodded, clutching her arm as if it had betrayed her. "I am sorry Torin." She paused. "What happened to Ambrose? I need to know."

Okay, it made more sense now. How the hell was he so slow to catch on? He wished she had told him about all this from the start and he could have helped her.

"Ambrose was working for the House of Ravens. It seemed they contracted him to get rid of you. It's clear why now. But he wouldn't give any further information. Mage Shepard and your classmates witnessed him attack you and stab Erik, so it was enough evidence for the Archmage to take action."

"Is he going to jail?"

"No, it'll be worse than that for him. The Archmage kicked him and his family out of the Tower and it seems she called the House of Ravens to deal with his failure before the Paranormal Justice Unit could get there."

"So, what will happen to him?"

"Not anything good." In truth, they would probably kill Ambrose and his family, even if his family had nothing to do with it. His value was solely held in being a spy within the Tower. With that gone, he was nothing to them. But Azalea didn't need to know that.

"But Erik's okay?"

"Yes. He's fine."

She relaxed back into the bed. "That's good. I'm really sorry about all this, Torin."

Somehow, he knew she meant it, and there was something very odd about that.

))) ● (((

A week passed and Erik was still in hospital. Azalea realized she hadn't updated Isaac on all the craziness, but she had reluctantly told her mum who immediately suggested Azalea should come back home. But that wouldn't fix anything.

Azalea called Isaac early on Saturday night, hoping he hadn't gone out yet.

"Azalea! You're calling to come out for a pint, right?" Isaac said as soon as he answered.

"Sorry, old chum," she said in her fake posh voice. "But I do have a lot to fill you in on if you're free."

"Go on then. I've got an hour before I'm off. But it better not involve you dying," Isaac said.

"Well . . ." Azalea proceeded to fill him in on her Shadow Magic lessons, the Ambrose incident and Torin finding out about her House, which she still felt sick about. Her thoughts went straight to Torin, wishing she had just told him rather than waiting till he found out this way.

Apparently Torin was out of the hospital but hadn't messaged at all. Hopefully, he'd come around soon.

"—so I was given the all clear after one day and spent Sunday resting at home. Other than some scrapes and bruises, I'm fine," Azalea said.

"Bloody hell. Your life is so much more exciting than mine."

"I didn't mean for it to sound exciting. It's been stressful. Torin isn't talking to me, these ghosts are freaking me out, I'm no closer to finding my dad, and Erik got stabbed. Plus, his stab wound was way more serious than Torin made out. According to Van, he needed a shit load of healing magic to get him right." Which also meant she had to wait all week to get the chance to thank him. But today Erik was out of hospital and had asked if she wanted to grab a pint in the caf tonight. She was nervous about seeing him. What would she even say? *Hey mate. Thanks for getting stabbed for me?*

"So, what about your teacher? Did she get in trouble for not listening to you before?" Isaac asked.

"No, I didn't tell anyone that. She basically threw herself at my feet, apologizing after class on Monday. It was kind of pathetic. I mean, I don't want to wreck the poor woman's life or anything." Hopefully, she learned a lesson for the next time a student asked for real help.

"You're a nicer person than me. I would have had her fired."

"No, you wouldn't have. Actually, I'm surprised the Archmage didn't wait to question me before throwing Ambrose out. But he confessed to working for the House of Ravens. The fuckwit was proud of it; apparently, he was bragging about being their man inside. Remind me not to fuck with the Archmage. She sounds kind of scary."

"You should let me come over more. I want to be part of your magic melodrama."

"I don't want you involved, Isaac. I wouldn't be able to forgive myself if anything were to happen to you, plus you're not meant to know about any of this, remember?"

"Roger that. Well, let me know how your date goes tonight. At least kiss the bloke or something," Isaac said.

"Yuck, no, it's Erik. It isn't a date."

"The bloke got himself stabbed for you. It's a date."

"Whatever, Isaac. I'll let you go off on your shenanigans now. Have a fun night."

"Wait, what are you doing for your birthday?"

"Nothing. There's a big winter solstice party going on here, but I think I'll skip it. Too many spirits for me to concentrate or have fun."

"Your life is so weird. Night!"

"Night Isaac." She ended the call.

It was not a date. Was it? She hoped not. It was just as likely her other classmates would be there too. It was just a pint, she told herself, and maybe some fish and chips because she was starving. Still, she needed something decent to wear. Not that she wanted to impress him—she just didn't want to look like she chose whatever was lying around on the floor.

She opted for one of the few things that was not on the floor: a thin cashmere sweater that was maroon colored, she guessed, with black jeans and black boots and her black leather jacket. Pretty similar to her everyday wear, but the sweater made her feel a bit fancier—fancy enough for a pint somewhere outside of her flat. Wow, she needed to get a life. Perhaps after she found her dad and sorted out these spirits, she'd be able to live like a normal uni student.

))‚◑⟨⟨⟨

The caf was bustling with a Saturday night pub vibe. The fake sky was lit with twinkling stars instead of the usual daylight, and the waterfall glowed a luminescent blue—fancier than any pubs Azalea had ever been to, though that wasn't many—only the two that had been near her house. She'd stopped going to them once her friends turned into arseholes.

Erik waved. He was sitting on one of the smaller picnic tables near the pond. He was wearing a white button-up shirt with a navy blazer that instantly made Azalea feel too casual. But that was just Erik. *You don't have to dress up for him*, she reminded herself. Others around the room were dressed to go out clubbing later, though a few were wearing jeans and t-shirts, which made her feel a little better.

"I didn't think you'd come," Erik said as he stood up.

"Why would you think that?" Azalea sat opposite him, and he sank back into his seat. She was feeling well out of her comfort zone. This place was way different from its day-time vibes, and this definitely felt like a date—whether it was or wasn't. She needed a beer.

"Because you hate me." He said it almost like a challenge, wanting her to prove him wrong.

"I don't hate you. I came because I want to say thank you and to make sure you were okay. So, thank you for saving me, and I'm sorry you got stabbed." *There. Done.* That was about as sentimental as she could get. She stood up. "How about a beer?"

He grinned as if he already knew she'd say that and waved his hand at her to sit back down. "You are most welcome, Azalea. But sit down, love. I'll get the beers and we will get this date rolling. Would you care for any food?"

Date? Ugh, she was so hungry though. Would it make it seem like she was into him if she ordered food? Would that send the wrong message? Her stomach grumbled at her. Food always won. "Not a date, Erik. But fish and chips please, we can split the tab at the end."

"Whatever you say, love." He sauntered off to the bar, chatting to every person he saw along the way.

This was too weird. Why was he being so nice? Why had he stepped between her and Ambrose? She glanced around to check that none of their classmates were in there. It wouldn't help classroom relations for Livia or Millie to see her with Erik.

She didn't see anyone she knew. Secretly, she'd hoped to spot Torin, but of course he wasn't there. He was probably resting at home, avoiding people as usual.

Erik got back and placed two giant pints of beer on the table. *No messing around.* "Why did you help me, Erik? How did you know Ambrose would do that?"

He sighed and flicked his hair back with his hand. "To be honest, I didn't realize how dangerous he was until that day." His voice lowered, and he leaned in. "The first week we started classes, he told me he was working for someone. He made it sound like a good deed that we were getting rid of you. But I'm pretty sure someone was blackmailing him, or controlling him, or something. I backed off once I realized how serious he was. That's when I started keeping an eye on you. That's why I followed you the day you tried all that Shadow Magic. But in class, when you were fighting him, I realized why he must be out to get you. I knew you could do Shadow Magic, so I figured you must be a Snake, and afterwards they told me he was working for the Ravens, so that made even more sense. Anyway, it was clear then he was going to kill you, but I don't think Mage Shepard realized how serious he was. So, I jumped in. I couldn't just watch that happen."

"I don't know how to thank you. I didn't expect you to do that, not really." It was above anything she'd ever expect anyone to do for her.

He shrugged. "I was feeling pretty guilty too. I was a right arsehole to you when you arrived. Ambrose seemed pretty adamant you were the devil herself, but I shouldn't have listened to him. I'm very easily swayed," he said with a sly smile.

"Did you hear what happened to him?" She ignored his last comment as her fish and chips arrived.

Erik took a chip off her plate straight away. She'd let him have that one, just this once. "Yeah. I heard the Ravens got him." He didn't sound the least bit remorseful. She realized how betrayed he must be feeling. Ambrose had been his friend for years. "I wish I'd punched the bastard in the face before he went." Erik rubbed the stab wound on his back. Well, maybe more vengeful than betrayed.

There it was. Normal Erik.

"I'm sure he's getting what he deserves," she said. She didn't want to think about it, not really. Time for a change in subject. She bit into a hot chip. It had a perfect crunch. "You know, it's nice that someone knows about my Shadow Magic, and for some reason, you haven't told anyone. So, thanks for that too."

"Well, you never told anyone about seeing me in the hospital after my accident, so let's call it even and start over, yeah?"

"Sounds good," she said, meaning it. He held out his hand, and they shook on it.

"To the start of our relationship."

"Not a relationship Erik. We're just friends."

"Whatever you say, love . . . Cheers to that," he said as he held up his glass. Azalea reluctantly clinked it and took a swig.

CHAPTER 35

AZALEA WATCHED THE SHADOWS of a flickering candle flame on her bedside table. Music from outside drifted in despite her shutting all the windows and curtains to try block it out. It had been snowing since before night fall and she felt a lingering chill in the air. Pulling the patchwork quilt from the end of her bed, she wrapped it around her, feeling sorry for herself. She imagined everyone out there dancing and chanting around the great bonfires and gigantic decorated Yule trees set up on the Tower green, all celebrating the winter solstice. Everyone but her.

There was no way she could be out there in the open with all those spirits. They remembered her now and Torin *still* wasn't talking to her, so she hadn't learned any spirit warding. Better to stay safe inside where she wouldn't expose her true house or look like a crazy person dodging all the weirdo spirits.

She shouldn't be depressed. Her birthday had been great—wonderful in fact. And now she was nineteen; *very much an adult now,* she told herself as she snuggled her toy dinosaur. Her mum and RoRo had turned up unexpectedly and showered her with homemade teas, jams, candles, various elixirs, and new skin care products RoRo had made. Then Azalea took them for brunch in the caf. Surprisingly, RoRo knew half the people that they stumbled across.

Her mum didn't cause any waves, and they avoided talking about anything to do with Shadow Magic. It worked well. Sometimes ignoring your problems fixed them (for now at least) and Azalea was thrilled to see her mum.

Suddenly, she sat up straight with an idea. Shuffling across the bed, she pulled out the Shadow Atlas. If the Atlas could track Hollows and celestial events, maybe it could also track spirits?

Reaching for her elemer, which was now always nearby, she cut into the Shadow Dimension. The alluring smell of lightning and storms rushed over her as her room filled with shadows.

The Shadow Atlas could track spirits. It had to. She couldn't explain how she knew, but this crazy book was in her head all the time now. It was like it was part of her. Maybe she'd fed it too much of her blood, or maybe she was going crazy.

Either way, it didn't hurt to try new things. Azalea wrote instructions to find her father's spirit. She poured memories and thoughts of her father into the book, willing it to find him.

She could feel it working. Illuminated borders appeared on the page first.

Despite the darkness, she could see the page as clear as day. The ink trickled into a map of London but added something new. Tiny pin pricks of light drifted around the streets and buildings. She was almost certain they were spirits, but she couldn't be sure.

The Tower of London grew clearer as Azalea pinched the image in closer with her mind. One area glowed brightly, and there were a few specks scattered around the Tower. She couldn't be sure they were spirits. She would have to check, but not tonight. There were too many people out.

A loud knock came from the front door. Azalea nearly jumped out of her skin. It wouldn't be Van. It was far too early, plus she wouldn't knock. Her mum and RoRo had driven home before dark and everyone else would be at the solstice celebration.

The knock came again. Azalea tossed the Shadow Atlas under her pillow and realized her room was a mass of shadows, something she had gotten used to, but others did not need to see that. Throwing her fluffy purple dressing gown on over her short pajamas and t-shirt with no bra, she opened her bedroom door and shut it rapidly behind her to keep the shadows in.

"Who is it?" she called, tiptoeing up the hall.

"It's Torin," the familiar low voice sounded.

"Just a sec!" *Shit. Just what she needed*. She probably looked like crap. Glancing in the mirror behind her, she tried to tie up her mass of hair that needed a cut. Her eyes were all black. She stopped to stare at herself. It was as if her eyes weren't there. It made her feel powerful, like a real mage.

"Azalea, please let me in. I just want to talk."

She didn't even have a hair tie on her wrist. Flattening out her hair as best she could using her fingers as a comb, she then turned to open the door. He was going to tell her he wanted to stop her lessons, she just knew it.

"Hi, Torin. Please come in." Azalea's breath caught. It was as if a fancy Regency era gentleman was transported right to her doorway. He wore a well-cut suit with a waistcoat of silver and sapphire, complete with a pocket watch chain. He looked amazing, though his leg was still in a cast and the crutches ruined his time traveler image. She gestured to take his coat, which was covered in light flakes of snow. His gaze fell straight to her eyes. It felt like he was drilling into her soul.

"Been practicing?"

She nodded. He looked nervous. She felt nervous. This was weird, and why wasn't he at the party? She led him into the kitchen/ living room, and he shuffled his way to the nearest chair at the table. What did Van usually do when they had visitors? Her mind was going blank. *Duh, make tea.* She started the kettle boiling.

He rearranged the candles in the center of the table as Azalea cleaned two mugs.

"What are you doing here? Shouldn't you be at the celebrations?" she asked.

"I was there for ten minutes, but I didn't see you. Figured it was because of the spirits."

He was right about that. But it didn't answer her other question. She needed to apologize but didn't know how to start.

"Look, Azalea . . . I'm sorry for the way I reacted to finding out your House. I should have worked it out myself. I mean, it was all rather obvious in hindsight." He winced, as if struggling to get the words out.

The kettle boiled, and the kitchen was silent. Awkwardly silent. She didn't know what to say. It was clear neither of them liked admitting they were wrong or talking about anything remotely emotional.

Out with it, she told herself. "Peppermint tea or normal?"

"Normal, thanks."

She dunked the tea bag once, then turned to face him. "I'm sorry I didn't tell you. I thought it was the right thing to do, but it was stupid. Of course you needed to know. I'm an idiot and I keep doing stupid things, but I can't help it. My judgments with magic, and people, for that matter, seem to be way off. I didn't want to lie to you, though, and I understand if you want to stop our lessons," she blurted out.

She turned back, not wanting to see his reaction, and threw the tea bags in the sink then set the cups on the table and sat down.

"I don't want to stop our lessons. I said I'd help you and I like to keep my promises. I'm sorry I left it this long. I know you need help with the spirits and I'm the reason you can't be out there enjoying your birthday. So, sorry for that, too."

He knew it was her birthday? How? "That certainly isn't your fault. Don't think that for a second. This spirit thing is bizarre, but it's no one's fault." Although it had gotten much worse since Torin had brought her back from the dead, and she couldn't help but wonder if those people in her dream had something to do with it.

"Well, anyway. Happy Birthday." He placed a bag on the table that must have been on the floor. It sounded like a bottle. He got her a present?! That was unexpected and rather sweet. She wouldn't have a clue when his birthday was. Danni or Maiken must have said something.

But he was standing up before she could open it.

"Lesson tomorrow then," he said as he slid into his crutches and went to the door to get his coat.

"You're welcome to stay longer," she said. She should have offered him biscuits or one of Van's muffins. He hadn't even drunk all his tea.

"No, I have some work to do tonight, anyway. I'll leave you to it. See you tomorrow?"

"Of course. Night," she said as she closed the door. She didn't have time to celebrate her lessons starting up again. Her phone rang, and she followed the sound to her bedroom. The shadows were all gone. The Shadow Atlas must have been hungry. *Good.*

She grabbed her phone off the bed, and saw it was Fabian. After all this time he was finally checking in. All it took was for her to turn nineteen.

"Hello?" she answered.

"I need to talk to you. Are you free tomorrow?" Fabian said.

"No 'Happy Birthday, Azalea'? 'How are you, Azalea'?" she said. *Rude.* Just like him to stay away for months and not even know it was her birthday.

"Happy Birthday, Azalea. Now look, can you meet me tomorrow?"

"Um, sure. What's the rush?"

"I'm on a big job, but I'm in the area tomorrow. Meet me at the pub down the street at 10 am. Danni will escort you."

"Certainly." She hung up with a sigh. *What a grump.* She suspected whatever he wanted to talk about wasn't going to be fun.

Her shoulders slumped. *Screw this.* She wasn't going to sit here moping on her birthday. She was going to get drunk, even if it was just with her cat. To be fair, Van had offered to hang out, but she didn't want to wreck Van's night. And Isaac had gone back home for Christmas, though he had offered to come back for her birthday. So, it was just her and Faraday.

She grabbed the bottle out of the bag on the kitchen table and cleaned another mug. The bottle said it was whiskey, and it looked fancy. She had no idea if it was though. Pouring a large cup of it, she slumped into the couch and found the cheesiest Christmas movie to keep her entertained while she drank alone.

"Happy Birthday Azalea and cheers to you, Dad!" She held the mug up in the air. "I'm coming to find you! I promise." She chugged back the whiskey. It was awful, but it had just the brain numbing effect she was after.

CHAPTER 36

A ZALEA'S HEAD POUNDED. SHE rolled out of bed and caught a glimpse of the tattoo above her breast in the mirror as she stood up. Weird, it was glowing. A hazy memory flashed across her vision of Christmas movies and whiskey.

She stumbled to the bathroom and got in the shower, remembering she had to go meet her uncle for breakfast. The cascade of water and clouding steam cleared the fog from her brain a little. She studied the snake tattoo on her left arm, not wanting to leave the hot water. It had changed in the last weeks; she wasn't sure if she should be concerned. The perfectly neat knot the snake used to be had unfurled and spread into a winding creature that coiled around both the front and back of her arm. Its head still sat at the pulse point on her wrist, facing the crescent moon, but the end of it wound all the way up her bicep. The tattoo on her chest was different, too. It didn't pulse with magic like her arms, but sometimes it grew warm for no reason and glowed spontaneously. Just another weird magic thing.

She dressed in jeans and an over-sized gray sweater and just had enough time for a coffee. She was about to throw out the bag Torin had given her, when she noticed a blue velvet box right at the bottom. Ooo, interesting . . .

Pulling it out, she lifted the lid thinking it would be some sort of jewelry, but Torin didn't seem like a jewelry-giving kind of guy.

But she was wrong. It was a delicate silver locket. She gently removed it as the silver chain pooled in the palm of her hand. The locket clicked open as her heart skipped. Not a locket, but a tiny, ornate watch. It had mini rubies set in the face and the prettiest watch hands she had ever seen. It was smaller and far more delicate than any watch she'd ever owned. He won best gift giver by far, but she was sure she'd only mentioned her pocket watch obsession to Torin once.

She slipped it around her neck.

Danni came knocking at the door at 9:50am with a warm, "Morning, Sunshine!" as Azalea opened the door.

"Morning," she grumbled, not looking forward to meeting Fabian.

"Aren't you a box of rainbows today? Off we go, then."

They walked the short way up the road to the pub, and if Azalea weren't feeling so lousy, she would have enjoyed leaving the Tower for a change. Danni saw her in the door and turned around.

"You aren't leaving me alone with him, are you?" Azalea asked.

"He wanted to talk to *you,* and I've got a few errands to run. You'll be alright. Have fun," she said and ran off grinning.

Fabian waited in a booth in the secluded corner of the pub. The smell of stale beer mixed with the morning smells of coffee and bacon was overwhelming. Maybe she'd had a little too much to drink last night.

It was hard to believe it had been four months since he left her at the Tower. This wasn't the best time to demonstrate her progress. She squared her shoulders, attempting to look confident. No doubt he was still thinking he'd done the right thing in pawning her off to the Initiates' program, and he was probably right. She mumbled "good morning" but didn't look him in the eye.

"Good night last night?" He gave her a disapproving look.

"It was fine. Not that you even knew it was my birthday," she said.

"Very true. Take it from an expert: order the full breakfast and a coffee. You'll thank me for it later."

She took his advice. They both ordered big breakfasts and sat in silence as they waited for the food to arrive. He asked a few questions about her training. She answered that it was fine, giving no specific details. It seemed neither of them were morning people, and she wasn't exactly in a chatting mood.

Once the food came out, Azalea perked up. Perhaps it was the hangover, or that this was possibly the best breakfast she'd ever had. The bacon was perfectly crisp, the sausages were juicy. Even the toast was just how she liked it, and the eggs were perfectly fried with golden yolks that burst and oozed out as she poked them with her fork.

"You seem to have perked up a bit," Fabian said.

"Coffee and food have that effect on me," she said, placing her knife and fork together on the plate. Since her life bars were restored, Fabian set about quizzing her on Echo Magic. His questions were way too easy. At least that made her look good.

He asked to see her tattoos. Keen to show him, she peeled up the sleeve of her sweater to show the bee tattoo. It hadn't shrunk, at least, and it was as beautiful as the first time she saw it. The azalea flowers were bright and the bee with geometric designs had grown on her wrist recently. He nodded, clearly impressed.

"How about the other one?" He nodded to her other arm.

She swallowed, hesitant to roll up that sleeve. He'd know what it meant, but she didn't want to hide it. Slowly, she slid the fabric up her arm.

His face fell blank.

"You've been doing Shadow Magic."

"Yes. Because I had to learn to control it. *You* wouldn't teach me." A flicker of guilt appeared for a microsecond before he went back to frowning. Changing the subject was a good idea. At least now he knew.

"Do you have news about the House of Ravens? Did they keep looking for me?" she asked.

He blinked as if coming out of some deep thoughts. She hoped he didn't feel too bad about ditching her at the Tower. She didn't blame him, though of course she would have wanted him to teach her. That would be the next best thing after her dad.

He glanced around, checking no one was listening. "I did my best to make them think you were gone. But I don't know if it worked. I've been up to my eyeballs in this bloody gallu hunting. No doubt you've heard about it."

She only knew what Livia and Millie had told her and had never got 'round to finding out more.

He took a large gulp of coffee. It looked like he hadn't slept in days.

"That's partly what I wanted to talk to you about. This gallu isn't like the others. It's almost like it's toying with me. It comes just in range, but it seems to know exactly what I'm going to do. I've missed it three times already. It's dangerously close to becoming corporeal."

"What does that mean?" Azalea asked.

"If it goes corporeal, it's pretty much over for me. I'm out of a job."

"But what will it do? What will you do?" This sounded dangerous. Would he go back to working with Danni?

"Call through more gallu, I suspect. Go on a rampage. Once they're solid, they don't just have to feed on spirits. They can kill humans and take spirits themselves. Not something you want to see, but I've got something else in the works if it goes pear-shaped. Don't worry about me."

"But you can catch it, right?" she asked.

"Of course I can. I just need to outsmart it. It won't trick me again." He didn't sound that confident. Something about this made Azalea uneasy.

"Anyway," he said. "The reason I wanted to meet is to tell you I'm setting up Blackbourne Manor as a safe house for House of Snakes families. I've got a few people in there now. It has the highest level of security wards and can't be found by anyone who isn't invited. If you ever find the need to go there, just message or call me and I'll find you."

"Okay, but why would I need to do that? Why are you telling me this?" she asked.

"I've had threats from Korbyn Dumont—"

Wait a minute, Dumont? Suddenly it clicked; he was talking about Torin's dad. Torin's dad might be a lunatic, but she was one hundred percent sure Torin had nothing to do with all this.

"—he's outright said he's going to kill me this time, and he's already gone after a few others. Burned down their houses. Two of them didn't get out." He swallowed hard and looked down at his coffee.

"Why are they doing this?" Azalea asked, thinking back to Ambrose. He was out to get her just because she was part of this group, this *House* she knew nothing about, they didn't even know who her father or uncle were.

"Korbyn Dumont blames our House for the death of his wife. There's a lot more to it than that, but he swore revenge and he's set on getting it."

"There was a break in at the Tower recently," she said. Fabian tilted his head. "They were trying to get something from the Artifacts Department. I heard rumors it was the House of Ravens." *And Ambrose tried to kill me,* she wanted to add, but didn't. If she told him that, he'd make her leave the Tower and she'd never find her dad. She had to stay.

"What happened?" he asked.

She sat up a little straighter. "Wouldn't you like to know?" she said, smirking.

"Just tell me, Zaels. They were after the relics, weren't they?" he said.

"I have no idea. No one tells me what's going on. But they got away and took nothing. Torin stopped them, but he won't tell me anything more about it."

Fabian's face dropped. His eyes flashed black, and the color drained from his skin. The vein in his forehead was pulsing.

Oh crap. She should not have mentioned Torin.

He took a breath and placed his rolled fists on the table in a slow, deliberate manner.

"Torin who?" he said through a clenched jaw.

It was her turn for the color to drain from her face. She felt it trickle away like icy water. So, mentioning Torin was definitely a bad idea. She might be used to him, but he was still from the House of Ravens and her uncle wasn't in an understanding mood.

She cleared her throat and sat up confidently. "He's my tutor," she said quietly.

"What is his last name? And don't lie to me." It was clear Fabian already knew the answer.

"It's Dumont." *Obviously.*

He slammed his fist into the table, causing the plates to jump and clatter back down.

"Danni," he growled to himself. "I can't believe she would let you near that man and think I would be okay with it."

"I'm old enough to decide who I spend time with. It's not Danni's fault."

Overreacting much? Best not to add fuel to the fire by telling him about the whole Shadow Magic mishap. It was all in the past now, anyway.

"You don't know what he's done, Zaels," Fabian said through his teeth. "Horrible things. He's a monster."

"I know he's done bad things. He told me as much. But he's not a bad person. He's helped me a lot, and you weren't around, so you can't exactly yell at me for going to the only Shadow Mage I could find."

"I doubt he told you everything or you wouldn't be defending him. You have no idea. It's in his blood and he can't change. Just stay away from him. I'm glad you've learned the basics, but leave it at that for now," his voice was forceful. He wasn't giving her a choice.

No way he could come in here and tell her what to do after everything she'd gone through alone, all the mistakes she had made trying to do the right thing.

"Tell me exactly what he's done and give me a reason to stop doing Shadow Magic or I'm walking out of here," she hissed.

"I can't tell you Azalea. I'm trying to protect you. Please understand that. Because knowing won't help you, it will make you more like me and that's the last thing I want."

What? She was going to turn into an alcoholic gallu hunter if she found out what Torin had done? "I won't stop training with him unless I have a reason to."

Throwing down her napkin, she shuffled across the booth to get out. Fabian grabbed her arm and pulled her back into the seat.

"You will stop, or I'll make you stop," he said. "Listen to me." His voice grew louder.

"No! He can teach me what I need to know. He fixed whatever was in his past. It doesn't matter."

"Some things can't be fixed, Azalea!" He choked on the words. "Some things can never be taken back, no matter how much you want them to be."

She'd never seen him like this. He was starting to scare her.

"Whatever. I'm leaving and I'll just have to ask Torin myself." She stood up and this time he didn't stop her.

"Zaels," he called after her. "If I see him anywhere near you, I will kill him."

She looked back at him in disgust. A chill ran through her, seeing that he meant it. What could Torin possibly have done to him that was so bad? So bad he wouldn't tell her? People around them were staring and muttering. She stormed out and her head started pounding at twice the speed it was before. She needed sleep, and to forget whatever just happened so she could start her spirit surveying with the Shadow Atlas.

CHAPTER 37

A ZALEA TRUDGED ACROSS THE frosty ground toward Danni and Maiken's place for their small Yule get together. She'd spent the morning on phone calls to her mum, RoRo, and Isaac. It was nice to get outside. Christmas carols rang from the St. Peter ad Vincula Royal Chapel as people gathered inside and out. The lightest sprinkling of snow filled the air, not enough to settle, but the perfect Christmas atmosphere for a short walk. Christmas and Yule had always blended into one holiday when Azalea was growing up, and it seemed similar here in London.

Azalea kept to the other side of the grounds to avoid any spirits. As she walked, she couldn't get Fabian's comments about Torin out of her head. She hoped he would be at Christmas lunch so she could tell him about it. She'd been too hungover the day after her birthday, and he told her to wait till after Christmas to start their lessons again. It gave her time to think at least, though she'd spent the last two days watching a map of the Tower, trying to predict movements of spirits. She had yet to test her theories.

She made it to the Hospital building. Zoe and Ava almost bowled her over when she entered the flat. Their rapid-fire reports of everything Santa had brought them overloaded her brain in seconds. Standing near the door, they proceeded to 'make her prettier' with tinsel bracelets, a tinsel necklace, and a glowing reindeer headband.

"Thank you, I love it," she said, giving a spin in front of the mirror to prove it.

"Okay, now you can come in," Zoe said. They dragged her to the sofa and sat her next to Torin.

"Doesn't she look pretty?" Ava said, demanding an answer from Torin for her handiwork.

Azalea did her best not to laugh.

"Azalea looks lovely, as always," he said without missing a beat, almost as if he wasn't forced into the compliment. The twins giggled and Azalea felt a slight blush rise in her cheeks.

"Here, you two take these to the tree." She handed the girls her bag of presents and they squealed and ran to add it to the mountain of already opened gifts.

Danni and Maiken must have spotted her sparkling tinsel form. "I see they Christmas-a-fied you good and proper," Danni said as Azalea stood up and greeted both women with a kiss on the cheek and the usual Christmas and Yule greetings.

"I feel much more festive now," Azalea said with a laugh, and meant it. It made her miss her mum and RoRo a little less, though she'd seen them just a few days ago.

Maiken and Danni refused any help and ordered Azalea and Torin to relax and enjoy the hot mulled wine. They did as they were told even though the mouth-watering smells of roasting potatoes and glazing ham had Azalea wanting to follow the two women into the kitchen just so she could pick at the food.

Instead, she relaxed into the comfy sofa. Festive aromas of cinnamon and star anise filled her senses as she sipped her drink; the spices and red wine were sharp and warm on her tongue.

She shuffled back next to Torin, feeling strange in a setting that wasn't his office or the salt circle of torture.

"Hitting the piss hard again, I see," he said with a mocking smile.

"It was my birthday—a perfectly appropriate occasion to be drunk. Plus, it was your present!" she said. She suddenly remembered and pulled out the necklace from under the neck of her black sweater dress. "And thank you for the watch! I love it so much. There are so many details. Did you know the rubies set in the face make up the Corvus constellation? It's brilliant."

"I hadn't noticed that," he replied. "But I'm glad you like it. How was your head the next day? You didn't do any magic, did you?" His lips danced around a smile.

"It wasn't the best, and no. I don't think I could have done any magic if I tried. It was a terrible morning, made much worse by having breakfast with my uncle."

"Sorry to hear it." He didn't sound the least bit sorry.

"Actually—" she started. "I *may* have mentioned to my uncle that you were tutoring me in Shadow Magic." She took another sip of her drink.

"I imagine that went down well," Torin said. He drank down half his cup.

"To say he was pissed off is an understatement. In fact, he lost it, right in the middle of the pub and ordered me to stop doing lessons with you." Better to leave out the bit about the death threat.

Though Torin's posture didn't change in the slightest, she noticed his eyes fall to his hands. She suddenly felt horrible for bringing it up. The twins ran over and placed sticky cookies, which they had just been busy decorating, in Torin's and Azalea's hands. Azalea thanked them, welcoming the break in tension. They giggled and ran off again once they'd had enough praise for their decorating skills.

"So, you want to stop the lessons?" he said.

"Don't be stupid. I'm not listening to him. I'm sorry he said those things about you. He doesn't know you."

He drained his cup, then held his hand out to take Azalea's for a refill. She handed it to him. He took his time coming back and sank into the couch and handed her drink back.

"He's right, Azalea. You won't be safe if you continue training with me. You've progressed well over the last few months, but you should think about this." He turned to her. "You know I'm from the House of Ravens, but that isn't the only reason people hate me. My reputation could hurt your chances of getting ahead. You know how small this community is. They'll either assume I'm teaching you Shadow Magic, or that we're sleeping together. Neither is going to put you in a good light."

Her eyes widened at his unexpected frankness. "But I want you to teach me. We can tell people I'm studying history with you. You're the only one who can help me, and I don't care what they think. It's as simple as that."

"Nothing is ever that simple."

"Then simplify it for me. Tell me what was so horrible that you can't forgive yourself for?" *It couldn't be as bad as Fabian made it out to be. Could it?*

"Innocent people died because of me. I hope you never know what that feels like."

She swore she could feel the guilt radiating off him. "What happened? I'm sure it wasn't your fault, was it?" Even if it wasn't, he'd probably confess.

He looked away. "It was my fault."

Okay, but there had to be an explanation. "How did they die?" she whispered. Her chest tightened, and she sat back a little.

"I had to kill someone to pass my Initiates' test," he said.

She tensed without meaning to.

"I don't want to talk about it." He started to get up. She needed him to know she didn't care. It was all in the past, and clearly, he regretted it. Azalea laid her hand on his in sympathy, but a jolt shot through her arm. They both froze, and Azalea shook the numbness out of her hand.

"Um, that was weird," she said.

He shook out his own hand, and concern flashed across his face.

"But don't think you're getting out of it that easy. Just tell me—please," Azalea said.

Torin slumped back into the cushions.

"I thought it would be just the one man, not the others. My father made me do it, and he hadn't told me the extent of his plan. It was after that, that I left the House of Ravens for good. He'd lied to me. He said the man had killed my mother. I was only sixteen, so of course I believed him. I later found out it wasn't true. Several other people died that night, too. I turned myself in and got locked up for a few years. I'm only out because of Danni and the Owls. I owe them a lot."

How horrible. But he was so young. Still, she had no idea how this affected Fabian. Torin glanced over at the kitchen. "Since I was so young at the time, I continued my education in a reform camp. The Paranormal Justice Unit handles cases like mine and were happy with the way I reformed. After that, it was Danni that got stuck with me. I have her to thank for everything."

Azalea gripped her cup. No wonder he was so defensive around people. His dad sounded like a right arsehole. "You were a kid. How can people blame you for that?"

"It's in the blood, apparently. People hate my family, hate my father. What I did just proves them right."

"You can't still believe it was your fault."

He exhaled. "I was the one who did it. I can't change what happened."

"No, you can't, but you can change what happens now," she said, a pang of sadness stabbing at her chest.

"Thanks, Azalea. I know you mean well. But there will be consequences if you continue to study with me."

"Thanks for the warning. But I'm not as fragile as you think." Sorting out her spirit problems was more of a priority right now, anyway.

"That's not what I'm worried about." He gave her a strange look. "Let's just forget about this nonsense and enjoy Christmas. How about that?" he said.

"Sounds good. Enough serious talk. Merry Christmas and Happy Yule." She held up her glass.

He shook his head and clinked his glass against hers. "Merry Christmas, Azalea. Honestly, I'm surprised you're still sitting next to me. So, thanks."

"Well, I *do* need someone to teach me still," she said with a small shove and got a hint of a smile out of him.

Van arrived with a mountain of Christmas cookies and raised an eyebrow at Azalea sitting next to Torin. Van knew nothing about him except the horrible stories everyone whispered. She'd never actually met him.

Azalea pushed thoughts of Torin's past away as the other guests arrived. Torin's boss, Brandon Guildford with his wife Hazel, and the Ravenmaster, showed up to complete the party. They were bubbly, loud, and their Christmas spirit was infectious. Soon everyone was smiling, popping Christmas crackers, and wearing flimsy paper hats. It was nice to forget about the spirits and her dad, even if it was just for an afternoon.

The Christmas lunch was a feast worthy of the Queen herself. Maiken and Danni had put on a shiny glazed Christmas ham, crispy potatoes, devils on horseback, mountains of roast vegetables, and the most scrumptious gravy. For dessert, Azalea managed a small amount of fragrant plum pudding, a mince pie, and a bit too much icing as she helped Zoe and Ava decorate gingerbread men. She was about to burst.

It was a lovely afternoon. She hadn't heard from her uncle since their fight and was glad he hadn't turned up unexpectedly—for both her sake and Torin's. Evangeline soon got over her fear of Torin after her curiosity won out. Azalea introduced them, and Van did a good job of chatting away and keeping him occupied with her theories on mythical creatures that lived in the Thames.

After they were all stuffed and sleepy, they piled onto the sofas and Azalea lounged on cushions on the ground with Ava and Zoe piled on top of her. Faraday appeared and hopped between

Torin's and Van's knees as they sat down to watch the Queen's speech.

She was stuffed from an afternoon *and* evening pigging out on food. Everyone, including Torin, had drained the mulled wine and moved on to red wine, and then port after that. Azalea has stopped at the mulled wine.

She couldn't stop thinking about the Shadow Atlas and the spirits. Too excited about testing her idea to drink anymore, she excused herself after the third round of dinner.

Back at the flat, she opened the Shadow Atlas and fed it some blood and shadows to put it in a helpful mood. It was time to check if the dots of light in the book really were spirits.

It was dark outside, and the light snow had turned to sleety rain. She found a clear bag in the kitchen to cover the Shadow Atlas and dug out one of Torin's umbrellas from the hall cupboard. Her black Wellington boots did not match her knee-length sweater dress at all, nor did her yellow raincoat.

Smiling to herself, she stepped outside, clutching the book to her chest. The cobbles were slick, and her breath misted in the air around her as she approached the area with the most light dots on the map, right outside the chapel, which was now very dark. With her head down, she skirted around the path and crouched on the steps of a house with no lights. Hopefully, the residents weren't home and wouldn't mind her sheltering on their doorstep for the sake of research.

The Shadow Atlas was safe in its bag and still open to the map. She watched the group of spirits. There were about twenty of them. They stood in the same positions as the dots on the map and moved at the same time. Hope rose in her chest, along with a plan. She focused on each dot one at a time. As she did so, she got a mental image of the spirit; a sense of who they used to be and what they looked like.

Focusing on one dot, an image of a middle-aged man appeared in her mind: he died at the Tower and had been executed for standing up for his beliefs. She sensed he wanted to move on but didn't know how. His sorrow, old and dulled, brushed over her in a wave of sadness that struck her heart. She glanced up. He was staring at her, and he wore a triangle shaped hat, dark robes, and a wide gold chain across his chest—the exact same way she'd seen him in her mind.

It had worked! It was him.

She didn't make eye contact, hoping he would go away. So, the dots were ghosts. All she had to do now was scour as many maps as she could to find her dad. Hopefully he hadn't traveled too far. Plans whizzed around in her brain. Once she found him, she could go get him. Then, if she was lucky, he would be different than the others. He would remember.

If not, she could lure him back to the Tower and hide him amongst the spirit community until she worked out a way to get him to remember.

A chill ran through her. She wished she'd put on an extra sweater. Her hands felt like icicles as she tucked the Shadow Atlas into her coat. She picked up the umbrella, ignoring rain dripping from the eaves of the roof.

A woman materialized in front of her.

Her heart leaped into her throat. "Bloody hell! You scared me," Azalea said, lowering the umbrella when she saw it was B.

"I know thou sees me, girl. I remember your face. Why does thou cower there watching us?"

"I was looking for someone. Maybe you've seen him?" Azalea said, taking a page out of the ghost book of conversations.

"I too seek a man, my brother George," B said, in an understanding tone.

"I know," Azalea said. She might as well try. "I'm looking for Samael Blackbourne. He's a tall bloke with dark hair, gray eyes. Looks kind of like me, maybe?"

B gazed thoughtfully into the rain as it passed through her. She turned back to Azalea. "I do not believe I have met such a man. But I shall inform thee if I do. You are a most unusual girl. I recall seeing a gentleman, your husband, I presume. He does not see me, but I wonder why you do? Others are starting to recall your face and you become clearer with each passing day. I think you will help us."

Azalea studied the woman's face. Her eyes were crafty and determined. "I'm not really here. I'm a spirit," Azalea lied. "I can't help anyone in your world. I'm sorry. But I think I saw George go into the chapel. Perhaps you can catch him?"

B considered Azalea's strange statement. It's funny what people did when you mentioned spirits, even if they were one. She shuffled uncomfortably and stepped back as her hand clutched her necklace.

"Please leave me be spirit, I don't want any trouble. I shall go to George now."

Perhaps her lie bought her a little time. Chills crept deeper in her bones. Azalea popped the umbrella and walked home as fast as she could. The holidays would allow her freedom to track her dad. He was out there somewhere, and she was going to find him.

CHAPTER 38

A FTER ONE WEEK OF lessons back with Torin, Azalea was starting to remember why she hated them. The night air was crisp as she made the dash from Torin's tower past the chapel. She refused to make eye contact with spirits or to stop and listen to their bellowing. Apparently, more of them remembered her now.

It was only Thursday, but it was New Year's Eve, and everyone would be distracted. It was the perfect time to go find her dad.

She'd spent the entire week glued to the Shadow Atlas. It was like being reunited with an old friend, but her old friend was an unhelpful book that spoke in riddles and gave her a headache. But she'd managed to get it to track ghosts around the Tower all week, learning how to pinpoint individuals while keeping well out of their way. After a few days she widened her search on the map to the larger area of London, and golly gosh (as her mum would say), there were a lot of spirits.

After hours of meditation and tediously learning how to filter out spirits like a search engine, she finally got somewhere. She was finally able to narrow it down to one spirit.

Her dad. At least she hoped it was.

His spirit felt different from the others. It was a purple dot and gave off a strange feeling when she focused on it, like it was linked to her somehow. The problem was he traveled a lot more than the other spirits she tracked. His movements seemed more purposeful. He wasn't just floating around the same areas like most ghosts. This gave her hope.

Nervous energy buzzed through her. She dressed in layers, her thickest jeans, with a long-sleeved running top, a black fleece and black puffy jacket on top. She had no idea how long she'd be out. It was finally time to do this thing.

It was after nine when she left the Tower. Van was going out with her apprentice friends. Danni and Maiken invited Azalea to come with them to the big party in the caf, but she declined, saying she wanted to stay in and call her mum at midnight. Torin said he was having an early dinner with Danni and Maiken, then staying in, probably reading, or doing some research.

It felt strange leaving the Tower after so long. Her hands pressed into her lap as she rode the tube across town, hoping her dad would stay where she'd last spotted him and not travel too far. She couldn't exactly whip out the Shadow Atlas on public transport. She studied the tube's tangled mess of colors on her app and was careful to get off at Archway station. She'd thought about attempting to make a Hollow to get there, but she was too scared. After a bus ride and walk, she finally reached the towering gates at the aptly named *Highgate Cemetery.*

The night air was so still. Goosebumps prickled at her arms as the quietness of the cemetery crept in on her. It was too quiet after the noisy bus of partygoers.

Shivering, she opened the book. *Don't freak out*, she told herself. Hanging out in one of the most haunted graveyards in Britain was a perfectly normal thing to do on New Year's Eve. Thankfully, the purple dot was still there. Why did he have to be right in the middle of a dark cemetery surrounded by a collection of yellow dot spirits? "They're just spirits. They can't hurt you," she whispered to herself. Though she wasn't so sure about that anymore.

Going through a Hollow to get in would be the obvious choice but they hadn't covered those lessons yet. It would have to be the fence.

She hoisted herself up the iron bars and pulled herself against the big stone pillar between fences. Tucking her foot into the top of the bar, just below some nasty looking spikes, she hoisted herself up and hugged the rounded top of the pillar as she pivoted around and swung her legs to the other side. It was not very graceful, but it did the trick. She landed with a soft thud and peered into the darkness, half expecting guards or dogs or vampires to jump out.

Stay focused. Just track the dot. It was a cloudy night and trees loomed still and silent overhead, adding to the darkness. Victorian monuments and tombstones leaned against each other, as the grass crept through cracks in tombs while other shone with polished marble that was too bright in the darkness. It might be pretty in the day, but the night only conjured images of monsters in the shadows.

The main pathway led through winding lanes of graves. Keeping her eyes forward as to not look for shapes and spirits in the shadows, she felt like she was tiptoeing through a stranger's house.

Her heart drummed in her chest. What would she say when she found him? Would he even recognize her? She'd thought about everything leading up to this moment but hadn't planned what to do when she found him. Talk to him? Lure him back to the Tower somehow?

A great atone archway covered in vines loomed overhead, and Azalea psyched herself up to walk through. This was it. He was in there.

CHAPTER 39

FABIAN HAD BEEN CHASING this gallu for months, but it was smarter than anything he'd tracked before. It was always one step ahead. But it wouldn't get away this time. It was too close to being corporeal for him to let it. This time he had a foolproof trap.

He set up at a cemetery, as usual. This time he had picked one of the oldest cemeteries in London—Highgate, a favorite of his. Instead of setting the black diamond shield gems just around the body, he had placed concentric circles of weaker gems starting outside the mausoleum. As the gallu crossed each one, it would become more tangled in his web without knowing it, unable to go back.

Now, he waited.

He'd borrowed so many gems that if this went wrong, or he lost them, he was well and truly screwed. He couldn't afford to replace them. Not to mention he'd lose his credibility as a hunter if this creature got away. He rolled his flask over in his hands before placing it back in his jacket. He'd need every drop of magic he could muster tonight.

Perching on a stone wall, he shrouded himself in a shadow cloak. His eyes were well adjusted to the night. He wanted to see the creature coming. Slowly he took calming breaths, lowering his heart rate, and pushing his ears to hear every inch of sound on the still night air. Faint footsteps sounded in the distance, but it wasn't the gallu.

His hands were going numb. He rolled his shoulders and tried to think warm thoughts, hoping the creature would show up soon.

The body in his trap was an old man who had died of a heart attack that day. He was extremely talkative and doing a good job of attracting other spirits to him. Ghostly figures made their way across the quiet cemetery. Some babbling to each other, others just looking lost, wandering aimlessly since they forgot their purpose in life, and now in death. He had stopped feeling sorry for them long ago.

He never understood why anyone would choose to linger when the grand adventure after death waited. They were all cowards without the bollocks to move on. Children were the exception. They often kept a bond with a parent and couldn't go on alone. Them, he felt sorry for.

His spinel ring began pulsing long before he saw anything.

In the distance, near the edge of his gem web, a dark shape moved. Fabian narrowed his vision and watched as the creature crept closer. It lifted its head to sniff the air and let out a chilling laugh. His skull prickled. Gallu never laughed.

Then something unexpected; a woman's voice calling out. "Dad, are you there?" He couldn't tell if it was a spirit or not. They often called out for their loved ones, but this sounded different.

He jumped off his perch, keeping the gallu within sight. It hadn't noticed him yet and was heading straight for the spirits.

The ghost gathering had grown, all flocking around the newly dead man whose name Fabian hadn't bothered to find out. The gallu moved through the gravestones, weaving in and out with ease. It had bulked up since he saw it last. Its hide was thick and rough, no longer oozing and oily. A very bad sign.

"Dad!" the voice called again, more desperate this time. He was sure it was human, and she was heading right for the gallu. He rushed to the other side of the courtyard and was about to call out but stopped dead in his tracks.

Azalea.

"Shut up!" he hissed and raced over to her. She spun around, eyes wide with fright. She clearly hadn't been looking for him. Panic flooded him. Then what the hell was she doing there?

"Uncle Fabian?" She stood there, stunned.

He grabbed her wrist and yanked her behind a column. "It's not safe here. You need to go." He poked his head out to check that the gallu was still heading toward the spirit trap.

"No, I need to be here. My dad," she said as she rubbed her wrist. "He's here."

Fabian's stomach dropped. It couldn't be true. He would have surely known if his brother had returned as a spirit. "He isn't here. You need to leave. I need to catch this gallu, and I've only got one shot. I can't have you screwing this up or getting yourself killed by mistake.

She clenched her jaw and stood her ground. "He's one of those spirits there and he's going to get eaten. You need to help him."

Great, just what he needed. No way his brother was a spirit. He turned back to the gallu which was nearly at the spirits. He had to act now, whether she was there or not.

"Stay here," Fabian ordered.

"No, I'm coming with you."

"This thing could kill you." He clenched his elemer. "I can't watch you and catch it."

"Don't, then. I'll just stay behind you. I can make a shadow cloak. I'll hide. Just get on with it."

His blood raged. She was still taking lessons with Dumont. He would bet his best whiskey that murderer had no idea who Azalea was. Maybe Fabian should tell her the truth? That would scare her off.

He cursed under his breath. Azalea would have to stay. He couldn't wait.

CHAPTER 40

T HE SHOCK OF FABIAN appearing nearly gave Azalea a heart attack. It couldn't be a coincidence they were both there. It had to be her dad drawing them in. She peered around the edge of the stone column as Fabian crept between the shadows. She had never seen that many spirits in one place. All lively and rambling on as if they knew it was New Year's Eve. Fabian must have lured them for his trap, and her dad was one of them. She was sure of it.

She knew how important catching this gallu was, but she didn't want her dad to be one of its next victims.

Fabian crept around the edge of the old tombstones, slowly closing in on the gallu. Azalea choked back a cry when she saw it. The monster was nothing like the descriptions she'd read about. It wasn't a fresh ghostly wraith, nor did it have an oily sheen of the secondary phase. It looked like it was comprised of thick leather that had been stitched together. Its head was an unformed blob that was vaguely humanoid, though there was nothing human about the rest of it. It had dark hollows for eyes, no mouth, no ears, and slits for a nose. It jerked its head unnaturally, as if sniffing in every direction. It was terrifying and every inch of her told her to get the fuck out of there.

It neared the congregation of spirits and attacked without hesitation. Bile rose in Azalea's throat as it tore at the spirit's limbs, ripping them apart and shoving them into tentacles that protruded from its body.

They crouched behind an angel statue, and she glanced at Fabian, whose eyes were wide and fixed on the monster. "This is bad." The way he said it shot ice through her veins, adding to the growing chill from the spirits.

"Please, for the love of the gods stay here. I need to seal in each barrier circle as it enters so I can trap it. Don't interfere. I've only got one chance, and this is the closest I've ever seen a gallu to being corporeal. There won't be a second shot."

Panic rose in her chest. His trap might hold it, but the spirits were hostages as much as the gallu. Being eaten by this creature wasn't something she wished on anyone, not even the annoying spirits. She scanned the group for her dad, half hoping to see him, half hoping she was wrong, and he wasn't there.

Fabian slipped closer and held his position as the gallu neared the innermost circle of his trap. To anyone passing by, the cemetery would have appeared as silent and serene as ever. They wouldn't hear the horrible screams.

The gallu loomed closer, plucking up stray spirits as it went and tearing them apart to absorb them into its deformed body. Azalea wanted to scream at them, to tell them to move. But she knew they wouldn't listen.

A few started shrieking as the gallu neared, and they realized what it was doing. They scattered in all directions but found themselves trapped in Fabian's circle. Fabian took no notice. He moved in, sealing each circle with what she assumed were gemstones.

Spirits crashed against the invisible barriers, screaming to be set free with no understanding of what was holding them. They saw Azalea and pleaded for help. She avoided their eyes and noticed the bait at the center and stifled a scream with her hand. A human body was spread across a grave. An old man sat on top of it—the body's owner.

Azalea swallowed back vomit. Fabian must have put it there. She watched in horror as the gallu made it to the body. The spirits were in full panic mode, their usual creepiness replaced with gut retching screams of terror and pain. Some tried pleading with the beast, others clawed at the unseen walls, a few tried to protect the child spirits but they were all fair game to the gallu.

It ripped and tore its way through the crowd. Azalea continued to search for her dad, but she couldn't see him. He wasn't one of them. She studied their terrified faces, but Fabian was right. He wasn't there. So where was he? She had been so sure about this.

The gallu neared its prize in the center and Fabian pulled something from his pocket. As the creature moved in on the fresh spirit, he crouched with his elemer out, holding a small bottle in his other hand. The gallu paused at the edge of the circle and made a hissing noise before gliding into the trap.

The old man stood over his body, yelling at the gallu, trying to protect his corpse. But that wasn't what it wanted. Azalea wanted to rush over, yell at the stupid man to run, but he had little to no hope if these were his survival instincts.

Fabian shot out with lightning speed and sealed his trap with the gallu in it.

The monster wrapped its leathery limb around the arm of the old man's spirit, pulling it in close. It didn't rip bits off like the others. Instead, it rubbed its face over the old man as if drinking in his smell.

Fabian's eyes were closed in concentration. She could tell he was building up a spell cloud to prepare to seal the gallu. She stayed quiet.

He stepped out from behind the stone and faced the beast. With a rapid cut, he threw a wave of magic so strong that Azalea felt shock waves roll out from it. The low vibration resonated through every cell in her body. Horror gripped her as Fabian forced more and more power into the gallu with a stream of purple electric light. She imagined the power searing like ice through his veins. Bloody hell, that was a lot of power. There was no way he could keep this up. The gallu fought back, thrashing its limbs, and backing to the edge of the barrier. Its body jerked around, trying to throw off the magic link.

Fabian severed the spell and shot back behind Azalea's safety gravestone. Breathing heavily with sweat pouring down his face, he threw a cloak of shadows across the inner circle.

"Is it working?" she asked.

He shook his head, trying to catch his breath. "It's so strong. My spell was powerful. It shouldn't have been that hard. I heard the gallu's shell start to crack, but it wasn't enough. I'll have another go at it," he said between breaths.

"Let me help. Can I lend my magic somehow?" She was desperate to do something.

He gave her a disapproving look. "Just stay back. If it breaks out, it can kill us. Keep a shadow cloak around you and run if you have to."

He turned away and darted back between stones. Azalea peered through the shadows and made out the shape of the gallu. It held the old man's spirit in its grip, dragging him around like a rag doll and scanning with its hollow eyes into the darkness to find its attacker.

Fabian positioned himself closer to try another shot. He held up his elemer but froze. The gallu spoke.

Azalea caught her breath. It wasn't a raspy, leathery voice as one might expect, but a familiar, human voice. A slight hiss was the only giveaway that it was a monster.

"Fabian, I know it's you who huntsss me."

Fabian's face fell in a moment of shock before he regained his composure. He aimed his elemer at the creature's chest. His spell went straight through the old man's spirit. Azalea felt the wave of power once more, but stronger this time.

The gallu roared as the spell tried to dismantle it from within. It thrashed and slammed against the barrier, raging, and dragging the spirit with it. Fabian was struggling to hold the connection as it moved. He couldn't seem to keep a clear line of sight. The spell broke. Azalea felt the retraction of energy as Fabian stumbled back, scrambling to get upright. He was too slow and too close to the barrier.

Sitting around and waiting was killing her. Why didn't she know anything useful? She didn't want to hurt Fabian or make things worse. The gallu snatched Fabian and tossed him hard into a stone wall. Azalea heard the breath knock out of him. She remained under her shadow cloak, her brain whirling with useless ideas. Adrenaline pushed her muscles forward, and before she knew it, she was weaving between headstones until she was directly behind Fabian, but out of sight.

"You will listen to me Fabian," the gallu said.

"I don't give a rat's arse what you have to say. I'm here to do one thing, and it sure as hell isn't to listen to you." He struggled to his feet.

"Don't you recognize me? Don't you want to hear my tales of the afterlife and how I came to be in this world?"

Azalea felt the bile rise in her throat at how human it seemed and how it was enjoying this. Was this normal? Fabian didn't speak. All the simple elemental magic and Shadow Magic she knew seemed useless in this situation.

"Don't you recognize me? I'm insulted, though some time must have passed. I am not so familiar with this mortal plane. Perhaps I look a little different, but deep down you know who I am? Yesss?" it hissed.

Coldness latched onto Azalea's core. She knew that voice, though Fabian wouldn't have heard it in years. Her throat felt like it was closing, and she couldn't swallow, couldn't breathe. What had Elam said about gallu—*they can retain the memories of the spirits they eat. They get smarter as they consume more spirits. They can even use the memories of the spirits' loved ones and go after them.*

Vomit rose in her mouth, and she threw up against the back of a gravestone.

The creature lashed out and clasped its leathery protrusion across Fabian's ribs, crushing him into the stone.

The haunting sound of the gallu's laugh tore through every cell in her body. "Come out, little girl. I know you're hiding in your shadows."

"Azalea, stay back!" Fabian wheezed.

Azalea had to do something. She couldn't just let him die. Not when it was all her fault. She gripped her elemer tightly and stepped out from behind the stone.

"There you are." It sounded sickeningly pleased. "You know who I am now, don't you? I can see it in those stormy eyes."

"You're not him." She heard the waver in her voice.

It laughed again. "No. But he is part of me." It turned its empty face toward Azalea, then jerked back to Fabian and hitched him higher against the stone. Fabian made a choking sound.

"Have you worked it out yet? *Brother.*"

The words stabbed through Azalea's heart, and from the look on Fabian's face, he felt the same way. His expression crumbled as realization hit him.

"Samael?"

She had done this. She had let this monster trick her into bringing it here. She had let it manipulate her, let herself believe her father was out there. It had used his memories, his voice against her. He'd known about the book; known she would use it. It was this sick creature all along. The gallu had eaten her dad's spirit.

CHAPTER 41

"SAMAEL," FABIAN CHOKED ON the word.

A sob escaped Azalea at the sound of her father's name. Realization cascaded down and crushed her chest like an avalanche.

"Do you want to know how I came to this mortal plane, Brother?" it said.

Azalea could feel the tears streaming down her cheeks. The still night pressed in around her, hauntingly silent.

The creature's face slid down to Fabian's eye level.

"I don't care how you got here. Azalea, get out of here!" Fabian tried to move, but the gallu pressed harder, crushing his lungs.

"No, she should stay," it hissed. "You see, it was my sweet daughter that brought me here. She sought me out one equinox. I was in the Hollow, hoping for a weak point to appear in the veil, but what I found was much better. She wanted to help me. I promised to teach her Shadow Magic if she succeeded. Last equinox, she got the chance." He let out a grating laugh that splinted through Azalea's bones.

Fabian didn't speak. He kicked out and with a burst of energy, threw his spell at the gallu. His eyes were wide and black as purple light poured from his elemer, and the gallu staggered back and screeched into the night air. Fabian stumbled and fell back to the barrier. A flicker of light surged, and Azalea knew the barrier had fallen.

Fabian lost his hold on the spell. The creature realized its advantage and lunged at Fabian in full attack mode.

It ignored Azalea as Fabian ran. He was trying to lure it away from her. She sprinted to the other side of the courtyard and climbed onto a mausoleum roof and hid behind the triangle piece at the front. The gallu moved with surprising speed, closing in on Fabian's tail. He narrowly dodged the arms that shot out like leathery octopus' limbs.

Cracks of defensive spells rang through the cemetery. Fabian threw blue fireballs and uplifted gravestones behind him as he ran. Nothing stopped it.

It seemed amused by Fabian's attempts. It slunk around as if it were toying with him, working him up to exhaustion. It seemed to be working. Azalea watched helplessly.

Fabian was stumbling on tree roots and rocks. The way the gallu had crushed his ribs, she was surprised he could run at all. He dropped to the ground and Azalea couldn't hide any longer. She jumped down the wall but ended up half sliding, half falling down the uneven surface. She landed hard on her ankle and scraped her arm and hip against rough concrete. She got up and started hurling dirt at the gallu.

"Get away from him!" she screamed as she called to the plants to draw on them with Echo Magic, but she was so surrounded by Shadow Magic that they didn't respond. The gallu turned and laughed.

Fabian was on the ground, gasping for breath. Azalea rushed over to him and tried to help him up. He only pushed her away. "Just leave, Azalea. Get the fuck out of here and tell someone what happened."

"No, I won't leave you!"

She pulled through as much Shadow Magic as she dared and raised a shadow shield between them and the gallu, bigger than she'd ever done before. She made cuts to both dimensions and pulled moisture from the ground and mixed it with shadows and forced it through her elemer. A jet of ice blasted out and coated the gallu. The magic burned in her veins, a beautiful and painful searing of power. It froze the gallu on the spot.

She released the magic and ran to Fabian. Together, they struggled backward.

A sickening crack of ice echoed across the cemetery. The gallu lumbered toward them, straight through her shadow shield, then stopped.

"Thanksss for the feast and the fun. But I must be going now. It would be too easy to kill you now." It let out a low, maniacal laugh and lumbered off.

Fabian slumped against a headstone, his breath rasping. What the hell had just happened? She didn't want to believe that this vile creature held part of her father's soul. Deep hatred burned in her chest.

She reached out to prop up Fabian, who was about to pass out. His face was void of color and dripping with sweat.

"Hold on, I'm getting help." Her hands were shaking as she rummaged through her backpack for her phone. She called Danni and tried to keep herself together. She told her where they were, and that Fabian was having trouble breathing.

"You need to cut into the Hollow, Azalea. It's the fastest way," Danni yelled against the background noise of the party.

"I don't know how." What if they got trapped in there? How would they get out?

"You can do it. Just cut through and get Fabian inside. Then get Fabian to cut through to the Tower. He knows the right spot. Is he awake enough to do it?"

"Maybe," Azalea said weakly. He would have to be.

As she pressed end, a crack thundered across the sky. She ducked and looked up. It was only fireworks. Midnight bells tolled, and the sky burst into colorful explosions. Fabian took no notice. He just growled as Azalea tried to help him up.

She told Fabian the plan, but he pulled himself up the stone, rather than accept her help. She forced the last of her energy into cutting a Hollow. Making a wide arc big enough to fit through, she held the silky edge open as Fabian went through first. She stumbled in after, barely able to hold the portal open. It sealed behind them and she felt the absolute silence of the Hollow swallow them up. She had done it, but it didn't feel like much of a triumph.

At least Fabian was still conscious. He didn't speak. Just cut another Hollow then collapsed to the ground. Azalea held her elemer against the ghostly doorway and almost sobbed in relief when she heard familiar voices. Danni and Maiken were there and in a flash had him out of the Hollow in the tunnel under the hospital.

They eased him into a wheelchair, his head lolling to the side. They sprinted up the hall to the elevator. Danni stayed behind to explain the sudden activity that would attract guards.

Maiken and Azalea were upstairs to the flat before anyone knew they were there. Maiken didn't ask what happened. She got Fabian onto the sofa and held her elemer over his chest. As she moved it along different parts of his body, it changed color. She stopped longer at places where it turned red. The part over his lungs was the darkest.

Maiken put her hands and the elemer over his chest and pressed into it. Her eyes turned black, and her face strained as a faint flow of magic entered the room. It only took a few seconds. Maiken doubled over and started coughing. Red veins shone bright, glowing against her dark skin, and spread around her eyes like tiny branches. "Get those pills on the counter, please," Maiken asked.

Azalea grabbed the pills and quickly filled a glass with water and handed it to her. Maiken recovered quickly and sat back up, her black eyes turned bloodshot.

"What happened? Is he alright? Are you alright?" Azalea asked, genuinely concerned about Maiken after what just happened.

"He's fine. Just a few cracked ribs. I healed them just enough to help his breathing and put him to sleep so he'll be out for a while. I'll be fine, it wasn't too much damage."

"Thank you," Azalea said, meaning it wholeheartedly. Everything was her fault. She couldn't deal with Fabian dying or Maiken getting sick because of her.

Azalea sank to the floor. Maiken watched her but said nothing. A few minutes later, Danni came back, her eyes wide and panicked.

"Are you both okay?" Danni asked.

Azalea nodded.

"Torin was over here before in a tizzy that something had happened to you. I have no idea how he knew, but we searched high and low for you—"

"We're just glad to see you back in one piece," Maiken cut in. Perhaps she could tell that Azalea was on the edge of collapse, barely holding back the tears.

Danni agreed, then jumped up. "I'd better call Torin."

Once Danni got back, Maiken updated her on Fabian's condition and reached for her first aid kit on the coffee table and patched up Azalea's various scrapes and scratches. Azalea was starting to hurt all over.

"You need to tell us what happened. Don't leave out any details, okay?" Danni said kindly.

Azalea's lip trembled as she talked. Without intending it, everything tumbled out at once. How she had been learning Shadow Magic with Torin, how she could see all the spirits, how she never lost hope her dad was out there, and how she thought he might have been at the cemetery.

Azalea didn't say how she tracked the spirits, but made it sound like she knew Fabian would be there. She paused when she got to the part about the gallu speaking. Tears rolled down her cheeks, and she wiped her nose with her sleeve. "My dad wasn't there. He wasn't a spirit." Sobs wracked her shoulders, but she had to say it. "It was the gallu. My dad was the gallu, and it used me, it used the knowledge from my dad's spirit." She couldn't say anything else.

There was a stunned silence. All she could hear was her heart drumming in her ears and the sobs heaving her chest so hard she couldn't stop.

"Oh, Azalea," was all Danni said.

This was bad, and she hated herself for not realizing, for not listening. She was going to get arrested or kicked out for sure.

"What's going to happen now?"

"We'll see what Fabian has to say in the morning. For now, I suggest you go home," Danni said. Her usual attitude of waving off problems was nowhere in sight. Azalea had never seen her scared before.

"I'm so sorry," Azalea said through tears as she pulled herself up and stumbled out the door.

CHAPTER 42

A ZALEA CRIED HERSELF TO sleep but was plagued with horrible dreams of talking gallu and screaming spirits. She turned on the bedside lamp and stared at the ceiling. She was drained. Drained of power, drained of tears, drained of emotion—drained of life. She wanted it to be morning, but also wanted the night to go on forever, so she wouldn't have to face the next day. Face Fabian.

The dawn came too soon. A loud knocking filtered through her dreams and had her stumbling out of bed to answer the door. It was Fabian. Already.

"Are you okay?" she asked as she rubbed her eyes. Her heart pounded. She had fucked up and probably cost him his job, and he was about to tell her she was kicked out.

"No. My bloody ribs are broken." That wasn't what she meant. She knew he wasn't okay, and she felt terrible for it. Fabian wouldn't look her in the eye as he sat down on the sofa. She mindlessly switched on the kettle.

Fabian glared at her. "Do you have any idea what you've done?"

At least no one else was here to witness this. She nodded, the guilt creeping up. "I'm sorry." It felt pathetic to say so little, but she didn't know where to start.

His eyes drilled into her. "How the hell are you still alive?" He didn't give her time to answer. "Correct me if I'm wrong, but you performed an advanced, not to mention, *illegal* necromancy spell with blood magic in order to try bring your father back?" He shook his head as if not believing his own words. "Which failed because it was never your father. It was a fucking gallu." He spat the words like poison.

She sat like a river stone, cold and solid, letting the words flow over her like a current. She deserved whatever he said next.

"As stupid as that is, I believe it. What I don't understand is how the hell you are still alive? Do you understand how impossible that situation is?" He winced as he tried to straighten up.

"I don't know how," she mumbled. She couldn't explain how Torin had saved her. Her uncle wouldn't focus on the saving her part, he'd focus on the illegal necromancy Torin also performed, and she didn't want to give him any more fuel against Torin. How was she so blind to the truth? She hadn't even considered it might not be her dad.

"I told you not to use Shadow Magic. I told you not to use the real elemer. I didn't think it was necessary to tell you not to use necromancy or blood magic, but here we are. I'm sorry Azalea, I should have taken you somewhere else and taught you myself. This is my fault." Guilt was plain across his face.

She stared at him, shocked. "This isn't your fault. It's mine, and I'm so sorry. I had no idea what I was doing. I thought it was my dad for real. 'Course I was going to listen to him over anyone else."

His expression dropped as his guilt and anger washed away, replaced with unmistakable pity.

"I forget how little you know about all this," he said sadly.

This was worse than being yelled at. He should be yelling.

"You have to understand it was never your father in there. It must have consumed enough of Samael's spirit on the other side to manipulate his memories. That's how it knew us both. How it knew how to use you. You can't blame yourself."

Images of her dad being ripped apart flickered across her mind. Same as those poor spirits last night. Reality came crashing down on her. She had done this. She had screwed everything up. She tried to calm her jagged breathing but felt silent hot tears creep down the side of her face. Sliding onto the sofa, her forehead fell into her hands. Her father was dead, and he wasn't coming back.

She couldn't look at Fabian.

Why had she been so stupid, so gullible? Her dad was dead for real, and it felt like she was drowning. She was a failure. Everything she learned; it was all pointless. Her dad would never come back, never teach her Shadow Magic. They would never become great mages together. She had failed. Failed in the most epic way possible and set a monster loose on London. People would die because of her.

"Fuck, what have I done?" she mumbled under her breath, wishing she could go back to the night she had apparently died, and just stay dead.

Fabian groaned as he moved. "You've fucked me over, that's for sure." There was no sympathy in his voice. "I've failed my job and I'll have to get a team of hunters in to help me. There'll be no work for me after this."

Another layer of guilt jumped on her shoulders. "What will you do? You can still catch it, right?"

He shrugged. "I don't know, Azalea. At least they'll still need me for the next full moon when it summons more wraith gallu through. After that, who knows?" Fabian said.

"More gallu?" Shit just kept getting worse.

"Yes. But you just worry about yourself. You've got enough problems heading your way."

"Like what?" her voice came out as a squeak. She had to find a way to help him fix this, it was her fault.

"Danni was obligated to inform the Archmage about what happened. This is too serious to sweep under the rug. There will be consequences."

"I'm going to get kicked out." Her stomach dropped to her feet. She'd be back to where she started, cowering at home, hiding from spirits the rest of her life. No way Fabian would take her in now and Torin hadn't taught her spirit warding yet, so she was pretty much fucked.

"Probably. Can't say you don't deserve it." He stood up and started shuffling out. It felt like he'd stabbed a knife into her heart.

She apologized once more, but it felt meaningless. She couldn't make up for what she'd done. For the people that might die at the hands of the gallu because of her.

Then Fabian was gone. Azalea slid down the wall in the hallway and broke down sobbing.

)))●(((

The morning seemed like it had been another horrible dream in a chain of horrible dreams. She woke late in the afternoon and forced herself up. She made a bacon sandwich and sipped her tea through trembling lips as a dark feeling boiled in the pit of her stomach.

The Archmage would be turning up any minute now to kick her out. Maybe it was better to get it over with, rip off the plaster and leave without a fuss.

She checked her phone. No messages from Fabian. Some from her mum and Isaac wishing her happy new year. She'd forgotten all about that. What a fucked-up way to start the year, certainly a bad omen.

What was surprising was the 50 or so messages and missed calls from Torin. They started late last night and went right up till this afternoon. She skim-read through the thread, starting with the first one, asking if she was okay. They got more and more concerned as she read on. Then before midnight, he said he was coming to look for her. How the hell had he known something was wrong?

She had to find out and had to tell him what happened before someone else did. Leaving her tea, she yanked on a black hoodie and jeans and stepped into the chilly air of the new year. She tugged the hood over her head to hide her red, puffy eyes and set off for Torin's place. She darted past the chapel and the spirits, ignoring their cries, and shot up the stairs to Torin's tower.

She knocked on the door and within seconds, Torin was there. His face was a stony mask, but she could swear she felt anger and betrayal radiating off him—so much so that if she reached out, she was sure she would feel it like real flames. It was clear he already knew what had happened.

"I'm sorry, Torin."

"That's all you have to say?" He folded his arms and didn't invite her in.

"I want to tell you what happened. I thought my dad was one of the spirits." She knew it was no excuse, but she wanted him to understand why she did it.

"Gods, Azalea! I told you it wasn't possible he was out there. You've studied this. You knew it wasn't possible." His biceps flexed as he tightened his fists.

"I know. But I can't take it back now!" She looked up at the converging clouds, willing herself not to cry. "It's all my fault. It was me that released the gallu."

"Danni told me everything. You're a bloody fool. Do you have any idea how bad this is?" he said through clenched teeth. "That gallu is going to kill people. And all for your stupid experiment you knew nothing about. I've put everything on the line to protect you. My job, my reputation. Teaching you was supposed to make you think about your actions, but you could have been killed *again* last night." His eyes drilled into her, filled with disgust. "Do you care so little about your own life?" He cracked his fist into the door frame and turned away.

"I'm sorry I didn't listen to you, Torin. I'm sorry I didn't trust you."

"Just go, Azalea. Danni told the Archmage everything, so please, just stay away." He shook his head slowly, as if he didn't want to close the door in her face. But he did it anyway. The door clicked shut.

"I want to help fix things," she yelled at the closed door and rested her forehead against it. She had to make this right. She was sure she could feel his guilt shining through from the other side. He still blamed himself despite everything being her fault.

She trudged down the stairs and nearly bowled over an old woman on the way down. "Gosh. I'm so sorry," she said in reaction, reaching out to make sure the woman was okay. She was holding a cane but straightened herself up in a split second.

"No harm done, girl." The woman had fierce silver eyes, a short bob of pure white hair, and a look that said, *don't fuck with me*. It was hard to tell if she was fifty or one-hundred years old. She was spry with barely wrinkled skin, but those eyes . . . A cold chill ran down every inch of Azalea's spine. This was the Archmage. "You are Azalea?" she said as if accusing her.

This was not a good start. "Yes. It's so nice to finally meet you, Archmage. Sorry I nearly knocked you over." Her palms were sweating. This was it. She was going to get locked up or expelled, or something equally bad. This woman was terrifying.

"Sit with me." The Archmage took Azalea's elbow and guided her onto the cold stone step alongside her. She sat with her wooden cane out in front with both hands resting on the carved owl on top.

Silently freaking out, Azalea tried to appear calm and not on the edge of a meltdown. Suddenly, a force struck her mind like a lorry running straight into a brick wall. She doubled over in pain. Her skull felt like it might be ripped apart with the pressure.

It stopped. Azalea slumped over and reached for the wall before she fell over. A bony hand gripped her bicep. Ow! This witch had fingers of steel.

"There are no secrets that can be kept from me," the Archmage said in a cold, steady tone.

Azalea froze, not daring to move under her grip. She realized what had happened. A new level of fear washed over her. That woman had been in her brain. Had helped herself and pillaged her memories. It took a second for reality to catch up, but Azalea saw everything she had seen.

She tried to shuffle toward the wall, but the grip on her arm tightened.

"There, there, girl. No need to fret. You don't become Archmage by sitting around quietly and letting others run the show. Nothing goes on in the Tower without me knowing. You'd do well to remember that."

Azalea was dumbfounded. Why would she need to remember that if she was getting kicked out?

"And no. I will not be expelling you from the program. I have need of you. And you know what they say . . . two Shadow Mages are better than one." She dropped Azalea's arm and wiped her hand on her gray tweed coat.

Did people say that? She suspected not. Was this good or bad?

"But why?" Azalea blurted out, wishing she had come up with a more coherent sentence.

"You, little snake, are going to help me. You will continue your lessons with Mage Dumont. You will continue to learn Shadow Magic. And you will watch for me."

If anyone was a snake, it was this woman. Azalea could feel her thin eyes drilling into her. She tried to raise her mental shields but couldn't.

"What will I be watching?" It seemed better to go along with whatever this was than make things worse.

"You will watch Mage Dumont and you will report to me. You will work your way into his confidence and assist him in his mission. But first you will need to earn his trust."

A sudden tightness in her chest told her this was a bad idea. But what choice did she have?

"Thank you, Archmage. I truly appreciate this opportunity and I will help you any way I can," she said, hoping the Archmage believed her. This time, she forced up her mental shields. No way she would let this woman see she was lying. She wouldn't betray Torin; she would do everything she could to help him.

"Of course you do. Now go. I must speak with Mage Dumont."

Azalea didn't need telling twice. She was up and ready to get the fuck out of there.

CHAPTER 43

A ZALEA THOUGHT SHE COULD hold it together until she got home but as soon as she passed the chapel, she lost it. Shouldn't she be happy she was staying? Shouldn't she be grateful the Archmage was letting her and Torin off the hook, despite what she knew?

She tried to remain inconspicuous, sitting on the edge of someone's steps behind a potted plant, crying. It was pathetic. Uncontrollable sobs racked her body, and it was made much worse by the fact she was in public and surrounded by tourists who were probably staring at her. Fortunately, the people kept most of the spirits away. She ignored them all.

Wiping her eyes, she was unsure of the main reason she was crying. Was it Torin slamming the door in her face? The Archmage drilling into her brain with her sick mind magic? The fact that her dad was actually dead? The gallu out there ready to kill people because of her?

She didn't deserve to wallow. She should be fixing things. Forcing herself up, she stumbled toward home with her hood over her face. Suddenly, someone tall appeared next to her.

"Hey Zalea, you alright?" *Erik.*

"I need to go home," she said through gritted teeth, trying not to cry again. He pulled her in and wrapped his arms around her like a cocoon. A cocoon she so desperately wanted to climb into and disappear. His blue sweater was soft on her cheek, and she practically melted into his warm chest, but he reeked of alcohol. Why was she hugging Erik? This was weird, but his arms wrapped around her felt nice, even if it was just for a minute.

She detached herself from him and stepped back, suddenly feeling silly.

He put his arm around her shoulders and steered them home. Without a word, she opened the door, and he followed.

She went to the bathroom to wash her face. It was just her luck to have Erik there to witness her meltdown. Gods, she looked terrible. Black bags hung under her eyes and her hair was a mess from sleeping and not brushing it.

Go talk to Erik, she told herself. *Keep it together.* Back in the kitchen, Erik was making tea and seemed quite at home. He told her to sit down, and she sat at the table with her head in her hands.

"You want to tell me what happened?" he asked, bringing the tea over.

She shook her head. "No. It's all a bit much. I'm not even sure what I should do now," she said.

"How about we watch telly?" Erik suggested. "I've got a killer hangover anyway."

Right now, putting on pajamas and crawling into bed was what she really wanted, but an even stronger feeling told her she couldn't be alone. She couldn't face the voices in her head or reliving last night over and over. Erik was a distraction, and a distraction sounded good right about now.

"TV sounds good," she said and dragged herself to the sofa, pulling a soft blanket off the back. Erik settled in next to her and turned on the TV. He chose *Spirited Away* to watch. Lucky guess. It was one of her favorites.

Erik leaned back on the sofa. Should she offer him the other half of her blanket? He moved closer and helped himself to it, anyway. As he did so, he glanced at her arm of her rolled-up sleeve, her bee tattoo arm. A frown creased his forehead.

Her skin was crisscrossed with angry red scratches and cuts from scraping over rocks and through bushes last night. Not to mention the large purple bruise around her wrist from when Fabian had hauled her up behind the statue. She hadn't even noticed.

"How did this happen? Who hurt you?" he said.

That was an unexpected reaction. "It's just from training," she lied, hoping he'd drop it.

"Like hell it is. Something's not right. You're one of the toughest people I know, and I've never seen you cry. But here you are, falling apart and covered in bruises." He was holding her arm, examining it. "We should go to the hospital." He stood up.

She caught his arm, pulling him back to the couch. "No, please. I've already been there. Let's just stay here." She couldn't face leaving this room, let alone face Maiken again.

Reluctantly, he sat back down and crossed his arms after he reclaimed half the blanket. They watched in silence for about five minutes before Erik spoke up again.

"It was Mage Dumont, wasn't it? Are you actually going out with him? Did he do this?" he said in a low voice.

"No! It's not like that. This isn't his fault." Trust him to jump to crazy conclusions.

"If you say so," he said, holding his hands up in defense. "You don't have to tell me. I'll shut it now."

That lasted about a minute. "Look, if you're not going to go to the hospital, at least let me fix up the cuts?"

It was clear he wasn't going to give up, so she agreed. She was in no mood to argue. He took his time finding the right items in Evangeline's extensive medicine cupboard in the kitchen. He wiped all the cuts and bandaged them in the correct herbal bandages.

When he wanted to look at her other arm, panic shot through her, and she nearly punched him in the face.

"Sorry, gut reaction," she said as she pulled up the other sleeve, revealing her snake tattoo and an arm free of injuries.

"Wow," he said. "That is one sexy tattoo."

She smiled, suddenly feeling shy. How was it he accepted things so easily? He never once made her feel bad about her House, unlike Torin's reactions to everything.

She began to relax again until she glanced at the clock.

"Shit, we're supposed to be in class in five minutes for the sunset ritual." She groaned and couldn't think of anything worse than welcoming in the year right now. If it was starting like this, there wasn't much hope for the rest of it.

"Stay put." Erik dashed out the door. She was not at all motivated to move. He returned ten minutes later, saying he had talked to Mage Shepard. She didn't ask him what he told her, and she didn't care. Right now, she was having a hard time staying awake.

The movie finished and Van still wasn't home. Erik happily agreed to another movie.

Azalea fell asleep in the first ten minutes and woke to find herself leaning on Erik. He smelled more like tea than alcohol now at least.

"You should go to bed," he said, shaking the feeling back into his arm as she sat up.

No. He couldn't leave. She couldn't be alone. What if the spirits came this time, while she was so weak? Her imagination ran wild in the dim light. Spirits and gallu forcing themselves through the front door, squeezing in through the tiny windows.

Erik stood up.

"Please don't go. Please stay. I mean, could you stay until I fall asleep?" She knew she sounded desperate but didn't care. "I don't want to be alone."

"You sure?" He sounded uneasy. "Are you sure you're okay? You don't want me to go find someone for you?"

"No, please. I just don't want to be left to think. I know it sounds stupid, but Van won't be home till late."

She couldn't face anyone else. This seemed like the best immediate solution and right now, she needed sleep.

"I'll message my dad to tell him I'm over here," Erik said.

"Thanks, I'll get ready for bed. Then we can watch another movie in my room if you want?"

She got into bed and collapsed. Erik lay on top of the covers as Faraday placed himself strategically between the two humans. Minutes went by and she forgot how strange it was that Erik was lying next to her. He looked rather at ease in her room. She suspected he didn't mind the excuse to miss the class ritual, especially with his hangover.

Before long, her warring thoughts all merged together, and she drifted into a fitful sleep.

CHAPTER 44

AZALEA WOKE TO FIND something warm against her back. Erik was still in her bed and Faraday sat at the end, looking royally pissed off. Poor Erik was lying on top of the covers, curled up like he desperately needed a blanket.

Erik had been downright pleasant the day before, but that's because he didn't know what she'd done. Everyone else should hate her. She deserved it. She left Erik to sleep and draped a blanket over him, cursing herself for asking him to stay. Things weren't quite so scary in the light of day.

She stumbled into the kitchen and bumped into Van, whose eyes instantly went to Azalea's bandaged bee tattoo arm.

"Wait there."

"But I need some tea first," Azalea complained.

Van appeared back in the kitchen with her oversized medical bag. They sat at the table as Van unwrapped the bandages and began putting new, strange smelling things on Azalea's arm as she tried to drink her tea.

"Soo, where did you get these cuts and bumps?" Van asked.

Sick of all the lies, she told Van everything. Van had a million questions, which Azalea reluctantly answered. Though she left out the bit about the Archmage, Torin, and the Shadow Atlas.

So, not everything. But it felt good to tell the truth, and though Van seemed wary of her, at least she hadn't turned on her.

"I'm such a failure."

"No, you're not, Azalea," Van said firmly. "Though this is all a little shocking. We all keep secrets for a reason, and it's okay when it's protecting others. So, I won't hold that against you."

"Thanks, Van." Azalea reached over and hugged her.

"So why are we whispering?" Van asked after the marathon explanation session.

Azalea couldn't help her face going red.

"Do you have someone in your room?"

"Yes. But it isn't like *that*. I was a little upset last night, and you weren't home."

Van's eyes filled with concern. "I'm sorry, hun. There's something else you aren't telling me?" she said as she studied Azalea.

"Do you know anything about gallu?" Azalea asked.

"I know a little."

She was going to take a risk. "That gallu that escaped. I need to stop it," she said.

Van turned white. "Nope. You should stay the hell away from it, that's my heartfelt advice. There are professional hunters out there. Leave it to them."

"There aren't going to be enough hunters. It's fully corporeal. Soon there are going to be more than they can cope with, and I know how to track it."

Van sat there blinking. "You should tell someone that."

"My uncle thinks I'm a walking disaster, and I was going to tell Torin . . . but he isn't talking to me now. It's the thought of him hating me that I can't handle right now. I don't even know why." Saying it out loud made it hurt more. Her thoughts kept going back to him.

"It was an accident, Azalea. Don't blame yourself for everything."

"But the gallu can kill people now. My uncle said on the next full moon it will bring more through." She checked the moon cycle on her phone. "That's on the 28th of January, just under four weeks away."

Concern was written all over Van's face. "No. This is too dangerous. I see that you feel responsible for whatever reasons. But you should leave this to the professionals."

But they don't have the Shadow Atlas, Azalea thought to herself. She was relieved when Erik walked in, so she didn't have to explain further.

"Morning." He sat down at the kitchen table as if he lived there.

"Morning," Azalea and Van rang out at the same time. Azalea started to regret asking him to stay—he looked far too pleased with himself.

"So, you're the mystery man in Azalea's bed," Van said with a grin.

"That's me. I'm Erik, nice to meet you." They shook hands, and Erik turned to Azalea.

"You okay?"

She nodded. "I'm fine. Van's patched me all up."

"I told her to go to the hospital last night, you know. She wouldn't listen," Erik said to Van.

"Yes, she's a stubborn thing. You did a good job, though. And it's lucky she has me here to look after her." She patted Azalea on the head condescendingly.

"Guys, stop talking about me like I'm not here," Azalea said.

They both looked at her like she was a lost puppy.

"Anyway, I better get to training. I'm late. You should go back to bed." Van jumped up and winked at Azalea as she slipped off to her bedroom.

Erik made himself a cup of tea and sat down, looking right at home. "Better this morning?" he asked.

She nodded and forced a weak smile, feeling self-conscious that she had just woken up and spent half the previous day crying. "Thanks for staying. Sorry, I was such a mess yesterday."

"Don't mention it. But if it was Dumont who did that to you, you should really tell someone and stay away from him."

"It wasn't him, Erik."

"Then why were you running from his house crying?"

"It was my fault. I did something really stupid." She shook her head, wanting to shake all the memories out as if none of it happened.

"Want to tell me about it yet?"

She paused. She thought about telling Erik everything. After all, he was the only one who knew about her Shadow Magic and didn't seem fazed by it. But she couldn't bring herself to do it. "Maybe another time. I'm not really in the mood to talk about it."

He just nodded. Lately he'd been less arsehole Erik and more understanding Erik. He drained his tea. "Message me if you want to get out of classes again. I'll make up another story for us." He gave her a sly smile and hopped up to leave.

"Wait, what? What story did you tell them? Erik—?"

He was out the door in a flash. Azalea rested her head on her arms. She could see a whole lot of problems in her future.

CHAPTER 45

TORIN KNEW AZALEA WAS in the library the second he walked through the door. He sensed her, and the very thought of that made him uncomfortable. It was also the reason he was there. Not to talk to her, but to research something he had only figured out two days before when she nearly got herself killed a second time. *Soul bonds.*

It wasn't a good thing. A soul bond was rare, and something so archaic and taboo it had been buried in history. But it was the only thing he had found that explained his connection to Azalea. It would explain why he could sense her presence, or feel her emotions, or know when she was in danger. He suspected it had accidentally formed between them when he brought her back from the dead.

He spotted Azalea set up in an alcove with her computer, and with Erik. Torin glanced at her, and she turned around. She would have sensed him too, not that she would know what it meant. Their eyes met briefly. A flash of her pain and grief washed over him and he turned away, walking faster to get to the end of the vast room.

He shouldn't have spoken to her so harshly. The truth of finding out about her father must have crushed her, and he just slammed the door in her face. He was regretting that and wondering what sort of bargain she had made with the Archmage to keep her position in the Tower. Nothing good, he bet.

He reached the right section: *Marriage and Relationships.* Stepping down the aisle he found the book with a stiff leather spine: *Practices of Marriages and Magic for Nobility.* There were gold embellished hearts around the edges. "Bloody hell," he muttered to himself before he flicked it open. Nobility and magic went hand in hand throughout history. He flicked right to the end.

Soul bonds.

A Soul Bond will only form between those equal in soul and magic. By means of a blood binding, magic is called upon and tested by trial of death. Only in death is the true intention revealed. An act of love, a vow, and a knot will seal the binding. Great power will arise.

They had the blood and trial of death part down, but equal in soul and magic didn't seem right. The good news was, if it was a soul bond it hadn't been sealed if it required an act of love, a vow, and knot. It sounded very much like marriage. So there was still hope to undo it. But there was nothing written about *how* to undo it. He took a photo of the one page and put the book back.

An uneasy feeling crept up his spine. He wasn't even sure how it was possible to form an accidental soul bond. Soul bonds had been made illegal during the Victorian times, an era well known for the free use of magic in society. Back then, the penalty was death. He didn't know what it was now, but he assumed it wasn't any better.

He browsed the shelf mindlessly as he considered how a bond like that could have been made in the first place. Something had gone wrong with his spell, with the blood magic. His intention had been to call her back to him, not bind her to him. The zircon had been there for that very purpose, to bind her to the earth, to her body. Perhaps because they were in a Hollow, she couldn't bind to her body and the earth? Or there was another influence. He could only speculate.

He should probably tell Azalea . . . but keeping her in the dark about this seemed like a better idea. That way, if anyone found out, only he could be blamed. Perhaps ignoring it would weaken the bond until he found a way to break it. He rubbed his forehead, feeling the stress of the last few days building up. What he needed was a drink.

Everything was going to shit. With the gallu on the loose and the Archmage looming over him, demanding the next relic, his life was turning to chaos. He still had no idea why the Archmage had kept him around after everything with Azalea. One thing was for sure, that devil-woman had an agenda.

Giving up his hunt for any further info, he strode up the long central passage of the library, passing Azalea, who appeared deep in her studies. But he could tell she wasn't. He thought about going over to talk to her, but this was too public of a place. He'd wait another day. Right now, having a drink—or five— sounded like a good idea.

CHAPTER 46

E RIK ASKED AZALEA IF she wanted to meet up in the library to study. Right now, she'd take any distraction she could get and agreed to meet him at 11 am.

Coffee was what she needed today—or perhaps something stronger. She settled for the coffee and a blueberry and courgette muffin, one of Van's new experiments. She couldn't complain and it stopped the growl in her stomach. Packing up her laptop, she made her way to the library, not even noticing or caring what the weather was outside.

The glow of library lamps welcomed her as she entered the long stone room of books and spotted Erik in her favorite alcove.

"I knew you couldn't resist my charm for long," Erik said as he moved to the armchair, and she took the desk.

"With so much modesty, how could I?"

"Hey, you were the one who asked me to sleep over." He held his hands up. "Which you are welcome to do again, I might add."

She refused to let her cheeks go red. "I'll keep it in mind," she said, trying to sound casual. That cheeky smile of his. It was hard not to like him, but she wouldn't let herself forget what a dick he could be. She had no time for that sort of thing right now, anyway. She had enough on her plate.

She got out her computer with the intention of at least opening her Engineering Principles assignment that was due next week. Erik settled into his chair, playing some sort of shooting game on a tablet . . . So much for studying.

Staring at the screen, it was obvious she was in no state of mind for problem solving or complex theories. What she should be doing was using the Shadow Atlas to track the gallu. *That bloody book.* She hated the thought of opening it again, of feeding it magic and shadows after what it did to her. All it wanted was to be fed. It didn't care that it wasn't her father she found. It didn't care that she nearly died following its information. Still, it was her only hope of making things right, and she was determined to undo this mess she'd made.

A chill ran up her back and a wave of anxiety flooded through her. She turned toward the door, somehow already knowing it was Torin who had just entered. They held eye contact for a split second before she turned away, eyes set firm on her screen. *Strange. Torin didn't seem angry.* He looked concerned.

Their moment didn't go unnoticed by Erik.

"So, what was up with you and Mage Dumont? Are you ready to tell me what happened?"

She shifted in her seat. Of course, he wouldn't let it go that easily. "He was teaching me Shadow Magic."

Erik stared at her. "Why would you want to do that? And with him?"

"What's wrong with him?" she said, surprised at how that got her back up so fast. "Would you rather I was shagging him?" she said defensively.

Erik leaned on the chair arm with his chin on his hand, staring up. "Gods no. I'm actually rather relieved. But you know, it's all the stuff they say about him."

Wow. He wasn't subtle. She didn't want to get into an argument about any of this—she didn't have the energy.

Erik glanced around. "It's just that . . . after that time you nearly died. Why the bloody hell would you want to go anywhere near that stuff again?" he whispered.

"That 'stuff' is Shadow Magic, and it's not something to be scared of. I need to learn to control it."

He raised his eyebrows. "If you say so." He pulled a packet of crisps out of his bag and started eating them loudly. "So, what happened the other night that had you all upset?"

She was sick of secrets and there was no one else around to listen in. "I went on a gallu hunt with my uncle," she whispered, debating telling him the whole story.

"You what!"

Might as well tell him. Perhaps she would feel better to get it all off her chest. She lowered her voice and told him about the gallu, how her uncle hunted them, how she released one, the whole horrifying experience. She left out the parts about the Shadow Atlas, instead telling him the locket around her neck could track gallu. A silly lie, but a harmless one. He even seemed genuinely sympathetic when she told him it was all her fault and how she'd accidentally summoned the gallu.

By the end, he sat solemnly as if thinking it all over. "I'll keep your secrets, Azalea. Don't you worry about that."

She found she believed him, and it was like a weight lifted from her shoulders. He was so accepting. So easy to be around, except for this eating in the library thing. Erik was the opposite of Torin with his constant assessments and judging eyes. She kept looking behind her as if she could feel Torin lurking back there.

"It seems like having magic comes hand in hand with keeping secrets," she said.

He leaned further over the arm of his chair. "Sometimes I swear this Tower is built on secrets. If you took them away, it would crumble to nothing. Secrets keep our world running. Secrets and corrupt bloody House politics," he said.

"You're probably right." The Archmage was the queen of secrets and corruption, apparently. Though that thought wouldn't be wise to say out loud . . . or even in her head.

They went back to 'studying,' and Azalea did her best to ignore Torin's constant presence. She wondered if he'd put some sort of tracking spell on her, or if he could read her mind. It was a strange feeling she couldn't shake.

Azalea made a small start on her assignment, but her brain just wasn't in it. After another twenty minutes, Torin left.

She couldn't stop thinking about him. How she had screwed up his life, put his job at risk, then agreed to spy on him for the Archmage. She was a horrible person. After another ten minutes, she couldn't sit there any longer.

Torin had been right all along. Every warning both him and Fabian had given her was for her own good, and she had ignored them both. This whole time, she'd acted like a selfish brat who thought she knew everything about Shadow Magic. She slammed her laptop shut. She was a horrible person, and she had to make it up to him. He had trusted her and all she had done was disappoint him. Well, not this time. It was her turn to trust him and tell him the truth.

"Sorry, Erik, I've got to go."

"You're going after him, aren't you?"

"Yes. I need to make things right."

"Good luck," he said without much enthusiasm.

She dashed out of the library and bolted up the stairs of the Barracks, taking two at a time. Then she realized she needed some sort of peace offering. She darted through all the tourists and made it to her flat in record time.

She hunted under her bed and in the hall closet and collected an armful of umbrellas. Making a beeline for Torin's tower, she ran past the spirits and shot up the stairs, not stopping for anything.

She knocked. He was slow to open the door, and he blinked into the afternoon sunlight. He wasn't dressed for work anymore; he was wearing workout clothes, a nicely fitted black t-shirt, gray jogging bottoms, and bare feet. But he didn't look like he had any plans to workout based on the glass of dark liquid in his hand.

"Hi. Are you okay?" She shuffled nervously.

He ran a hand across his shaved head. "What are you doing here, Azalea?"

She looked him straight in the eyes, telling herself to be brave. "I came to apologize. Here." She handed him an armful of his own umbrellas. "I'm sorry, Torin. I want to make things right."

He knocked back his drink. "You might as well come in."

At least he hadn't told her to piss off straight away. His office was cold.

She followed him upstairs and relaxed a little as she entered the familiar warm room, drawn to her favorite chair by the fire, but found it covered in a mountain of books and papers. Torin shuffled the pile to the floor and slumped into the other chair. More paper and books were strewn across the coffee table and stacked in a precarious tower leaning against his chair.

"Sorry about the mess," he said half-heartedly. This was chaos-state-Torin.

Her eyes darted to the kitchen. It was far messier than she'd ever seen it. Empty wine and whiskey bottles lined the bench, and empty food packaging burst from the rubbish bin.

"I'll make tea." It would be better to have something to do, and Torin didn't protest.

While the kettle boiled, she filled a glass with water and brought it over to him. Their fingers touched as she passed him the glass. A fuzzy spark ignited where their fingers met, just as it had before, and Azalea drew her hand back swiftly. Torin's eyes widened. But he didn't acknowledge anything had happened. She stepped back and pulled her hand to her chest.

"You said you were here to apologize. I'm listening." His face didn't change, but something about him made Azalea think he wanted to apologize to her.

"Look, Torin. I'm sorry I didn't listen to you. I'm sorry you had to save me and that I keep wrecking things. And I'm sorry I lied to you about my House and didn't tell you when I went to look for my dad." A lump caught in her throat. "But I want to make things right. I want to be honest with you."

"Well, you can start by telling me what bargain you made with the Archmage to keep your place here, and mine for that matter. I know I didn't do this. I was expecting to be thrown out alongside you, but she asked me to keep teaching you. Why?"

So, he knew exactly what type of person the Archmage was. She went to get the tea. "She said that two Shadow Mages were better than one," Azalea said genuinely. But how could she tell him the bargain she made without the Archmage finding out? But they needed to trust each other, and she had to tell him. "She was in my head. She ripped everything out." A trickle of fear ran through her at the memory of that woman clawing through her brain.

Torin twisted in his chair and stared at her in horror. "She did not," he said, almost stunned. "I didn't think she'd dare."

Azalea carefully carried the tea to the fireplace and set Torin's next to him, though he seemed set on drinking whiskey. She sat in the chair across from him. "I'm scared she'll do it again if I tell you the rest. Then we'll both be out of here."

"There's a potion you can take. I never thought you'd have a need for it, but desperate times. I take the potion every morning, and you should start too. It keeps your memories safe, and I'll teach you a technique for projecting only the memories you choose. Just tell me the truth, Azalea. I need you to do that."

That was just the news she needed to hear. At least one thing was going her way. She had to start trusting people, and this was the start of it. She took a long breath. "She asked me to spy on you. She said to continue our lessons, and that I was to gain your trust, then report back to her on your progress, or whatever it is you're doing."

Torin downed his whiskey. "So, she really doesn't trust me," he said with a laugh, though he clearly didn't find it funny.

"Why not?" She hoped he was pleased that she told him. Either way, they had to start their lessons again. But she preferred for him to want her there, not to be forced.

"She doesn't know where my allegiance lies. She probably thinks I'm a spy for my father, which I am not."

"Oh. Well, I have no intention of spying on you. So do you still want to do lessons?" she asked.

"What you did was incredibly stupid, Azalea. But I'm hoping you have learned your lesson since," he said, but with none of the rage he had the last time. "But since I don't have a choice in the matter either way, I suggest we start working together rather than fighting."

"I will make it up to you, I promise."

"Well, you do need to promise me something."

She held his stare.

"Next time you're about to do something stupid, just tell me about it first."

Relief filled her chest. She hoped there wouldn't be a next time. A hint of guilt clawed up her back. She just hoped Fabian would accept her help once she told him about the tracking. If not, she'd have to go after it alone and suspected Torin wouldn't be open to helping.

"Thanks, Torin. I truly am sorry, and next time I'll tell you." His eyes met hers. A strange feeling came over her, as if he was reading her mind. She pushed her thoughts behind her vault, just in case.

"Or you could work on there not being a next time?" He raised his eyebrows.

She gave a weak laugh. "So, when can we start training again?" she asked optimistically.

"Give me a day. How about Tuesday night?"

Today was Sunday, Tuesday she could deal with. "Sounds good. Now, how about I clean up in here? You have a shower, then we can get your work back down to your office before the Archmage realizes what a mess you've made."

He rubbed his face and looked around. It was a lot of mess for a few days, and she knew a large part of this was her fault.

"Things haven't been going well. I'm a lot further behind the Archmage's expectations of finding these relics than I need to be," he said.

Was he finally going to tell her about them? She sat as still as she could as if he were a wild animal that might spook.

"It's not going as planned. I need to find this collection of relics before the House of Ravens gets to them. It's important. I keep hitting dead ends and the next one might be dangerous to get. I'm not looking forward to it."

"I'm here if you require an assistant, any time—day or night."

"Thanks. I might have to take you up on that," he said reluctantly. "After I get you that potion."

She smiled. Things weren't as bad as they seemed when she woke up that morning. Now all she had to do was see past the Shadow Atlas betraying her and use it as a tool to find the gallu once more.

CHAPTER 47

AZALEA BOUNCED HER LEG under the table as she sat in class on Tuesday night, trying to focus on melting the marble into a blob of glass. It remained very much a marble no matter how hard she tried. Fire symbols beyond simple candle lighting were out of Azalea's reach. They seemed the opposite to everything her magic wanted to do. Of course, Elam and Erik could melt a marble, no sweat. Erik had gone a step further and reconstructed his into a tiny glass cat with the streak of blue through the center—*showoff*.

"For you, my beloved," he said with a Shakespearian accent and a bow as he handed the cat ceremoniously across the table to Azalea. "It's good luck."

Her cheeks threatened to turn red as Millie and Livia's eyes seared over her. They had nothing to be jealous of. Erik just liked teasing her. She accepted the cat with a polite thank you.

Might as well make use of his current friendliness. "Can you melt my marble so I can leave, please?" she whispered.

"Why? Got a date?" he teased.

"No, I've got another lesson to get to." One she was very nervous about attending.

His back straightened, and the sparkle left his eye. "So, you made up with him, then?"

She nodded. Maybe she shouldn't have told him. Erik reached across the table and slid her marble into the crucible in front of him and melted it without hesitation and slid it back. "I'll walk you over there." He pushed his notes into his bag. "Mage Shepard, Azalea and I are done. Can we leave, please?"

She glanced at their crucibles and gave a nod. "Of course. Well done, you two. Off you go, then."

Azalea slipped the glass cat into a safe pocket and packed up her stuff. She was out the door with Erik in a flash.

"You don't need to walk me," she said as they climbed the steps of the Barracks.

"It's fine. I wanted to give you the opportunity to invite me over for another movie night."

"You don't hold back, do you?" she said as they passed through the Barracks' lobby.

"What the point? Life's too short to not say what you think."

"Fair enough," she said as she pushed the heavy door open to the wintry night air.

"So, you want me to come over tonight?" Erik asked.

Before she could answer, she nearly crashed into Torin, who was standing on the front steps. He stepped aside and raised his eyebrow as she steadied herself.

She was flustered. "Um . . . Hi, Torin, this is Erik. Erik, Torin."

"We've met. Though not under the best circumstances," Torin said, staring Erik down. The memory of Torin hovering over Erik's corpse-like form flashed across her mind.

"Oh. Right. Sorry," she said.

Erik stood and smiled at Torin. "Right. Thanks for that, mate. Lucky for both of us, you're always around."

She suppressed a groan. Torin didn't need reminding of these things.

"Yes. Well, you're as stupid as each other," Torin said.

Azalea rubbed her temple. "Aren't we meeting at your office?"

"I've got something else planned."

"Right, then. I'll be fine from here, Erik. I'll see you tomorrow," she said, picking up on Torin's wish for Erik to leave.

"You sure?" he asked seriously.

"I'm sure." She hoped he would take the hint and leave.

Erik nodded. "No worries then. I better get home. Let me know when you're done if we're on for some movies tonight."

"I don't think I will be," she replied, sure she would either be exhausted or most likely sick at the end of this. Movies sounded much more fun than whatever Torin had in store for her. "Bye, Erik."

He flashed her a winning smile. Hopefully, he got the message about not having a movie night.

He sauntered off behind the Barracks toward the back end of Mint Street. Torin started walking toward the chapel, and Azalea had to jog to keep up.

"You're not *seeing* him, are you?" Torin said.

"No, I'm not. Not that it's any of your business."

"Just be careful."

"I know how to be careful. I've met enough arseholes to know that."

Torin turned to her with a look that said otherwise.

"What? He's nicer now," she said.

"He's an idiot."

"So am I. You said it yourself."

Torin left it at that. They neared the chapel, and Azalea felt the familiar chill and eeriness of spirits getting closer. Instead of walking faster, like they usually did, Torin stopped. Spirits started turning their heads.

"Can we not stop here, please?" Her voice came out as a squeak.

"Today's lesson is spirit warding."

Azalea's insides plummeted. She'd been dreading this day and was in no way prepared for it. *This is not a punishment*, she told herself. Though she suspected Torin might get a little enjoyment from it at her expense.

"I'm not doing this as punishment, Azalea."

Her stomach dropped further. He was so reading her mind that time. "Let's get on with it then," she said, pushing away those thoughts. She needed to be focused.

"It'll be easier now, while your resistance is weaker than usual. Better now, than after intense training."

She swallowed. It made sense. But it didn't make it less terrifying. People from across the Tower grounds moved toward her as they stopped on the cobblestones outside the chapel.

Whatever Torin had planned, she hoped it didn't make her look like a mad woman. A few of the people were Yeoman Warders doing nightly rounds, she knew they weren't spirits.

She stepped closer to Torin as the spirits moved in.

"You can't always use me as a shield, Azalea."

She resisted the urge to clutch onto his arm and do just that. The sickening coldness teased her as more spirits joined. The closer they came, the more her lungs tightened. Even Torin gave a shiver.

"Focus, Azalea. How many are there?"

Her vision began swimming as ice fogged her mind. Fear rose up, pulling at her throat with frosty claws. It was just like the cemetery, all those spirits. But these were much closer and here there were no barriers. She swallowed. "Maybe twenty," she said weakly. She wasn't able to focus her eyes enough to count.

"Focus." Torin's stern voice brought her back for a second.

She inched closer to him.

"Imagine your aura of magic around you. Can you see auras?" he asked.

She shook her head. She'd read that some people could, but she wasn't one of them.

"Me neither. Just imagine your aura is a wide cloud of magic around you. Imagine it the same color of your magic in spell clouds if that helps."

She did as he said and closed her eyes, imagining a purple cloud of energy around her.

"You need to pull that cloud of magic back into you. Right now, it's an uncontrolled tangle of power leeching out. You need to contain it. Imagine doing that now."

She imagined her skin like a magnet, sucking in all the magic around her and sticking it back in.

"I've not seen you of late, girl." A haughty voice pulled her out of focus. Azalea reached out for Torin's hand in panic, and with a jolt, the warmth from his skin seemed to flow into her as his fingers entwined with hers. He flinched as if he'd received the same shock. Azalea opened her eyes and B was standing right in front of her with a look that demanded attention. Azalea ignored her and squeezed her eyes shut, trying to will her away.

Torin gave her hand a squeeze, and her eyes flashed open. He was shaking her hand in excitement and actually smiling.

"Azalea. I can see her. I can see them all," Torin said, his voice full of awe. Wonder and confusion flashed across his face. She could almost feel his amazement as if it were her own. For a moment it scattered her fear.

"It is rude to not acknowledge my presence when it is clear you can both see me," B said.

"How can you see them now?" Azalea whispered.

He inched them both back a step as B took a step forward. "I have no idea, but I'm starting to understand your issues here," he said as the looming crowd of spirits crept closer.

Torin's eyes darted across each spirit moving in. Her heart gave a quick jump, knowing he was seeing them too. The feeling didn't last long as it was replaced with a sharp pain, like ice being stabbed into her shoulder. She jerked back.

"B just grabbed my shoulder!" Azalea stared down the ghost. "What the fuck was that?" she said, glowering at the self-important spirit woman.

"You should not be ignoring me," B said, narrowing her eyes.

Azalea's shoulder was numb, though it had been the briefest touch. Torin's amazement was turning to concern. He started guiding them out of the crowd.

But B was a spirit on a mission and Azalea had no idea what that was. All Azalea knew was she never wanted to be touched by a ghost again. It was like she had been frozen to the spot in both pain and fear.

More spirits started closing in with a wave of chilling air and nonsense questions that were getting louder and louder. Azalea couldn't move or fight it.

Her own thoughts couldn't get past the endless chatter and brain-numbing cold. Her eyes shut again as she tried to imagine the magic around her and pull it in. But it was too much. She couldn't think or hear over the chaos.

Azalea's eyes shot open just in time to see B lunge forward. Torin spun around and hoisted Azalea up, and they were moving. The cold dissipated as Torin rounded the corner behind the chapel and placed Azalea down on the steps. Still in shock, she followed him to the top of the wall, her legs working on autopilot.

The spirits hadn't followed. They couldn't get into the courtyard for some reason. She let out a breath of relief and the clouds in her mind blew away into the night as they went inside. "Sorry, maybe that was a bit much to start out with," Torin said, looking nervous. "I should have explained the concept first."

"It's fine." She forced a weak smile to let him know she was okay. "I get the idea and it might have worked if B hadn't touched me." She shuddered again at the thought and fell into the chair by the fireplace that sat cold and dark. Torin sat down at his desk.

"That's the B you always talk about? Do you realize who she is?"

Azalea laughed. "Yes, she's Anne Boleyn. I just don't want to give her the satisfaction of letting her know I know."

He shook his head in disbelief. "I didn't realize quite how bad they were."

"Well, I did tell you."

"Yes, but seeing for myself is a rather different experience," Torin said.

"I'm glad you did. Weird though, right?" She traded a glance with him. "That when I grabbed your hand, you could see them. Did you take some of my ghost seeing powers or something?"

"That isn't a thing, Azalea. I have no idea what happened." He looked away, and Azalea could feel that he was keeping something from her. Right now, she didn't care or want to know.

"So. That was a bust. What's next in spirit warding lessons?"

"If you can learn how to pull in your magic close, you should be able to control when you can see them. But it's going to take a great deal of concentration and as you build up more power, your warding will need to get stronger."

"Great. You better be prepared for more running away, because I have a feeling this isn't as easy as you made it sound." Plus, she needed to master this in the next three weeks if she was going to be around spirits when she found the gallu.

"Hmmm. Perhaps not," Torin said.

CHAPTER 48

A DAY HAD ALREADY come and gone, and Azalea found herself once more lying on the floor of Torin's living room as weak as a tadpole on land. "Just leave me here to die," she said as Torin sat by the fire with a book, without an ounce of pity. He placed her old friend the bucket next to her and went back to reading. His lack of sympathy was annoying. As soon as she stumbled up and recovered from the Shadow Magic torture with a cup of tea, Torin gave her the new memory potion with a brief explanation to use it each morning. A few minutes later, he was hustling her out the door.

She had falsely assumed he was being the gentleman and offering to walk her home but no. Their new schedule included a spirit warding lesson on the way home. She forced herself not to cry as they got closer to the chapel. Her stomach only had the tea sloshing around in it, and she was shivering from the cold and the exhaustion of forcing out Shadow Magic into that stupid, tiny stone for the past three hours. But she knew she had to if she had any chance of getting her Shadow Magic back up to scratch in time for the full moon.

Dread hung over her, and she wished she could just sprint through and be done with it. She regretted agreeing to it as soon as they neared the first spirit. Memories of the last time flooded back. Glacial fog closed in around her. But she couldn't take it. She had nothing left.

She felt herself falling before she could tell her body to react, and the world tunneled into nothing.

A warm light filtered behind her eyelids—much too bright. She opened her eyes to find herself on her soft bed rather than the cold cobblestones that she expected, with Gerald's puppy-dog-dinosaur eyes looking straight at her.

"Good, you're awake." Torin was sitting on the edge of her bed examining the glass cat on her bedside table.

"How long was I out?"

"Just for a few minutes. I carried you home and Evangeline let me in. I assured her you were fine, that you just overdid it."

"I didn't even get near any that time. I don't think I'm very good at warding off spirits."

"I don't think you got the chance to try." He was looking surprisingly cheery. "Don't worry, you'll do better next time."

She groaned loudly. "We're going to be doing this every day, aren't we?"

"You just need practice." He stood up to leave.

"Wait. Torin. Did you see them too?"

"I did," he said cautiously. There was an unmistakable hint of worry behind his dark eyes. "Don't worry, you'll have a few days off to recover. I'm off tomorrow to find another relic. Nothing waits for the Archmage."

"You'll be safe, right? It isn't dangerous?"

"I'll be fine. Just practice drawing your magic in, but away from spirits. Can I trust you to do that?"

"Of course. Night, Torin." She wasn't going to let him down.

He shut the door. She didn't have the energy to get undressed. She just pulled the blanket over her and lay there cuddling Gerald as her blood pulsed with the shock of the sheer amount of Shadow Magic she had channeled earlier.

Faraday crawled in next to her as she extracted the Shadow Atlas from under her pillow. She needed to be spending more time with the stupid book, tracking the gallu and trying to learn its behavior. A drop of blood slid from her finger from a prick of her elemer and absorbed into the ancient pages.

Despite being nearly drained, she added some shadows to its meal and asked it once more how she could defeat the gallu.

Blood-red writing crept onto the page.

The one you called who once was blood.
Draws strength at moon so bright.
But weakens once its kin is called.
One chance you'll have this night.

She assumed that meant it would be weakest after it called through the weaker wraith gallu. Good intel. But how to get that info to Fabian? She didn't want to go after it herself, but if no one listened to her, she would have to. She started searching the Atlas for the purple dot she now knew to be the gallu.

All she had to do was keep up with her tracking and keep up her strength for the next few weeks. One way or another, it was not going to survive past this full moon. Even if she had to try take it down herself.

CHAPTER 49

A ZALEA SAT AT HER desk in her bedroom and shuffled uncomfortably, unsure how long she'd been sitting there. Torin said he'd only be gone a few days, but it had been a week. For some reason, she felt like he was alive and well, but occasionally she got crippling pains through her chest that made her think something was very wrong. She figured it must be panic attacks—which honestly was not surprising after the last few months.

Every waking minute she had was now spent tracking the gallu in the Shadow Atlas. That little dot that used to give her a thrill of hope of seeing her dad now only brought on rage and hatred for that creature. Soon she'd have to tell someone that she could track it and knew when it would be weak.

Her phone buzzed on the desk. It was Erik, but the message was in a group chat with Elam, Millie, and Livia. Weird.

Hey team. Meet at my place after class. I've got a proposition you won't be able to say no to!

This couldn't be good.

))) ● (((

"Let's do this," Erik said, rubbing his hands together as they filed out of their Friday night lesson.

"What exactly is this?" Livia asked. "Why aren't we going to the pub?"

Azalea trailed out of the classroom behind Elam, who didn't look pleased with either idea.

"Yeah, I could do with a pint, and I'm starving," Millie said.

"You'll forget all about food when you hear my idea!" Erik said.

Azalea had no idea why they were meeting like this, but she was sure it wouldn't be good.

Erik led them out behind the Barracks and through an alleyway in the inner fortress wall. They came out on Mint Street, which took a ninety-degree angle and ran perpendicular to Azalea's part of the street.

Cars were parked all the way up the road in front of the red brick flats, much in need of a pressure washing. Time had crept up the walls, leaving a footprint of lichen and moss that gave the facade a gloomy, forgotten feeling.

He waved them into a doorway lined with an archway of white painted brick and shut the door behind them. "Come on." He thundered down the stairs, and the others trudged after him.

A wave of heat and smoke rushed over Azalea as she stepped into the underground room. Everything smelled of hot steel. Even her mouth tasted metallic as she breathed in the stifling air. One wall was lined with furnaces and open fires, another brick wall was lined with various wooden handled tools and leather protective wear. She remembered that Erik's dad was a famous elemer maker . . . elemer smith? Whatever the title, he was the number one elemer bloke in the world. The room was deceptively large, with a footprint that must go right under the road. The center was filled with wooden benches and storage shelves, all lined with elemer blades and metal-working materials. It was probably best not to touch anything, though her fingers itched to examine all the tools. She hadn't been able to work on her watches for over a month. She missed using tools and making things.

"Why are we down in this dungeon? What's wrong with the caf?" Millie said, turning her nose up. Azalea was wondering the same thing. This was an odd meeting place.

"It isn't a dungeon. It's a forge, and we're here because my dad is out, and no one can overhear us down here." Erik boosted himself onto a tall bench and sat there happily, with his legs dangling. Azalea and Elam leaned against a wooden bench. Livia dusted metal shavings off two stools with a rag for her and Millie.

"What are those?" Azalea asked, spotting stacks of long metal staffs with Sumerian cuneiforms down the sides—definitely some sort of magical device.

Erik shrugged. "My dad's current project." It was clear he had no idea what they were. She suspected Erik wasn't meant to bring people down here at all.

"Let's get to it, then!" Erik slapped his hand on the table a few times to get everyone's attention.

"As some of you may or may not know, the House of Eagles have put out a decent bounty on hunting the gallu," Erik said.

Azalea could see where this was going and did not like the sound of it.

"It's killing people. Why the hell would we go after it as well? They've brought in tons of hunters now," Millie said.

"Yes, but we won't be hunting that one. They've predicted it will be bringing loads of the weaker wraith gallu through on the full moon. Too many for the hunters to be everywhere. Plus they'll be trying to get the big one. They'll have to set multiple traps all over town. It's just like fishing, so we might as well set our own trap and try our luck."

Azalea held back a groan. Just what she needed—her classmates out there trying to get themselves killed on top of everything else she was dealing with.

"I propose we join the hunt and catch a few of our own," Erik announced.

This was met with a long silence.

"You can't be serious?" Livia scoffed.

"Oh, I'm serious." Erik leaned back, looking proud of himself. "It's five grand a catch. And that's just for the easy ones. If we get the big daddy, it's 50k."

Erik flicked his head toward Azalea, and she shook her head slowly and clearly. No way they could get involved in this.

"No way," Millie said, for the first time looking serious about something. "There are hunters out there getting them. We wouldn't have a chance."

"But we do," Erik said. "The hunters are all focusing on the big money gallu, but they can't be everywhere and there are too many wraith gallu out for them to bother with. They want non-hunters to do the easy ones and leave the dangerous one to the pros."

"I don't know, Erik . . . This seems dangerous, we don't have any training in this type of thing," Millie said.

"Yeah, and how are we supposed to find them?" Livia said.

"Azalea has a way to track them—a magic pocket watch that detects them." Azalea groaned inwardly. Why had she told him that?

Erik continued, "Azalea told me how her uncle makes the traps. Then it's just a matter of surrounding each one and then sucking it into a bottle like a genie. Easy peasy."

"A magic pocket watch, aye?" Livia raised her eyebrows skeptically. Elam remained silent, but it was clear he was thinking about it, or he would have said no right away.

"No way," Azalea said, her jaw clenching. The last thing she wanted was for the situation to get out of hand, or her classmates to be thrown face first into danger because of her.

"How did you get this 'magical' watch, Azalea?" Livia asked.

"You know, I don't think this is such a good idea," Azalea said.

"Show them the locket, Azalea," Erik said.

Reluctantly, she pulled the locket out from under her black sweater. "It's a family heirloom. I found it in my grandmother's closet, and she doesn't know I have it," Azalea said. *More lies* . . . but better than telling them about the Shadow Atlas, or that it was Torin who gave her the locket.

Elam still hadn't said anything, but Azalea could feel his eyes on her. He studied the reactions of everyone. She straightened her back and put up her mental walls, trying to pull her aura in around her like a safety blanket. Elam turned to his sister. Azalea's neck bristled. She could tell they were speaking telepathically.

"Fine, me and Elam are in," Livia said. "We could do with the challenge, and we all need to pay our student loans. We can't pass this up."

"Don't you want to think about this more? Consider all the risks? At least plan a little?" Azalea said, shocked that they agreed so easily. They might be shallow and idiotic sometimes, but they were intelligent people.

"I've read extensively about gallu. If they are only wraith gallu, they will be weak enough for us to handle. Setting traps is simple enough," Elam said confidently. "Plus, I've been saving up to visit the Vatican. I talked to a mage there who has access to the secret archives. I can't pass that up. If I had that money, I could afford to go there."

"Yes! Millie, you in?" Erik flashed a smile to Millie, shamelessly charming an answer out of her.

"I could use the cash . . . But you guys are crazy if you think I'm spending it on bullshit like student loans or geek field trips. I'll be getting a whole new wardrobe, thank you very much." She let out a dramatic sigh. "If you guys think it's a good idea, then I'm in."

Oh dear. This was not ideal. They were all set on the money, not the actual monster hunting part. If Azalea ended up having to hunt the dangerous gallu herself, she'd have her classmates to worry about on top of that.

"Azalea, are you in?" Livia said, using her practiced peer pressure look.

She didn't exactly have much of a choice. This was all her fault, and she felt responsible for these idiots. Whether she went or not, they would do it.

"I guess I'm in," she said reluctantly. At least if she was there, she could steer them away from danger and maybe set a trap that ensured they were all kept safe inside.

Erik slammed his hands on the table and pushed himself up. Darting to a small fridge in the corner of the room, he came back with a six pack of beer that he handed around. "A toast!"

Everyone raised their bottles. Erik's enthusiasm was infectious. They clinked and Erik delved into explaining gallu trap strategies. Elam added tips wherever he could get a word in, being his know-it-all self. They did seem to have most of it covered with surprisingly well-thought-out tactics.

Azalea sipped her beer, mentally going over all the things that could go wrong. At the same time, she couldn't shake the unwavering feeling that something wasn't right with Torin. She took another swig of beer. It was bitter—not really her taste, but she enjoyed the way it slowed down her brain.

CHAPTER 50

A ZALEA SLUMPED ONTO THE bench next to Elam and rested her elbows on the table. He was the least likely to talk to her of the bunch. Erik was too much to deal with for a Monday night class. She couldn't think when he was near her. He made her mind buzz, and she couldn't help but notice the warmth of his leg so close to hers, or his hand resting on the table, or the way he glanced at her. *Too distracting.*

Torin still hadn't returned to the Tower, and it had been over a week. She tried to keep her mind off him by keeping busy and planning the gallu hunt. She couldn't quite budge the feeling that something was wrong. A dull aching in her chest constantly plagued her, and it was distracting.

She practiced Shadow Magic training as much as she could on her own, but she couldn't do anything close to the levels of summoning she did with Torin. Without his safeguards and supervision, she didn't dare go anywhere near burnout.

The Echo Magic lesson today was hard: controlling a rotating ball of water overhead. She tried to concentrate as she was not keen on getting soaked, but a weak ten-minute interval was all she managed. Her neck ached as she looked up at the circling ball of water. She tried not to think about Erik, or the gallu hunt, or Torin.

Looking up at the swirling, bulging bubble was making her dizzy. Her eyes were trying to catch up when a lance of stabbing pain shot through her chest. She drew in a gasp as a burst of frigid water crashed down.

"Good one, Azalea," Livia muttered, wiping off her shoulders as if that would clear away the water. Elam was the one who was soaked.

"I'm sorry," Azalea muttered.

"Are you okay, Azalea?" Mage Shepard came over.

"I'm fine. So sorry." The pain in her chest intensified, and she hunched over, trying to ignore it and collect up the water. Mage Shepard took over much more efficiently. She waved her elemer over Azalea, Elam, and Livia, and soon had all the excess water out and back in the bottle.

She gave Azalea a questioning look. Better to stay quiet and not sound like a crazy person. But that pain had something to do with Torin. He was back at the Tower; she was sure of it and had no idea how the hell she knew that.

"Can I please be excused, Mage Shepard?" Azalea asked, trying not to look panicked. She had to find Torin right now, or prove she was going mad.

"Of course, Azalea. But I suggest you get some rest. You look like you might have been overdoing it lately."

"Thanks. I'll do that."

She packed up and left quietly as to not disturb the floating water balls above her classmates' heads.

Stumbling into the bathroom in the hallway, she locked the stall behind her. Her chest was burning. She pulled down her top, half expecting her skin to be on fire, but it was the moon tattoo. Pulsing with heat, the intricate lines of the knot in the moon were glowing with white light. She shoved her hand over it. It dulled a little from the pressure but didn't change much. Bile rose in her mouth, and before she knew it, her face was over the toilet bowl, barfing up her lunch.

Stumbling out of the loo, she splashed cold water on her face and stood there with her eyes closed. What the hell was wrong with her? She couldn't stop thinking about Torin. Her mind focused in on him and she couldn't concentrate on anything else. Where the hell was he? Then, clear as daylight, she knew he was in the hospital. She had to go there. Now. If he wasn't there, they could cart her off to the loony bin for all she cared.

Retying her ponytail with shaking hands, she headed down the tunnel to the hospital and slid into the ward without anyone noticing. She peered into every room. At the third door, she found him.

Van was in a white coat with amber cuffs standing over the bed, adjusting a drip. The other three beds in the room were empty. Azalea crept over and her heart skipped a beat with shock. She froze in place. Torin was lying there as still as a corpse and not looking much better than one. His cheeks were sunken in, his skin was dull and clammy. Azalea's hands shot to her mouth, and she must have let out a noise because Van swung around.

"Gods, you frightened me, Zalea." Van looked between Torin and Azalea. "He'll be okay," Van assured as she finished doing whatever it was with the drip.

"What happened?" Azalea walked a few steps closer. "I'm not supposed to say."

Van's eyes darted to the door. "But . . . he was bitten by a Bashmu—basically a snake monster. A really big one. How did you even know he was here?"

"Um, he messaged me before. I knew he was coming back," Azalea said, hoping it sounded at least a little convincing.

"You shouldn't be here. Archmage Norwich has orders for no visitors."

"Can I just sit with him a minute?"

"One minute. You have until I finish writing up this paperwork," Van said.

Azalea nodded and Van pulled the curtain around the bed. Forcing herself to move, Azalea stood next to Torin. His chest moved up and down in quick breaths. He was asleep, but his face twisted with pain. Azalea reached out to touch his hand. As her skin met his, a searing flash rushed across her eyes. She pulled away, but the bile rose in her throat once more. She gripped the bed to stabilize herself.

"What happened to you, Torin?" she whispered, but he was deep asleep, and it felt as if he was far away. She reached for his hand again, only this time there was just a quick initial jolt of pain, but she maintained her grip and squeezed her eyes shut, willing it to go away. She took a few deep calming breaths, then opened her eyes.

The pain in her chest stopped, and the sick feeling subsided, but her limbs went heavy as lead. She could have curled up right there on the floor and slept. She patted Torin's hand. "Sleep well Torin. I'll be back tomorrow."

She slipped through the curtain and Van gave her an apologetic look. "You better get home before someone sees you here.

I'll be here all night, but I'll update you later. Don't come back till Maiken says it's okay. Got it?"

Azalea nodded, trying to keep her eyes open and stay upright.

"Go get some rest."

Azalea walked home through the tunnels feeling, and probably looking like the walking dead. What the hell had Torin been up to? Clearly, his relic collecting hadn't gone according to plan.

)))●(((

Azalea didn't hear anything about Torin all the next day. Van didn't come home, and she didn't get any messages from Danni or Maiken. She was completely shattered in the morning and as soon as she got home from morning training, she conked out on the couch and woke up four hours later. She messaged Torin in hope that he had woken up but heard nothing.

Pacing the tiny space between the kitchen and her bedroom, she wondered if she should go to the hospital again. She didn't want to get Van in trouble or have people asking questions about how she knew Torin was there. Maybe Danni would know, but first, she needed to call Fabian. She had been putting it off far too long, and it was only nine days until the full moon.

She sat on the edge of her bed, getting more and more nervous with each phone ring. The words went round and round in her head, her telling him she could help track the gallu. He never answered. She rang RoRo to see if he would answer for her. She tried, but no luck. He was probably busy tracking the gallu's destruction across the city. More guilt piled on when she thought about the innocent people it was killing, and it was at least one or two every day now, according to the House of Eagle's news updates she got via text.

Next, she called Danni.

"Hey, Azalea," she answered cheerily. "If you're calling about Torin, Maiken told me he's awake but not allowed visitors. But he'll be out today."

That was one weight off her mind, at least. "That's good to hear. Thanks for letting me know. Actually Danni, I wanted to ask you about something else. You see, I have a way to track the gallu, but I can't get hold of Fabian. I know I can help, and I want to make things right, but I don't think he'll listen to me."

She heard a long sigh through the phone. "Azalea. You need to stay out of this. You're lucky to still be here as it is. I wouldn't push your luck."

"But—"

"Sorry Azalea, but I'm firm on this. I know you think you're trying to help, but it's just too dangerous. Let the hunters deal with it."

"But the gallu needs to be caught after it lets the others through. It will be weakest then."

"It will be caught before the full moon. They're closing in on its tail now. Just stay out of it, Azalea. I mean it. Look, I've got to go."

Azalea didn't believe any of that. It was clear Danni wasn't going to help. "Okay, thanks anyway," Azalea said, and the phone went silent. She groaned and stared at the floor.

It was looking more and more like she would have to go after it herself. Maybe she would go after it and once she was there, she would tell Fabian where she was so he could get it. Then he'd have to come.

With more pressure weighing down on her, she spent the day tracking the gallu and practicing shadow cloaks in her bedroom, then in the afternoon she practiced meditation and spirit warding. She couldn't do much without practicing with real spirits. It was impossible to tell if it was working or not and she had only nine days to master it. She couldn't afford to be distracted or compromised by spirits during the hunt.

She threw the elemer down on the bed. Even if Torin was getting out of the hospital he wouldn't be in any state to worry about her and her spirit problems. It was up to her to master this. They were just spirits, after all. She should be able to handle them by now. The sun had already slid away, and she decided it was time to face her fears. She tugged on her black hoodie and grabbed her dad's elemer.

It was colder than Azalea expected. She huddled into her hoodie like a turtle and headed straight for the chapel. This time, she would get this right.

A tightness clawed at her gut as she neared the old church. She pulled a shadow cloak around her to blend in with the night. A gathering of spirits had already formed.

B somehow spotted her. "There she is! The young witch I told you about," she cried out.

An icy chill ran through Azalea's blood. Something was very wrong. Azalea made a weak attempt at a ward, but their mass presence was overwhelming.

She doubled over as at least 50 spirits charged toward her like an army on the battlefield but stopped just short of her on B's order. B stood in front of her and crouched down. "You are the one we have been waiting for. You have awoken us," she said. Then turned to the rest of her spirit followers. "Follow my lead!" she sang out.

Azalea tried to roll over; to somehow escape. But dizziness clouded her head.

"Please don't do this," Azalea said. "Don't hurt me." She didn't have time to pull in her aura or try to shield them away with magic.

"I'm sorry, my child. I remember George now. He left long before me," B said sadly as she stepped forward. She reached out her hand with a look of deep yearning in her eyes. Azalea froze as B reached out. Her icy hand hit hard into Azalea's chest. Right into her heart.

Azalea's breath stopped as if she had been plunged into frigid water. Her heartbeat paused in time, and she struggled to capture the lost breath. B was gone and Azalea saw images of B's life flash across her vision. Where the hell had she gone?

Scraping her hands across the stone, Azalea tried to claw herself away. Murmurs rippled through the ghostly crowd. "She was right," one priest said. "This child will deliver us to our lord! Follow the Queen," he announced as he stepped toward Azalea. She shuffled back; her eyes locked on the priest.

"Keep away from me," she spat. Whatever they thought she was, they were wrong. She needed to get out of there.

"Forgive me. I remember all that I have done. I just want it to end." The priest kneeled and placed his hand on her shoulder.

Azalea's heart choked. Her vision sparkled and with her gasp of breath, the priest was gone. A whimper escaped her lips as more spirits stepped forward. The spirits were going through her. With each one she saw their lives parade across her mind in a painful reel. There was nothing she could do to stop them.

A soldier came up and asked to be absolved of his sins and with a sob he touched her, and the pain rippled through her once more. She struggled to catch enough breath before the next ghost stepped forward. "Please don't," she cried. She couldn't move. Couldn't sit up, and the spirits kept coming. Her chest was tight. Each time a spirit touched her, her heart stopped with a tight pinch. With each one, a little of her life ebbed away. She knew she was going to die.

))◗●◖((

Torin sat up straight. His soup spilled across the bed, and he swung his legs out.

"Please remain in bed, sir. You shouldn't be up." The healer looked at him like a scared deer.

"I have to go," he said. His heart stopped for a split second, and he doubled over. Something was very wrong. He ripped the drip from his arm and sprinted into the hallway, up the stairs, and pushed out into the freezing air wearing just his pajama bottoms. Pain spiked his heart and his leg threatened to collapse under him as he stumbled toward the Chapel.

"No, no, no!" He saw a slumped figure on the wet grass. He forced his legs to go faster and skidded across the ground.

Azalea.

He cradled her head in his lap. Energy buzzed into her hair where his fingers rested. He crouched over as pain shot through him and sat up, gasping. Hundreds of eyes fell on him. People.

No, not people, *spirits*. They crowded in, their eyes hungry and pleading. What had they done to her?

"Back off," he growled as a man inched toward them. He swung his hand out in warning and it passed right through a man's leg.

"I'm not missing my chance," the man said and pushed through Torin and crouched down to touch Azalea's cheek with surprising tenderness. Her skin glowed warm yellow, and a jolt jerked her body in his arms. His heart felt like a hand had momentarily squeezed it and the man was gone. He had gone right through her.

"Everyone, back off," Torin said, terror pulsing through him. It was rare to be in a situation where he was this weak and confused. He had to get her out of there. Scooping Azalea up in his arms, his legs trembled as he attempted to stand with her added weight, but he stumbled forward. He could barely walk himself, and more spirits were closing in. The way to the hospital was blocked, but there was a clear path behind them.

"If anyone else touches her, you'll be going straight to hell," he warned, hoping they were a religious bunch. "Now move," he bellowed. Spirits were just people after all, and he knew how to be intimidating when he wanted to. They parted ways, and Torin used every ounce of energy to carry Azalea back to his flat.

He found the spare key in the wall and got them just inside the door, then collapsed to the ground. Azalea tumbled out of his arms. Her head lolled as he slammed the door shut with his foot and crawled to her side.

"Please be alive," he said, placing his fingers on her neck. Her pulse was so faint he wasn't even sure it was there. He lowered his ear to her heart and heard a solid thump. He closed his eyes and rested his forehead on her chest. He felt a faint breath on his head and looked up.

She was staring at him. "I'm alive?" she asked.

"Yes," he choked out. "I think so."

She let out a sob and threw her arms around him. "Thank you," she said. He pulled her in and had never been so glad to hug someone in his life. He moved back and let her sit up. They sat on the floor, as she stared at him in disbelief.

"I'm glad you're alive too, Torin. I knew something had happened to you. I found you in the hospital as soon as you arrived, but I couldn't explain how." She shook her head and turned away in guilt. "Something's wrong with me. I don't think it was a dream when I went to that other place. You pulled me back from somewhere. They did something to me."

Torin swallowed. She was wrong. This was his fault. It had something to do with the soul bond, he was sure of it. "Where were you? What did you see?" he asked. Hoping it would reveal something about how their bond was formed.

She bit her lip before speaking. "I was in a room, like a lab. A woman put her hand on my chest and said there would be a price for sending me back, for keeping the balance. Damu, the tall guy, said someone was calling me back," she said as tears streamed down her face. "If I hadn't tried that stupid necromancy spell, no one would be in danger from the gallu and the spirits wouldn't be doing this. They did something to me, changed me."

This was bad. He recognized the name Damu. He was a god of healing, son of the great Goddess Gula. Azalea must have crossed over to the Shadow Dimension, and that's where he pulled her back from. The gods might have had something to do with their bond. "It will be okay. We can work it out. Now tell me what happened when the spirits touched you?"

She sat cross legged with a sorry look on her face. "I felt the spirits go through me. It was like they were using me as a doorway. I felt their relief and their last thoughts as they went through. It was terrible and wonderful at the same time, but I knew it was killing me," she said as she wiped a tear away.

"This isn't your fault. We will find out what's happening to you. I've read about this happening a few times in history, and if we can find the records we can see if there's a way to reverse it," he said.

He didn't want to say yet, but it was possible she had been turned into a portal for spirits to enter the Shadow Dimension, and the reason he was linked to her might be to help keep her alive—he was an extra source of power. Guilt spread through Torin like wildfire. It was his fault. He had broken the rules and brought her back and now they were both cursed. "Don't blame yourself. We will find out what's happening to you," he said.

He knew he should tell her about their soul bond right then, but a knock sounded on the door. Torin was suddenly aware of the fact that he was sitting on the floor with no shirt on and blood was seeping through the bandages across his chest that covered his more recent tattoo. Before he could get up, the door burst open.

Danni spotted them sitting on the ground. "What the hell happened?" she asked.

Azalea started laughing and shaking her head, then started crying. Torin glanced at Danni, who crouched down and pulled Azalea into a hug.

Torin just looked at her. "I honestly don't know," he said. This wasn't something he could explain until he knew how to undo it.

"You're lucky Maiken sent me to look for you instead of the hospital guards. You two look a proper mess."

"Nothing a cup of tea and good night's sleep won't fix," he said, not believing that at all.

"You need to learn when to stop, Torin. Fortunately for you, Maiken said if I found you alive and without further injuries you would be allowed to return home. Which I see you have already done." She rubbed Azalea's back and sat down next to her. "And you, missy? What's wrong with you?"

Azalea explained what had happened with the spirits, leaving Danni lost for any logical explanations. Fortunately, Azalea didn't mention that Torin could see the spirits too, and no one asked how Torin had known to find her. They sat there in silence before Danni spoke. "Maybe we should keep all this to ourselves?" she suggested. "Until we come up with a reasonable explanation."

"B was the only reason the spirits remembered. Without her, they might all forget me by the morning," Azalea said hopefully.

Torin got up on shaky legs and went to the window. Spirits were gathering at the edge of the courtyard. Since Danni didn't know he could see spirits now, it wasn't something he wanted to get into explaining. "Maybe you should stay here tonight, just to be sure," he said.

Azalea looked at him gratefully. "Thanks. I didn't really want to go out there again. Do you know what it feels like to have your heart stop?"

"No, and I don't want to," Torin lied. He had felt it alongside her.

Danni stared at them both in disbelief. "I'm getting Maiken to come over to check you both out. This is not normal."

Torin caught Azalea's eye, and she smiled and shrugged.

"Torin, go to bed. Azalea, I'll make up the couch for you. I don't want you to go outside again. Upstairs, both of you," Danni ordered.

Torin followed Azalea up the stairs while Danni stayed downstairs to call Maiken. When they got up to the living room, Azalea turned around and blocked him from going to the next floor to his bedroom.

"Tell me what's happening between us. You know what I'm talking about, so don't pretend you haven't noticed. You knew I was in trouble, the same as I knew the moment you arrived in the hospital. And this—" she grabbed his hand, and a jolt sparked between them. He flinched and pulled away. "That isn't normal," she said.

"You're right. There's some sort of bond between us. I'm not denying it. I just don't understand it yet."

She let his hand drop and tilted her head. "Okay . . . good. I'm glad I'm not going crazy."

"What you said about where you went when you died. I think it was the Shadow Dimension and I think you're right about them doing something to you. Once I work it out myself, I'll tell you. I promise," he said.

"That's all I ask. I was so scared when I found you in the hospital. I knew it was real."

"It's real, but it's not a good thing," he warned.

Her face dropped.

"Let's just keep it to ourselves for now," he whispered as he brushed past her, hoping Danni was still on the phone and not listening in. A hint of Azalea's power radiated toward him like it was trying to pull him back. He ignored it and went upstairs.

"Goodnight, Azalea," he said back. He'd have to tell her the whole story soon. But how could he even explain the soul bond? He didn't understand it himself, and it's not like they were in love. She was his student, and he was sure she didn't feel that way about him. He didn't even know how he felt anymore, what was real and what was the bond.

Those were things to worry about later.

In the meantime, the aftereffects of the Bashmu venom were pulsing through his veins and he was glad to be home. He would never take on a giant snake alone ever again, no matter what it was guarding. Maybe he did need an assistant.

CHAPTER 51

AZALEA DUMPED AN EXTRA bag of salt across the doorway to her flat and set a protection spell on it. No way in hell were any spirits getting in. She spent the whole week sleeping on Torin's couch because she didn't want to be in the flat alone while Van was at work. Too bad his spare room was all boxes and dust, or she might have moved in permanently. The day wasn't as bad as the night. She stuck to the buildings and traveled underground to keep out of the path of spirits. So far, none had sought her out.

Relieved to be showered and in clean clothes, she still felt extremely unprepared for whatever they were going to face during the full moon tonight. She was starting to have her doubts about her classmates being out there, especially since she hadn't convinced Fabian or Danni that she could help track the gallu. Now she would be with her classmates, potentially putting them in danger and having to make sure they didn't get hurt because of her. She needed to talk to Isaac.

He answered the phone straight away, and she slumped onto the bed. Faraday bounced up beside her. "Isaac, I'm really starting to wonder if I'm doing the right thing. Do you think I should call the hunt off? I don't want anyone to get hurt."

"Well, good evening to you, too. Maybe you should. It seems pretty dangerous Zaels, and after everything you've told me about these gallu, maybe you should stay away from them too."

Should she? Would Erik even listen to her if she told them not to go?

Isaac continued, "I can tell from your silence that's not what you wanted to hear, so I will add, that if you don't go, it sounds like your friends will probably still go without you. Either way, they could get hurt. At least if you're there, you'll have some control over the situation and won't feel guilty about it later."

He always knew the right thing to say.

"They probably would go without me. Plus, I plan on telling my uncle and Torin where the gallu is as soon as I know, and it's weakened."

"Sounds like a plan. And have a little faith in your classmates. You don't have to do everything yourself. You might find it's fun having help."

"As if," she said, but felt a little better already.

A louder than necessary knock sounded at the door. It could only be Erik.

"Got to go. Thanks, Isaac. I'll message you after."

"You better, and I'm coming over tomorrow to make sure you're alive. Stay safe Zaels." She hadn't told him half the bad stuff, just a light version of recent events. She didn't want him involved in any of this and promised herself to make it up to him after this craziness was over. She'd buy him all the pints he wanted.

Azalea let Erik in and led him into the living area where she attempted to tidy up her piles of books and stack Van's thousands of colorful cushions so the others would be able to fit on the sofa.

"I haven't seen you in days. You know what we're doing tonight, right?"

"I know, I'm so sorry. I've been staying at Torin's due to a minor spirit problem," she said, though minor was an understatement. "But not to worry, it won't affect our plans tonight. In fact, I think I can use it to my advantage. Maybe attracting more spirits will attract more gallu."

He frowned and there was a hint of skepticism behind his eyes. "If you say so. Are you sure you're alright? You look like you could do with a sleep, no offense."

"Yup, no problems here," she said confidently, though inside it felt like the butterflies in her stomach were in an epic battle. Soon enough, Elam, Livia, and Millie turned up. No going back now. She pulled out the locket.

"Sooo . . . the locket somehow senses the gallu and leads me to it. I can't explain how it works, but it does." Azalea swallowed hard and looked around the room, making sure to keep the truth far from her thoughts, though none of them had ever tried to read her mind.

Elam gave her a suspicious look but didn't say anything. Erik went over their roles in the hunt for the thousandth time. Even Livia was quiet as he spoke.

"We'll have a wide area in an open park with gems set around the outside for the trap. I'm on attack to herd the gallu to the right spot. Elam is lookout and will help me herd. Millie and Livia, you'll be setting the gems to close the trap at the edges once Azalea gives the all-clear. Then you all help catch them.

Azalea will be in charge of tracking, luring, and coordinating the attack. Got it?"

"How are we going to lure any gallu if we don't have a fresh body with a fresh spirit to use as bait, like the hunters do?" Elam asked.

"Azalea's locket and the sapphires should do the trick," Erik said.

Azalea tensed up. Elam was smart. She hoped he didn't think too much into it.

"That isn't really an explanation," Elam said.

"The locket will draw spirits and gallu to wherever we want it to go, and Livia was kind enough to liberate some sapphires from your mum to direct the spirits," Azalea said, hoping her voice was steady enough to sound convincing. She knew from studying the Shadow Atlas that the gallu kept coming back to this area and would bet her money that's where it would go again tonight. There was a higher-than-average spirit population in the area, and she had no doubt she could draw them in, and in turn, they would draw the wraith gallu in.

Her plan was to do the opposite of spirit warding. She needed to throw out a net of magic and summon them to her. The thought of it made her stomach turn, but it should work. The hard part would be making sure the spirits didn't touch her. She certainly didn't want them to realize she was their ticket out of this world.

Sooner than Azalea would have liked, the sky went dark. Nerves bubbled under her skin, and bile rose in her throat at the thought of stepping outside and facing the spirits without Torin, let alone intentionally drawing them in from miles around and then having to face the gallu.

Images from her dreams clouded her thoughts. She saw flashes of corporeal gallu ripping apart her friends and family like rag dolls. It was hard to block out.

Nervous energy filled the room. Millie looked like she was about to cry, and everyone else was far too silent. Before any of them could object, Erik clapped his hands and marched them out the door. Azalea slipped the Shadow Atlas into the inside pocket of her leather jacket before she left.

Torin was at Danni and Maiken's house for an early dinner and Azalea had promised them all she would stay inside. He was still recovering from his snake bite, and she hadn't seen him do any magic since he had returned. She suspected he was a lot sicker than he let on.

But she wasn't going to break her promise to him this time. She would tell him what they were doing. But only when she was sure the plan was going to work.

Azalea's heart thudded louder and louder as they merged with a group of tourists leaving the Tower. A short way up the street, they hopped into the Uber Erik had ordered. They sat in heavy silence as the van pulled into traffic.

CHAPTER 52

"Where are we off to then?" the Uber driver, a small, cheerful man, asked.

"Charter House Square, thanks," Erik said calmly. Azalea had checked the Shadow Atlas in her room before they left. The spot she picked was close to the area where the veil to the Hollow was thinnest tonight. There were lots of spirits and it was where the gallu seemed likely to hang out.

Azalea drummed her hand on her thigh. She didn't know how Erik could be so relaxed. He chatted away to the driver as if they were off clubbing. Everyone else remained silent until they pulled up next to a park with streetlights around the edge. They all filtered out onto the footpath. Her classmates' eyes darted around as if a gallu could jump out at any second.

"They aren't here yet," Azalea said, trying to reassure them as much as herself.

"Why would they come here, anyway?" Livia said, looking around, frowning. They stood in front of a lush park bathed in silvery moonlight. The large established trees sent shadows across the lawn in dense patches of night, and light spilled out from the border of buildings, both old and new.

Azalea pulled her leather jacket in tighter. "There's an old plague pit near here. There should be lots of spirits here to attract." But there were none in sight, yet. "You all just need to make sure you stay within the trap, stay in the circle and we'll all be safe, okay?"

Everyone nodded. Erik clapped his hands together. "Right, team. You know the drill. Let's set up our traps."

"Go team," Livia said sarcastically, but was the first to step onto the neatly trimmed grass and march toward the center of the empty park.

The others followed and soon had their circles of diamonds arranged on white hankies so they could find them again. Livia and Millie positioned themselves on the farthest edges of the trap, ready to place gems once the wraiths were inside.

Ice trickled down Azalea's spine. Spirits were near. *What the hell had made her think this was a good idea?*

Erik put a hand on her shoulder and a pleasant shiver ran through her. She spun around. He took her hand and looked down at it, lightly stroking the top of her fingers. "Now, you're sure about this? I know I kind of roped you into it all. I'm sorry, I get carried away sometimes. But we can do this, right?"

Her palm felt sticky against his.

"We can do it," she said, but couldn't quite look him in the eyes as she said it. The truth was she had no idea what would happen, or if the big gallu would turn up. If it did, she would make sure it stayed away from her friends. The plan was to allow only a few wraith gallu in the trap—an amount her classmates could handle.

Erik leaned in as if he were about to kiss her. Instead, he brushed her hair behind her ear. "When this is over, there's

something I want to ask you." A smile tweaked at the corner of
his mouth.

"You can just ask me now." Her heart raced. He was going to
kiss her; she was sure of it. And right now, filled with adrenaline
and the strong feeling that something was going to go wrong,
she wanted to kiss him. You know, just in case she died tonight.

"Trust me, it'll be worth the wait." He stepped back.

"Fine." *Don't look disappointed*, she told herself firmly. She
wasn't going to make a fool of herself just in case she didn't die.
Who knew with Erik anyway? She didn't even know why she
suddenly had the urge to kiss him. Must be a die-with-no-regrets
thing.

Focus, Azalea, she told herself as she fished out the bag of
sapphires that Livia had borrowed and placed them in a bowl
in the middle of the trap. Hopefully this would act as a muster
point for spirits, so they didn't converge on her. Azalea stood a
few meters away from the bowl. A chill set over her bones and
she sensed the ghosts coming before she could see them.

With her elemer in hand, she moved away from the sapphires
and threw out her power in a wide net, imagining her purple
aura spreading and calling them in. Now to wait . . .

She pulled out the Shadow Atlas and cut her finger to feed it
some blood. The map came up instantly. Lots of yellow dots of
spirits showed up. Scattered further out were faint purple dots,
the wraith gallu. She took out her phone and sent a group chat
to the others, so she didn't have to yell: *Spirits coming now.*

Azalea cast a wall of shadows around the outer edge of the
park. The world beyond the park blacked out into nothingness.
A void at the edge of the green so no one could see in.

Livia messaged: *What the fuck was that?*

Erik: *It's part of the plan*

Azalea was glad she couldn't see any of their faces in the night. Only Erik knew about her Shadow Magic, but the others would work it out soon enough. Azalea checked the Shadow Atlas again. Dots began to appear all over.

Figures moved through the shadows toward her as fear twisted in her stomach. Every muscle tensed, telling her to get the fuck out of there. But she stood still as a statue. Gaunt faces of plague victims ambled across the park like zombies. She hadn't expected actual plague victims in numbers like this. Alongside them walked more modernly attired spirits. All were drawn to Azalea's energy but headed toward the sapphires as Azalea cut off her magic and did her best to suck her aura back in while backing away.

The rabble of questions started as more and more spirits arrived in the square. Azalea stood frozen on the spot. Ice filtered through her veins and the memory of B going through her set Azalea's heart leaping into her throat. There was little chance of her getting out if they caught her now. But they didn't seem to sense what she was.

She unlocked her phone with shaking hands, the screen light blocking everything out around her. She prepared a message to send to Torin in case she had to leave quickly to go after the big gallu if it showed.

Hey Torin. Just letting you know I'm at Charter House Square with my classmates. We're only getting the wraith gallu so don't worry. And dont be mad at me. But I have a way to track the big one. I dont plan on going after it myself but I'm going to track it until my uncle can get there and catch it :)

She saved the draft and stuffed the phone in her pocket and glanced down at the book. More gallu were showing up, which meant the big gallu was now at its weakest. First, she had to make sure her classmates were okay.

"They're here! Wait for my mark!" she yelled across the field, continuing to pull her magic back into her like a magnet, at this point praying to every god that the spirits would ignore her.

The unwitting spirits meandered toward the center point. Behind them, the wraith gallu, presumably fresh from the Hollow, drifted in from the shadow wall, crossing the grass like wisps of thick smoke following the trail of spirits. Azalea held her breath. At least they couldn't harm her friends in this lowly state. They were heading straight for the spirits like a pack of lionesses going in for the kill.

A squeal came from nearby. Millie must have spotted them. Her classmates couldn't see the spirits, but they could see the wraith gallu.

"Holy shit," Erik said from somewhere nearby.

"Azalea!" Millie called.

"It's fine. Just stay put. They're focused on the spirits," Azalea called back, hoping that much was true.

In a split second, the wraiths lunged at the spirit group and began ripping into the weakest spirits. Azalea had a sickening flashback from a dream.

"Now!" Azalea yelled across the field as one last wraith passed through her barrier. This was a safe amount for her classmates to handle.

Erik called to Elam, and both boys raced in without hesitation, like a couple of pros. She had to give them credit—they had good hustle. Erik threw fireballs, herding the gallu toward the center, while Elam used wind and air to do the same.

The wispy wraiths barely had faces, just dark cavities in the smoke where their eyes should be, and shadowy mouths that opened with unhinged jaws to lock onto the clueless spirits. So different from the leathery later stage.

From the edge of the massacre, Azalea estimated about 50 spirits were huddled together, screaming, and fighting to get away. There were about 20 wraiths on the outside circling the group, crowding spirits in tighter like sheepdogs herding sheep. They seemed to be working together.

Erik and Elam were pretty close to them, but the wraiths ignored them as they closed in on their prey.

"What are they doing?" Livia yelled, running up to join Azalea.

"They're about to attack the spirits," Azalea said. She started walking forward. They shouldn't be too hard to catch while they were so occupied.

"You can see the spirits?" Livia said, disgust clear in her voice.

Millie joined them. "What do we do now?" She was out of breath from her run over and her voice was shaking.

"Everyone, surround them," Azalea called.

Livia sprinted off to the other side and took her place near Elam. Millie stayed close to Azalea but didn't back away from the job.

"Now!" Azalea called.

Erik took out the first wraith with ease as he blasted one with a fireball and ran at it with a bottle of black liquid. He summoned it in with the correct spell as if he'd done it a thousand times.

Azalea nearly froze, half expecting it to turn on him and do something. But it worked.

"Got the sucker!" Erik called out as he waved the bottle in the air. Azalea couldn't help but smile.

This seemed to give the others courage. Elam and Livia raced in at the same time. Azalea didn't see how they did it, but two more wraiths were gone. The rest were busy feasting on the spirits.

Her turn. Azalea blasted purple energy and shadows at the nearest wraith—her uncle's spell. The wraith gallu spun around and as soon as it did, she sucked it into the tiny bottle. It was almost too easy.

Millie had joined the mix after watching how to go about it.

It was like a chaotic animal pen, but only Azalea could see the spirits running around like a broken flock of sheep as the wraiths realized what was happening.

Spirits screamed in agony as smoky protrusions shot out from the wraiths like mist tentacles, clasping on and tearing away ghostly limbs.

Her classmates were unaware as they ran straight through the tormented souls getting their limbs ripped off. She was jealous. It would be easier to only see the wraiths. She had the added problem of having to dodge the frantic spirits that escaped the pack, hoping they wouldn't touch her.

Her classmates seemed to have it under control. Azalea glanced down at the book. The solid purple dot. It was him—the corporeal gallu. A rush of cold terror ran over her as she sensed the new darkness. Tendrils of fear curled into her stomach as she repressed the overwhelming urge to run. The monster was outside the barrier, but her friends were safely inside. Just as she planned.

There were only a few wraith gallu left. She had to lead the big gallu away from this place. Cold adrenaline shot through her veins, it was time for her to leave and finish this. She sent her text to Torin.

Erik ran up to her, bottles clanking in his pocket. Two dangled between his fingers as he clinked them together. "I've got like eight in here," he gloated.

"That's great, Erik, looks like that's all of them now. I've got to go take care of something. Can you make sure everyone stays in this circle till I get back?"

"Anything you want, love. We're rich!"

Panic was setting in. This was it. Better to just walk away before she gave away just how terrified she was, how much she didn't want to die tonight.

"One more thing," Erik said as she turned to leave.

Suddenly he was in front of her. His eyes were as black as night and his gaze lowered to her mouth.

"Can I kiss you now?" he asked.

Holy crap, he was going to kiss her, and right at the worst possible time . . . but she wanted it. In answer, she tilted her head toward him and pressed her lips to his. His fingers slid to the back of her neck, and her heart raced against her rib cage. Shoving all thoughts of death and gallu aside. Bloody hell, either he was really good at this, or she had forgotten what it was like. She felt him smile against her mouth, then pull away.

"Aren't you just full of surprises," he whispered.

"Well, you were the one who said life's too short." She smiled up at him as a wave of heat spread through her. The park flooded with moonlight as the full moon slipped from the clouds. A scream rose from the center of the trap, and her heart nearly stopped. It was just a spirit. But the moment was over, and panic shot through her. They were in a public park surrounded by mutilated ghosts. *What the hell was she doing?*

"Shit. I've really got to go, Erik." There would be time for kissing later, if she survived. Erik's mission for the night might be finished, but hers was just getting started.

"I knew you wanted me," Erik said smugly as she slipped out of his arms and away from his warmth.

"Way to ruin the moment," she teased, trying to get up the courage to leave. It was better he had no idea what she was walking into.

"Come back with me. We can celebrate at my place."

"I can't explain right now. Just stay in the circle until Torin gets here."

"Torin?" Erik wrinkled his nose.

What else could she say? Staying there and kissing Erik would be much more pleasant than being killed by a gallu, but she didn't have much of a choice.

Azalea raised her elemer and let the shadow wall around the park dissolve until the streetlights were visible once more, and she was sure the gem barrier would hold, keeping it safe for her friends.

"You're getting good at this Shadow Magic thing," Erik said.

"Thanks. I'm not sure everyone else is so impressed." She nodded toward Livia and Millie who were giving her death glares. Though that could also be due to kissing Erik.

"There's one outside the circle!" Elam yelled.

Azalea whipped around. "Elam, don't! It's too dangerous. Stay inside the circle!" she cried. He was too far away to hear. *Bloody hell.* "Erik, make sure everyone stays in the circle. I'll get Elam," she called out in panic.

Elam left the gem barrier and sprinted across the road as the leathery gallu turned and laughed. *Shit*, it was leading him toward an alley.

"Elam, get back here," Azalea shouted. She didn't even notice the spirits come up behind her. But the shock of their touch froze her in her tracks as her heart squeezed, stealing her breath away. She saw three lives flash before her eyes, and then they were gone.

"You okay?" Erik was suddenly at her side crouched over her, concern plastered across his face.

"I'm good," she wheezed as her breath returned. Straightening up, she caught big gulps of air as she raced across the road and into the alley without a look back.

Cold sweat plastered her shirt to her back by the time she rounded the corner to the dark lane. There was no sign of Elam. Her eyes flicked to a shadow behind a skip bin. It slowly emerged, and her heart plummeted to her feet. Elam was hovering high in the air as if he were on a crucifix held up by two leathery protrusions. The dark body of the gallu slid into the moonlight.

Azalea stifled a scream as Elam's head lolled to the side.

"This one will make a nice addition to us. His magic is so sweet, quite the treat. We thank you, daughter."

"I'm not your daughter. Drop him now!" she screamed. He didn't deserve this. Not sweet, quiet Elam. He still needed to go to the Vatican to see the stupid archives. He didn't deserve this.

"Too late." Another protrusion emerged from its body and drove into Elam's spine with a crack.

Azalea froze in place. This couldn't be happening. Elam's body dropped and his head hit the road with a sickening thud.

Hot rage exploded through her.

"You're going to pay for that!" She spat out the words. The gallu laughed and didn't even attempt to go after Elam again. It just turned its leathery back and ripped into the Hollow. Blood thundered in her ears as she staggered toward Elam.

Suddenly, his arm moved. He was sitting up. She stumbled and the road bit at her hands as she crawled toward him.

"I thought you were dead for sure." She choked out the words.

"So did I," he said, relief plastered across his face.

She reached out to him. A pain shot through her chest like a hot knife. She winced as she pulled Elam into her chest in a hug. Her heart froze.

"Tell Livia I'm sorry," he whispered.

Her breath caught, and her voice wouldn't come as she tried to pull him in, but she couldn't feel him, he wasn't even there.

"Elam!" she let out a moan.

His body lay there, left behind in the dirty alleyway, like he was nothing. In that second, she'd seen his life. She saw him growing up in the Tower, following little Livia around like he worshiped her. Tears blurred her vision. The gallu was gone. Elam was gone.

Now she was sure the creature was teasing her, playing a sick game. It hadn't even tried to take Elam's soul.

Her hands curled into fists at her sides, and she pressed them into the gravel as she forced herself up. That monster was going to pay, and she would be the one to take it down, no matter what it took. All she knew was she had to follow it into the Hollow.

CHAPTER 53

A GNAWING FEELING WRITHED in Torin's gut. He stared down at his dinner. He was at Danni and Maiken's place and wanted to be polite but couldn't face eating anything.

Danni looked over at him. "It's all right if you don't want to eat, love. It will take you a while to come right after what you've been through. You're lucky to just be up again after a Bashmu bite."

Maiken glanced at him with concern.

"Are you sick, Torin?" Ava asked.

"I'm just tired, little one, no need to worry," he said.

"I'll give you some of my broccoli. Mum said it makes you strong, so you might need it more than me," she said.

"No, eat your own broccoli. Look, Torin still has lots of his own," Maiken cut in.

Torin tried to smile, but a flash of cold fear drove through him. Something was very wrong. His knife and fork clattered to the table, and he couldn't help but squeeze his eyes shut in pain.

"Excuse me," he said as he pushed back his chair and headed straight for the bathroom. *What the hell had Azalea done now?* He doubled over the sink until the wave subsided and he pulled out his phone.

The blood drained from his face as he read the message from Azalea. Sharp corners of panic prickled through him. He stormed back out, his vision blurring.

"Sorry I've got to go. Azalea's gone after the gallu and dragged her classmates into it. That stupid girl." He'd believed her this time and was an idiot for not seeing this coming. And he was certain a spirit had just gone through her, but worse than that was the sickening terror building. He could almost taste her fear, and he had to get to her before it was too late. At the front door, his hand found the rough fabric of his coat.

"I'll call for help. You go get her. Where is she?" Danni said, up in a flash.

"Charter House Square. Bring backup, lots of it," he said, his feet already leading him out the door.

"I'll meet you there," Danni called after him. He sped down the stairs to the Hospital and into the tunnel.

He cut a Hollow and stepped through, then made another cut and appeared on the edge of the park at Charter House Square. At least she'd had the decency to tell him where she went.

He could hear people yelling and raced toward the voices. Erik was there with two of Azalea's classmates, all looking rather pleased with themselves.

"Erik," he called out. "Where's Azalea?" he said as he tried to catch his breath. Bloody poison had him well off his game.

"She followed Elam off that way." He pointed. "One of the gallu wasn't in the trap," he said calmly.

Rage boiled under Torin's skin. "Do you not see how dangerous this is? Just stay inside this bloody trap until help comes. Do not leave it. Understand?"

"Sure, but I don't know what you're stressing about. We got 'em all. Look." Erik held up a handful of bottles with a smirk.

"Those aren't the ones you should be worried about, you idiot. Just stay here." Torin marched off as voices traveled on the night air from behind him.

"Bloody hell, that's Mage Torin Dumont," he heard one of the girls say, not at all quietly.

"I bet it's no coincidence she's been learning Shadow Magic. She's shagging him. I said that, didn't I?"

"Shut it you two. You don't know what you're talking about," Erik said.

"Worried he'll murder you for snogging her?" one of the girls taunted.

Torin ground his teeth as he walked away, doing his best not to clench his fists. He shouldn't care if she had been kissing Erik, it's not like they were together. There were more important things to worry about and those fuckwits had no idea the danger their friend was in. He raced off toward the alleyway Erik had pointed at. Rage pulsed through him, stronger than before. He knew it was coming from Azalea. She was close. He burst into the darkened street and saw her.

Relief washed over him. She was alive, but not okay. That much was clear. She was standing over a body. As she turned toward him, her chest heaved with a great sob. Rage and sorrow rippled through her and into him.

"I'm sorry, Torin. It killed Elam. I'm going after it," she said as she turned away and cut a Hollow into the night air. Torin sprinted toward her but the Hollow closed before he got there.

Air stalled in his lungs as he stood over Elam Frost, the Archmage's grandson. A gruesome hole was ripped into the boy's chest and blood pooled around him, trickling down the cobbles in a black stream.

He couldn't waste any time. He sent Danni a rapid voice message to tell her where to find Elam, then used his meager reserve of magic and cut into the Hollow. He stepped through. But where had she gone? He cleared his mind and focused on finding Azalea. He slowed his breathing and reached out for it with his elemer. He was sure he cut into the same path she'd left from.

It took precious seconds for him to gather the strength to cut into the Hollow again. By the time he ripped through the subspace and stepped out onto a neatly trimmed lawn, she was long gone.

His eyes adjusted to the moonlight, and he scanned the wide-open expanse. "Azalea!" he shouted. His voice echoed around the vast space—a stadium.

At the center of an oval, stands rose around him, empty and filled with shadows. A large pavilion stood at one end. It was familiar somehow—it was Lord's Cricket Pavilion. He'd never been there, but he knew it well enough from TV.

A slamming door drew his eyes to the entrance of the building. He ran toward the sound, his body protesting every step. He had to get to her, he couldn't let her die. He staggered up the aisle between the white chairs and crashed through the double doors. He stilled his breath, his heart pounding in his ears. She was in there and he was going to make sure she got out of this alive, even if it killed him.

CHAPTER 54

A ZALEA HAD TO DO this alone. The moment she saw Torin in the alley and felt the panic radiating off him, she knew. She knew he wouldn't let her do this and knew if he followed and something happened to him, it would be her fault. As she stepped into the Hollow, away from Elam's body, away from Torin, she knew she wouldn't be coming back.

The gallu was just toying with her, luring her away. But she didn't care, as long as it got the hell away from her classmates and Torin. They wouldn't be the ones to pay for her screw ups.

Torin's eyes pleaded with her silently as she stepped into the Hollow and the chill of winter wrapped around her. She didn't look back as the shadow doorway closed behind her.

A slit of moonlight caught her eye, and she lunged with her elemer to stop the gap the gallu had gone through from closing. Forcing magic through her arms, she ripped through and tumbled out to a grassy field flooded in moonlight. The Hollow sealed as if it was never there. A dark hulking form in the distance lumbered through the doors of a huge sports pavilion at the end of a field.

For a second, she remembered she should tell Fabian where she was, but she realized she had no idea herself. She couldn't lose it now. This was the monster at its weakest, and it was her only chance to bring it down, and she was the only one there.

She raced after it until she reached the building, taking long strides up the stairs between stadium seats. At the top, she threw open the door. A cackle broke in the distance. She turned toward it, wincing with each echoing footstep across the wooden floor.

It felt like a decade passed as she crept up a long hallway. One side was bright with moonlight from rows of windows, and the opposite was dulled by the night with wood-paneled walls and cabinets of cricketing things. She searched for movement as she walked painstakingly slowly across the creaking floorboards with only portraits of old cricket guys to witness her last march.

The mass of black, leathery evil slid into her path. It had been waiting for her. She wanted to run, scream, but her body betrayed her as if she had turned to stone.

"You should have listened to me, little girl. I could have made you great. I would have kept our bargain, you know. Told you the secrets your father kept, taught you his Shadow Magic. I have all his memories. But now you will never be the great mage you imagined. You'll never have Daddy's approval. Never be good enough. You will die a failure, a nobody. *Powerlesss.*"

"Keep your lies to yourself. I don't give a shit about power or becoming a mage. All I want is to destroy you. If I can keep you from hurting the people I care about, then I win!" she said with everything she had.

"You'll make the tastiest dessert," it replied. "A tasty dessert in your father's favorite place. What fun memories for us all."

"You're going back to whatever hellhole you came from," she said as she caught her breath.

"I don't think so, my dear. I'm far beyond killing. My dear brother is the best hunter out there and even he couldn't stop me. What makes you think you'll do any better?"

"Because I don't care if I go down with you."

A door slammed and Azalea darted toward the wall. Footsteps closed in on her. Her heart sank when she saw it was Torin. He was in no state to battle anything.

"Azalea, you can't do this. Get the hell out of here!" Torin yelled as he stepped into a moonlit square. How had he tracked her here? She was sure the Hollow had closed behind her. His breath was ragged, and Azalea swore she felt a wash of panic radiate from him as plain as she felt it herself.

"It killed people. It killed Elam," she choked.

"Let me help," he said. "Just come over here. Please just trust me."

"No, you'll make me leave." Every inch of her wanted to go to him, to trust him. But he could just as easily whisk her away in a Hollow and she'd lose her shot.

A cackle rang from the end of the long hall. "I'll just have you both," it said, its voice serpentine and cold.

Azalea had to make a choice now. She looked back at Torin. She did trust him. Before the gallu could move, she pivoted around and darted to Torin's side.

"I'm so sorry Torin. I didn't want to drag you into this."

He reached out and his fingers curled around hers. An instant jolt of power rushed through her and something cold pressed between their palms.

"Just trust me. I'm not letting go. So, you might as well just take my help," he said with a squeeze of her hand.

If she was going to trust anyone, it was Torin. She nodded. A tingle of blue magic spread into her palm and trickled up her arm. Closing her eyes, her head tipped back as magic flooded her veins and drove into her heart like nothing she'd ever felt before. Her eyes flew open and met Torin's. His were jet black and wide with fear she could feel as clearly as her own.

She turned to face the gallu, and Torin moved alongside her, not letting go. Azalea held her elemer out and drew on a spell cloud, different to any she'd done before. It was a complex pattern of power symbols, consisting of many that were new to her. It swirled in her mind as clear as if she had another eye. The power built in every cell in her body, spiraling like an electric cloud inside her, drawing in energy from Torin.

His grip on her hand grew weaker as they closed in on the gallu. She sliced her elemer into the Shadow Dimension and pulled in more magic. She inhaled and aimed straight at the gallu as it laughed, not even bothering to move.

Power shot from her hand and rattled every bone in her body. Every inch of her pushed her will on this horrible creature to die. She forced more and more into it. It stumbled back, hitting the wall hard. That would teach it to underestimate her.

Time stopped as she shook with effort. An electrical storm of blue and purple power blasted out of her, and the thick smell of electrical energy filled the air. Windows shattered and furniture splintered apart around them. A vortex filled with paintings swept past. Her hand was slick with sweat as she tried to keep her grip on Torin. She could smell Elam's blood on her clothes and skin which only enraged her further.

The gallu lashed out, finally realizing it was in trouble. It forced its leathery body against the deluge of energy. Her cells hummed, and Torin's hand began slipping from her grasp. Something dark moved through a shard of moonlight.

This was getting to be too much. She screamed as she cut her power source and dropped to the floor. Torin fell limp next to her. His elemer clattered at his side.

"Torin, get up," she yelled. She glanced to the side. The gallu was convulsing in the corner. She tried to drag Torin up, but he didn't move. Something dropped from his hand with a small thud. *Her practice ruby.* She grabbed it and shook Torin.

"Please get up, please. I need you."

She knew it was now or never. The monster was weak, but it would soon be up again. A flash of black darted across the room toward the gallu.

She glanced at Torin. "I'm so sorry. Please don't die."

She sprang to her feet and sprinted toward the corner. She reformed the spell cloud in her mind. It was much harder this time.

"No more playing around." Its malicious hiss cut through her.

She wasn't going to waste energy talking to it. Summoning the spell cloud as the ruby pressed into her hand, she cut into the Shadow Dimension and propelled the magic forward like a jet engine. It tore through her veins, burning her hand as it seared out. To her left, a dark shape materialized, darting back and forth in front of the gallu. Azalea was losing control. She realized with a shock that it was Faraday racing around. He moved like lightning. She wanted to scream at him to leave.

The gallu lashed out at him. It was working. Twisting around wildly, the creature went for the cat and Azalea heard herself scream. It hooked Faraday and sent him flying across the room.

There was a loud thud, but she couldn't look away to check he was okay. The gallu retreated further into the corner as Azalea drove it back with deliberate anger fueling her steps forward. The stream of purple lightning and shadows aimed straight at its heart. Or where a heart should be.

She felt it the moment it began to break. Her power hammered away at its outer shell, crushing it open like a sledgehammer on a walnut. Every cell in her body screamed at her to stop, but she pushed forward and drew a last drop of power from the ruby until she felt it give.

The gallu shattered. A wave of energy slammed her back, and she was thrown across the room with the force of a bomb. Black shards splintered out and a puddle of ooze blistered the floor. Then everything was still.

CHAPTER 55

AZALEA'S BODY DECIDED THAT was enough. She collapsed to the floor like a dropped puppet. When she tried to sit up, a wall of dizziness slammed her in the face. She had to get to Faraday and Torin and get the hell out of there. Glancing around, she couldn't focus enough to find them. *Don't panic, finish the job*, she ordered herself as she remembered what she needed to do.

She crawled across the floor with every part of her body shaking. Stretching the bottle out at an arm's length, she tapped the glass opening against the edge of the dark oily puddle that smelled of tar and burned leather. She used her last ounce of power to pull the essence of the gallu into the vial. Hopefully, killing it had released all the spirits it had eaten. She had no idea how to tell. Sealing the bottle, she let out a shaky breath.

It was done.

She shuffled over to Torin, who was lying in a patch of moonlight from a shattered window. "Torin, please wake up. Please." She took his hand and placed the ruby in his palm. She folded her hand into his. *Please, please, any god listening, let him wake up*, she prayed. Salty tears trickled into the corners of her mouth.

She looked around helplessly. "I'm so sorry Torin. It was meant to be me, not you."

"I don't die that easy," a faint whisper slipped from his lips.

Azalea threw herself across his chest and sobbed like an idiot. His hand fell gently on her back.

"Please stop crying. I'm uncomfortable enough as it is. What happened?"

"I got it," she said, sitting up and not quite believing it herself. "Faraday helped too. I don't know where he is."

"He'll be fine. You know him," he said, not quite awake.

"Can you sit up? I was worried I took all your magic and killed you. You should have stopped me."

"It was worth it," he said as he shuffled against the wall, leaning heavily on Azalea.

"Here." Azalea pushed the small bottle into his hand. "I'm so sorry about everything. I know you must hate me."

"I don't think I could ever hate you Azalea," he said drowsily. He looked down at the tiny bottle. "I can't take this. You did all the work."

"You know that's not true, and you keep stopping me from dying, so you might as well make it worthwhile."

He rolled the bottle around in his palm. "It is unlikely either of us will survive another year at this rate."

"True," she said, unsure how they'd even survived this. She felt like she'd been cooked from the inside out and her muscles plucked away strand by strand. Torin tried to give the bottle back, and she pushed his hand away. He looked down in confusion and pushed his index finger into the palm of his other hand.

"Why do you do that?" she asked, wanting to block out the pain.

"It's a test to see if I'm in a dream or not."

"And are you?"

"Apparently not." He sounded genuinely surprised. "Why would you give this to me? The money, the honor that comes with it . . ." He stared at the bottle again.

"Torin, there is no way I can explain how I did this, but people will believe you did. So just take it and make it easier for both of us. You'll get some brownie points with the Archmage, and I won't be forced to explain anything. It's not a favor—it just makes sense. Just say I followed you here because I wanted the money for the gallu, but you stopped me and heroically saved my life." Torin deserved this far more than she did.

"Look Azalea, there's something I've been meaning to tell you. But you have to trust me that I can fix it, okay?"

"Of course I trust you, Torin. I'm sorry I keep letting you down. I don't know why I think these things are good ideas."

"Just be quiet and listen. The truth is, we're cursed. I've cursed us both," he said, all seriousness. He took her hand like people did in movies when they were about to say that someone had died.

Maybe he'd hit his head. She didn't feel cursed, but from the look on his face, he wasn't kidding.

"That night I brought you back—it all went wrong. More wrong than you can imagine. The magic I did was illegal, Azalea. Just as bad as what you were attempting to do. I don't know what I was thinking." He raked his hand across his hair. It was sticky with blood.

"You were trying to bring me back, Torin. Which you did. I can't blame you if something went wrong."

"You say that now." He ran his thumb across her hand. She suspected he didn't know he was doing it as he stared down blankly. "I tried to do a necromancy spell to bind you to your body and the earth. But there was so much blood, and we were in a Hollow. The spell wasn't quite right." He looked into her eyes, and she felt his guilt, clear as day—this was about their weird bond thing.

"I didn't just bind you to your body again. I bound you to me as well."

His finger sent slight shocks through her hand she was finding hard to ignore. She tried to process in her muddled brain what Torin was saying.

"Okay . . . so what does that mean? A bond doesn't sound as bad as being dead, which was my other option," she said. The pain in her head was only being added to, did they have to talk about this now?

"I created a soul bond between us. Something very illegal, very taboo, and something no one can ever know about. If the High council found out, we would be locked up, or probably worse."

"You're starting to scare me, Torin. So this is why I can some-times sense what you're feeling, right? Can you read my mind?" At least he seemed to have an explanation for this now. She pulled her hand away. The contact seemed to pull his emotions through to her.

"I can't read your mind. But yes, we can sense each other's emotions. It took me a while to work this all out."

At least he couldn't read her mind. One good thing.

"I've put us in this position, Azalea. It's a bad one. I've been trying to find a way to fix it and I didn't want to tell you about it until I knew how. But—."

"It's okay, Torin," she said, trying to cheer him up as she felt both their panic levels rising. What they needed to do was get back and get him to the hospital.

"It's not okay Azalea, this is bad. If people found out—" his face paled.

"They won't find out, okay?" she snapped. She got out her phone, but then wasn't sure who to text or where to say they were, though she was sure it was in London somewhere. She couldn't focus over Torin's urgency to talk about this. She could feel it radiating off him, now that she knew that, it was highly unsettling. A thought hit her. "The people in the Shadow Dimension. You said they did something. If they did this to us, it can't be your fault. I'm sure we will find a way to break it," she said, hoping he would buy her false optimism. She did not need this right now. They could sort it out later.

He shook his head, and she could feel the hopelessness rolling off him. They sat in silence. She knew they'd have to leave and face reality soon. She wasn't ready but was pretty sure they both needed a doctor.

"It probably saved us, you know, the bond. It kept us alive fighting the gallu. Our magic together was amazing. We could use it."

His face contorted with revulsion. "We can't use it again, Azalea. We shouldn't have shared magic. It was wrong. So wrong." He shook his head. "I thought we were going to die. I was giving my power over to you . . . I didn't. . ." He was unable to get the words out, but Azalea suddenly knew what he meant.

She leaned away from him, then folded her arms to try to cover her reaction and glared straight ahead. "I get it. We were never meant to have this conversation."

"No, you don't," he said, laughing. "I can't even explain it."

"No, I get it," she said as anger welled in her chest. "You would rather have died than be in this situation, right? That's how bad this is."

A guilty look flashed across his face. "What we need to do is make sure the bond doesn't get any stronger until I work out how we can break it."

"Fine, let's just continue to pretend it never happened. I'm sure you'll work it out," she said. It couldn't be that bad. Shouldn't he just be happy he was alive?

"I'm sure we will," he said, obviously trying to end the conversation. Well, now she wasn't ready to let it go.

"I just realized my tattoo gets warm when you're around as well," she said, not sure why she said it, but it felt relevant.

"What tattoo?"

She unzipped her jacket and pulled down her sweater to reveal the tattoo across her chest above her left breast. The half-moon tattoo with intricate knots glowed white. She looked down at it self-consciously.

"Shit. It's a Mark of the Gods. We were both marked."

He pulled down the collar of his shirt to reveal the exact same moon tattoo, though in the reversed direction. Azalea reached out without thinking and ran her finger over it. A buzz of magic and warmth ran through her. She swallowed, and Torin's eyes filled with concern.

"I don't think this is a good sign."

Footsteps sounded right in front of them. Azalea backed against the wall.

"Well, well, well. Isn't this cozy?" a shadowy figure appeared in front of them, tapping a cane rhythmically on the wooden floor.

Torin slid forward and pulled Azalea behind him, though he could barely sit up. Azalea leaned against him with her shoulder to keep him upright. He clearly knew this man.

"Leave her out of this. If you've got a problem with me, spit it out or piss off. Our friends will be here soon."

Azalea pulled her phone out, but the blood on her fingers stopped it from doing what she wanted. Wiping her hand on her jeans, she quickly swiped away the dozens of messages and missed calls.

"Where are we?" she whispered.

"Lords," Torin said back, not looking away from the stranger.

Using Torin's back as a shield from the man, she messaged Danni: *Send help please. We're at Lord's Stadium.*

Danni messaged instantly: *Thank the gods you're alive! Help is on the way now. Hold tight.*

"I see you've finally learned to stand up for yourself. Good job, Son."

Torin's whole body tensed, and Azalea grabbed his shoulder to keep him up. This was Torin's dad. This was the man who murdered her father. This was Korbyn Dumont, and he'd finally come for her.

Korbyn chuckled, but Torin remained silent.

"My dear boy, the truth is, I didn't even know you were here. Just a bonus, I suppose. And don't worry about your friends, they won't be turning up anytime soon. I took the liberty of warding this area against Hollows. I was either going to come out of here with a prize gallu, or a prize girl. That's you, deary." He chuckled, too lightheartedly for the situation. No wonder Torin hated the man. He had a hateable vibe about him and one of those faces you just wanted to punch.

His large cloak and cane were obviously for show. He had speckled gray hair and a villainous goatee. She suspected he spent too much time on crafting his look. He didn't look nearly as scary as she'd imagined him in her head, but she might also be suffering some major head injuries right now.

Azalea didn't dare move. He was here to kill her, and help wasn't coming. She couldn't let Torin get in the way. She pivoted around to Torin's side and let him fall back against the wall. He growled but didn't move. She suspected he couldn't.

"It's me you want," Azalea said.

"Smart girl, this one."

"I'm not letting you anywhere near her. Leave her out of this," Torin said.

"Funny that. You protecting her? I'd like to hear how this relationship came about. I've got the time. Do tell."

"There's nothing to tell," Torin said bluntly.

"You know who I am," Azalea said, staring at Torin's father's black, inky eyes.

"I do. And I think you know why I'm here," he said with a smirk.

"Because you're a sick bastard who has nothing better to do than come after people who've done nothing to you," she spat. If this arsehole was going to have a go at her, she wasn't going to go down easy. Though she didn't particularly want to fight the notoriously insane Dark Mage. At this point, all she had were words.

Korbyn sneered. "I see you're as rude and arrogant as your father was, young lady."

Torin turned to her. "You know my father?"

"I know *of* him." Azalea was shaking all over but couldn't look at him. She never blamed Torin for his father's mistakes. She didn't want to bring him into her family's past.

"Oh, Son," Korbyn said, shaking his head. "Do you really not know who this girl is? Who her father was?" He let out a manic chuckle. "Marvelous."

A sick feeling was building in the pit of Azalea's stomach. Something was way off.

"Let me be the one to break the news. This, my rehabilitated son, is the daughter of the one and only Samael Blackbourne. The man you murdered."

Torin flinched. A mix of disgust, panic, and horror washed over him and into Azalea.

She couldn't move. No, this wasn't right. It wasn't Torin that had murdered her father. It was Korbyn. It must be a trick. He was trying to get between them. Torin's hand fell away from her wrist.

"It's not true," she whispered.

Torin snatched up his elemer from the ground. "Liar!" Torin lunged at his father with more strength than she thought he had. Azalea was too slow to react. Shadow ropes shot out of Korbyn's elemer and tangled up Torin in seconds, suspending him in the air like a fly in a spider's web.

Azalea shot up, her unsteady feet barely holding her. Shadows pressed her against the wall, and she had no strength to fight it.

"Let him go! If it's me you want, just take me, and get it over with!" she screamed.

"No, no, no, deary. This is too good for it to all be over at once. No. I've got a new plan. I'm going to let you both go so you can torture each other. How nice of me, you say?"

He lowered Torin to the ground, but the shadows remained around him. Azalea swayed and grabbed the wall for support. This was certainly a trick.

"But I'll leave you with an offer, my boy. A one-time offer to return to the fold of the House of Ravens. Bring me the girl and bring me the relics, and you shall be reinstated as my heir. Something to think about."

"I'll never come back," Torin spat.

"Have a wee think. I'll be back in the near future. But I shall take my leave now, as I believe you two have some catching up to do." His shadows slowly unraveled from Torin. "And don't worry, young Azalea *Blackbourne*. I'll be coming back for you if my son doesn't deliver. I always keep my promises, and I made one to your father long ago—I would end his family line." He gave a wide, shit-eating grin and winked at Azalea.

"You're sick," Azalea said.

With a wave of his elemer, the remaining glass in the windows and cabinets shattered and sent a shock wave across the room, presumably destroying his temporary wards. Azalea ducked to avoid the hurtling shards.

"*Au revoir*," he said as he opened a Hollow right behind him and stepped into the darkness.

He was gone. Just like that, and the rain of glass settled into deathly silence.

Torin collapsed to the floor and Azalea rushed over but stopped right before him.

"Is it true?" she asked.

He squeezed his eyes shut and turned away. The same pain rippled through both of them.

Azalea's heart dropped to the floor. So it *was* true. Torin had murdered her father. Her chest tightened. Breaths came in short sharp jerks and hot tears stung at her eyes.

"I'm sorry. I didn't know who you were. Your name, it's different. You took your mother's name. I didn't make the connection and I didn't know you were from *that* House of Snakes family," Torin said.

His feelings of guilt were thrust away in a tsunami of Azalea's own anger. She hoped he felt the firestorm that was building in her chest right now. How could he not have known? She ground her teeth, brain whirling, trying to weld together words that could express how she felt. All she could see was red. Then Torin passed out.

She didn't move. He'd murdered her father; he'd lied to her this whole time. But no . . . he hadn't known.

Azalea sunk to the floor. She should help him.

A chill of cold air rushed behind her, but she didn't have the strength to move.

"Thank the gods, you're alive!" Danni screamed, and arms wrapped around her from behind.

Azalea was numb. More people streamed from the Hollow behind her. Someone went to Torin. Fabian crouched in front of her, fatherly concern plastered across his face. Now he came to help her, when her life had already amalgamated into a screwed-up mess.

"Azalea, can you hear me? Are you hurt?" someone asked.

Azalea stared blankly into the darkness. She had a soul bond with the man who had murdered her father. How had neither of them known that?

One thing was for sure. She would have a very interesting chat with Torin once he woke up and he would find a way to break this ridiculous soul bond so she could get the hell away from his fucked-up family. A weak meow brought her out of the daze.

"Faraday!" she yelled out with sudden clarity in her mind, tears threatening to cloud her vision.

"You need to stay sitting, Azalea. We need to check you out," Maiken's stern voice seemed distant.

Azalea stumbled to her feet. Cold panic washed through her as her eyes darted around the dim room, looking for any black shapes that could be a cat. She spotted him under a table, but he wasn't moving.

"Faraday!" she called out as she slid onto the floor next to him and pulled his limp body onto her lap. He was still warm. She put her ear to his chest and heard a faint rumbling purr. He started shaking all over. Maiken crouched next to her. "Is he okay?"

"He's alive. Can you check him please? Can you heal him?"

Maiken laid her hand on his back and ran her elemer across the air above him. "He's in shock and had some minor injuries. I can heal him now, if you promise to listen to me and let me check you."

"I promise, I'll do everything you ask."

Maiken closed her eyes and a brilliant white light expanded out from her elemer and seeped into Faraday. Maiken let out a satisfied sound. "Cats are easy," she said. "He'll be right as rain. Now come with me."

Azalea cradled Faraday in her arms as Maiken pulled her up. Her legs were ready to give out under her. Torin was being loaded onto a stretcher while Fabian frowned over him. He spotted Azalea and rushed over and pulled her and the cat into a hug. "Thank the gods you're okay."

She welcomed his warmth around her. "He killed it. The gallu." Her voice cracked.

"Dumont killed it?"

"Yes. He saved me." As much as she hated Torin right now, she didn't want Fabian following up on his death threats. At least she knew why he hated Torin so much.

The world seemed fuzzy—almost unreal. Like a parallel universe. It was a new reality now. Everyone would know she had Shadow Magic, and the Archmage would have no choice but to kick her out. A new wave of guilt crashed over her at the thought of Elam. He would be alive if it wasn't for her.

And now there was Torin's dad to deal with. He was going to kill her, but it was nice of him to give her warning. Oh, and she couldn't forget the minor problem of spirits using her as a doorway to the great beyond. What she didn't want to believe was that Torin had murdered her father. It was hard to see past that right now.

Were these normal issues for the average uni student? How had her life become so screwed up? She had a sudden urge to giggle at the ridiculousness of it all.

One thing was for sure, tomorrow was going to be one hell of a day.

The Shadow Atlas Book #2

Preorder now!

available at
amazon

Acknowledgments

It turns out writing a book takes a lot more time and a lot more people than I ever would have guessed, and I want to say thank you to everyone who helped me along the way!

A special thanks to you, the reader! You give me a reason to write, and I hope you will continue this journey alongside me in future books.

To my husband, Michael—Thanks for helping me follow my dreams off into my own fantasy worlds. I wouldn't even have a book right now if it wasn't for you—I probably would have thrown it in the rubbish if you hadn't helped me sift through those first edits! One thing for sure, I wouldn't be able to do this without your amazing support.

To my sisters Lucy and Rosie—Even though we all live in different countries, our obsessions with fantasy books, Harry Potter, and travel will always bring us together! Thanks, Lucy, for being my number one supporter and first fan! And thanks Rosie for taking the plunge and reading the first chapters of this book when it was in it's early days!

To Manuia Heinrich—You read the very first version of this book when it was a mess of plot holes and terrible grammar!

Thank you for your feedback and all your amazing encouragement and support starting from my first NaNoWriMo back in 2018—you were my first writer friend :)

To Bethany Arliss—Beth, you are the best critique partner I could hope for! I'm so glad I found you and that we are on this publishing journey together. Thank you for all your wonderful support, and cheers to many more books!

To Liz Frederick—Thank you for using your amazing powers of editing on this book! My sentences (hopefully) make a lot more sense because of you. One day I might learn how to use commas correctly . . .

To my beta readers—Manuia, Liz, Heather, Rosie, Jess, Jenny, and Kim. Whether you read a few chapters, or the entire book, every bit of it was helpful and I am so grateful for your time.

To my Granny, Val—Your short stories are what inspired me to start writing in the first place. Thank you for all your love, support, and wonderful childhood memories.

To my Dad, Dave—A love of books seems to run in our family. Thank you for all your support and for buying me so many books as a child! I look forward to the day we can sit together on your boat and have a long overdue beer.

And saving the best for last (or second to last)! To my Mum, Maggie—You set an example of how to lead a life filled with magic and creativity. After three years apart we are overdue for many tea and bullet journaling sessions. Thank you for your unending support and for raising me to follow my dreams and to always have lots of books!

Last but not least, a big, big thank you to anyone who reviews my book! Especially all the wonderful ARC readers, bookstagrammers, and book bloggers out there. Reviews make the world go round for authors, and I appreciate every single one of them.

If you enjoyed reading this, please leave me a review on Amazon or Goodreads, that would truly make my day!

About The Author

Jenny Sandiford

Jenny grew up in small town New Zealand on a steady diet of fairytales and fantasy books. She lived in Mongolia for nine years with her husband where they spent the unfrozen months of the year living on the edge of the Gobi Desert mining gold. When she isn't writing, Jenny enjoys hiking, meeting new animals, and loves to curl up in a sunny corner with a cup of tea, a cat, and a book. She is currently in the United States with her husband and their two street cats from Mongolia.

CONNECT WITH JENNY ON:

Website: jennysandiford.com

Instagram: instagram.com/JennySandifordAuthor

Facebook: facebook.com/JennySandifordAuthor

Goodreads: Jenny Sandiford

WANT THE LATEST BOOK RELEASE NEWS?

Sign up for monthly updates!

jennysandiford.com/subscribe

Made in United States
North Haven, CT
08 May 2022

18990605R00275